HUNTER SHEA

GHOST MINE

This is a **FLAME TREE PRESS** book

Text copyright © 2019 Hunter Shea

FLAME TREE PRESS
6 Melbray Mews, London, SW6 3NS, UK
flametreepress.com

Distribution and warehouse:
Baker & Taylor Publisher Services (BTPS)
30 Amberwood Parkway, Ashland, OH 44805
btpubservices.com

Thanks to the Flame Tree Press team, including:
Taylor Bentley, Frances Bodiam, Federica Ciaravella, Don D'Auria, Chris Herbert, Matteo Middlemiss, Josie Mitchell, Mike Spender, Cat Taylor, Maria Tissot, Nick Wells, Gillian Whitaker.

The cover is created by Flame Tree Studio with thanks to Nik Keevil and Shutterstock.com.
The font families used are Avenir and Bembo.

Flame Tree Press is an imprint of Flame Tree Publishing Ltd
flametreepublishing.com

A copy of the CIP data for this book is available from the British Library and the Library of Congress.

HB ISBN: 978-1-78758-208-8
PB ISBN: 978-1-78758-206-4
ebook ISBN:978-1-78758-209-5
Also available in FLAME TREE AUDIO

Printed in the US at Bookmasters, Ashland, Ohio

HUNTER SHEA

GHOST MINE

FLAME TREE PRESS
London & New York

'Good judgment comes from experience,
and a lotta that comes from bad judgment.'
Will Rogers

'Go to Heaven for the climate, Hell for the company.'
Mark Twain

For you, Dad. I miss you.

CHAPTER ONE

This was Billy's favorite time of the day. The whistle had sounded some time ago, signaling an end to the shift in the mine and that all was well. Most of the men were in either of the two saloons *blowing off some steam*, as his daddy liked to say. His ma forbade him to go anywhere near those places, lest he get caught in the middle of something he was too small to extricate himself from.

That was fine by him. The men, and sometimes even his daddy, scared him when they came out of the saloons.

Billy had spent the better part of the day trying out a new slingshot on the field mice behind their small temporary house. The little critters might be tiny and fast, but he'd still managed to bag a couple. His pants pockets were laden with rocks and his slingshot poked out of his waistband.

A cold breeze swept across the plain, tilting the shriveled blue-green wheatgrass. Only two weeks into fall and already they could tell that a brutal winter was on the way. Pretty soon, he'd be confined to the house or, worse, Ms. Betty's school.

All the more reason to have as much fun as he could now.

He looked up at the sun, realizing he didn't have much time until it dipped for good.

His ma would be calling him in for supper before he knew it.

He ran to the small crop of hills on the rear side of the mine, to the cave that, as far as he could tell, was unknown to all but him. He'd found it by accident a month ago when he was out riding on his horse, Sugar. Something had spooked her bad and she'd reared back, throwing him from the saddle. He'd gone ass over heels through a patch of cattails over six feet high. He'd braced for impact as he hit the air, sure he was going to splatter against the unforgiving sharp face of the hillside.

Instead, the cattails cushioned his fall and deposited him into the mouth of a dark, cool cave. Fear for his life was quickly overcome by wild fascination, as can only happen in the heart and soul of a nine-year-old as wild as the creatures that roamed the prairie. The cattails had formed a perfect, impenetrable barrier to the cave's mouth. If it weren't for that stupid horse, he'd never have found it.

He'd been coming back ever since, stealing candles and a few matches from his house so he could explore the cave a little deeper each time.

When the men blasted the charges in the mine, he could hear their echoes in the cave, feel the ground shake. He wanted to be a miner like his daddy. For now, this was as close as he could come.

One thing he'd discovered early on was that the cave was home to some of the biggest rats he'd ever seen. They chittered about in the darkness, fleeing from his meager candlelight, sometimes scampering over his bare feet. Disgusting varmints that would have sent his ma on top of the table, screaming her head off.

Because of the chill, he'd worn boots today. Their slick, furry bodies wouldn't have him hopping this time around. Today was payback time. He struck a match against the side of the cave's mouth and lit one of the candles he'd ferreted into his pockets when his ma wasn't looking. They were both down to their nubs, which is why he thought it best to grab two.

The amber glow from the candle's flame was swallowed up by the obsidian depths of the cave. The usual frigid breeze wafted from somewhere beyond his explorations. If they were still here come spring and summer, he might tell his parents about the cave. Seemed to him a good place to store food away from the heat and the rot that it brings. His daddy might even take him out for some candy for coming up with such a great idea.

Billy took several confident steps into the cave. The reverberation of his footsteps caromed off the uneven walls, disappearing into its unfathomable core.

A pile of loose rocks on the left, just fifteen feet into the cave, would make for a good place to sit and wait. The sun's dying rays didn't dare come this far into the cave. In here was the blackness of a starless night. He tilted the candle and poured some hot wax onto a flat rock by his feet and planted the nub in the wax.

With his hands now free, he laid out a few of his choice rocks and fitted one into the slingshot's pocket holder. He pulled back on the rubber, stretching it as taut as he could, feeling the small burn in his muscles.

Reaching into his front shirt pocket, he found the crumbs of bread and cheese he'd secreted off his supper plate the night before. He scattered the morsels of food in front of him.

Now all that was left was the waiting.

He kept as still and quiet as the stones around him. He breathed through his mouth because he had a tendency to whistle through his nose. Even the tiniest noise was made large by the acoustics of the cave.

It didn't take long. He heard the rats well before he saw them. Their enhanced sense of smell drew them to his trap. Their squeaks and squeals filled the cave with the sounds of starvation.

The first pink snout, whiskers twitching madly, stepped into the candlelight. Billy saw its round, black eyes and pulled back on the slingshot.

Just a little closer, he thought.

The rat was as long as his forearm, but so skinny he could see the outline of its ribs through its matted fur. This would be a mercy kill.

Squinting his right eye down the Y sight of the slingshot, he let the rock fly. It zipped through the air fast as a hummingbird. The rat yelped and flipped onto its back. It clawed the air, wailing in pain. He watched with morbid curiosity as it struggled to turn itself over. Each time it tried, it scraped its wounded belly against the floor. The pain sent it reeling onto its back, leaving small droplets of blood in its wake.

It flipped and flopped like this for several minutes. Its protests scared the other rats back into the depths of the cave. Billy waited until the rat stopped and became silent. Extracting the candle from its wax holder, he knelt down to take a closer look.

The rock had pierced one side of its scrawny belly and come out the other. He could see the pink of its guts pushing their way out of the hole. It was dead all right.

It was the biggest animal he'd ever killed for fun. The tail alone had to be six inches. He lay on the ground next to it and stretched his arm alongside its still form. Lining up the peak of its snout with the tips of his fingers, he looked up his arm and saw how the tail ended past his shoulder.

"You're a big son of a bitch," he said, getting back to his feet.

Son of a bitch, a bitch, a bitch, called back to him.

For a moment, he felt sorry for the rat. Killing little critters was one thing. For some reason, it didn't seem altogether right, taking the life of something this big without it being in self-defense or to put on the family table.

Maybe I should give it a nice burial.

That would make it right, help ease his conscience. He'd bury it within the cattails. After being in the dark so long, it would appreciate spending eternity under the sun and stars.

He picked it up by the tail, feeling it slap against his thigh. He hoped it didn't get any blood on his britches. His ma would kill him if she saw that.

Something heavy crashed in the Stygian depths behind him.

It was followed by a large thud. Then another. Billy felt it in his chest, as much as he heard it with his sunburned ears.

A boulder of phlegm and bile lodged in his throat.

Footsteps! Something was walking inside the cave. And it was coming toward him.

Thump. Thump. Thump. Thump.

His knees, locked at first, flexed and he started to run. The rat was still in his grasp. A voice called out from the dark.

"*Uh-uh-uh, Billy. It's not nice to take away my pets.*"

The words didn't echo because he heard them *in* his head.

Stunned into immobility, Billy turned to face the man. Those ponderous footsteps continued. No man could walk that heavily.

His chin quivered when he looked up toward the ceiling of the cave. A pair of red, menacing eyes hovered there, some nine feet in the air. He couldn't make out a body. The eyes narrowed, and the thunderous footsteps stopped.

Billy's hands shook, and the rat fell to his feet. It sprang back to life, chirping angrily. An irregular line of blood stretched into the dark as its bony body scampered back to where the red eyes glared.

He tried to scream, but nothing would come out. All he wanted to be was home, safe with his ma and daddy. Hot tears streaked down his grime-covered cheeks.

The candle in his hand sputtered out, and the darkness took him into its cold and empty embrace.

CHAPTER TWO

It'd been two years since my first and last visit to Sagamore Hill. I remember it taking a good two days for my hangover to hit the road after spending the night with the Colonel. His being the president and all now didn't change things much in my mind. Old dog. New tricks. He was still the Colonel, or better yet, Teddy, to me.

The train to Long Island had been hot and crammed full of sweaty men and women anxious to be home for the weekend. I hate trains. The rocking motion never fails to make me sick. I'd take a gimpy horse over a train any day.

I used my finger to pull the collar from my neck so cooler air could run down my shirt. The Victorian house looked just as it had three years ago. It was big on the outside, but filled with so much stuff inside that it actually felt homey. Gravel crunched under my boots as I trudged up the lane. I saw a man standing on the front porch and smiled.

"We didn't call for no copper," he barked.

"And I didn't call for no trained gorilla," I shot back.

Scott Goodnight, tall and thick with a bushy mustache that connected to his equally bushy sideburns, clomped down the wooden stairs to greet me. We shook hands until he pulled me in for a bear hug.

"Been a while," he said.

"Hey, you're the one who's in Washington and Lord knows where else most times. Me, I'm always here."

"Watching that man is a full-time job," he said with a sly smile, his head jerking to the house behind him. "He's out for his afternoon ramble. Come inside and set for a spell till he gets back."

Scott had been Teddy Roosevelt's bodyguard ever since he'd been named vice president under McKinley. I recalled that I had been offered the job but politely refused. I had no stomach for politics. Washington was my idea of hell on earth.

Inside, the house was too quiet. The Roosevelt brood were a rambunctious bunch. "Teddy here alone?" I asked.

"Wife and kids are in Westchester visiting friends. They'll be back tomorrow. You want a glass of lemonade?"

I followed Scott into the study and ran my hand over a pair of elk tusks that were mounted on the wall over a set of bookshelves. They were pretty damn big and smooth as polished leather. The room was filled with books and hunting trophies and an array of mismatched furniture. I thought of my East Side apartment with my one book on police procedure, bed, chair and the small table I used for eating and as a catchall. Spartan was what the one woman who'd been to my apartment called it. She'd been a pretty redhead who'd wrongly thought she could tie me down. Guess I'm just not much for collecting things…or people.

"If by lemonade you mean whiskey, neat, then yes, I would like a glass."

Scott cocked his eyes at my police uniform. "Hell, I'm off duty. And even if I wasn't, I still want that whiskey."

He laughed. "I'm just messin' with you, Nat. Wanted to see how much of this regimented city life had taken hold of you. Be right back."

I slumped into one of the many rocking chairs in the room and heard it creak so loud I thought it would break into kindling. The more I settled in, the less it protested. Staring at the pattern of the Oriental rug on the floor, I wondered, not for the first time, why Teddy had sent an urgent message for me to come. Far as I knew, we weren't at war with the Spaniards again. Not that I'd mind getting another crack at that nut.

The sound of a door slamming caught my attention and I was about to ask Scott where the hell my drink was when the man himself came bustling into the study like a force of nature.

"Nat Blackburn! You look remarkably fit. I'm so glad you came."

His grip was like a vise. Teddy was always good at letting folks know who the top dog was in the room. I didn't mind it at all because he had proven to me many times that he could stand behind the things he said.

"Far be it from me to deny a presidential request," I said.

Teddy was dressed in a heavy three-piece suit. He wiped his pince-nez clean with a handkerchief. He'd put on some weight since we last met, but it seemed to be all muscle and collected around his broadening chest. There wasn't a drop of sweat on him, even though he'd been out walking in the summer sun. It was over ninety degrees, without a lick of a cool breeze, even out here on Oyster Bay.

Scott came in with two glasses of whiskey. "Pour one for yourself and have a seat," Teddy said to him. He was only too happy to oblige.

Teddy sat in an overstuffed leather chair and fiddled with an ivory-handled knife that was on the side table. I took a sip of my whiskey and winced. Damn, it was good. Better than anything I could buy on a cop's salary.

"How have things been on the force?" Teddy asked me.

"Never a dull moment. Just yesterday I caught a kid stealing bananas from a fruit vendor over on Twenty-Second Street. Kid stomped on my boot and got it all scuffed. He got an ear twist for that."

Teddy blew out a tremendous laugh. "God, I miss your sarcasm. When you get to be president, people talk to you differently. You're no longer a flesh-and-blood man. Mind you, there does need to be a code of conduct, but it's always refreshing to talk to my men. What a lot we were."

The *men* he referred to was the First US Volunteer Cavalry. Folks called us the Rough Riders, and even though we weren't too keen on the moniker, it kind of stuck. Men came from all over the country, itching to fight the Spaniards. Everyone from old cowpokes like me to professional soldiers and rich dandies made up the ranks. All were exceptional when it came to riding and shooting. We'd seen the best and worst of war in a very short time. It was the quickest and hottest summer of my life in some ways.

Colonel Roosevelt and I had shared a moment during the siege of Kettle Hill that I guess had bonded us for life. He claims I saved his life. I say I was just doing what I came to do – kill Spaniards and protect my fellow Rough Riders. He did a good job taking care of us during and after Cuba, getting folks like me settled in New York with jobs and futures. I was damn proud to call the president a friend.

Seeing Teddy brought back the smells of gunpowder and the cordite from the smokeless powder guns the Spanish used, quite successfully when they were sniping from trees and dugouts. The phantom taste of the horrendous canned roast beef the military provided us made me scrape my tongue against the roof of my mouth to exorcize it. If it weren't for the Colonel buying us edible food out of his own pocket, we all would have starved or died from food poisoning.

Scott returned with his drink and we shot the shit for a time. Scott and I knew each other from a brief stint in the Apache Wars while we were out in Arizona and much younger men. He'd gained some measure of infamy with the Cibecue Indians in his time. Now, here we were, in suits sitting with the president in a study that was half trophy room, half library. You never can figure what the hell life is up to.

"So tell me, Nat, how have you found your time in New York?" Teddy said. He paced around the room, all nervous energy, running his fingers along the leather spines of his books. "I know it's a far cry from what you're used to."

I shrugged. "Not much to say. It has its good and bad points."

Teddy wrinkled his brow and pointed at me. His naturally high-pitched voice had dropped a bit, thanks to the whiskey. "I look at you and do you know what I see? I see a God-honest cowboy trapped in a blue uniform. Truth be told, I never thought you'd last this long. After Cuba, I wanted to give you a chance to rest, add a little padding to your bank account, see a city that will be the brightest light in this nation. I assumed that once you'd had your fill, you'd be on the next train to New Mexico or California."

"I'm an old man, Teddy. Old men need a place to take root before they get laid to rest *with* the roots."

"Nonsense! You're not much older than I am and the last thing I want is to take root." Scott said, "You're younger'n me, Nat. You think I should be fitted for a rocker?"

I laughed, bringing up the point that he was currently *in* a rocker.

Teddy slammed his glass on his desk a mite too hard. Good whiskey splashed onto his shoes.

"We're in the prime of our lives, Nat. We have wisdom to go along with our experience and courage. I'm afraid that by letting you stay here, you're in danger of becoming an old codger. Which is why I'm sending you to Wyoming!"

CHAPTER THREE

"Wyoming? Now what could possibly be in Wyoming that has you all fired up?" I said.

Now it was my turn to get up and walk about the room.

Teddy poured two more fingers of whiskey and said, "Opportunity, that's what's in Wyoming. But in order to take advantage of it, we need to clear out a small problem."

I felt a little tingle at the base of my neck. That was the tingle that told me whatever small problem was on Teddy's mind was a mite bigger than he was letting on. And to be honest, I was a tad intrigued. Maybe he was right. I'd spent my entire life wandering across the West, first on cattle drives with my father who was a cook on the Shawnee Trail, then doing some rustling of my own, mostly on the Chisholm Trail, running cattle from Texas to Kansas. Life had always been a battle, whether I was fighting the elements, cattle, shady men in shady saloons, Apaches, Spaniards, you name it. Got so it was in your blood, all this fighting.

"What kind of small problem we talking about? Indians? I thought most of them were settled by now."

"I wish it was Indians. Better the devil you know."

"I'm kind of relieved at that. We fought with some good Indians back in Cuba. Don't know if I'd have the same feelings toward them on the open range."

Teddy nodded. "No, the situation in Wyoming is unique and I wish I could be the one to go out there, but the country needs me here. You ever hear of a town named Hecla?"

"Doesn't ring any bells," I said. I looked over at Scott who shrugged his shoulders. "Back about twenty years ago, it was a mining outpost, west of Cheyenne, out by Laramie.

"Prospectors found great stores of copper and other minerals. The place was bustling, ready to establish itself as the premier source for copper in the entire state. There was even talk of making it a stop on the Union Pacific line. It didn't happen of course. Hecla didn't stay around long enough for the honor. The copper vein petered out."

"Happens all the time with mining towns," I said. I watched the last orange rays of the sun melt over the treetops outside the study window.

"You're right, it does. But not when miners strike gold." That got my attention.

"You mean to tell me the miners left even though they knew there was gold to be had?

"That doesn't make sense. You sure that's not just some tall tale?"

Teddy gripped my shoulder and offered some more whiskey. "I can assure you, gold was discovered in Hecla. For a period of time, it was all people in the area could talk about. I first heard about it during a hunting trip to the Sierra Madres about seven years ago. The locals I met spoke about a gold mine that was there for the taking… if anyone was bold enough to do so."

"So why did everyone pick up and leave? Were they afraid of getting rich?"

"That's the problem. No one knows why. Anyone who has stepped foot in Hecla has disappeared."

In my experience, there was one sure, logical explanation behind this whole Hecla story. I pinched the corner of my upper lip between my teeth and asked, "You sure there aren't any Indians left out of the rez that take offense to white men pillaging their land? In my experience, when folks are run off and others disappear, there's usually an angry and motivated tribe of reds somewhere in the mix."

Teddy grew serious and stared off, his mind somewhere beyond the room. It wasn't often that I saw him pull inside himself like that. I plopped into one of the leather chairs scattered around the room. The mounted head of a brown bear, his black gums curled over sharp teeth, loomed over me.

He said, "I sent a small squad of troops to investigate several months ago, just after my inauguration. The country needs gold, and if private companies weren't going to bring it out, I didn't see why we couldn't. They reported that even the Indians wouldn't go near

Hecla. Nearby townspeople refused to talk to them. And then the squad, too, disappeared." Now, my first instinct was that the boys in that squad chased off the Indians, dug up some gold and took off out West to retire under a new name. Loyalty was hard to come by, especially if there was big-time money involved. I was going to tell Teddy just that but something made me keep my trap shut.

"You want me to locate your missing soldiers?" I said instead.

Teddy stomped over to one of the bookshelves and pulled one out. He said, "That's not your primary mission, but by all means, I would like to find out where they've gone. I need you to go to Hecla to find out what the blue hell is going on there and what we can do to get that gold from the mines. I don't know many men who've been to the places you've been and come out with their scalps intact. You may not know Wyoming, but you know the land. I can't think of anyone I'd trust more to find the truth."

He dropped the faded brown book onto my lap. I picked it up and turned it over. The raised gold lettering on the spine read, *Konungs Skuggsjá: King's Mirror.*

"Reading material for your train ride," Teddy said. "I've already spoken to your sergeant and advised him that you would be in the service of your country for the foreseeable future. I could tell that he wasn't too pleased but knew enough not to voice it to me. You'll take the Union Pacific to Laramie, which is the last town east of Hecla. I'll make sure you have horses and all the provisions you'll need waiting for you."

My mind was spinning, and it wasn't from the whiskey. In the span of several minutes I'd been drafted and thrown into a mystery that could be hazardous to my health.

It sounded good to me.

I knocked back the rest of my drink and nodded. "Can I take Teta with me?"

For the first time since all this talk of Hecla started, Teddy smiled. "I had a feeling you'd say that, so I made plans for him as well. You might want to tell him tonight before he reports for duty tomorrow."

"When do we leave?"

"The day after tomorrow. I figured you'd need a day to put everything in order."

I smiled. "More like five minutes. That'll give me and Teta a chance to have one last night on the town."

Teddy motioned to Scott, who pulled a fat envelope out of his vest pocket and handed it to me.

"Your night on the town and all expenses for the trip are on me. If you need more, there are instructions on how to reach me in Washington inside the envelope."

I stuffed it into my shirt, where no one could easily get at it during my ride back to the city.

We shook hands on the deal. "Guess I'll go find Teta now," I said.

"If I know him, that should be an adventure," Scott said. I laughed in agreement. "Wire me when you get to Laramie," Teddy said.

As I walked out of the study, he added, "You're welcome, by the way."

I tipped my hat and made my way into the night. A soft breeze came over me, heavy with the smell of jasmine.

CHAPTER FOUR

I was on my fourth bar along Madison when I heard someone shout, "So help me God, Noel, if you let that spic win I'll kick your arse clear across the Hudson!"

A crowd had formed at the back of the bar and even though I couldn't see who was at the center of the soon-to-be melee, I knew I'd found Teta.

The men chanted, "Three, two, one, go!"

A violent concussion of shouts, cheers and curses practically shook the walls of the bar. The wood smelled like stale beer, vomit and varnish. Someone was playing a fiddle like the devil was on his ass and the sound of glasses slamming onto the bar top could just be heard over the din.

Leave it to Teta to rile the Irish. I motioned to the bartender to pour me some bourbon and settled on the vacant end of the bar. I'd wait for him to finish what he started.

Half the gin- and beer-soaked men whooped and raised their arms in victory. I watched paper money exchange hands as they parted, the winners dropping their winnings on the bar and ordering enough booze to make walking home a high adventure.

The face of the man I presumed to be Noel came into view. He stared hard at someone to his right. It was a look that said things were about to get uglier than a dead coon's ass.

A fat man with wild, white hair stepped away from the bar and I could finally see Teta, his brown skin in stark contrast to the pale complexions of the several dozen men around him. His scraggly black mustache was peppered with peanut skins. Four large and empty mugs had been turned upside down in front of him. Traces of white foam slid down the glass onto the bar.

Teta saw me and raised his chin, smiling. His lack of concern about the storm brewing beside him was like that of an innocent kid, happy that he'd won a game of marbles. He knew what was coming. I was tempted to let him go it alone. The man was small and lean but strong as an ox and, when prodded, vicious as a bobcat.

A messy pile of bills lay between Teta and the simmering Irishman. I saw Teta's eyes flick toward his winnings. So did the Irishman. The big man slapped a fat hand on top of the bills, sending a few onto the tacky floor.

"You even think of touching that, you cheating spic, and I'll fook you up so bad, your own *madre* won't recognize ya."

Teta reached over and pinched his thumb and forefinger atop the man's hand, slowly lifting it off the money. The Irishman was too stunned to react. It would wear off quickly.

"My madre's dead."

He swept the money off the wet bar and into his shirt pocket. Picking up a black bowler hat from the floor – the left side had been dented in – Teta tipped it to the burly Irishman and walked toward me. A few men, those who had bet and won on him, slapped his back as he passed.

"Having fun?" I asked when he sidled up to me. "*Sí*," he replied with a sly grin.

"Don't expect Noel and the boys to take kindly to your walking off with their money, whether you won it fair and square or not."

He made the sign of the cross and pointed to his heart. "I never cheat. I just drink fast." I watched Noel gather a few of his *compadres* around him. They cast furtive glances our way. I knew from experience they were talking themselves into taking action. They were probably wondering where I fit into things and who would take out whom. "You do understand you're an officer of the law," I said.

"So are you."

The Irishmen, five of them now and one bigger than the other, had formed a tight formation and were steadily making their way down the bar.

"I take it you don't want to make them aware of said fact," I said.

"Not if you don't."

"This is your fight, Teta. I only came to talk. We have big plans, you and I."

"How big?"

"Big enough to get us out of this city."

A hush settled over the bar. The man with the fiddle stopped and put his instrument in its case for safekeeping. All eyes were on the band of men dead set to make Teta regret invading their turf. Not surprisingly, he was the only one who didn't seem to care.

"When?" he asked.

"Day after tomorrow."

"No more police?" A glimmer of hope lit up his face.

I shook my head just as Noel tapped him on the shoulder with a finger as fat and round as the handle of a bullwhip.

Teta turned his head, smiled wide and said, "Yes, yes, yes, I know you want to talk to the complaint department. But you're being rude. I'm in the middle of a conversation with my friend here."

I got up from my seat and took one step back from Teta, my gaze trained on the men at his back.

Noel narrowed his eyes. Thick beads of sweat ran down the tight crevice of his brow and along the sides of his nose.

"I don't give a fiddler's fart what yer doin'. When I—"

With a blur of concentrated fury, Teta lifted the barstool and hoisted it over his shoulder, mashing the guy's face and clipping a black-bearded grizzly of a man to his left. Both went down before they could draw a breath of surprise.

He kicked the man to the right on the top of his kneecap. I heard a pop and a crack as the bone fell to pieces. The man lay on the floor, wailing in pain and clutching the area where he used to have a fully functioning knee.

That left two. I took a sip of my bourbon, rotgut in the truest sense and nothing like what I had been enjoying earlier at Teddy's estate. I nearly dropped it when Teta grabbed a man with a bald head and nasty scar that bisected his face, slamming him facedown on the edge of the bar. He slid the unconscious body in my direction.

"Hey!" I said, stepping aside and holding my drink up high like a matador with his sword.

"Sorry," Teta said with an upward shrug of his shoulders.

The remaining man, much younger than the other four but with a chest that could double for an anvil, stood opening and closing his fists. His head swiveled from side to side as he took in the condition of his fallen mates.

Teta leaned his back against the bar and said, "I'll give you to the count of five to walk out of here on your own." There was no menace in his voice, no trace of an accent to mark him as a foreigner. He'd gone to great pains to not sound like a drifter from the Dominican Republic. It was the voice of a man offering a choice, and in that choice, some sound advice.

"One."

The kid flexed his arms, took a deep breath. "Two."

He wiped the sweat from his brow with his forearm. "Three."

I watched him shift his feet and bend his knees. It was a fighter's stance. "Don't do it, kid," I offered.

He looked my way and spit on the floor, missing my boots by an inch. I raised my glass to him.

"Here's to your future kids who'll be a little…off."

Teta said, "Oh fuck it, five!"

When Teta raised his fist, the kid made to block the punch with his left and counter with his right. His eyes were so fixated on Teta's upper body that he never saw the kick knifing to his balls. A geyser of vomit whooshed out of him and he fell to his knees on legs made of watery grits. His breath hitched in his chest as he struggled for air.

It'd been one hell of a shot.

"Gentlemen, it's been a pleasure," Teta said. He walked over the kid, who had curled into a fetal position.

I put a few extra bills on the bar. "For the cleanup."

The night air felt cool and welcome, compared to the stifling atmosphere in the bar.

Teta and I walked side by side down Madison toward lower Manhattan. "You still got that piece of lead in your boot?" I asked.

Teta laughed. "I never go to bars without it."

"If he's lucky, he'll have cross-eyed kids of his own one day."

"Yes, but maybe he'll teach them to stay out of bar fights that aren't their own." Teta the philosopher.

"So tell me more about this big thing. Where are we going and why?"

We had over twenty blocks ahead of us until we got to our flats in adjoining buildings. I wouldn't be sorry to put them behind us. It didn't seem right, living in such close quarters with so many folks. Getting a moment's peace was as strange and alien there as a cow running for mayor. And the smells. It was no wonder I'd lost a good deal of weight over the past couple of years. My gripes were too many to name.

"While you were out carousing like a common wino, I was meeting with the president."

I told him everything Teddy had relayed to me. Teta was wary, but anxious to leave city life behind. He was born in a shack on a farm and raised more by the animals and elements than his parents. His stint in New York was against his nature. But no matter how many times I told him to skedaddle, he stayed by my side like a tick or a bedbug. Blood brothers, he called us. I was never sure if he meant it in the traditional sense or if he was referring to the prodigious amount of blood we'd shed together.

We parted company in front of his tenement, agreeing to meet around noon the next day.

And for the first time in a long while, I slept like a baby.

CHAPTER FIVE

I was up early the next day. I splashed some tepid water on my face and dumped the rest out the window. My suitcase, a battered old thing that needed four leather straps to keep it in one piece, as well as to prevent my belongings from spilling out, was under my bed where I had stowed it two years earlier.

It felt good to put on my denims, boots, button-down shirt and leather vest. I'd been wearing a police uniform so long I'd forgotten how much I missed my old one. I looked in the mirror and winced.

When did I get old? My father's face stared back at me, though my lined face was a mite paler and my mustache a little thicker, with more flecks of gray. At least my hair was still thick and chestnut brown, like my mother's had been. I ran my fingers along the stubble on my jaw and chin and decided to skip shaving.

I gathered my cop gear and put it all in a paper bag. I pulled my bronze-colored Stetson from a nail I had driven into the wall and secured it on my head. It felt a little tight. I'd break it back in just right.

The Polish family next door was awake as well. Mr. and Mrs. Rakoczi were shouting at one another and their kids had to scream even louder just to be heard. They were normally my alarm clock, but my eagerness to be on my way beat them to the punch. I hammered my fist on the wall for old times' sake and they quieted down a bit.

Teta waited outside holding a similar brown bag. A black sombrero lay against his back.

"Where'd you find that old thing?"

"Where I put it," he said.

"Where'd you put the nice Stetson I got you when we were camped in Santiago?"

"I lost it on a bet. I like my sombrero better. It gives me luck."

From the way he told it, he'd been hired to capture or kill a

Mexican bandit who had held a two-bit town in terror for several months. I couldn't remember the town, but it was somewhere in the western end of Texas. Working alone, Teta strolled down Main Street, telling everyone he met to let the thief know he was there to put him in a box. He'd be waiting for him in the saloon.

It all sounded like something out of a pulp novel, but with Teta you never know.

Sure enough, the Mexican storms into the saloon with a gun in each hand, firing away like he had all the bullets in the world. Luckily, the saloon was relatively empty, so no one got hurt too bad. The Mexican figured the best way to handle Teta was to shoot him in the back. No need for talking. No standoff in the streets. In real life, you had to take your opportunities when they presented themselves.

Unfortunately for him, Teta had just stepped out of the bar to hit the outhouse in the back. He was turning the corner of the saloon when the Mexican busted in.

No dummy himself, Teta walked behind him and shot *him* in the back. The Mexican was dead before his knees buckled.

As the Mexican crumpled to the floor, according to Teta, a harsh wind blew down the street and into the saloon. Somehow, it plucked the sombrero from the Mexican's head and deposited it on Teta's own noggin. He saw it as a sign that the Mexican's spirit held no ill will toward his murderer. Teta worried a lot about the untethered souls he'd set free, assuming they all had designs on haunting him.

At least with the Mexican he knew there was one soul that would let him be.

He'd been wearing the hat ever since, until we came to New York where sombreros were not appreciated on the police force or in the streets.

"I hope you don't plan on wearing it today."

"It needs airing out."

We stopped at the precinct to hand in our badges and guns with little fanfare. Everyone knew that we were fish out of water and our time as New York police would be short-lived. For a while there, I thought maybe I had managed to get myself stuck in an unstickable rut.

Teddy had helped us a good deal by getting us on the force, and had saved us by providing a way out. Teta had stuck around this long not only for me, but because there were several states that would have been none too pleased to see his ugly tan face, Kentucky, Colorado, Florida and Virginia among the batch. We were pretty sure the heat he had stirred up had cooled down enough for him to emerge from hiding within law enforcement, of all places. After that, we went to Mulberry Street to hunt up some food. The street was a mass of people and food stands and pushcarts. Voices blended into a riot of sound, almost none of it English. We got some fresh oranges from one pushcart run by a man dirtier than a sewer rat. But the orange slices were cool and sweet and hard to turn down.

Teta grabbed a couple of potato pancakes wrapped in newspaper from an old woman dressed in black, complete with heavy scarf over her head. Lots of widows in this section of town.

"Anything special you want to do?" I asked.

"I think I'm going to get a trolley to the Astor Library and do some reading. I doubt there'll be anything like it in Hecla or Laramie."

"You want to meet for drinks at Mulligan's tonight?"

"Sí. I'll see you around six."

For a Dominican who had spent the better part of his life as a ranch hand and gun for hire, Teta, whose real name was Nico Delacruz, was about as book smart as any man I knew, with the exception of Teddy Roosevelt and some of the officers we'd fought with in Cuba. He liked to play the part of the dumb foreigner so people would underestimate him. That smoke screen of underestimation was what had kept him alive through more scrapes than he could recall.

The libraries in New York were the one thing that he loved out here in the strange East. More so even, he once told me, than the wife he'd left behind in San Pedro de Macorís. He never talked about her much, just that she could be the best woman a man could want one minute, and the meanest alley cat in the whole Dominican Republic the next. He had a scar that ran down his right arm from the time she'd stabbed him with the filed edge of a coconut. Knowing Teta, I figure he'd had it coming.

CHAPTER SIX

Being a man who had no love of rail travel, the trip to Wyoming was guaranteed to be unpleasant for me. I had resolved myself to it and didn't bother griping to Teta. I just had to keep reminding myself that I would happily be back in a saddle in a few days. Teddy had been generous enough to get us top accommodations, with a sleeping car big enough for four. Nursing slight hangovers from the night before, we took a couple of shots from the bottle of whiskey we brought on board and settled in for the long ride ahead.

The train left Grand Central Station with a sudden lurch and Teta slipped off his seat. He'd somehow managed to land on his sombrero, squashing it pretty good. He didn't appreciate my laughter.

"That's a bad omen," he said, punching it back into shape and hanging it on a hook.

"For your cap, it sure is."

"I'm going to sleep. You want another shot?"

I nodded yes and we each took another belt. Then Teta settled into the narrow bed, closed his eyes and was asleep before we emerged from the tunnel.

The heavy rocking and monotonous clanging of a train was like a lullaby for many, my partner included. It just made my stomach queasy. The only good thing about it was the nice breeze coming in from the window. I leaned against it and breathed in the last sharp, acrid smells of the city. I couldn't say I would miss it. There were a lot of places I'd been I wouldn't miss. Something about the disjointed facts given to me about Hecla had me thinking I'd be adding that town to the list when all was said and done.

We traveled south into Pennsylvania then headed west. I somehow managed to nod off for a spell. When I woke up, Teta's head was hidden behind a big book. It was something called *The War of the Worlds* by a fella named H. G. Wells.

"Picking up some battle tricks?" I asked, rubbing the crust from my eyes with my knuckles.

"I hope not," he said. "I don't think we'd do well if this book came true."

"What's it about?"

"Creatures from the planet Mars landing on Earth and taking over England. Very brutal. If we had their machines in Cuba, the whole thing would have lasted three minutes, tops."

"You would have been out a considerable sum." Teta had been hired by the rebels during the Spanish-American War to help smoke the Spaniards from their nests. He charged by the day. We Rough Riders adopted our little mercenary because he'd done more than his share of fighting and saved quite a few of our hides. Plus, he made Teddy laugh with his stories about traveling the country and all the scrapes he'd gotten in. "Sounds like a hell of a book," I added. I couldn't see why a man would want to waste his time reading about invaders from Mars, but like I said, Teta liked to read. "You steal it from the library? I might have to turn this train around and take you in to the chief."

"I thought about it. I started reading it in the library yesterday. But I decided it was bad luck to do something criminal on the same day I stopped being the police. So I went to a bookstore and picked up a few for the trip." He tapped a crumpled brown bag on the floor with the heel of his boot.

"So you got a bunch of books, and only one bottle of whiskey. I'm starting to regret my decision to have you tag along."

"You want one? I have *The Sign of Four*, a Sherlock Holmes mystery. You like him."

I had read one of his stories back when we were in quarantine on Long Island when we got back from Cuba. The Red Cross provided food and medicine because a lot of the men were awful sick at the time with malaria. They thought there might have been an outbreak of Yellow Fever, which is why they kept us so long. Some of the volunteers brought us books. That Sherlock Holmes story was the first what they call fiction book I'd ever read. It helped pass the time, but I never felt a desire to read another.

"That's okay. I actually have one of my own."

Teta raised his dark, bushy eyebrows in surprise. "Are you bullshitting me?"

"The president himself gave it to me. Said I should read it before we get to Wyoming. I figured I'd start tonight. Maybe it'll help put me to sleep."

I opened my leather bag and gave him the book to look at. "*Konungs Skuggsjá: King's Mirror.* What kind of book is it?"

"It's a book about some Norse legends. I don't know. Why don't we stretch our legs and see if we can get something to eat?"

"You're the *jefe.*"

It felt good to move, even if I was jostled from side to side as the train rolled along. Looking out the window, all I saw was empty space, with green grass that stretched on until the sunset. The air smelled like honey, which was more than welcome since Teta stunk like a bear cat. I'd told him to freshen up before we left because I didn't want to have his stink as a third party in our sleeping car. But we did drink a lot the night before and there wasn't much time to get up and make the train.

An older couple squeezed by us as we entered the dining car. The man – short, balding with a white pencil mustache – saw us heading his way and reached out to grip his wife's hand. Can't say I blamed him. We were dressed in our range gear. With me well over six feet and Teta having honed the dark and dangerous look, it was easy to misconstrue our true personas.

It must have been around seven o'clock and the dining car was just about full. Chattering and the sharp clink of utensils on plates and cups hit us like a hot blast from a coal furnace. I was grateful that my earlier headache had left me during my nap.

I spied a small table toward the rear of the car and headed over. As soon as we sat down, a waiter came to hand us menus and asked if we wanted a drink.

"Two bourbons," Teta said.

"Very good. I'll be back in a moment with your drinks," the waiter said and turned to leave. He was young, barely able to grow out a proper mustache with light-blond hair cut high above his ears.

"Wait!" Teta shouted.

The kid turned around, looked nervous. So did the pair of couples at the table next to us.

For a moment, it seemed everyone had stopped to see what would come next, but I think that was just me being paranoid.

"You didn't ask my friend what he wanted to drink."

"I…I just assumed—" the kid stammered.

I said, "Not a problem. You just bring me the same. We've been cooped up too long and got pretty thirsty. And I'll have a glass of water too.

"See how you make people nervous?" I said, flicking a crumb off the white linen tablecloth.

The bourbons arrived in record time and I ordered the cold chicken plate. Teta asked for the roast beef, as rare as they could make it.

A table of four unattended ladies was seated behind Teta. I caught the eye of one of them, a fine brunette with dark, curious eyes, apple-red lips and a long, graceful neck that looked as soft and pure as milk. The other three were blondes, one more buxom than the other. Teta had a thing for blondes. And blondes had a thing for Teta. It was that whole opposites-attract thing.

I raised my glass in a toast to the pretty brunette, saw the burn on her cheeks. She whispered something to her companions and they leaned their heads into the center of the table and tittered.

"I smell fresh *chicas*," Teta said after he downed his first glass.

"Your nose still works."

"As do your eyes." Teta closed his own, tilted his head back and breathed deep through his nose. "Two, or is it three blondes?"

I'd known Teta for years and I was still unnerved by his strange ability to tell what a woman looked like just by using his flat yet talented nose.

"Three."

Now the brunette and the blonde next to her shifted their eyes to me, both smiling and looking away right quick.

I put my tobacco pouch on the table and rolled a couple of cigarettes. The blonde, I noticed, looked on with barely concealed fascination. Now we had bourbon, good smokes and the attention of four ladies. The only thing that could have made it better was a good meal, and that came before I could finish my cigarette.

The chicken was passable. I assumed Teta's roast beef was as well, judging by the speed with which it disappeared off his plate. The waiter brought the ladies' supper at the same time, and while I worked on rolling another couple of smokes for us, they picked away at their plates with long forks.

"What's your move?" Teta asked with a green broccoli sprout stuck between his front teeth.

"It'll present itself. No need to rush things."

We ordered another round of bourbon just to kill time. It was getting late and the dining car started to empty out.

The ladies finally finished their dessert and when they got up, all four looked in our direction.

Suddenly, the train lurched, pitching the brunette forward. I reached my arm across the aisle and gently caught her by her midsection. Her stomach, even beneath her dress, felt warm and soft, yet firm. I helped her to her feet. She smelled like wild flowers.

"I'm so sorry," she said. "I can be so clumsy."

"Wasn't your fault. These trains can be unpredictable."

"Well, thank you. You're pretty fast. It's a good thing!"

Her breasts had swelled from the top of her dress. They heaved up and down with the rhythm of her breath. They were very nice to look at, but I made sure not to stare.

"If you want, I can walk you back to your car. You never know when the next bit of warped track is going to come up."

She narrowed her eyes, but I could see the curiosity still burned there. She said, "Where are you from?"

"New York."

"I assume that's where you're coming from, but where did you grow up. You are most certainly not an easterner. In fact, I'd say you were an honest-to-God cowboy." She looked down at the spurs on my boots.

"Guilty as charged. I grew up out in New Mexico. Been here and there most of my life."

Teta eyed the three blondes like a starved dog slobbering over a side of beef. He had all the subtlety of a donkey's kick.

"I have another idea," I said. "Would you ladies be interested in staying for a drink? It's a mite too early to turn in and my friend and I would appreciate the company of four beautiful women."

The brunette and I rocked in tandem as the train came around a bend. She considered my offer without consulting with her companions.

The corner of her mouth curled and she said, "It'd be rude to turn down a chance to drink with a cowboy, now wouldn't it?"

⋆　　⋆　　⋆

Her name was Rebecca. She and her girlfriends were going to Chicago to be teachers.

They had gotten jobs at the same school.

I wasn't thinking much about this as I drew her dress over her head and pulled her close. Her tongue tasted sweet from the after-dinner wine. My hand wandered down her back and settled on her round and supple ass. Her hands worked at the buttons on my shirt and jeans. Before I knew it, we were both naked as newborns. I was a lot taller than her, so my hard-on pressed flat against her stomach.

She moaned in my mouth as I cupped her breast and stroked my fingers over her nipple.

It stiffened at my touch and I bent down to lick it. "Oh yes, Nat," she whispered.

She reached out and wrapped her fingers around me, stroking me long and slow. I returned the favor by pressing my fingers into the slick warmth of her pussy. Two of my fingers slid in with ease and I felt her nails dig into my shoulder.

"I want you in me."

Keeping my fingers inside her, I lifted her in my other arm and laid her on the bed. She surprised me by turning onto her stomach and drawing herself up on her hands and knees.

"Like this," she husked.

She spread her legs and slid her hand over her ass, her fingertip resting just above where she wanted me.

Rebecca screamed when I entered her, rocking back and forth with an almost-feral abandon. I put my hands on her soft hips and took the lead from her. She buried her face in the pillow to hide her squeals.

For the first time in my life, I kind of liked trains.

CHAPTER SEVEN

We had to get off to change trains in Chicago. I gave Rebecca a polite nod as we parted company on the crowded platform. Rebecca winked and flashed me the same grin she had given me after our third go-around last night. It was enough to make a weaker man soft in the knees and ready to change his immediate plans. She and her friends headed to their futures as shapers of minds in a new city. I had to give them credit for guts.

Teta had dark circles under his eyes but it was hard to notice them above the smile on his face.

"You have fun last night?" I asked.

"Yes. I think I'll name my next horse Charlotte. She had tits a man could die between."

Teta liked to name his horses after special women in his life. I'd noticed how he never mentioned naming a horse after his wife.

"You do know how to flatter your ladyfolk."

He had spent the night in Charlotte's sleeping car, on account of ours being full. The other two gals spent the night in Rebecca's. We were all tired, but for a good cause.

The smell of coal smoke was overpowering on the platform, so we ambled into the station. People moved in every direction like ants, all in a hurry to get somewhere other than here. I got a newspaper so I could see how crime fared in Chicago. Call it professional curiosity.

We settled onto a long bench and Teta's eyes were closed before his ass finished settling. I scanned through the paper, peeking above it from time to time to watch the menagerie of folks around me. It was a very well-dressed, civil crowd. Nothing like I suspected would be waiting for us in Wyoming. There wasn't much call for suits and fedoras out there.

It didn't take long before I fell asleep.

The old man with the white pencil mustache woke us both up when the call went out to board the next train.

"I like your spurs," he said. "Always wanted a pair myself when I was younger."

"How do you like my sombrero?" Teta asked.

The man gave a polite smile and hurried to join his wife.

"Guess he doesn't know how lucky it is," I said, popping my knees as I got up from the bench.

★   ★   ★

The rest of the trip was uneventful, which was fine by me. We passed through Iowa and Nebraska. I caught up on some much-needed sleep and set about reading that book Teddy had given me. My first attempt put me to sleep in less than ten minutes. When I woke up, the book was on the floor and Teta was happily reading about Martians.

For the life of me, I couldn't figure out how a book about Norse legends would have any connection with our little mission. It wasn't written in any kind of English that I could comprehend and sure as hell had nothing to do with mining towns. I gave up when we entered Wyoming and stuffed it in my bag.

The weather got hotter and the land dustier as we pulled away from the station at Cheyenne. Laramie was the next and, for us, last stop.

I spotted the conductor and asked, "How much longer to Laramie?"

He checked his pocket watch and said, "About three hours or so. We should pull in around half past six."

Teta pulled his sombrero over his face. "That sounds like enough time for a good nap."

"You've been asleep more than you've been awake since we left New York."

"A man must always take advantage of opportunities to piss and sleep. I've done the one, now it's time to do the other."

I tried to follow his lead but sleep didn't come easily. I was anxious to get back on solid ground. The closer we got, the more anxious I felt. Hecla was a mystery that had swallowed up U.S. troops and scared off anyone who dared to venture there. The sooner I could see things for myself, the easier I'd feel.

We stopped in Laramie right on time. The station was nothing like they had in places like Chicago or New York, but very much like every other station we'd passed through during the long trip. It was a fair-sized wood-frame building with a long porch dotted with benches. A few folks milled about. The horizon was pink and laced with low clouds.

Teta said, "I think it's too late to get horses and supplies."

"Me too."

I walked to the station agent's window. My spurs rang with each step. He looked disappointed that only the two of us had gotten off the train. I guess we weren't much to look at.

"Excuse me, is there a place we can put up for the night?"

He used the rubber end of a pencil to scratch his forehead, pushing his cap in the process. A fly buzzed around his head and landed on his lip. He didn't pay it any mind. "Hotel's right up the street." He pointed to my left.

There was a series of connected three-floor buildings not more than a hundred paces from the station.

"Thank you kindly. I'd also like to send a wire."

He pushed a piece of paper and a pencil toward me. I wrote to Teddy that we had arrived safely and would set out in the morning. I passed my message and a coin back to the station master and we walked to the hotel.

Rectangular plots of grass were set up in front of the hotel and fenced in by long metal posts. In the center of each was a small tree. Very ornamental.

There was a sign for a lunch counter but the door was closed. We'd missed lunch by a good number of hours.

The front desk clerk wore a heavy wool suit despite the heat. He was bald and pale, which told me he didn't leave the hotel much. It was hard to avoid the sun in Wyoming in the summer.

"We need a couple of rooms," I said.

He sucked his teeth and cast a disapproving gaze at my sombrero-wearing companion. "There a problem?" I asked, at the same time communicating with my eyes that there'd better *not* be a problem. He broke his gaze quicker than a cat in a staring contest. I wasn't in the mood for his bigoted bullshit.

"You're in luck. I happen to have two available. How long will you be staying?"

"Just tonight."

We signed his ledger and I paid him for the night with the money from the envelope Teddy had given me. He gave us our keys from a pegboard. I looked at one of the notes that had been stuffed in the envelope and asked, "Can you point us in the direction of the McCallum Stable?"

"Yes, I thought that might be where you were headed. Do you men break horses or something?"

"Something," Teta replied.

Realizing that was all the information we were going to give, the clerk continued, "Just make a right out the front door and your first left onto Weed Street. You'll pass the Methodist church on your right, the school and a few houses. McCallum's is at the end of the road."

We stowed our gear in our rooms and headed to a restaurant across the street. The steaks were rare and creamy as butter. There weren't many people in the restaurant or about the streets. We tried the local beer, deemed it worthy and had a few more before heading back for what was most likely our last night in a decent bed for a while.

★   ★   ★

The next morning broke hot and humid. Teta and I left the hotel early and headed over to McCallum's. Laramie was very much alive this time of the day. Men walked in every direction, some heading to the brickyard, others the plaster mill or slaughterhouse.

Folks gave us queer glances as they filed around us. I didn't see a solitary Stetson in the herd. I felt like a man out of time, more so than I had in New York, because Wyoming was so close to my old stomping grounds. I'd only been on earth for fifty years and in that time I'd gone from riding in a rickety chuck wagon, herding cattle, to having to sidestep loud automobiles with tires skinny as a rat's behind.

As we walked, Teta pulled a folded paper from his back pocket and handed it to me. "The *Laramie Weekly Boomerang*. What the hell kind of a name is that for a newspaper?" I asked.

Teta shrugged his shoulders. "I like it. It's different. Not sure if you'll like it, though. No crime to report."

I stuffed it in my bag. "Might come in handy for something other than reading later."

A bunch of kids were running around outside the school. One of them kicked a can our way and I sidestepped so it could skip by me. The Methodist church was across the street and I could see the sign for the small stable ahead.

We were met by a man as old and weathered as a deerskin coat. His skin was shriveled and lined like jerky, but I could tell none of his strength had been sapped by years or hardship. In most cases with old ranch hands like him, a life of hard work made them tougher than a one dollar steak.

"You here about them horses?" he asked as we strolled up to the round horse pen. He was shoveling piles of shit into a wheelbarrow.

"We are."

"Court McCallum. Pleased to meet you. Got them waiting for you out back."

This was a man I could take a shine to. I hadn't run across many honest, old-time ranchers in New York, or any to be exact.

"That's two Appaloosas, two quarter horses and one mule, plus tack. They were ordered by a man called himself Theodore Roosevelt. No chance that would be the president, is there?"

"They would be one and the same," I said.

"No shit. You just cost me a dollar. I told my daughter it was just someone with the same name." His ice-blue eyes, still clear and honest as the morning sky, took us in with newfound interest. "You and your *vaquero* friend don't exactly look the presidential type, if you don't mind my saying so."

Teta, who had been staring at the ranch house, said, "That's why we left the job for Roosevelt."

The old man considered him a moment, then jerked with an internal laugh. He shouted, "Selma!"

I heard a woman shout back, "Just about ready!"

"That's my daughter. She's getting everything fixed up for you. I also picked up the list of supplies. You should be all set to go. Hasn't been much call for our services lately. Folks would rather drive those fancy cars. I swear people are going to get themselves killed on those things."

"Thank you." I decided now was a good time to see what he knew about Hecla and the troops that had been sent by Teddy. I had toyed with the idea of staying in town for the day and talking things up, but my desire to get my ass in motion was greater. "Were you the one to supply the troops that came here a few months back?"

"Troops? Can't recall having any soldiers come through. At least not to my stable. Any reason why they would be in Laramie?"

"I'd heard about a squad passing through. Just wondering if you'd done business with them."

"You a soldier too?"

I shook my head. "Not anymore. We did about four months of soldierin'. That was enough for us."

I heard the steady clop of horses and spotted our cow ponies. There was a dun-colored quarter horse with rippling hindquarters leading the way. She looked strong and fast, and had just a hint of wildness in her dark eyes.

"I'll take that Appaloosa," Teta said, pointing at the spotted stallion. Its front quarters were chocolate brown, but the rest looked like a can of paint had been tossed over it. It wasn't pretty, but I knew Appaloosas to be damn fine horses, especially in rough terrain.

Standing in between them was an almond-skinned woman with jet-black hair tied up under her hat. She had full, black eyebrows and a round, pretty face. Selma possessed a comely body that amply filled her clothes. She looked like she'd done her share of a man's work. She smiled with teeth so white they reflected the sun.

"Thank you, Selma," the old man said, taking the reins from her hands.

I think it was safe to say he'd taken on a Mexican beauty as a wife some, oh, thirty-odd years or so ago. My old heart did a little dance as I took her in.

"Thank you, Selma," Teta mimicked. He struck his casual-but-dangerous pose, hoping to get a rise out of her.

She nodded in his direction and said to me, "You've got four of our finest, Mr. Blackburn. They'll take good care of you."

She wore a blue-and-white shirt tucked into tight denims. The buttons along the front of her shirt were working hard to keep things together. I actually had to take a moment to catch my breath. I'd only once before been taken by a woman like this and the feeling was like standing too close to a lightning strike.

She mistook my silence for confusion and added, "I remembered your name from the order. And you're Mr. Delacruz, right?"

Teta tipped his hat.

I had to get while the going was good. Any more time around her smile and I'd be helpless.

"They look ace-high. Appreciate what you've done."

She patted the dun horse and gave us some carrots. "A little something to help you bond." She flashed that smile again. It was hard reconciling that this half-Mexican beauty was the old man's.

"We'll have plenty of time to bond on our way to Hecla. I looked at a map and it seems to be about a half day's ride from here. That sound about right?"

The old man's demeanor changed as quickly as a flash flood. He turned to his daughter and said through clenched teeth, "Best you get inside. I have a feeling those biscuits are about to burn."

Selma's smile vanished and her hand flew to her mouth. She started to say something, stopped, then turned and jogged to the ranch house.

When the old man saw she was out of earshot, he leaned over the pen fence and said, "I have a mind to keep these horses and save you the trip."

"There a problem with Hecla?" I asked.

He ignored my question. "But seeing this was all ordered by the president, I don't suppose I should stop you. I voted for the man and I'm not one to say I know more than him. All I can say is good luck to you."

With that, he opened the pen and made a bowlegged walk to the house. "Another bad omen," Teta said as he mounted his Appaloosa.

"Just another log for the fire. *Giddup!*"

With our spare horses and loaded pack mule in tow, we headed for Hecla. I was growing less enthusiastic by the minute.

CHAPTER EIGHT

As I suspected, my horse still had a bit of a wild streak left in her. She tried to rile me with a quick twitch a couple of times and fought the bit, but I held steady, letting her know this wasn't a Sunday ride with a pretty girl.

It was obvious that the area had been going through a dry spell. The switchgrass wasn't as tall as it should be and was turning a light brown. My nose felt like it was packed with dust. I tipped my canteen to let some water splash over my face.

"You hot?" Teta asked. He and his stallion rode in lockstep beside me.

"Not yet. Just clearing the airways."

I breathed the water into my nose then turned my head and snorted it out.

We rode on a flat plain under a sun that felt inches above our heads. I could see the outline of what I figured to be the Deep Rock Hills in the far distance. That was where most of the mining had taken place in Hecla. Might as well rename them the Disappearing Hills.

I spotted a cloud of dust to our left and saw a small herd of antelope taking flight. There was a time you couldn't set foot in Wyoming without seeing a buffalo. We'd yet to spy a single one.

"I suppose we'll have our pick of places to shack up," I said.

"Unless the soldiers decided to move in for good and aren't the sharing kind."

"Unless that."

"How long has it been since anyone did any mining there?" Teta asked.

A red-tailed hawk sailed high overhead. I lost him when he crossed over the sun. "Few years. According to Teddy, one day the townsfolk were there, working the mines, next day they weren't. No one knows where they went, but we both know it's easy to make yourself disappear out here."

"How many people were in the town and working for the mine?"

"About a hundred fifty or so, including the women and children."

"Seems like a lot of people to take off without someone turning up somewhere." He had a point.

"Maybe they did turn up, but no one's really looking for them. What's important is what's under those hills."

"You think gold is worth more than a person?"

"It is for a good number of people I've met."

Teta laughed. "Me too. Don't know many people who would trade a bar of gold for me." In fact, I knew a few, myself included. Back in Cuba when we were starving from the lack of rations, hard tack was scarce, canned meat was revolting and beans were running low. It was Teta who worked beside Teddy, rounding up food from among the villagers, keeping our bellies full for a long, rough week. He was also the one who took out a Spanish sniper that had been fixed in a tree, happy as a murderous monkey. That damn sniper had shot one of my men in the face and nearly took off the top of my head.

When we made the charge up Kettle Hill, Teddy shouting, tall in his saddle, begging for a bullet, Teta had joined the madness after mounting a horse that had lost its rider. I thought we would all be killed that day. Teta, a man who by nationality had no dog in the fight, just a small mercenary fee that never materialized, jumped into the fray without a care for his own well-being. Before it was over, we would both save each other's lives more than once.

He was worth his weight and more in gold.

I just didn't give him the satisfaction of telling him that. I didn't want his head to outgrow his sombrero.

We came upon the bone orchard about a couple of hours after noontime. It had been placed on the outskirts of the temporary town and judging by the number of crooked wooden crosses planted in the loose soil, the Hecla mines were a tad more dangerous than most.

Teta made the sign of the cross as we inspected the graves. He stared at me until I did the same. His eyes grew wide and I followed his gaze. Two fat crows were perched on a pair of neighboring crosses.

"Bone orchards are always full of birds," I said to him. I wasn't in the mood to hear anything else about omens. "Good a place to rest as any."

"I count one hundred fifty-nine graves. How long did you say this mine was open for?"

"I think it was only a few years. It only takes one big accident to claim a lot of men. But I'll give you that it does seem like a lot for a place small as this. They must have had as many dead beneath the ground as living above in the end."

We rode into a series of half-collapsed houses a stone's throw from the graveyard. They were all leaning to the left. A windstorm must have swept through and had its way with the abandoned structures.

It didn't take long to get to the town proper. It wasn't much to write home about, with just a few structures on either side of the street. Glaringly absent was a church. Even the smallest mining towns usually had a church.

Teta dismounted to look inside one of the houses.

"Nothing but dust and broken furniture. I don't even think rats would stay here," he said. His hand was on the butt of his pistol. Just because a place *looked* empty didn't mean it *was* empty. I laid my rifle across the saddle, just in case.

"I'll check a couple more."

The only sound was the sharp *chink* of Teta's spurs as he carefully inspected all of the houses. There wasn't a lick of a breeze and the silence was this side of unnatural. When my horse snorted, I gripped the rifle tighter.

Get a hold of yourself, Nat.

I remembered a similar day when I was with a patrol of scouts looking for the White Mountain Apaches that had started to cause some concern among the enlisted at Fort Apache. Their medicine man, Nock-ay-det-klinne, had roused them all up, swearing he was going to raise some Apaches from the dead. His secretive ghost dances had begun to sway the Apaches who worked as scouts for the fort. They thought if he could bring the dead back to life, he would be the most powerful Indian leader in the world, more powerful than any white man. It was time to choose sides, and it wasn't hard to figure out which direction their wind was blowing.

I was sent with two other men to find out where Nock-ay-det-klinne was holding his ghost dances, since the Apaches who were still loyal to us refused to disclose his whereabouts or describe what was involved with the ghost dance. I guessed it was some form of Apache magic. My concern, all of ours, was that belief in that magic would lead to very real and violent action.

We tracked them to a cave. The day was like this, hot as a whorehouse on nickel night and quiet as death. We'd left our horses behind an outcrop of fallen rocks and crept to the mouth of the cave. There wasn't a sound coming out of that hole in the hill. But we knew they were in there. We crouched outside, too afraid to move or even breathe. Caves were a terrible place to conceal sound, but somehow they managed it. I only needed one of them to so much as cough so I could have the proof I needed to report back to the fort.

We waited for them to do something, anything. Day bled into night, and still not a sound. I wasn't about to take a French leave, even though my companions kept motioning for us to skedaddle.

The first Apache scream tore out of that cave like a flock of mad bats and made our hair stand on end. A fire was lit deep in the cave and we could only make out dark, twisted shadows as the ghost dance began.

We were the first and only white men to ever see Nock-ay-det-klinne's ghost dance. It looked like any other Indian dance to me, but to them Apaches it meant the coming of a new age and the end of the white man and our rules.

We hightailed it back to Fort Apache and told Colonel Carr where he could find them. By the time the troops mustered out, the Apaches were gone, but they couldn't hide forever. Nock-ay-det-klinne never did bring those men to life, and he was eventually shot in the throat and died. He'd fought hard, like a true warrior. At the time, I was worried his death would only make things worse. Lucky for us, it didn't.

Those Apaches showed me that an enemy could hide anywhere, beyond the reach of your senses. I was kind of sorry Nock-ay-det-klinne never did what he set out to accomplish. It would have been a hell of a trick, and I couldn't blame him for wanting to establish his place in the world.

Teta woke me from my daydream when he shouted, "All clear!"

"Let's move on to the next. Must be a dozen more to the east. I'll help you look them over."

I dismounted and tied my horse to a withered ash tree and joined Teta's side. Together we poked around the homes. All of the doors were open, most of them hanging off their hinges. Practically nothing had been left behind, not even a stray dish or wash basin. I'd been to my share of abandoned mining towns and you could always find something left in the departing miners' wake.

I looked down the parallel row of frame houses and one-room cabins and noted their coloration, worn and sanded down like they had been in a month-long sandstorm. The rooftops were in sore shape, many of them caved in. Hecla was like a fish that had been cleaned and gutted, and left to dry and rot in the unrelenting sun.

If I hadn't known better, I would have sworn this place had been left behind forty years ago.

Teta must have felt the same way, because he turned to me and said, "You sure we have the right place? Nobody's been here since I was working on my *padre*'s farm."

I pointed to a building slightly larger than the others, to our north. It had a raised but warped porch with a pockmarked sign above the opening where a door would have been. It read *HECLA MERCANTILE.*

"I'd say that's our proof, unless a twister picked that store up and dropped it here." Teta holstered his gun and rubbed his arms as if he were cold.

"Come on, let's check out the rest."

Hecla had been a small town on the outskirts of the Deep Rock Hills. By all appearances, it was a mite tiny for a place that had gone from copper, to gold, to population zero. The moment gold had been discovered should have sparked an influx of miners and their families, all hell-bent on getting rich. Mining towns always, and I mean always, exploded at the mere mention of gold. Most places burst at the seams with houses, saloons and throngs of people stricken with fever. Gold towns grew and grew until they went bust.

There wasn't much left here, but everything we had seen and heard about Hecla didn't add up. If any lesser man had sent us here, I would have thought we were being played for fools and turned back to Laramie.

This place was a ghost town, nothing more.

We pressed on. There were two saloons, though the second was barely big enough to seat a dozen men. It looked more like a sitting room with a bar top. Other than the mercantile, these were the only businesses in town. Mining could be a temporary operation, so towns got by on the bare minimum. Far as I was concerned, more than that was wasteful. Places like New York had too much to distract a man.

The edges of the sky were turning a light purple when I said, "I think it's safe to say no one's home."

"You want to hole up in one of the houses for the night?"

"Not necessarily, but I'm not sure I want to be out in the open."

"How about that one, jefe?"

He jerked his chin in the direction of one of the few houses that still had a door, stable roof and even glass in the windows. There hadn't been a stick of furniture inside.

"Better than most."

"I'll get some firewood, start supper," he said.

"I spied a water pump and trough behind the saloon. I'll take care of the horses."

Teta narrowed his dark eyes and said, "Be careful. I know we haven't found anyone, but that doesn't mean someone isn't here. And if they're hiding, it's not for a good reason."

"You don't have to tell me twice."

I swung my rifle over my shoulder and grabbed the reins of the horses to lead them to the saloon.

It only took a minute of pumping to get the water flowing again. It came up surprisingly clear and cool. The horses dipped their muzzles into the trough. It had been a long day.

After filling a spare canteen, I walked to the house. Even with the sun sliding behind the hills, it remained hot and still. I turned on my heels a couple of times because I couldn't shake the feeling that someone was at my back.

Teta had a nice fire going and was cooking a can of beans and pork. "Do we at least have water?"

"That we do," I said.

"I laid your bedroll out inside. Even the mice don't hang around here."

"That's one good thing about this place. I'm not fond of them crawling around me. The older I get, the more I appreciate the comfort of a nice bed."

We talked more than usual as we ate, trying to fill the silence. Growing up just shy of wild animals, we were both used to spending the night in the middle of nowhere. But even in the dead of night in the midst of some untamed prairie, the night had its own kind of music that let you know life went on while you slept.

Here, it was more like being sealed in your own coffin and lowered into the ground.

Teta pulled a thick piece of jerky with his teeth and said, "You want to check the mines tomorrow?"

"Might as well. At least one of them. Teddy said there may be as many as a dozen entrances."

"You ever gone in a mine before?"

"Nope. All my life's work has been done above ground."

"Me neither. I don't like not knowing what to expect."

"Shit, Teta, I have a feeling even if we had twenty years' experience in mines, we wouldn't know what to expect here."

I pitched the dregs of my coffee into the fire and listened to it sizzle as it struck the hot center. When I got up, my back cracked as I straightened.

"Old bones," Teta said, grinning.

"Laugh all you want. Your bones aren't far behind. I'm going to get the horses, tie 'em up by that patch of grass."

By the time I got back, the fire was out and Teta had a hurricane lamp going in the house. He was on his bedroll, reading his Martian book.

"Not tired?" I asked.

"I am, but I want to read a little before I sack out. You forget you're with a *muy inteligente* Dominican."

"How can I? You never give me a chance to forget."

I was dead tired myself, and fell asleep the moment I put my hat over my face.

CHAPTER NINE

Sometime during the night, a strong wind kicked up, whistling through the cracks in the planks of the house's walls. A cloud was over the moon, and at first I couldn't see my hand in front of my face.

Teta was sawing logs somewhere in the dark.

What woke me up?

I'm a light sleeper, but it takes more than a little wind to wake me. I waited for my eyes to adjust, scanning the room from right to left until I could make out Teta's shape under his blanket. The temperature had dropped considerably. It was the kind of thing that happened more in the desert, not the plains of Wyoming.

There was a sharp chill in the air that I felt down into the center of my gut. Like everything else in Hecla, it didn't seem right, didn't quite belong.

One of the horses nickered outside and I heard them shuffle about.

Clunk.

My hand went to my pistol when I heard what sounded like a boot stepping on wood outside the front door.

I waited. If someone was about to come in, it was better I let them come. They wouldn't be expecting me to be awake and ready. Leaves skittered against the thin panes of glass in the window.

Clunk.

Steadying my breath, I slowly pulled my blanket over my body so my gun hand was free.

The wood groaned as if a heavy weight had shifted on the other side of the door.

I'd been right to be cautious. Someone was listening, waiting. I had to keep a mind to watch the window as well, in case whoever was outside had an accomplice.

The door handle turned, slowly at first. I aimed my pistol

midway up the frame, where a man's chest would be. If I was going to get the first shot off, I wanted it to count.

I could just make out the copper-colored handle as it turned clockwise.

Come on, just a little more.

There was a gust of wind and suddenly the door flew open. It stopped short of slamming into the wall.

I tightened my finger on the trigger and sprang to my feet. There was no one there.

I ran to the door, stopped and peered outside. Nothing. If someone had been there, I would have at least heard them beating a retreat. Even a skilled Apache made enough noise for a trained ear to detect.

I circled the house, looking for tracks, finding none but Teta's and my own. The town lay as silent as it had been when we first came upon it.

What the hell was that? Maybe my mind was playing tricks on me. I'd probably dragged a dream with me when the wind woke me up. And then the same wind forced the door open. The creaking was the wood of an abandoned house settling.

"Get your head straight, Nat," I mumbled and settled back onto my bedroll.

The wind had stopped. I listened for anything, straining so hard that my ears began to ring from the absence of noise.

I kept my hand on my gun and slipped it under the rolled-up blanket I used for a pillow. After a while, I drifted back to sleep, wondering what the hell I'd gotten myself into.

CHAPTER TEN

I woke up minutes before sunrise. I like to think that my body is aligned with the sun, and we both know when it's time to get a move on. Being out in the country had me back to my old self.

I gave Teta a gentle nudge. He'd fallen asleep with his book on his chest and it was still there. While I was hunting for shadows in the night, he'd slept like a dead man. It wasn't like him.

"Rise and shine, you odd stick."

He propped himself up on his elbows and looked out the dusky window with squinty eyes.

"Sun's not even up yet, jefe. Why are you in a rush to walk into some dark holes?"

"The sooner we're in, the sooner we're out. No sense wasting time. I'll heat us up a pot of Arbuckle's, get the blood flowing."

"Arbuckle's? I remember that stuff tasted like tar."

"That's because you don't know shit about making a decent pot of coffee."

For some reason, I was relieved to see the horses and mule were still where I'd left them. I hadn't realized I'd been concerned about their whereabouts until I saw them. Despite the fact that I hadn't spotted anyone snooping around, I couldn't shake the feeling that someone had been outside the house.

I started a small fire and put the kettle on. Teta emerged from the house the moment he smelled the fat strips of bacon I'd laid across the frying pan.

"You mind doing me a favor and taking over for a bit?" I asked.

He must have seen the look of concern on my face because he didn't protest. He just nodded and I walked off toward the mercantile.

I spent the better part of the next half hour reexploring every store, cabin and storage shed in the area. It was the only way to ease my concern. Even in its prime, Hecla mustn't have been much to look at. Now, it seemed less than a memory.

By the time I was done, Teta had finished eating but had set aside a plate for me. He'd even made a pan of biscuits. They were burnt on the bottom but there was no sense complaining. I'd burned my fair share of biscuits. My father always said the burnt parts were good for digestion.

"You find what you were looking for?" Teta said while he cleaned the barrel of his Colt.

"Unfortunately, I didn't. If Teddy sent a dozen men here not too long ago, they would have done what we have, right?" I pointed at the fire between us.

"Of course."

"And odds are they would have commandeered a few of the places here to act as a base camp and hole up for the night. If you were one of them, where would you go?"

"In this one. It's in the best shape from all we've seen." A glimmer of understanding colored his eyes.

"Does it look to you like there have been any recent fires in or around this place?"

"No one's used the hearth inside for a very long time."

"And I haven't seen any trace of a fire outside or inside any of the cabins. If they were here a few months ago, it would have been colder, especially at night. They would have needed bigger fires, both for warmth and to feed everyone. There'd be no sense to wipe the place clean because it wasn't like they were on the hunt or being tracked. They were here to do some recon on a damn mine. Even if you take them out of the equation, place like this is pretty enticing for anyone passing through. If I didn't know better, I'd swear to Jesus that no one has so much as set a foot in Hecla since Cleveland was president."

"Do you think someone is working hard to make sure this town *looks* deserted?" That same question had been nagging me from the moment I'd woken up.

"Did you hear me get up last night and go outside?"

"If I did, I probably thought it was better you take a piss without me."

He gave a weak smile that dropped when he saw I wasn't joining in the fun.

"I thought I heard someone outside the door. They walked up the steps loud as can be. I even watched the doorknob turn as someone tried to get in. I was ready to shoot first and ask questions later. Then it was like the wind blew the door open and I ran outside, looking for whoever had been creeping around."

"Why didn't you wake me up?"

"I think I was too amazed that you stayed asleep in the first place. I kept expecting you to get up, but you didn't even move."

Teta removed his sombrero and scratched his unruly, dark hair. "That doesn't make sense. I'm not a heavy sleeper, even when I've drunk myself stupid."

"All I know is that there wasn't anyone outside. At least not so far as I could tell."

We sat in silence while I finished my breakfast. There was no need to give voice to what we were thinking. I knew we were both on the same page. At least I hoped he wasn't thinking that his friend was getting too old and skittish to be out in the bush.

No, if he felt that way, he'd tell me, if only to keep me from harm. I said, "Guess we should see the mine."

Teta holstered his pistol and beat the dust off his pants. "Let's get it over with."

★   ★   ★

We rode the horses out to the multilayered Deep Rock Hills. There were plenty of houses on the outskirts of town, especially as we got closer to the hills. They looked in worse shape than the ones in town. It was fine country around the hills. Great forests of pine trees stretched as far as the eye could see in either direction. The closer we got to the mine, the more lush and green the vegetation became, as if this patch of land had been spared by the drought.

Or maybe it had long underground veins that drank the town dry.

We rode up the path that had been carved into the hills leading up to the mines. The trees petered out the higher we went. There were a lot of stumps, the trees having been clear-cut to make room for the miners and their equipment.

We slowed down to a trot. I saw the first open shaft dead ahead.

"Maybe this is where we should camp tonight?" Teta said, breathing deep. "At least it smells alive here."

We tied our horses to a half-broken hitching post. The trees were filled with birds, singing and fluttering overhead. The air here felt cooler, more humid.

"Hand me that lamp," I said. We each had full hurricane lamps, with spare candles in our pockets. I wasn't planning to go very deep because I had no idea what one needed to do in a mine and come out alive.

The wood slats that had been designed as a kind of covering for the mine's entrance lay on the ground. They'd been there awhile. Tall, sturdy weeds grew through the cracks.

A lintel composed of two-by-fours had been hammered into the mouth of the mine. I didn't put much faith in some chunks of lumber to hold up an entire hillside. Folks said that to be a miner, you had to be at least half-mad. Looking into the abandoned shaft, I came to the conclusion that miners had to be completely insane. It looked about as safe as walking into a pen of pissed-off bulls.

Old, dust-covered rail tracks led into the darkness. I looked to my left and saw one of the ore cars off the tracks and on its side, rusted from the elements. Teta bent low to look inside the car. He spit on his hand, swept it along the bottom and inspected his fingers.

"Nothing in there but dried ore. Definitely no gold."

"I don't expect we'll find any gold this close to the surface. Anyone who took the time to bring it this far would have taken it with them."

The steady *plink-plink* of dripping water echoed in the shaft. I took a hesitant step inside and squinted into the blackness. I couldn't see a thing beyond twenty or so feet. It was easy to imagine Nock-ay-det-klinne and his Apache warriors waiting in the depths to perform their ghost dance. I shivered, and it wasn't from the dip in temperature in the tunnel.

I struck a match against the rough wall, lit my lamp and handed the match to Teta so he could fire his up.

I motioned him forward and asked, "Would you care to lead this dance?"

He shook his head. "Teddy called you to come here. I'm just the sidekick."

Out of the corner of my eye, I watched him make the sign of the cross. "You got any prayers to go with all of that gesticulating?"

"I'm praying the ceiling doesn't cave in on us and we get back to our camp in one piece so we can share some of the whiskey I bought in Laramie."

"Sounds like a worthy prayer to me. And I like the whiskey incentive. Come on, let's get a wiggle on."

We walked in the center of the tracks, our bootheels and spurs making quite the racket. It gave me a sort of comfort, knowing that there was no way for someone to sneak up on you in the mine without being heard from a mile off. There was a bend to the right and when I turned around, the bright mouth of the shaft was replaced by dark walls. Timber pilings lined the walls and ceiling, the wood soft with decay.

"I'll give this one thing, it is a hell of a lot cooler in here. Feels better than a cold bath," I said.

"I'll settle for the bath."

The farther we went in, the narrower the passage became. The ceiling dropped and my Stetson caught on a finger of rock and flipped off my head. Teta was a good five inches shorter than me, so his sombrero was safe. I had to hunch down to keep from braining myself on the ceiling.

"I don't like this," Teta said. "It feels like we're buried alive."

"In a way, we are."

"Thank you, Nat. I needed your reassurance."

As we ventured deeper, more water ran along the carved floor. Our boots splashed through water colder than a well-digger's ass. My toes started to tingle. I'd never been much of a cold-weather person. My first winter in New York nearly killed me. I'd gotten frostbite more times than I could count while walking my beat.

I saw a few bottles on the ground and a dented miner's cap. I watched the floor carefully, mindful of any holes that had opened up. I wanted to avoid plunging to my death at all costs.

We came to a fork and stopped.

"I don't suppose you want to split up," I said.

"You suppose right."

"Right or left?"

"Right. I'll hang my bandana here so when we head back, we know we're in the right direction. It's so dark in here, I have no idea which way is up."

He hung his soiled red bandana on a splinter jutting out from a two-by-four. It didn't take long to see that this particular vein was just big enough to accommodate a medium-sized man and a small ore car. Now I had to bend at the knees and hunker my head down. My shoulders scraped against the jagged walls. Even Teta was feeling the pinch. He'd removed his sombrero and it hung down his back.

The more we walked, the colder it got. The water was up to our ankles in spots, barely a trickle in others. I held up my hand to stop.

"Let's just listen for a bit."

Even holding my lamp out as far as I could, its light was devoured by the impenetrable black of the mine. This was no place for men. This was where nightmares were stored, a place where secrets remained for eternity. I had a feeling that nature made it so alien, so inhospitable for a good reason. Everything about this place said, *BEWARE. COME NO CLOSER.*

But we had a fledgling country and we needed raw materials, as well as wealth. Warning signs had no place when it came to progress or prosperity.

"No bats," I said. "Or rats."

"Doesn't seem right. Not that I want to run into a flock of bats."

I looked at the tunnel walls, saw where pickaxes had chiseled away. The wet surface reflected my light like an oil spill. I saw different colors bending as I moved the lantern about.

The echoes of water, when we paused to take everything in, blended so they sounded like people murmuring in the far distance. It was unnerving.

"Ghosts," Teta said.

"Come again."

"Ghost voices. Can't you hear them?"

"I can hear water that sounds like talking because of the way it's bouncing off the walls."

"Maybe it's the tommyknockers."

"Is that something from your Mars book?"

"No, tommyknockers are real. I met a man in St. Augustine who had worked in mines until his lungs couldn't take it anymore. He spent his days drinking until he was full as a tick and nights playing cards. He was a damn good poker player. Anyway, he told me about the tommyknockers. Miners depended on them to alert them of danger or cave-ins. If they heard rapping against the rocks coming from an area where they knew no one was, they'd head for the surface. Sure enough, there'd be a cave-in or a full ore car would break loose. The tommyknockers looked after the miners. Those who ignored their warnings paid with their lives."

"And who are the tommyknockers?" I asked, hiding the fact that his little story had me on edge, even knowing the fella he talked to was probably three sheets to the wind when he'd spun his tale. Somehow, down here in the confining gloom, anything was possible.

"The spirits of the earth. The ghosts of miners who have passed. Little people. No one knows for sure."

I was about to tell him to stop being superstitious when we heard three soft cracks. It sounded as if someone had taken a small hammer to the shaft wall.

Tink. Tink. Tink.

CHAPTER ELEVEN

"Tommyknockers!" Teta hissed.

I shushed him and waited to see if the sounds repeated themselves. The tunnel was silent again.

"There's running water and chiseled rock. I sincerely doubt your tommyknockers are making themselves known the moment you start jawing about them."

"We should get back anyway. I don't feel safe here."

"I think we should go back to the fork, take the left tunnel, see what we see. No sense looking to shin out already. We have other openings to explore this week."

I heard Teta draw his gun. "I'll feel safer this way."

Turning and going ahead of him, I said, "Don't go shooting any of them tommyknockers. We may need them."

I chuckled but Teta didn't see my humor. I saw his bandana and veered into the other tunnel. It was more of the same, but there was a little more room to move. Still felt like I was creeping through my own coffin.

We didn't see much, heard even less, which was fine by me. There were no signs of gold veins in the walls. So far, I'd done a fair job convincing myself that the oppression and pitch black of the tunnels didn't bother me much. That veneer was wearing thin the longer we stayed underground. There was no telling how far down we were from the surface, but I could tell from the gradation that we had gone down a ways.

After a while, I wasn't even sure what we were looking for. Did I think the troops were camped out in the mine, picking for gold? Was I looking for the miners and their families? If there was gold, how would I really know?

The mines were the heart of Hecla, the reason for it ever being a town. I guess I just wanted to see if the heart was as dead as the rest of the body. In this place, death was everywhere. I could feel it in my gut, taste it in my mouth with every breath.

It was time to cut out, call it a day.

When we got back to the fork, Teta pulled his bandana off the splinter and stuffed it in his pocket.

He said, "It feels like we've been in here all day. I bet the sun won't even wait around for us."

"Place this dark makes you forget there was ever such a thing as the sun. I don't know how those men do this for a living. Makes me appreciate long, shitty cattle drives and getting shot at by Apaches."

"Does it make you appreciate being a cop in New York?"

I sucked my teeth. "We haven't been down here long enough for that."

I noticed we'd quickened our pace the closer we got to the mine exit. My feet were so cold I couldn't wait to get my boots off.

"Ah shit!" Teta cried out.

The tunnel got darker. When I turned around, he was holding his empty hurricane lamp at eye level. "Looks like we outlasted the oil."

We both looked at my lamp as the fire grew dimmer and dimmer. It was only a matter of seconds before the flame dipped down into the wick and disappeared.

It was a darkness so complete we could feel it swallow us whole. "Candles," I said as calmly as I could manage.

It was amazing how I instantly had no idea which way was out and which was back into the center of the mine. The totality of the pitch blackness in the tunnel was so foreign to me it disconnected my senses.

Teta struck a match and lit his candle. I tipped mine into his and the meager light was just enough to see by.

"I think if you turn around we'll be on the right track," Teta said.

We hadn't taken more than a few steps when a soft breeze whistled down the tunnel, blowing our candles out.

"That wind had to be coming from outside," I said. "We'll have to hold our hands in front of the flames until we get some daylight in here."

I relit our candles and we cradled the flame so close you could smell our skin burning.

Tink-tink.

The tiny sound of metal on rocks echoed from somewhere far behind us. "It's just rocks falling," I said.

"That's what you keep saying."

Because of the fragility of our candlelight, we had to take it slow. Teta was practically on my back, breathing heavily. I'd been next to him with hundreds of bullets whizzing by our heads and had never seen him the least bit afraid. Now, I could feel his fear pushing me forward.

"It didn't seem to take this long to get in here," I remarked. "But then we were able to move a little faster."

I thought I saw a bend up ahead, which meant the exit wasn't far. I felt the first rumble beneath my feet and stopped.

"Did you feel that?"

CHAPTER TWELVE

Another tremor followed, this one longer and strong enough to shake some rocks from the ceiling. They bounced off my Stetson.

Teta suddenly grabbed me by the back of my collar and propelled me forward with such speed and brute force my feet barely touched the ground. Our candles were forgotten as they fell to the ground. How he guided us without slamming into a wall was beyond me. When I tried to protest and regain my footing, he snapped, "Just go before we end up here for eternity!"

The light of day came into view and Teta hauled me up and launched us the last few feet out of the mine. As we hit the ground, my elbow cracked into one of the steel rails and stars exploded in my head.

A belching noise erupted from the shaft and the entire hillside gave a short jerk. A cloud of dust and debris poured from the mouth of the mine, sweeping over us like a dust storm.

We choked, gagging on the mine's regurgitation. When it settled, we were on our backs, facing the sun. The bright rays felt like hot pokers jabbing into my eyes. It did make me forget the pain in my elbow.

"My fucking head," Teta said. I could make out his shadow as he leaned over me. He was on his knees and holding out a hand to help me up.

"I think you broke my damn elbow."

"Better that than leaving you in there for an early burial."

It was hard to see his logic when my bone was smarting so badly I wanted to cut my arm off to make it stop. If it was broken, our little mission was going to be cut very short.

"Rub it fast and hard," he said. "I'll show you."

"Touch my arm and we're going to have a problem. Let me clear my head a moment."

The dust settled along the open mouth of the mine. The grass around us had turned an ashy gray.

"It's like the place exploded. I can't see how our walking around could trigger a cave-in like that," I said, wiping sweat from my forehead. The hot air outside felt more severe than it should because we'd been so cool, downright cold, in the mine.

"It doesn't take much, but when it goes, it can be bad."

"You learn that from a book?"

"Read a serial in a magazine about it. Very interesting. I never thought I'd get to experience it for myself."

"So you're telling me our wandering around could have set the whole place off?"

"I don't think it had anything to do with us. Miners make a lot of noise. Sound can't trigger something like that, jefe. That tunnel was either meant to collapse, or someone brought it down on us."

I thought of the person at our door the night before. Someone knew we were here. A well-placed stick of dynamite was a good way to make us disappear. Was that what happened to the troops?

My elbow stopped barking and I dusted myself off with my leather gloves I'd kept in my back pocket.

"I think that's enough mines for the day. We've got some work to do back in town."

★   ★   ★

We rode the horses at a full gallop on the way back so they could stretch their legs and lungs. A lazy horse was your worst enemy in a tight spot. I wanted to keep them fresh but active. Hecla's assortment of decrepit abodes was the same as we'd left it. Our spare horses and the mule were grazing beside the house we'd commandeered.

After feeding them some apples and getting fresh water, I rolled some cigarettes. "Where's that whiskey you've been hiding?"

Teta got a bottle from his bag, pulled the cork out with his teeth and took a swig. He passed it to me and I took an extra long pull.

"I don't know what in the hell happened back there, but I don't like it," I said, drawing heavily on the cigarette. "Teddy sent us here because he knows we get things done. Sitting-back and taking-the-lay-of-the-land time is over. We need to take control of the situation."

"Good," Teta said with a wicked grin. "What do you want to do?"

"First, we're going to scrub this area clean. Grab as much loose, fine dirt as you can find and spread it around, especially on the steps and under the windows. Next time someone comes around, I want tracks. Maybe we'll get a sense of how many folks are around. If there's gold in those mines, it stands to reason that some folks want to keep it for themselves. A man could die out here and no one would be the wiser."

The burn of the whiskey felt damn good and focused my thoughts. "We should sleep in shifts," Teta said.

"I agree. One sleeps here while the other stations himself in that house over there." I pointed to a cabin that was in such a state of disrepair it looked like a good sneeze would bring it to the ground. "They think we're spending our night in here because it's the only solid place in town. Let's keep their attention here while we have their backs in our sights."

"What about booby traps? I could set a couple up around the house."

Teta was an expert at rigging all manner of traps. He liked to find creative ways to break a man's legs and leave him for the wolves and vultures.

"Not tonight. I've got a feeling they won't do anything rash. Not after what happened up at the mine. They need to regroup, figure out a better way to get rid of us."

"But they could just come in and shoot us in our sleep."

"They could have done that last night. And even if they try it tonight, we'll have each other's backs."

Teta said he would take the first watch and brought his rifle, spare ammo and two revolvers to the busted-up cabin. The day was hot and long, and we spent a better part of the afternoon looking for tracks. Nothing but small critters had moved about recently, but that didn't mean bigger, two-legged critters hadn't covered their own comings and goings.

It was a relief for night to finally come. We both went into the house, with Teta slipping out the window to take watch. My nerves were still humming from the incident at the mine. I had to grab some shut-eye so I didn't nod off during my shift.

A coyote called out in the darkness. I strained to see if it was an actual coyote or an Indian mimicking their call. Another lonely cry echoed in the distance, then more joined in response. Coyotes always sounded sad to me. I could hear the touch of melancholy in their throaty yowls. Even a skilled Indian couldn't do that.

I closed my eyes and tried to empty my mind, but I couldn't shut it down. Something was going on in Hecla. Something odd. Something bad.

It wouldn't take long to get stranger.

CHAPTER THIRTEEN

The tiny knock at the door roused me from a troubled dream. It was just a couple of raps, but the sound was so out of place I immediately went on high alert. I grabbed my Winchester that I'd left propped against the wall and was on my feet before my eyes had even opened.

My head swam from getting up too fast. "Teta, is that you?" I whispered.

Why would Teta knock on the door? No, it couldn't be him. I calmed myself down, knowing he was across the way with whoever was at the door in his sights.

The knocks resumed. Two quick raps, then silence.

I crept to the door. The floor creaked loudly, potentially giving away my position. I stepped lightly to the right of the door.

Pulling the hammer back on my rifle, I reached out and slipped my hand over the doorknob. It was cold.

I didn't hear a sound on the other side of the door. Not a breath, not a shuffled step. I waited.

Knock. A pause. *Knock.*

I twisted the knob and threw the door wide open. Nothing could have prepared me for what I saw.

Two small kids, a boy and a girl no older than ten, stood in the doorway, their faces downcast. The girl had curly, jet-black hair that hung past her shoulders. She wore a faded dress that came down to her ankles and her feet were bare. The boy was barefoot as well. He wore a hat that had seen better days. One of his suspenders was broken and hanging down by his knees.

I looked over their heads to see if anyone else was behind or around them.

It was just the two of them. What the hell were they doing here? Neither reacted to the fact that they'd been greeted by a man brandishing a rifle in their faces.

"You kids need help?" My words came out scratchy, strained. It was hard to talk. My mind was in such a state that it was having a hard time telling my body what to do.

"Do you have any food?" the girl asked. "We could use some water," the boy added.

They kept their faces pointed at the floor. It was as if they were either afraid to look me in the eye or ashamed to be begging in the middle of the night.

"Come in before you catch your death."

"We just need some food," the girl said, "and water."

They didn't move. Something about them made me uneasy. I was a grown man with a rifle in his hands, and yet I was... frightened. But what was I frightened of?

I waved my arm so Teta could see everything was all right. I had to assume he did the same. It was too dark to see that far.

"Let me get some light on and I'll fix you up something to eat. You sure you don't want to come in, warm yourselves up? I've got a couple of thick blankets with your names on them."

They shook their heads and the little girl's curls waved back and forth.

I lit one of the lamps and dug around for some jerky and a canteen. Now that I could see them better, my consternation grew. They were filthy. It looked like they'd rolled in a pigpen and left themselves out to dry for a week.

Funny, there was no odor coming off them. Kids that dirty should stink to high heaven.

Of their skin, I could only see their hands and feet. They were pale as milk, at least in the parts not streaked with dirt.

"What are your names?"

The boy reached out and looped his pinky finger with hers.

"Do you know where you are? How did you get out here? Do you have folks nearby?"

I couldn't stop with the rapid-fire questions. They could have been with a family that was attacked by thieves, but I doubted it. Something about them seemed off, unnatural. If only they'd show me their faces. What were they hiding?

And where the hell was Teta?

I poured some water in two tin cups and held them out to the kids. They didn't move to take them.

"It's only water. Nice and fresh. I've got some jerky too. I can start a fire, make you up something proper. Come on, there's no need to be afraid. You came to me, remember? I just want to help. Let me see your faces, make sure you're not hurt or anything."

"Do you have some food?" the girl said again, her words falling to the floor. The boy followed with, "And some water."

It was like they were one of those recordings on a phonograph that kept skipping back to the same note. Were they foreigners? Was that the only English they knew?

The hairs on my arms rose like cactus quills.

I put the cups down and knelt down to their level. The shadows in the room made it hard to see their faces, even from that angle.

"Were you two at the door last night? Was that you trying to get in? Where have you been staying?"

A nonsensical question popped into the back of my mind. In normal circumstances, I wouldn't have given it a second thought. There was nothing normal about these kids.

I took a breath, waited to see if they would move or speak again. When they didn't, I asked, "You been up in those mines?"

The boy's shoulders twitched and the girl let his pinky go. Then, as one, they raised their heads.

I stumbled onto my ass when they met my gaze. Their eyes were black as coal.

CHAPTER FOURTEEN

"Nat. Hey. *Jefe!*"

The pressure of Teta's boot in my side woke me up. My back cried out in protest and I became aware of a dull chill in my bones.

"What are you doing sleeping on the floor like that?"

The lamp was still lit and the two cups of water lay beside it. I was in the middle of the floor, right where I'd been talking to the kids with the black eyes.

A shiver ran through me that shook me so hard my heart skipped several beats. Teta ran and got a blanket to throw over me.

"Are you okay?" he asked. "Did you pass out or something?" I looked at the cups.

"Where were you?"

"Across the street, watching the house."

"Why didn't you come when those kids were at the door?"

A sharp look of concern hardened his eyes. "Kids? What kids?"

"The ones who knocked on the goddamn door! Hell, I even waved you over."

Teta put his hands on my shoulders. "Nat, I never took my eyes off the house. I didn't see any kids. Why the hell would kids be out here in the first place? You're not making any sense."

My mind reeled and I pressed the palms of my hands into my eyes hard enough to hurt.

I needed the pain to straighten myself out.

"They kept on knocking. They wanted food and water. Said they were hungry. They…they wouldn't look up from the ground. They wouldn't answer me. Just kept asking for food and water."

"Where are they?"

"I don't know. I was trying to find out where they were from. Then, for some fool reason, I asked them if they'd come from the mine. I don't know why. Maybe I was trying to throw something out crazy enough to get a reaction out of them. And it worked. They finally showed me their faces. Except it was bad. Real bad. Their eyes were solid black, Teta. No whites to them, nothing but the deepest black I've ever seen. It startled the shit out of me. Next thing I know, you're here rousting me up."

Teta lowered himself onto the floor and sat Indian-style in front of me. He said, softly, "You sure it wasn't a dream?"

"There's the water I poured for them." I nodded toward the cups. "I lit the lamp to find them some food, see if they were hurt. I didn't dream that. How could you not have seen them?"

"I don't know."

"I'm not crazy."

"I'd never say you are, Nat."

I rubbed my head, chasing phantoms from my brain.

"The more I think about it, I'm not so sure I have your conviction."

★   ★   ★

There hadn't been much more to say, and after sharing a smoke, I took up my position for the rest of the night. Time went by without incident, though it seemed to take forever for the sun to rise.

Teta emerged when he smelled coffee. I could see by the heavy bags under his eyes that he didn't get much sleep. I was feeling pretty wasted myself.

He grabbed a cup and sat on the steps. "You want to ride into Laramie today, tell Teddy all's clear?"

"I can't tell him that."

"Why not? I'll give you that this place seems strange, but I don't see why it should remain deserted. Not if there's gold up there."

I stretched my back and tilted my neck so the sun could warm my face. "There're too many questions. I haven't seen a trace of gold. We still don't know what happened to the miners or troops. Teddy doesn't just want us to find them. He wants us to make sure the place is safe. I couldn't rightly say that at this point."

The fact that I left out the strange kids with the black eyes hung heavily in the air between us. We both knew *something* was here. It was just a matter of finding out who, or what.

Teta held his hands out, palms up. "If you want to stay, look around some more, I'm with you. I just...I just don't feel right here. And I know you don't either."

"I won't argue with you on that. But I'll bet that we get to the bottom of things soon. I'm getting that feeling you get just before a storm's about to break. The air feels different, charged."

"You want to ride around the hills, see what we find? I'm not *tan feliz* about wandering around the mines again."

"That sounds like a good use of our time."

We sopped up some beans with hard tack we'd let soak in their juices, finished our coffee and killed the fire. Teta got the horses saddled up.

It was another hot, though dry, day, and there was no sign of actual storm clouds. Hecla could use a good soak. Or, more like I'd heard a fair share of pastors say, a *cleansing*.

I was filling our canteens at the pump when Teta whistled. "Someone's coming," he shouted.

I dropped the canteens and jogged over to find him standing on the roof. I hoped he didn't fall through.

"I saw dust kicking up about a mile out. It looks like a lone rider. *Mierda*, he sure is beating hell to get here."

My tongue wanted to say, "Maybe it's the father of those kids," but I held it back. It wasn't just their unnatural eyes that made me feel they weren't what they appeared to be. It was the weird feeling I got the moment I saw them. I didn't have much experience with children, but I'd never met ones that made me afraid.

"Can you make anything out?"

"Not yet. Toss me my rifle."

Teta caught it with one hand and lay on his belly so our visitor couldn't see him. There was no telling what was making its way to us. It was always best to err on the side of caution. I crept around the house to look. The rider was really taking his spurs to his horse. I looked to see if there were signs of any kind of pursuit, but it was just the one rider tearing across the chalky plain.

"This place is full of surprises," Teta said.

"Who is it?"

"You're not going to believe it."

He jumped down from the roof and smiled. "You got your best bib and tucker on?" he said, mocking my old cowboy slang.

"What the hell are you talking about?"

"You'll see."

Teta splashed some water on his face, slicked his hair back and adjusted his sombrero. Was it Teddy he'd seen riding in? That couldn't be. Now that he was president, there was no way anyone would let him ride alone anymore. He was too important for that.

I held my hand over my eyes to block out the sun and saw what had Teta all worked up. It was a woman.

CHAPTER FIFTEEN

"I'll be damned," I said. "She bears a striking resemblance to Selma, old man McCallum's daughter."

"That's because she is."

Sure enough, when Selma saw us standing there, she eased up and came to a trot.

She was dressed in black from head to toe, cutting a fine, full figure of womanhood. A layer of dirt and dust hovered like a cloud around her. Her horse had worked up a good lather. If we hadn't been so well hydrated, I would have sworn she was a mirage.

"Gentlemen," she said, pulling back on the reins. "Do you have some water? Maria here has been working hard to get here."

Maria? I couldn't recall anyone naming a horse Maria. "Well, if it isn't Selma McCallum," I said.

"Smartwood," she corrected me.

She got down from the horse and slapped the dust off herself as best she could. Teta wasn't about to take Maria to the trough, so I volunteered.

"Thank you." She smiled with dark lips plump enough to lay your head upon.

The moment I turned my back, Teta slipped into his Spanish accent just enough to add to his exotic appeal. I'd seen him do it countless times. The problem with Selma was that, being half-Mexican, I didn't suppose it would have much effect on her, other than making her homesick for her momma.

Maria greedily nudged my horse from the trough and went to town.

I wondered why Selma had ridden so hard to get here. Could be she had word from Teddy. I hurried back to her before Teta really put the moves on her.

"What brings you out here?" I asked, a tad breathless.

Without her father around, I could really take her in. She was a stunner, with ample curves in all the right places and a face that could tame a wild horse. I could tell by the slight wrinkles at the edges of her eyes that she wasn't as young as I'd first thought, though she was still a mite more youthful than me.

Teta said, "I got the feeling from the way your father shooed you off when we mentioned this place that it was off limits."

Selma gave a nervous smile and clenched her bottom lip between her teeth. "You'd be right. If my father knew I was here, he'd skin me alive."

"There must be a very good reason for you to risk a skinnin'," I said, offering her a cup of water. She drank it down in one swig and handed the cup back to me.

"I came to ask you to leave. If it's gold you're looking for, you won't find any. Those hills are just dead and empty mines. Whatever gold was found is long gone, along with everyone who's come hungry for it."

"See, now that's a bit of a contradiction. I know that when folks find gold, they do everything they can to convince other folks that there's nothing to see. Scaring them off a claim, even killing a man, is all right in the eyes of the Lord when gold is at stake," I said.

"I...I..." Her eyes flicked back and forth between Teta and me.

The last thing I wanted to do was scare her, but that I did, in spades. I regretted the part about killing a man. After all, here was a woman, several hours' ride from help of any sort, with two strange men who stank like weasels, looked rough around the edges and spent their time poking around a deserted mining town.

"Let me put it another way. We're not here for gold. We wouldn't even know how to find it. If you want me to rope a cow or break a horse, that I can do. I'm simply saying that it comes off strange, you coming out here to assure us there's no gold and to tell us to vamoose."

The tension in her shoulders eased a bit and they dropped slightly. "You talk a lot like my pa."

"Us geezers have a language all our own," I said, chuckling.

Teta drew in a breath to pump up his chest. "I'm here to make sure Grandpa doesn't hurt himself."

She laughed.

I said, "Now, you care to tell me why you're really here."

Selma sighed and walked to the embers of our fire. She lifted a stick off the ground and used it to poke around. She was a bundle of nervous energy.

"I really do want you to leave. Hecla isn't safe. My father should have told you back at the ranch but he was too rattled to think straight."

"We scouted the town and I agree, the places here aren't safe, which is why we're staying in the one solid house left standing. And we did have a tunnel collapse on us in the mine. Not fun," Teta said.

She shook her head. "I'm talking about the land itself. It's not good. It hasn't been for years. People who come here vanish."

"That's partly why we're here. Some United States troops came to Hecla on a scouting mission a few months back. No one's heard or seen them since. You know anything about that?" I asked.

She paced back to the steps and sat down. "Yes. They stopped in Laramie, of course. It was all the talk for the one day they were there. It'd been a long time since we saw so many soldiers. They even brought their own horses with them. I saw a few in town when they stopped to eat. They never said where they were headed, so it didn't seem strange that they didn't come back to Laramie. Until now."

"I suppose you'd met the miners and their families when the mines were operational," I said.

"Yes."

"Anyone say what happened to them?"

"No." She got up suddenly and went back to pacing.

"You know of anyone else who said Hecla was in their intentions but never came back?"

"Yes. Once news about the gold got out, men would come by all the time, hoping to get rich. After the first fifty or so disappeared, I guess word got around and they stopped coming."

"Fifty or so?" Teta said. "Plus an entire mining town *and* troops. What have we gotten into?"

"That's why I came to warn you! I couldn't let you stay here in good conscience. There's something wrong with this place. Something…evil. I don't know how to explain it. I just know that it's no place fit for men."

"Or women," Teta said under his breath.

"Out of all the men that have come out here, why did you choose us as the ones to warn?"

She snapped a stick in two and threw it into the embers. "I don't know. There's something different about the two of you. A woman can see greed in a man from a mile away. It burns in their eyes like a sickness. You didn't have that look. It didn't seem right to leave you out here."

It was easy to see by the way her eyes shifted around the ruins of the town that she was spooked. Even if she turned around now, she'd be gone most of the day. Her father would surely give her hell. That spoke to her sincerity. And her courage.

"Look, Selma, as much as we'd like to leave—"

"I'd *really* like to leave," Teta interrupted.

"We can't just yet. You've done a courageous thing, coming out here all by yourself. For that, I'll level with you. We're here on orders of the President of the United States. Being the commander in chief, he doesn't like it when his men go missing. It's our job to find out what happened to them and scout Hecla for any potential hazards. And, of course, to see if the claims of gold are true. I'll admit, this isn't the most hospitable place I've ever been, but I haven't seen anything to be afraid of."

As long as I didn't think long and hard about tommyknockers or those black-eyed kids.

"You have nothing to worry about. Believe me, we can handle ourselves. It's best you head on home and tell your father I'll personally apologize for worrying you so when I get back to Laramie."

Selma pursed her lips and knit her brows. She wasn't buying what I was selling. "If you're not going back, I'm not," she said.

"But you said yourself this place is evil," Teta said. "Why stay here?"

"Because being here is better than being shuttered away on the ranch. I lost my husband to this place three years ago. If I can't convince you to leave, I might as well find out what happened to him."

CHAPTER SIXTEEN

"I'm sorry to hear that," I said.

There were no tears in her eyes, just cold determination. Now that the words had tumbled out of her, she finally stopped fidgeting and became very still. Teta gently put his hand on her shoulder and said, "Was he a good man?"

"He had his moments," Selma answered, her head hung low.

"Was he one of the miners?" Teta asked.

She shook her head. "He and his brothers decided to try their hand at finding the gold. None of them knew a thing about mining. They just knew that Hecla was empty and gold was there to be found. I told him not to go, begged him. He had the fever. He wanted out of Laramie. Hank dreamed of a big house in a big city, as far from Wyoming as he could get. In the end, having me as a wife wasn't enough for him."

I couldn't imagine any man leaving her behind. What was the sense of all that money if you didn't have someone beautiful to spend it on?

"What about his brothers? Did they disappear too?" Teta asked.

"Yes. All seven of them. Gone. It broke their mother's heart. When they didn't come back, she just withered up and died a few months later. It was hard on all of us."

I said, "Well, you're a grown woman. We can't force you to leave, even though I have my reservations. We were going to scout the perimeter of the Deep Rock Hills today. I'd prefer it if you came with us. I don't cotton to the idea of leaving you here alone."

"I'd like that."

"And maybe you can tell us what you know about this place," Teta said.

The man loved a good story, whether it was in a book or coming out of a pretty mouth. He'd cultivated a lazy, disinterested look that made a damn good smoke screen. While I was more about facing the moment, he was always trying to think one step ahead. Having Selma around could be to our benefit.

"Let's saddle up, then. The day isn't getting any younger."

★   ★   ★

The Deep Rock Hills cut a sharp, irregular profile against the blue, cloudless sky. They weren't high or wide. Plenty of evergreens, pines and conifers crowded around and up the hills as to camouflage them from the rest of the flat plain. I took the lead as we slowly plodded around them. From time to time, I dismounted to swipe away brush that at first appeared to have been placed intentionally to hide tracks. Each time I came up empty.

Teta did find a rusted crowbar not far from the entrance to one of the tunnels on the east end. We could just make out the shaft openings through the trees. It was like the miners were bees, entering the hive from as many shafts as they could make.

"What do you make of all these entry points?" I asked Teta.

"So far, the one we went into seems the largest. I'll bet that was the initial entrance when they were going in for copper. They must have found gold somewhere down there and decided to come at the vein from all angles."

"Seems that would make the whole works unstable. There's not much to these hills."

Selma's horse nipped at my horse's hide. She gave it a sharp, "Cut that out, you old crow bait."

Her horse, a young, brown filly with a blonde mane, was anything but crow bait. I bet that horse would cost a pretty penny if one were to haggle with her old man for it. I laughed and caught her eye. She flashed me a smile and tilted her head away right quick.

"You know, maybe you're on to something," Teta said. "Maybe the miners were too anxious to find the gold. Maybe they did weaken the interior of the hills. Could be they caved the whole works in. For all we know, they're all still in there."

"What's left of them anyway."

I thought of Selma's husband and winced.

I added, "But that doesn't explain where their families went. Selma, is Laramie the nearest town?"

"Yes. Their families usually came into town once a month for supplies. Then one month, no one showed."

"So you have half your mystery possibly solved," I said.

"I wish we had Sherlock Holmes here for the second half," Teta said.

Selma gave him a curious glance. "He's a kind of detective in mystery books," I said.

"Oh," she said.

It didn't take long to circumnavigate the hills, even taking it as slowly as we did. By noon, it felt like the sun was sitting on the brim of my Stetson. We were about to call it a day when Selma pulled up her horse and barked, "Look over here! What is that?"

Peering down, I saw a footprint of some kind. It was made by someone who had been barefoot because you could make out all the toes. Odd thing about it was that there were only four toes.

And it was big. Longer and wider than any foot I'd ever seen. "There's another one over here," Teta said.

About seven feet to the north of the first track was another. All told, we found six of them, though only two were deep enough to retain any kind of definition.

"*Qué demonios!*" Teta said, whistling as he walked around them. "I never saw a foot that damn big."

I jumped off my horse and bent down to get a closer look. "Awfully wide," I said.

"You can see there's a right foot and a left foot," Selma said, pointing to the nearest set. "And only four toes on each," Teta added.

"Let me see something, try to gauge the size." I put my boot next to the footprint. It was bigger than mine by a good five or six inches, and I wore a size twelve.

Selma said, "Maybe it's an old footprint. Time in the elements just wore it away enough so it looks bigger than it is."

Tracing my fingers in and around the best print, I shook my head. "Nope. This one's fresh. Couple of days old at the most. The ground up here is too dry to keep a print for long, even one that's as deep as this. Had to have been someone awfully heavy to make it."

"How do you know that?" she asked.

"He did this for a living, long time ago, back before you were born," Teta said with a wry smile.

"Then you think it's real?"

"The print is," I replied. "Can't tell you about the person who made it. Hard to imagine a man big enough to leave a print like that. Maybe he was wearing some weird kind of boot. Could be ceremonial for one of the local tribes. Not every Indian is on a rez. I hear there are still Cheyenne and Crow about."

I'd seen Apaches wear some peculiar stuff during their ceremonies. It wasn't hard to imagine an Indian sporting something like this, though the depth of the impression bothered me. Could have been a man with someone on his shoulders.

"But why would someone do such a thing?"

"I'm just a white man. It's hard for me to get into the head of an Indian. They have different dances and different ways of dressing for everything you can imagine. I've heard of some that believe in a wild man of the mountains. It's kind of like some big, hairy bear that's also part man. He's said to be taller than any man, stronger than an angry bison and faster than a mountain lion."

"Do you believe in it?"

Teta gave a quick laugh and I cut it off with a sharp look.

"No, I don't. But they do. And when they believe hard in something, they do their damnedest to make themselves look like it. What this tells me is what I've thought all along. We have some rogue Indians out here keeping the white men away from their hills."

The first cool breeze of the day whispered through the trees and shook the brittle leaves.

It sounded like small bones rattling in a jug.

Teta instinctively placed his palm on the handle of his Colt. "Suddenly, I don't like being here with so much cover."

"Me neither. Let's get back to camp. I have to rethink things."

Selma was quick to mount. Her head swiveled from side to side, anticipating danger everywhere. Poor girl had no experience with things like this. I had a good mind to bring her back to her father myself in the morning.

We had only gotten a few feet from the tracks when a piercing howl erupted behind us.

My insides went numb. All three horses reared.

I hoped to hell we didn't get bucked.

Not with whatever was at our backs close enough to raise the hairs on our heads.

CHAPTER SEVENTEEN

By some miracle, we all managed to stay saddled.

By another miracle, the howl was short and quick and not repeated. Our horses were spooked and all balled up. They snorted and whinnied some, but we managed to settle them down.

"What…what was that?" Selma said, stroking her horse's neck and doing her best to calm the filly.

"Coyote?" Teta said.

"I ain't never heard a coyote make a noise like that," I said. "Wolf?"

"In the daytime? Highly unlikely."

"Whatever it was, it sounded angry," Selma said. We had our rifles in hand before she finished the sentence.

"I'm a curious man by nature, but I pick my spots. Let's move out of here before the horses lose it again."

We started at a trot and took it up to a hard and fast gallop. No more ungodly sounds followed us as we sped into the empty town.

★ ★ ★

"There's never a dull moment here," I said after we had hitched the horses and found a patch of shade to sit under.

"I wouldn't mind one," Teta said. He'd found a forearm-sized stick and was working away at it with his knife. He couldn't whittle worth a damn, but he did know how to make a pretty pile of wood shavings.

Selma had regained her composure, but I noticed her stealing quick glances at the hills.

I asked her, "Any chance you'll reconsider going back to your ranch? We'll be happy to ride with you, make sure you get there safe."

Her face screwed up and she said, "It's going to take more than some Cheyenne boot prints to chase me off, Mr. Blackburn."

"Please, call me Nat. I'm feeling old enough as it is."

"And what about you, Mr. Delacruz?"

He put down his stick, removed his sombrero from his sweaty head and gave a small bow. "Everyone calls me Teta."

Her cheeks bloomed. "I'd rather not," she said.

He gave a short laugh. "Believe me, I could have been called worse things than a—" Teta struggled for the best way to put things. Most women we met didn't know a lick of Spanish, so they didn't think twice about the nickname that had all but replaced his God-given name. I enjoyed watching him squirm.

He cupped his hands over his chest to finish his explanation and Selma's blush grew a deeper red.

"I understand. I'm almost afraid to ask how you came by that name."

I held up a warning hand. "Don't ask and he won't tell. You don't want to know. Sometimes a little mystery is best."

Selma got up and said, "I brought something for you. Let me get my saddlebags."

She slipped into the house and came back with a bottle of bourbon and a burlap bag. "I figured you might want something good to drink and eat."

The bag was filled with eggs, apples, cans of beans, a sack of flour, bacon, a slab of beef, onions and bottles of different spices. We each grabbed an apple.

"Seeing as I'm the intruder, I'll prepare supper. In the morning, I can find some game to keep you both well fed."

"Good luck with that," Teta said with a mouth full of crispy apple. "Even animals steer clear of this place. Plus it's better if you stay close. Best to leave any hunting to us."

Tossing some kindling down in the fire ring, she said, "I'm not a child. I will have a rifle with me."

"We're not children either," he said, pointing an apple slice at me, "and we were hightailing it out of the hills just as fast as you before."

"Teta's right. We see anything, we'll bring it back to you. If you're going to stay here, you have to play by our rules." I looked her square in the eye to let her know there was no sense arguing. She huffed a bit but then left to find wood.

When she was out of earshot, Teta asked, "Nat, you have an idea what those footprints really are?"

"Something we need to keep an eye on."

After the best supper I'd had in a while, I rolled a smoke for me and Teta.

"Care to make it three?" Selma asked, scrubbing the pan filled with water over the fire.

The water hissed as it spilled over the edges.

I paused lighting my smoke and raised an eyebrow.

She said, "Don't think that a good after-dinner smoke is something only the boys can enjoy."

"No, ma'am," I said. "It's just that I've never seen someone—" I had to choose my next words carefully, "—like yourself take to tobacco before."

She steadied the pan on a flat rock and dried her hands on the front of her jeans. "Should I take that as a compliment?"

"Most assuredly."

I offered her mine and put the lit match to it. She took a deep drag and held the smoke for a bit. She blew it out in one long breath over my head. She rolled her neck and I could hear tiny bones crack. "That feels good."

Teta lay flat on the ground with his head on his saddle. He smoked his cigarette with his face to the sky and eyes closed. It was getting near nightfall and the pinks and purples bled across the horizon.

My stomach was full to bursting. Everything about Hecla and the mine had me on edge, but Selma's cooking couldn't be denied.

"Care to talk a stroll down the empty streets of Hecla?" I asked. She surprised me with a quick smile and said, "That sounds nice."

"We won't go far," I said to Teta. He raised a hand but didn't open his eyes.

I made sure to keep myself heeled. The last thing I wanted was to be caught without my gun in this place. I was tempted to give one to Selma as well, so we were doubly armed, but thought that might ruin the nice mood we were all in.

We walked side by side, Selma's arm occasionally bumping into mine. We finished our smokes early on and took to ambling down the main street and staring into the wreckage that was once the town.

"Can I ask you a question?" she said.

"You can ask me anything you want. I can't guarantee I'll give you an answer."

I kept a straight face but she saw through it quicker than a jackrabbit. She gave my arm a playful slap.

"Do you really know the president?"

"I sure do."

"How did you come to meet him? He must think highly of you and... *Teta* to send you both out on a special mission."

"Depends how you look at it. From my vantage point, I'm beginning to think he's not our biggest fan. I wouldn't send my worst enemy to this place."

We walked in silence until she said, "And you met Mr. Roosevelt when..."

"When we were fighting with the Spanish. I was looking for something to do. I knew a man who had signed up to be part of Roosevelt's cavalry and he asked me if I wanted to come along for the ride. I'm pretty good on a horse and not shy with a gun. Seemed like a good fit to me. So we headed out to Tampa, down in Florida, trained for a spell and headed out to Cuba. What I remember most about both places was the heat. It was so hot and wet it was hard to breathe most days."

"You were in Cuba with the Rough Riders?"

"How do you know about that?"

"Everyone knows the Rough Riders. We're not living underground. So I'm walking with an actual Rough Rider. Did you kill anyone?"

I nodded.

"Were you wounded?"

"Not in Cuba."

I could feel her looking up at me. I kept walking, watching the shadows grow amidst the rubble of the structures that dotted Hecla's streets.

"How did you and Teta meet?"

"In Cuba. He was a mercenary employed by the locals to help fight the Spanish. He rode with us, fought with us, saved my life, and I saved his. When the battle was over, his prospects weren't good. A lot of folks wanted to take a crack at him, put him toes up. I convinced Roosevelt, who was our colonel then, to informally adopt him and take him back to the States with the Rough Riders. Since then, we've been kind of stuck to one another. When you place your life in another man's hands and he comes through, well, that's a bond that's hard to break. Plus, he gives me a chuckle from time to time."

Her deep-brown eyes held me captive while I talked. "Do you have a wife? Any kids?"

"Almost and no. Unless you count Teta." She laughed, smooth as honey.

I'm a man of few words who rarely divulges any details about my past. For some reason, I was happy to tell her anything she wanted to know. It was like I'd known her all my life, and here we were, reunited and catching up on old times.

"Well, it's never too late." She put her hand to her mouth as if she were trying to shove the words back in.

"Romance is for the young," I said. "Whatever charm I used to have is long gone."

"I wouldn't say that."

Her words hung in the air between us.

She added, "I didn't know there was a limit to charm and romance."

"You have nothing to worry about. You're still young. It's easier for a woman, especially an attractive one."

I guided her into a U-turn so we could get back to camp. Especially with night closing in, I wanted to keep us all together.

I changed the subject and said, "Enough about this old sawhorse. On account of your being out here with us now, I'm assuming you and your husband didn't have kids."

"No, we were never blessed. Hank used to say he wanted a whole posse of boys. I secretly wanted three girls. I was raised with five brothers. I'd had my fill of boys."

"If you don't mind my asking, was your mother Mexican? You don't look much like your daddy."

She picked up a rock and threw it into a lone shard of glass that was left standing in a window pane in a cabin to our right. Everything had collapsed but the façade. The glass exploded with a crash that seemed louder because Hecla was devoid of normal night sounds.

"Good shot."

"You should see me with a rifle. To answer your question, yes, my mother was from a little town in Mexico called Orizaba. I'd love to go and see where she grew up, maybe meet family that I've never seen or even heard of before. It's a long way from here, and I couldn't do it alone. But I dream that someday, maybe after my father passes, the opportunity will present itself."

"It's been my experience that you have to make your opportunities. I've never been to Mexico myself. Fought some Mexicans off on cattle drives, fought *with* some against the Apaches. Food's a bit too spicy for me."

We turned a corner. Our fire blazed in the distance. Teta must have just thrown some more wood on.

"I hope my food wasn't too spicy."

I patted my stomach. "No, your cooking was just about perfect."

We stopped and faced one another. Selma's eyes were as dark as the patches between the stars, and just as impenetrable. She said, "Thanks for the walk. I think I'll turn in and get some rest."

Looks like you've gotten more than your fill of beauty sleep, I almost said.

"We'll be right out here if you need anything. Just going to watch the fire burn itself out."

There was an awkward moment where both of us made to say something else, stopped, then thought better of it. She bade Teta a good-night and stepped into the house.

"Have a nice walk, jefe?" Teta was nursing a bottle of bourbon that had about two fingers left swirling along the bottom. I took it from him and made it one finger less.

"Nothing like sitting around a fire with you, but it helped pass the time."

There was no need to tell him the feelings that Selma had stirred up in me. The man could read my face like one of his precious books.

CHAPTER EIGHTEEN

We set up watch again, with me volunteering to take the first shift this time. Teta was dead on his feet. At least I'd gotten some shut-eye before those kids came knocking. It was agreed that we not tell Selma about the black-eyed kids. She had enough on her mind, with wondering about her lost husband, Indians and the footprints in the hills.

Inside the house, Selma had set herself up in the far corner, opposite Teta, for propriety's sake. When I left them, she turned over and said "good night", while Teta found the book Teddy had given to me and hung the lantern on a nail over his head.

"Think I'll see why Teddy gave this to you. Something in here has to relate to Hecla."

I'd completely forgotten about the book and was more than happy to have him slog through it. "You all finished with Mars?"

"Sí. Things didn't go well for them. They died by getting sick. Makes you think, huh?"

"That it does."

I set myself up across the street, hiding in the shadows amidst fallen planks. The moon was barely a sliver but the stars were plentiful. The sweet scent of honeysuckle danced on the cooling breeze that whispered through the cracks in the tattered hideout. It was so quiet my breathing sounded like a heavy, steady scream.

The night went without incident. No kids. No Indians. Just darkness and silence. I heard Teta sneaking up behind me. He was good at keeping undercover. We didn't want any potential interlopers knowing we had set up a watch.

"That was pretty good," I whispered, keeping my eyes on the empty street. "I never saw you leave the house."

Something scuffed on the floor, like a boot being dragged. "Teta?"

I turned and saw only the ruins of the house.

My eyes were good and acclimated to the dark, but I couldn't make out a thing. It was like the interior of the house had somehow turned blacker than night, just like the endless gloom of the mine.

With both hands on my rifle, I held my breath back as much as I could, trying to keep stiller than a stone.

Scritch.

Easing the hammer back with my thumb, I tensed. I hadn't imagined the sounds. Someone was in here with me.

I tried again. "Teta, is that you?"

A rotted board shifted to my left. I swung the rifle in that direction.

It wasn't Teta. He was smarter than that. A man could get killed messing around with an armed man on night watch.

Whoever was creeping toward me was close. So close I should have been able to see them. The roof was missing, so even some light from the stars should have made its way in. What the hell was going on?

Wood groaned and I could feel it vibrate under my feet.

Come on, you son of a bitch. Step a little closer so I can see you.

It was more than just hearing things. I could feel the presence of someone close by. Even blind men could tell when someone sidled up to them. In essence, I *was* blind, and I knew damn well that I wasn't alone.

I waited, my finger pulled back on the trigger just enough so it wouldn't take much more to introduce lead to the creeper in the dark.

A hand dropped on my shoulder and I pushed back with my heels to drive myself into the person at my back. Crashing through the decayed wood of the front of the house, I landed on top of someone. He grabbed me by my shoulders in an attempt to roll me over and get the upper hand. Snapping my head back, I felt his face crunch against my skull.

"What the hell is wrong with you?" Crap. It was Teta.

I rolled off him and helped get him to his feet. We jumped back when the house groaned, shuddered, and finally collapsed on itself. A cloud of dust and splinters blew into our faces.

"That should do him in," I said.

"Who? Why did you hit me?"

Pointing at the rubble, I said, "Someone was in there. At first I thought it was you, come to relieve me. I called your name and when you didn't answer, I knew it had to be someone else. I heard them moving closer. When you touched my shoulder, my sense of self-preservation kicked in. Sorry about that."

Teta massaged his nose. A slight trickle of blood ran over his lips and down the stubble of his chin.

"You've got a head like a cannonball, you know that?"

"Is it broken?" I asked, pointing at his nose.

"No. Just smarts."

I turned my attention back to the jagged pile that was once a house. "I don't suppose whoever it was got out of there. We should probably check."

Using the tip of my boot to kick a plank away, I knelt down to see into the debris. Nothing. Not even the sound of settling wood could be heard. It was as if the spirit of the place had up and left and nothing remained to see or say.

"If someone's in there, they're flat as a flapjack," Teta said. His nose had swelled up and his voice had a nasal twang.

I was about to dig around a bit when something bright and soft, like a lit streetlamp in a blizzard, flickered into view at the other end of the jumble of timber. Squinting hard, I pointed it out to Teta.

"Fireflies?" I said.

"Can't be. It's too big."

We watched the faded light float behind the next building.

No sooner had we taken our first step in pursuit than something shrieked loud enough to wake the dead.

It was Selma.

CHAPTER NINETEEN

We raced over to the house, forgetting the odd light by the hideout.

Selma's screams came one after the other. I burst through the door to find her standing in the corner, her wide eyes fixed on the window opposite her. She had her hands balled into fists at her chest.

"Selma, what's the matter? Are you all right?"

A scream died in her throat, but her lips trembled and heavy tears rolled down her olive cheeks. She couldn't take her eyes from the window. I motioned with my head for Teta to check it out. He darted over, saw nothing, then dashed outside.

"What's the matter? Did you see something?"

I had to shake her a bit to calm her down. At first, when she looked at me, it was as if she didn't even recognize me. She blinked a few times and wiped her tears with the back of her hand. She was breathing heavily and I worried she might pass out.

"It's me, Nat. Selma, can you tell me what happened?" I felt her muscles relax under my hands.

"I saw him," she said. Her voice trembled, like a little girl's when she was hurt.

"Saw who?"

I staggered back as she threw her arms around me and pressed her face into my chest, sobbing. Holding her tight because I wanted to keep her on her feet, I gently patted her back.

Teta came back inside, huffing. He shook his head.

When Selma's crying ebbed a bit, I tilted her chin up and asked, "Who did you see that got you so worked up? We can't help you if we don't know what we're looking for."

Selma sniffed and squeezed her eyes tight.

"It was Hank. My husband was looking through that window. But it wasn't him. I...I can't explain it. The way he looked at me. It was...it was like he wanted to hurt me. I never saw such hatred!

Nothing about him looked right, but I know it was Hank."

"Was he alone?" I asked.

She nodded her head against my chest.

"Teta, hold her for a minute. I want to get a good look outside."

It wasn't easy passing her over to Teta. She had a good grip on my shirt. I grabbed the lantern and went out back to where she'd seen her missing husband.

There wasn't a track to be seen. Unless he'd floated on air, he would have left something behind.

A harsh breeze started to pick up, blowing bits of grit into my eyes. I had to hold my hat to keep it from flying off my head. I turned my back to the wind and smelled the air. It didn't have the scent of an oncoming storm. Spending most of my life on the range, I got to know when a storm was coming by sight and smell pretty good. If I was wrong, and this was more than just a passing wind, I hoped the house would hold up.

When I got back inside, Teta was handing Selma a cup of bourbon. She was on her knees atop her bedroll. Her tears had stopped but she was good and spooked.

"You spot anything, jefe?"

"Nothing. And if there are tracks to be found, that wind will wipe it all out." The house groaned against the oncoming blast. Small pebbles tinkled against the panes like hail. Teta eyed the roof, muttering a prayer in Spanish to keep it from falling on our heads.

I poured a cup of bourbon for myself and stood over Selma.

"You said you saw your husband, but that it wasn't exactly him. What did you mean by that?"

A little of the spitfire in her had returned and she took a moment to think. She chewed the end of her finger while she puzzled things out.

Finally, she said, "It was Hank all right. Same height, same build, and I know his face better than my own. There was just one problem, and it's what set me off shrieking, instead of running out to hold him and ask him where the hell he'd been."

Teta's spurs clinked as he walked to close the door. A good deal of dust was blowing into the house.

"It was his skin. It, well, it glowed. It wasn't natural. Even a full moon couldn't light someone up like that. But it wasn't the moon. That glow, it was coming *from* him, not on him. I know that's not making any sense. You probably think I'm just a hysterical woman who would be better off home doing woman's work."

"We're in the state that was the first to give women the right to vote. I'm not about to tell you what a woman's work should be," I said to lighten things a bit.

Selma flashed a short-lived smile. "It wasn't just his skin, though. It was his clothes too. I don't know. Maybe he had a lantern on the ground and the way the light filtered through that old glass made it look like he was glowing."

Now I had glowing missing husbands to add to the list with tommyknockers, weird kids, plus whatever it was I'd heard and seen in the house. I had a mind to tell Teddy tomorrow to send troops to blow up the town and mark it off limits.

"I think we've had enough excitement for tonight. Teta was supposed to have watch until dawn. Seeing as our hideout just collapsed and the windstorm is making visibility near zero, it's probably best we all stay in here."

Teta tipped his sombrero and took a position by the door.

As confused and concerned as I was about everything, I was also dead tired. "Best we get some sleep," I said to Selma.

She pushed her onyx hair from her face and nodded.

"You okay with me turning the lantern off?" Teta asked her. "I don't want to be seen."

"Yes. I'll be fine. Maybe it was just a dream."

Maybe everything here is a dream, I thought as I settled down and put my hat over my face. Then the dreams did come, and I went along for the ride.

★ ★ ★

At one point near dawn I startled awake. Something had nudged me in the side. I looked over to see that Selma had moved her bedroll sometime in the night and was now just a few inches from my side. One of her hands had flopped over and rested on my hip.

I saw Teta's silhouette against the first orange rays of the day.

"You still have an hour," he said. "Might as well enjoy it while you have fine company."

I was too tired to come up with a passable retort.

CHAPTER TWENTY

For the first time in as long as I could remember, I'd slept in and was still sawing wood at eight in the morning. The door was open and I could hear Teta and Selma outside talking. The smell of coffee got my ass in motion.

"Look who decided to face the day," Teta said. He sopped some runny eggs onto a biscuit and shoved it in his mouth.

"Why didn't you wake me?"

"For what?" Bits of biscuit sprayed out of his mouth. "It's not like we have a schedule. Besides, I figured the longer you slept, the more biscuits I get to eat. Selma doesn't burn them like you do."

Selma handed me a tin plate loaded with eggs, two biscuits, beans and bacon. "I wouldn't let him eat all of it." She gave Teta a playful snap with a small tea towel.

After putting a considerable forkful into my maw, I said, "Good to see you're in better spirits today."

She sighed. "In the light of day, what I saw last night seems less real. It had to have been a dream. If Hank really was here, why would he run away? And why would he look at me that way? It had to be my imagination running away with itself."

I didn't want to dash her rationalization. She could be right, but the more time I spent in Hecla, the more I realized anything was possible. Hank running from her was simple. He ran from her once before with his brothers. Stumbling upon her in Hecla, of all places, wouldn't change his mind. And if he was in Hecla, where was he staying? Maybe up in the mine. Maybe Teta's tommyknockers were really Hank's brothers and that cave-in was designed to get us to vamoose. They didn't count on a couple of stubborn old cowpokes with nothing else to do.

After I cleaned my plate, I said to Teta, "We should look into the mine again. I have a hunch I want to work out."

"*Dios mío.* I better have another biscuit if this is going to be my last meal."

"I'll come with you," Selma said.

"That you will. I'm not going to leave you here alone. But you can't go into the mine. You can wait for us outside, keep yourself busy doing women's work."

I smirked and got a tea towel whipping. She was pretty good with it. I figured I'd have a couple of welts on my upper arm later. "Why can't I go in the mine?"

"Because it's not safe. We shouldn't be going in either, but we have a job to do."

She wrapped the remaining biscuits in another towel and put them in her saddlebag. When she bent down I couldn't help but notice the ample swell in her jeans. Teta caught me looking and winked. It was hard not to admire a woman as sturdily put together as Selma.

"I still think I should go in with you."

A thought occurred to me and I suddenly became curious. "Say, shouldn't your poppa come looking for you? He didn't seem like an unintelligent man. I'm sure he suspects where you've run off to. I'm surprised he isn't here already. Maybe it is better you stay behind in case he comes here today."

Selma's eyes were downcast and she set about cleaning things up. "He won't come."

"Now, I don't have a daughter myself, but I know if I did I wouldn't let her run off like that, especially to a place where folks go and never come back."

"I'll saddle up the horses," Teta said in a graceful exit from what looked to be a difficult conversation.

"My father's not a young man. He's old and afraid. During his life, he's lost everything but the ranch and me. I'm just one more thing the Lord's taken from him. He often compares himself to Job, feeling like the hardships this life has given him will hold him in good stead in the next. Maybe's he's right."

I could feel the pain and sadness radiating off her like heat on a tin roof. I didn't know whether to tell her she had to be wrong, hold her or assure her that her father loved her more than anything in this world. But the truth was, I didn't know that. So I kept quiet and hoped she was wrong.

"I'll come up to the mine with you today and promise to stay outside. I don't want to wait around here."

I nodded and went into the house to get my guns.

When my foot touched the first step, I felt the earth move. Thinking it was the house about to collapse, I jumped back. Turning around, I saw Selma's eyes go wide.

It wasn't the house.

"You get earthquakes out here?" I said when everything settled. It only lasted a few seconds but it was enough to put a scare in us.

"Not in Laramie. I can't tell you about Hecla."

I was about to say something when a deep, chest-rumbling blast of noise ripped the morning in two.

CHAPTER TWENTY-ONE

The thunderous noise was so loud, lasted so long, we clapped our hands over our ears to keep our heads from splitting.

It paused for a moment, then picked up again, cacophonous as hell and painful to hear.

After the third time, it stopped. I removed my hands and my ears rang as if I'd had a gun go off by my head.

Selma walked in a slow, tight circle, her gaze settling on the distant hills. She said, "What on earth was that?"

The horses whinnied for all they were worth and I heard Teta trying to settle them down.

"I've been around a few quakes before and sometimes I've heard some strange stuff coming from the ground. A fella once told me that's the sound of giant rocks under the earth scraping against one another."

I wasn't lying, but I also wasn't telling her that what I'd heard before bore no relation to what just happened. "Everything under control over there?" I shouted Teta's way.

"Getting there!"

I sat down hard on the ground. If another rumbler was going to come through, I wanted to feel it at the source. My hands trembled a bit when I pulled out my tobacco pouch. I rolled a cigarette quickly before Selma could see.

"I think it came from the mine," she said, her voice so soft and distant it was like she was talking in her sleep.

"Maybe the whole thing collapsed. That'd be enough to make a racket like that." She wasn't buying it. Fact was, I wasn't either.

"Are you still set on going up there?"

I looked up and down the empty street. "Can't see much else to do around here. Like I told you, Teta and I—"

"Have a job to do. Is it something worth risking your lives over?"

I got up and masked the sound of my knees crunching by coughing hard. Selma was fussing with her hands, pressing them together and rubbing her palms like she was polishing brass. I took her hands in mine, feeling a slight tremor running through her body.

"Teta and I have been in much worse situations before. When I compare staring down the barrels of hundreds of guns or riding in the middle of a stampeding herd, walking through some old mine is filled with about as much danger as whiling the afternoon away in a rocker. Don't you worry about us. We can take care of ourselves – and you, for that matter. I counted eight other tunnels. The one we explored was about as empty as a freshly dug tomb. Just some tracks and timber and a mining car. Men leave behind a lot of things when they take off. Not here. I have a duty to the president to find out what's going on here. If you're going to stay, you just have to trust us and do what I ask of you. You all right with that?"

To her credit, she didn't bat an eye. All the fear swept out of her. Her fingers laced with mine and she pulled me close.

"Yes. I'll do whatever you say. I hardly know you, but I have faith in you. I could tell the moment I saw you at the ranch that you're a good man. It's the reason I—"

"Horses are ready," Teta said, leading them to us. "I'm not sure how happy they'll be if that noise kicks up again."

Our fingers untwined and we took a small step away from each other. Her deep-brown eyes still stayed on mine and I knew I was in trouble. Deep trouble.

★   ★   ★

Navigating through the pines, I watched Teta spend more time looking at the ground than straight ahead.

"Looking for more prints?" I asked.

"I'm not searching for my *Tía* Anelida."

It was another scorcher of a day. We'd packed extra water to get through the heat of the afternoon. Selma rode slowly to my right. Her hair was down and blowing in the arid breeze that did nothing but make you hotter.

"Might be better if you waited for us a little ways into the tunnel. You don't have to go that far for things to cool off. Better than waiting under this sun."

"Thank you. I think I will."

Since our short-lived hand-holding incident, she'd gotten a little more formal with me. I wasn't sure if I'd overstepped some boundary. Complicated women were never my specialty. I couldn't help comparing her to Lucille. I'd been young then, Lucille slightly older, much wiser and far more complicated than some kid off a cattle drive could fathom. I fell hard for her, and to my surprise, she fell just as hard for me. She was short and slight, but her personality made her ten feet tall. I remembered the way her blonde curls had a way of slipping over her eyes and how she'd blow them off with a puff of her lips.

Lucille taught me more about women and love and lust in our five months together than I'd experience over the next thirty years. No matter how far time managed to drive her memory into a hazy past, my heart would always belong to the smart-mouthed filly with a smile that could lead a man to do things he knew best not to do.

Selma may have looked nothing like Lucille, but there was a bit of her spirit in her. They both had courage and will that was akin to a force of nature. Far be it from me to stand in their way.

Lucille's end was her own, a horror and a tragedy that had set me on my own path, running *to* places other men ran from, staring my own mortality in the eye and daring it to move first. I'd never know why she decided to hang herself. She left no note, or any clues as to what could have possibly driven her to take her life. I was the one who found her, her face blue, her tongue swollen and filling her open mouth. I cut her down, but it was too late. In our last conversation, we'd talked about having a family. Nothing in the world had made much sense to me since that day.

I had to keep reminding myself that that was Lucille's story, and her ending. That didn't mean it would be Selma's. Visions of Lucille on the end of that rope had kept me from getting close to another woman. Maybe it was time to let it go, let it fade until I couldn't recall every heart-rending detail.

I hoped the Lord wasn't fixing to call Selma to dinner sooner than need be, just like he'd done to Lucille.

And if he did have designs on her, I'd have something to say about it.

The sun reflected off her raven hair and blinded me for a moment. When my eyes readjusted, I saw that she had moved ahead of me. I watched her back and a knot of concern twisted my stomach.

I got myself into the damnedest situations.

We stopped at a small tunnel entrance, a little south and west of the one we'd first gone into. The tracks leading into this one were broken and warped. The wood was splintered and the steel looked like it had been melted and reshaped. To look at it, you'd think it had been done in by cannon fire.

"Better watch our step, eh, jefe?"

"I'd hate to break my neck or leg out here."

"For you," Selma said, handing us four hurricane lamps. We'd learned our lesson from the first time. Aside from the backup lamps, we each had two candles and a box of matches.

I walked over to my horse and found my extra pistol in my saddlebag. I handed it to Selma.

"Take it. If anyone or anything tries to come up on you, don't hesitate to use it. Shoot to kill. Aim for here." I poked my chest with my finger.

She tried to hand it back to me. "I don't like pistols."

"You'll like it sure enough if the situation comes up where you need it. I'll feel better knowing you're heeled."

"Be careful," she said.

"That's all we can be," Teta said, tipping his sombrero.

★   ★   ★

The crunch of gravel under our boots ricocheted off the tunnel walls, fading into the center of the hills. I was loath to leave Selma behind, but I'd have felt worse if she were with us. What if that bellowing sound *was* the interior of the hills collapsing on itself? There was no telling how bad things were going to be.

We lit our lamps and started our slow trek down into the heart of the mine.

It was tough going, walking with our heads down, making sure the way was clear. A couple of times, we each smacked into outcroppings of rock. At one point, Teta walked his head right into a small but thick stalactite. It broke from the ceiling and crumbled into pieces on his sombrero.

"That hurt?"

He removed his hat and shook the debris from it. "Shit. It put a hole in it. Look." He poked his finger through a hole in the brim and wiggled it.

"Better that than your thick skull."

Again, I was struck by the fact that the miners had left nothing in their wake. Not a stray tool or bottle or anything that said men used to work and eat and drink in the mine. There was nothing but the warped track and blocks of wood that seemed to keep the whole thing from falling on our heads.

It was also bone dry. My feet were appreciative. That also meant it was completely devoid of any sound. No drips of water here. Nothing at all.

"Hey, you learn anything from that book?"

This was proof that I would talk about anything to break up the deathly silence of the tunnel.

"I didn't get through much last night. It's kind of hard to read."

"You're preaching to the choir. I don't know why Teddy just didn't tell me what was in there. It would save me a lot of trouble."

"Maybe he's not even sure himself."

"You could be right."

I felt the tunnel bend and slope deeper underground. I still wasn't sure what the hell we were looking for. At this point, confirming that it was all clear was good enough for me.

I heard Teta trip before I felt him crash into me. We went down in a heap, and this time the corner of my other elbow took the brunt.

"This is a habit I'd like to break," I said through clenched teeth. Teta didn't answer or move. He lay on me like a smelly bearskin.

I shifted from side to side to roll him off, but he stayed put. Our lamps were thankfully still lit, though both lay on their sides. If I didn't set them upright, the flames *would* die out.

Suddenly, Teta clamped his hand on my jaw and turned my head to face the tunnel ahead.

He whispered, "Nat, tell me I'm seeing things. Are those eyes?" I looked down the tunnel and my stomach turned to ice.

CHAPTER TWENTY-TWO

Two red, glowing orbs hovered near the ground. They were set too far apart to belong to a man, unless he had a head as wide as a horse's ass. Like Teta, I froze, mesmerized by the intensity and impossibility of them.

"They can't be eyes," I said softly. "Maybe it's just something reflecting the lamplight." Teta eased himself off and pulled me to my feet. We did it slowly, quietly.

"It's too far back for the light to go," he said.

The hammer of his Colt clicked as he pulled it back. I lay a hand across his chest.

"I'm not sure it's a good idea to start shooting in here. You could spark something off or cause the whole place to collapse. Let's see what it is first."

"I'm not going. You check it out. I'll cover you."

Ever since we'd gotten to Hecla, I'd been seeing a very different side of Teta. I'd never, and I mean *never*, seen him so skittish before. This was the same man who'd once taken on seven Spanish soldiers with nothing but an empty rifle and a cavalry sword he'd taken off a fallen Rough Rider, and lived to tell about it. But at least we could see the Spanish. There was no telling what was up ahead.

I took a tentative step and found myself drawing my own pistol.

My boot crunched into the grit of the tunnel floor. The sound danced around us like gnats. I paused, never taking my eyes off the red lights. Teta was right; they were too far away to catch the hurricane lamp's flame.

What the hell were they?

They were too big to belong to a possum or raccoon.

They blinked. My foot froze in midstep. My blood hammered in my veins.

I aimed my gun in the dark space between them. If it was an

animal, it had to be sick to have eyes like that. Eyes like that couldn't be found in nature. At least not the nature I'd grown up with.

My hand rose up as the scarlet eyes levitated. One foot off the floor.

Two feet.

Three.

Four.

Teta's shoulder rubbed against mine. He held the lamp ahead of him as far as it would go but it couldn't come close to penetrating the dark. He kept his gun hand loose at his side.

"What the fuck?" he hissed. Five feet.

Six.

The ceiling of the tunnel was maybe seven feet tops in this area. The eyes finally stopped hovering too damn close to its limit.

"Step back," I said from the corner of my mouth. We each took a short step, then another. It was hard to tell, but I could swear the eyes moved closer.

Two steps closer.

We stopped. Total silence returned. I could hear my own breathing in my head. "Back a little more."

The heel of my boot caught on a rock and I almost lost it. I regained my balance. The eyes still watched us, maintaining their distance from us.

"Teta, hold my lamp for a second."

He hooked a finger through the handle so both lamps were held by the one hand. He needed the other for his gun.

I reached into my shirt and got one of the candles. I lit it and crouched to the floor. After letting some hot wax spill on the ground, I pushed the candle into it and waited for it to harden.

"What was that for?"

"If it keeps pace with us, it'll step into the light of that candle. That way, we'll get a better look at it."

"I'm not sure I *want* to look at it."

I thought it best not to tell him I wasn't too crazy about it either. But if I was going to have to shoot, I wanted to know what I was shooting at.

I said, "Here's the deal. You're going to turn around and

make sure we don't break our asses. I'll lean my back into you and take your lead. If I pull the trigger, it's going to be louder than hell on a Saturday night. Start running unless I grab you for extra fire power."

Teta's head bobbed and his sombrero dipped up and down. It was almost comical. Almost.

"On a count of three, start walking."

"Let's just start now."

"Fine by me."

Teta took two quick steps and I walked in line with him, backwards.

This time, I could definitely tell the eyes were moving. They blinked again and tilted a bit to the right.

Either the animal wasn't making any noise as it moved, or our own boot steps were masking its advance. Teta kept walking. I could feel his anxiety rippling through the muscles of his back.

"Just a little more," I said.

The candle's flame flickered, caught in whatever breeze the animal's movement kicked up. I hoped it wouldn't blow out.

"See anything yet?" Teta said.

"Any second now."

We continued walking like a pair of Siamese twins. It was awkward, at best, but we managed to stay upright.

My hopes were answered when the candle did, indeed, stay lit.

When the creature stepped into its light, I wished I could have traded in that hope for something better.

★   ★   ★

Seeing the faint outline of the beast, I did as I'd instructed Selma earlier and shot near its heart. There was no sense waiting to see what its intentions were. At that moment, I didn't care if it was the second coming of Jesus. If that was the disguise he chose, his father couldn't blame me for taking a shot.

It was massive. The top of its head barely missed the ceiling, and its shoulders spanned the width of the tunnel. Long hair covered every square inch of its massive body. It stood on two legs, with arms the size of heavy logs that came down to around its knees.

At first glance, I thought it was the biggest bear I'd ever seen. But when I saw its face, I knew it wasn't any bear.

Those red eyes sat on either side of a wide, leathery nose. Only the face was hairless. It didn't have any lips, as far as I could see, just a horizontal slash that ran from left to right. And when those eyes narrowed at me, that slash opened to reveal two endless rows of sharp, jagged teeth.

If death had a face, this was it.

The concussion of the gun blast made my ears ring so hard I was dizzy. Teta whirled around and opened fire, putting three bullets into it.

All four bullets didn't even make it flinch. I wasn't even sure if they found their mark at all. It was as if something swallowed them up before they could reach their final destination.

It lifted a gigantic foot and squashed the candle, casting itself back into the darkness. But the eyes remained.

"Let's get the hell out of here!" I shouted.

We turned tail and high-stepped it as fast as we could.

When the creature did finally make a noise, it turned my insides to water. It let loose with a howl that was a cross between an angry mountain lion and a sick bull moose. All I could think was that it was just a warning before it charged.

I was right.

Heavy footsteps pounded behind us.

My heart was in my throat. We'd shot the damn thing four times and we may as well have tossed our dirty socks at it. If we turned and emptied our pistols, would that be enough to kill it? If we kept running, would it catch up to us? We had no chance in a hand-to-hand situation.

Run or shoot?

"Faster!" I screamed close to Teta's ear.

We came to a big turn in the tunnel and bounced off the wall. I felt my shirt tear. My upper arm burned as it was slashed open by the rocks.

The light from our lamps danced crazily along the walls. It felt as if we were close to outrunning the light, we were moving so fast.

Still, the footsteps were gaining on us.

I reached back and took a wild shot. I figured the monster was so big it would be hard to miss.

Like an angel of mercy, the sharp light of the mine's exit came into view.

Selma!

We were leading the creature right to her.

CHAPTER TWENTY-THREE

We hit the sunlight and I had to bow my head to keep from being blinded. "Selma!" I called out, sweeping my head from side to side, looking for her feet. She answered right away. "Nat, what is it? Are you hurt? I heard shots!"

Her fingers brushed against the wound on my arm. It stung like a hornet. "Stay behind me," I barked.

Teta and I pulled our hats as low as we could over our brows, faced the mine entrance and had our guns at the ready.

"What's going on?"

As my eyes adjusted, I pulled Teta's arm so he could follow me as I edged to where we'd hitched the horses.

"Selma, mount up." The mine stayed silent.

"Here, use this," Teta said, handing me my rifle. If the Colt was a pea shooter against the monster, the Winchester would give it something to really think about.

Selma hesitated. "I don't understand."

"You don't have to. Just do what Nat says," Teta said.

The leather of her saddle creaked as she swung herself up.

I was about to do the same when a shuffling sound bled out of the cave. My shoulders tensed and I had to concentrate to slow my heartbeat. Dead men let their nerves get the best of them.

The sound of footsteps grew closer.

I turned to Teta. "Empty everything you got into it."

"You don't have to tell me twice, jefe."

Heavy beads of sweat ran down his face like a waterfall.

My plan was to get off a shot, then swat Selma's horse on the rear to clear her out of the area. That way I could concentrate on what needed to be done without worrying about her safety. If I aimed right, and I was lucky, maybe one shot was all I'd need.

"Here it comes," Teta growled.

My finger tensed on the trigger. The sun felt like a branding iron against the tear in my arm. My horse nickered and pawed at the ground. It was kill-or-be-killed time. I was opting for the former.

A pale pair of trembling hands emerged from the darkness of the mine's entrance. "Please, don't shoot!"

It was followed by a quick bark.

A man with long, white hair and a matching beard stumbled out of the mine. Beside him was a mutt that looked like a patchwork of a dozen different dogs. You could see its ribs poking out from beneath its scraggly fur. I would imagine we would have been able to make out every bone of the emaciated man's body if he weren't wrapped up in a very loose shirt and britches held up by several loops of rope around his narrow waist.

His eyes were red rimmed but seemed unaffected by the brilliant sun. He was a sore thing to see. He looked like he'd been rolled into the mine and left to die of starvation.

Teta turned to me with a look that said *this can't be happening!*

"Stay right where you are," I said, keeping my rifle trained on the center of his chest.

He raised his hands as high as they could go and stopped. Even the dog settled onto its hind legs. We could see the man's knees shaking – either from fear or exhaustion, it was too hard to tell.

I wasn't sure what to say or do next. Clearly he wasn't what Teta and I had seen and heard back in the tunnel. How in the hell did he and his mutt get by the creature? It had filled the breadth of the tunnel. Even a rat couldn't have squeezed by it.

Maybe there were offshoots that we hadn't noticed. It was the only logical explanation. "Who are you?" I asked. Teta took a few wary steps toward him, his rifle going from the man to the dog. I'd seen plenty of mongrels take a fellow out to protect their master. You couldn't be too careful around them.

"Franklin?" Selma said.

She got off her horse and stood a step behind me. "Franklin, is that you?"

He looked around at first, as if he couldn't locate the source of the voice. He scrunched his eyes and peered in my direction.

"Selma?" His voice was hoarse, as dry as desert gravel.

"Oh my God, Frank!"

Selma blew by me and ran to the man, taking him in her arms. Teta and I swung our rifles down quickly.

He kept his elbows locked and arms straight above him while she wrapped her own around his upper back. I saw the beginnings of a smile amidst the wild, cottony hairs of his beard. I told him he could put his hands down.

When he did, the rest of his body followed suit. He would have hit the ground if Selma hadn't been there to hold him up. Teta moved in to help her. I kept my distance, my eyes on the dog, the mine and the man. I'd moved the rifle to my left hand so my right could pull my pistol out of the holster. If he made any sudden moves, I wanted to be able to take a tactical shot without harming Teta and Selma in the process.

"Bring him over here," I said, pointing with my rifle to a shady spot under an evergreen tree. There was a bed of brown pine needles that would make as good a place to sit as any. The dog followed them with its tail between its legs, sitting by Frank's feet when they laid him flat.

"I need water," Selma said. She ran to her horse and grabbed her canteen. She untucked her shirt and poured a little on its end. She dabbed at his lips with the moist material. His eyes fluttered a good bit and his chest rose and fell in a steady rhythm.

Moving behind Frank, she lifted him by the back of his neck and rested his head in her lap. Now that his head was elevated, she let a few drops of water from the canteen trickle past his lips. His Adam's apple bobbed up and down as the water worked its way down his throat.

Teta and I were now just spectators. I had too many questions to even know where to begin.

"This guy looks like Methuselah back from the dead," Teta whispered.

"Meth-who?"

"A very old man in the Bible. Where the hell did this guy come from? You and I both saw that…thing. He wouldn't stand a chance getting past it."

"The only thing I know for sure is that I damn sure don't know a thing anymore. And who is he to Selma? I'm a little bothered by the odds of her knowing him."

The man was a little more awake now and taking long sips from Selma's canteen. He pushed himself up on his elbows, looking around with wide, confused eyes. The mangy mutt got up and pushed his nose against the man's neck and beard. The man winced and tried to nudge it away with a shaky hand.

"We need to get him back to town," Selma said. "Can you help get him on my horse?"

"I think it's better he rides with me," I said. I didn't trust the man or the circumstances of his sudden and unbelievable appearance. Not by a long shot.

Selma looked like she was going to put up a fuss, but Teta broke her head of steam by moving over to get the man on his feet. "Come on, old-timer. We'll get you back to camp and put some of Selma's good cooking in that belly."

The man groaned as Teta draped his arm over his neck. I took my saddle off and dressed it over Teta's less-than-handsome stallion. It would be easier for me to ride bareback with the man in front of me. I lashed a leather strap around the both of us because he was so unsteady.

Before we left, I took one last look at the mine's entrance. It was dark and empty and silent. It would be a cold day in hell before I ever went back in there.

The dog scooted ahead of us and actually led the way into town. It knew the way without taking a single wrong turn. With our luck, the dog knew more about what was going on than all of us combined.

And it wasn't talking.

CHAPTER TWENTY-FOUR

Because of the condition of our guest, we had an early supper. Selma got started on a repeat of our breakfast while we set Franklin up in the house. He was asleep before his head hit the saddle we'd placed a blanket over as a pillow.

Teta tended to the horses, taking the rifle and shotgun with him so he could give them a good cleaning.

Selma squatted by the fire. She added eight fat slabs of thick bacon to the cast-iron skillet. They sizzled something fierce and the air instantly smelled like heaven.

"I hope you'll have plenty of biscuits to go with that," I said, deciding to take things slow and see where they led.

"You won't go hungry," she said, concentrating on getting the food together. She was all business now. It was easy to see she was upset.

"Well, Franklin's inside with his dog. They're both sawing wood."

"Thank you for helping him."

"It's not in my nature to leave a man when he needs a hand."

I rolled a cigarette and took a long drag, leaving silence between us, hoping she'd fill it. Instead, she fetched some water and started her biscuit batter. I was tempted to lend her a hand, just like I used to with my dad on the cattle trail. The man could cook. I had a tendency to think I could, but in practice I left a lot to be desired. A man can't be good at everything. Some were good at nothing.

Realizing that information was not going to be forthcoming, I took a new approach. There had to be a reason she wasn't volunteering how she knew the old geezer sleeping in our commandeered house.

When I saw that the food was good to go on its own for a bit, I walked over and placed a hand on Selma's shoulder. "I think we need to talk about your friend."

She looked up at me with quiet resignation, and a touch of what I could best tell was trepidation. She wiped her hands on the front of her jeans and nodded slowly.

"The big question is, how do you know this Franklin fella?"

"Do you remember when I told you my husband came out to Hecla with his brothers?" She paused, rubbing her eyes with the back of her hand. "Franklin is one of them."

So, she sees her husband looking in on her in the middle of the night, and now his brother shows up out of the blue or, in this case, black of the mine. Things were beginning to shake out. Could all of the mystery of Hecla be Hank Smartwood and his brothers conspiring to keep the gold for themselves by driving out everyone who came sniffing around? Or worse? "That has to feel good for you, then. It brings you one step closer to your husband."

Selma turned away and stared off at the hills. A sharp breeze picked up her hair, which danced behind her. It was tempting to reach out and run its velvety strands between my fingers. It was one of my things. Every woman I'd met appreciated that particular fancy.

"Everything's wrong about it," she said so low I couldn't be sure she wasn't just talking to herself.

"I'll agree his turning up, considering the prior circumstances, is a mite peculiar."

She spun to face me and there were tears in her eyes. They quivered at the brim of her eyelids but didn't fall.

"You don't understand. My husband was the middle child of eleven. When he left for Hecla, he was only thirty-four."

"What does that have to do with his brother?"

Her next words sent bitter shards through my blood. "Franklin is the baby of the family. He's only twenty-two!"

★   ★   ★

After Selma's confession, there wasn't much else to say. If I opened my mouth, only unanswerable questions would tumble out. I left her to fixing supper. Keeping her hands busy would prevent worry from digging deeper into her mind. I went round back to tell Teta the news.

"That man is not in his twenties. Maybe a hundred and twenty. I've seen bad things age a man, but not like that."

He cast a glance in Selma's direction and I could see the doubt creeping into his deep-set eyes.

"I don't know what else to tell you. I think we need to have a talk with young Franklin when he wakes from his beauty nap."

"My bad feelings about this place keep getting worse."

I removed my hat and scratched my head. My hair was a wet, dirty mop. "I know how you feel. Every time I think I have a handle on things, something else comes along and I get all balled up. Maybe this Franklin kid is sick with something he caught in the mine. At first, I thought maybe Hank and his little band of brothers were conspiring to chase folks from the mine so they could keep the gold for themselves. You think it's possible they're doing it to keep others from catching whatever Franklin has?"

Teta took a long while to think it over, absently brushing his horse down. "That might explain why her husband was looking at her the way he did through the window. He wanted to scare her off. If he loved her, and he knew it was dangerous, he would do whatever it took to keep her from harm, no?"

"Seems an odd way to go about it, but I've seen men do all sorts of things that don't make sense at first blush. I think we should hold off on the whiskey tonight. Be smart to keep our heads straight."

"That's one way of looking at it."

Teta smirked and headed over to the fire.

Within the hour, Selma declared supper ready. While Teta filled his plate, I went in to get Franklin. Selma stopped me, saying, "Maybe we should let him sleep. I can always save some for later, when he wakes up on his own."

I shook my head. "From the looks of him, he needs food more than a few winks. He can always go back to sleep when he's done. Your biscuits and bacon will set his stomach right." I tried to smile and knew I'd failed. Maybe he did need sleep more than a hot meal, but I was tired of waiting for answers. I needed him up and talking.

When I stepped into the house, he was standing by the window with his back to me. The sun filtered in through the glass and obscured his features, so he was only a scrawny shadow.

"Supper's ready."

He didn't acknowledge me. I walked closer. The clink of my spurs alone should have been enough to catch his attention. His dog was by his side, staring in the same direction; except the mutt wasn't big enough to see out the window, so it eyeballed the wall.

"Hey, Franklin, Selma cooked you up a nice meal. You want to come outside?"

His head twitched at the mention of her name and he slowly turned to me. He shuffled past without saying a word, his dog in tow. His body sagged in the dog's direction as he walked and I thought he might collapse on the mutt.

Selma handed Frank a full plate and a cup of water. He looked at his plate as if it were the first time he'd ever seen food. Selma had to put a spoon in his hand and help him scoop up some beans. Their dark-red juice ran over his lips, staining his white beard. He was in worse shape than I thought.

Teta balanced his plate on his thigh so he could keep one hand by the butt of his pistol.

I waited until Franklin got the hang of things before questioning him. His hand trembled when he brought a biscuit to his lips. Flakes broke off and peppered the ground.

"Selma tells me you're her husband's brother."

His eye shifted to me, but he continued to chew on his biscuit. I could feel Selma's gaze bore into the side of my head.

"You been out here all this time, in the mine?" Franklin let his dog lap some beans off his spoon.

"Did you hear or see anything in the mine when my friend and I were in there earlier?"

Selma started in by saying, "I don't think he's ready to—"

I held up my hand to shush her. It was beginning to feel like she was covering for him and, in turn, playing us for fools. Sure, it could have just been a woman's concern for a family member, but I couldn't afford to turn a blind eye to any angle.

"Franklin, I'm talking to you, son."

Even in his semidazed state, he could hear in my voice that I was at the end of my tether. He finally turned to me, giving me his full attention.

"You were in the mine the same time as Teta and me. Care to tell me what happened in there?"

Selma cocked an eyebrow. We still hadn't told her what had chased us out of the mine. Or at least what we thought had chased us. I suspected Franklin knew a good deal more about it.

"The mine is very – dark," he rasped. "Hard to see. You have to rely on your ears."

"It's a given that a mine is dark. What did you hear?"

"After a while, you don't even need eyes."

More of Wyoming's famous wind had kicked in, blowing tongues of fire Franklin's way.

I hoped his beard wouldn't catch.

I tried a different approach. "Where are Hank and your brothers? Are they in the mine too? Where have you all been hiding out all this time?"

"In…the…mine?"

"You've all gotten Selma sick with worry, not to mention your momma."

The film that had been over his eyes seemed to clear and he said, "Momma shouldn't be here. No one should be here."

Selma leaned into him and asked, "Franklin, please tell me what happened to you."

"Hank's gonna be mad. Oh. They are all so mad."

"Is Hank alive? Is he here?"

"No one's here. I'm not here. I'm not there."

"Teta, will you watch him?" I said, getting to my feet. I motioned for Selma to follow me to the house.

"The old man – I mean boy – isn't in his right mind," I said softly. The wind was blowing in Franklin's direction and I didn't want him to hear. "The only time he snaps to is when I mention either you or his dead mother. I need to get it out of him how he came to be in that mine."

"I can certainly try." She fussed at her lower lip with her thumb and index finger.

"But first, I need you to be straight with me. Are you hiding anything? Since your brother-in-law showed up, you've been acting strange. I can't have you keeping secrets."

Her eyes flashed hot with anger. "How am I supposed to act? I'm sick with worry, wondering what happened to him. What can turn a boy into that? I'm scared, Nat. And I can tell you are too. What was it that got you and Teta all riled up at the mine? Don't think for one second that's not weighing on me too."

I deflected her question and said, "Are you positive that's the Franklin you knew?"

"I've known him since he was born. Yes, it's Franklin."

I took a deep breath and stared into the sky. Long stretches of thin, white clouds passed by in a slow crawl.

A brief, bright flash of light illuminated the outer walls of the house, as if a bolt of thunderless lightning had touched down behind us.

The dog started barking and drew our attention to the fire. Teta lay on the ground, out cold.

And Franklin was gone.

CHAPTER TWENTY-FIVE

The dog growled at me when I ran past it to tend to Teta. If it made one move to snap at me, I had no reservations about planting a bullet right in its snarling maw.

Selma shouted, "Franklin!"

I lifted Teta's head and checked him up and down for any wounds. When I didn't see any, I gave his cheek a quick slap. His eyes snapped open and he leapt to his feet.

"Don't touch me!" he barked, drawing his pistol at the wind.

He looked at me and his shoulders relaxed. He slowly put the gun back in his holster. "Teta, what the hell happened? Did Franklin do something to you?"

He removed his sombrero and massaged the back of his neck. Selma was still calling out for her brother-in-law, walking in a widening circle in the middle of the unpaved street.

Teta spit on the ground and said, "The old man, he looked at me and said he wanted to tell me something. He raised his hand like he was going to cup it by my ear and whisper some kind of secret. I didn't like it, so I went for my gun. The next thing I know, you're waking me up."

"He didn't slug you?"

He shook his head. "As far as I know, he never got close enough to touch me. Everything got real white, then black. Is he gone?"

"Like the wind."

"Nat, no one in that kind of shape can disappear that fast."

"I know."

Franklin's mutt had calmed down and stretched out with its head on its front paws. The same dog that wouldn't leave its master's side now couldn't care less that he'd up and left. Even the damn animals in this town weren't right.

"Franklin!"

"Selma, come back here. I don't want you wandering out alone," I said. She stopped calling out for him and walked back with her hands on her hips. I could have sworn she looked partly relieved. No matter how you sliced it, Franklin's appearance and disappearance were distressing.

"Where on earth could he have gone?" she asked.

The three of us were left staring at the deserted streets of Hecla without a clue. I walked around a bit and couldn't find a single track from Franklin, other than his steps from the house to the fire. It was as if he'd hitched a ride on a passing eagle and flown away.

"At any rate, he knows where to find us," Teta said, sending a chill down my back.

★   ★   ★

We mounted up and did a quick search of the immediate area, but as I suspected, we found nothing. The dog remained by the fire. I'd hoped he would run off and join his master.

He didn't.

It was getting close to nightfall so we headed inside. Teta rummaged through the debris of the collapsed house across the street and brought some of the sturdier boards over along with some nails he'd found scattered on the ground.

"I'm sealing us in tonight," he said.

He unloaded his pistol and used it to hammer the nails into the board that he had slanted over the door. I gave him a hand.

"Now we just need to worry about the window, jefe."

Despite Selma's objections, we left the dog outside. Anything that came out of that mine was not welcome. When I thought about the creature we'd seen, I shivered and thought the board wasn't going to be enough if it wandered out of the mine and into town. Because of Franklin's miraculous emergence from the mine, Teta and I hadn't had a chance to discuss what the hell was living in the tunnels. With Selma around, and the state she was in, we'd have to wait for a chance to talk tomorrow when she was out of earshot.

I checked on how much lamp oil we had left and decided it would be smart to stick with using just one lamp until we settled in for sleep. We put our bedrolls around the lamp as if it were a campfire. Selma's eyes were tired and puffy, and any attempt at conversation was met with one-word answers or head nods.

I said, "Why don't you close your eyes and get some sleep? Teta and I will be up keeping an eye on things. You've had a hard, strange day."

A weary smile lightened the dark cast of her features and she laid her head down atop her hands. "Thank you, Nat. And you too, Teta. I'm sorry if I've seemed off. Franklin was always so young and sweet. He used to follow me around like a kid brother. I just don't know what to make of everything."

"That makes three of us," Teta said. He had Teddy's book on his lap and was paging through it.

Selma closed her eyes. It didn't take long for her to wink out.

My body was tired but my mind was on fire. I was trying to put all of the odd-shaped pieces together and even if I chewed off the ends, I couldn't get a damn thing to fit. I was going to need a few belts of whiskey to shut myself down, but that wasn't in the cards.

"I'll take first watch if you want," I said.

Teta's lips moved as he read. "I couldn't sleep now if I tried. I'm hoping this book will do the trick."

"Find anything interesting yet?" He nodded, his lips still working.

Lowering my voice, I said, "If Teddy only knew what he sent us into. We've all seen and done our share of unusual things, but this takes the cake."

Without taking his eyes from the book, Teta replied, "I'm not so sure he didn't know it."

"What do you mean by that?"

"I don't know yet. If you stop talking, I can figure it out."

I left Teta to the book, more than a little curious about how it pertained to our situation. In the meantime, I cleaned my pistol, smoked a cigarette, tried to count the stars outside the window and spent a good deal of time gazing at Selma's peaceful face. Her lips had parted slightly and every now and then her breath hitched with a short snore.

Instead of counting sheep, I counted the seconds between each of her breaths. Sleep crept up on me and took me under to a dark, dreamless place.

★   ★   ★

When I woke up, the room was as pitch black as the tunnels back in the mine. I craned my neck to peek out the window. Heavy clouds had settled in during the night. The stars and sliver of moon were nowhere to be seen.

Teta must have put the lamp out before going to sleep. My chest tightened with uneasiness.

Why didn't he wake me for my shift on watch? I reached over and lifted the lamp. There was still plenty of oil in it, which meant Teta had had enough presence of mind to turn it off before going to sleep. He should have woken me.

Selma and Teta were vague outlines in the dark. I only knew they were there by the sounds of their breathing.

But there was something else.

It sounded like panting. Heavy, quick breaths in rapid succession. Like a dog.

I reached in my pocket for a match and scraped it against the floor.

Even with its feeble light, the entire cabin came to life. I immediately went for my gun.

Franklin's mutt was in the house. It hovered over Selma. I had to rub my eyes to make sure I was seeing right.

The dog's jaws were open so far and wide the hinges had to have snapped into pieces. A glistening film of drool dripped down its yellow teeth. Hunched over, it poised its unnatural mouth over her head as if it intended to swallow it whole. It watched me with black, dead eyes.

Darkness returned when the match fizzled out against my thumb and finger. I cursed, found another and lit the hurricane lamp.

The dog's black lips curled back even farther from its diseased gums and it gave a low, menacing growl. Its head moved closer to Selma's but it never took its eyes from mine.

Selma sighed in her sleep. A long line of thick drool dripped into her hair.

I pointed my pistol at the dog. Something was very wrong with it. I'd seen my fair share of rabid animals, but this was entirely different. Its fur stood on end, like a porcupine. The flesh and fur of its face stretched thin over deformed bone. I'd seen something like it once before when I'd smoked peyote with a couple of Ojibwa scouts working for the army. I'd known then that it was just my mind playing tricks on me.

That was far from the case this time.

When I pulled the hammer back, the dog stiffened and its eyes darted to the barrel. I wasn't going to let it move another inch closer to Selma. If it didn't back off in the next few seconds, its head was going to paint the walls.

I croaked, "Your move, you ugly fucking mongrel."

Its jaws opened wider and I heard the sharp crack of displaced bone. It may have been a trick of the flickering light, but it looked like its incisors were growing longer, the tips tapering into deadly needles.

The threat of my gun wasn't going to stop it. In fact, it seemed to be doing just the opposite. It was as if it had waited for me to wake up so it had an audience to the atrocity it had in store.

There was no sense waiting. I had to shoot now, while there was still some distance between it and Selma.

Naturally, she chose that moment to wake up screaming.

CHAPTER TWENTY-SIX

Selma's eyes flew open and she shouted, "Hank!"

I jerked my arm up and shot at the roof. Her sudden scream came too quickly for me to lay off the trigger. The shot brought Teta scrambling to his feet, his own gun in hand, sweeping the room. It also choked Selma's screams in her throat. Her body was as rigid as a stone and she stared at me with a cross between fear and confusion.

The dog had backed off and was sitting on its haunches. Its face was back to normal. A pink- and black-specked tongue lolled out of its half-open mouth.

"What happened, jefe?"

I was on my feet now too. I held a hand out to Selma and brought her behind me. She did it without the slightest protest.

"It's the dog," I said.

"How did it get in here?" Selma asked. I felt her press against my back. "I don't know how, but there's something not right about it."

The dog looked back at us with typical dog indifference. There was no reconciling it with the grotesque varmint that had threatened to put an end to Selma just seconds ago.

Teta checked the door and window. "There's no way it came through here. Could it have been hiding in a corner when we were setting up before?"

"I don't know. But I'm not taking any chances."

I leveled my gun and pulled the trigger. The dog yelped and flipped backwards. Blood and bone and fur erupted against the barricaded door. Selma shrieked and pounded my back with her fists.

"What's the matter with you? What kind of man shoots a defenseless dog? You're sick!"

Her words sounded as if they were coming from far off. I watched the dog's legs twitch as it went into its final death spasm.

Its bowels emptied onto the floor. The stench of that and the blood was overpowering.

"You didn't see what I saw," I said, walking over the dog's body and pulling at the wood over the door.

Selma sobbed behind me. Teta helped me get the door open and carry the dog outside.

We dropped its corpse behind one of the ramshackle cabins across the street.

Teta didn't ask me what I saw or why I did what I did. I was grateful for that. I filled a bucket with some water from the pump and splashed it on the floor. Blood and brains and shit went out with the tide, trickling down the steps. I made seven trips to the pump, and by the time I was done, you could breathe in the house without swallowing back bile.

Selma watched me with cold hatred.

"I'll stand watch outside the rest of the night," I said. "There's still about three hours before sunrise."

I closed the door behind me and leaned against the house. It was best no one said anything until morning. Maybe a new day would bring some clarity.

★　　★　　★

I put a small breakfast together and Teta and I shared a strong cup of coffee before Selma awoke.

"Did she say anything?" I asked.

"Not a thing with her words, but I could feel a lot coming off her after you walked out."

"That wasn't an ordinary dog." I told Teta what I saw, how the dog transformed into a damn nightmare that was all mouth and malicious intent. He stroked the stubble on his chin while I talked, taking everything in.

"Did it look like that thing in the mine? Like maybe a smaller version?"

I shook my head. "Not even close. It was clearly still a dog, just twisted and re-formed. It could have taken Selma's head easily. What we saw in the mine, that was different. That looked just like the wild man the Indians talk about. I've seen drawings of it on rocks and wood carvings. As odd as it is, at least it has a reference point. The dog is a complete mystery to me."

"What the hell is going on here?"

"Too much."

"And I don't understand how I missed my watch. You know that's not like me."

"Don't beat yourself up about it. Neither of us are ourselves. It's like living in a fever dream."

The clouds from the night before had trailed off and the sun was bright and low in the sky. The air was still and dry. Hecla seemed emptier than usual. It was like entering a funeral home after everyone had left. It was just us and the cooling corpse of the ghost town.

"I think we need to go back," Teta said. "This is too much for just the two of us. Tell Teddy to steer clear. There's no evidence of gold. As far as I can tell, it's just a rumor that has led to bad things happening to the people who come here. Let's leave while we're still alive to do it."

I've never been one to give up, but for the first time in my life, it seemed the best option.

What the hell did I know about what was going on here? None of it made any sense.

I squared my hat on my head and tossed the rest of my coffee onto the ground. "You're right. I have a feeling if we stay any longer Hecla's just going to swallow us whole. Teddy has bigger fish to fry. Leave this place for the buzzards, if they'll even come."

Teta could barely conceal his relief. We'd been knocked into a cocked hat since the moment we set foot in Hecla. Feeling confused and inadequate made me angry, and when I got angry, people tended to get hurt.

Just ask the dog.

★　　★　　★

Selma slung a steady diet of daggers my way as she got everything together. It was hard to tell if she was relieved we were moving out through all of the hatred over what I'd done to the dog, if you could rightly call it that. I left Teta to help her load up her horse.

I was happy that we were going to put Hecla behind us. I may not have known what I'd be doing next with my life, but I did know that I would never set foot in Wyoming again. When you got to a certain age, there was such a thing as a little too much adventure. Maybe it was time to ask Teddy if I was still bodyguard timber.

Teta and Selma came out from behind the house on their horses. The spare horses and mule were tied up and in tow. I was going to let them take the lead so I could spare myself the dirty glances that would be burned into my back.

Our horses had started kicking up dust when Selma shouted, "Wait!" I stalled behind her horse.

Her head snapped around. "Did you at least bury it?"

"Pardon?"

"The dog. Did you have the decency to bury the dog?"

I pulled out a handkerchief and wiped some of the sweat from the back of my neck, chasing a cluster of mosquitos away for the moment.

"I can't say that I did. I didn't see much need to go digging a hole."

"Of course you didn't," she spat, turning her horse around. "Where did you put it?"

"We don't have time for this. I want to get you back to your father's ranch and plant my ass in a bed at the inn before nightfall."

"Then feel free to run on back to Laramie. I can take care of it myself. Teta, can you please be a gentleman and show me where you left the dog?"

He looked at me, caught between a rock and a hard place. I rolled my eyes, resigned to the fact that our return to Laramie was about to be delayed by a few minutes.

"Follow me," he said.

The mule at first didn't want to go, but after a few tugs, we all went back behind the crushed cabin.

Teta let out a loud, long whistle and said, "I'll be damned. You're not going to believe this one, Nat."

I eased my horse between his and Selma's and looked down.

The dog's body wasn't there. In its place was a pile of black, foul-smelling sludge that bore a striking resemblance to freshly sprung oil. A mass of thick-bodied bottle flies had gathered atop the ooze like bathers in a swimming hole.

"You must have put it somewhere else," Selma said. She brought her mouth up to cover her face and nose. The air was pungent enough to put you off breakfast for life.

"Nope, this is exactly where we dropped it," I said, pointing at the clump of sagebrush to the right of the rancid puddle. "It slipped out of our hands and dropped into that brush. See where it's crushed a little. We picked it up and put it down right there."

"What happened to it?"

"Whatever it was, it happened after we carted it here. I know you think I'm a cold bastard, but I'd never shoot an animal unless I had a good reason. There's your reason."

I didn't add that what was left of the dog was a sight better than the way it had looked back in the house before I put an end to it.

"No sense burying that," Teta said. He made a sign of the cross, then spit into the center of the oily mess.

"You have any objections to our leaving now?"

Selma stared at what was left of the dog and shook her head.

"Then let's skedaddle."

My horse didn't need any coaxing from me. She spun right back towards the way home and picked up the pace. I had to rein her in a bit so the rest could catch up.

None of us so much as gave Hecla a parting glance as we left the town, passing the bone orchard. Every grave marker was lined with silent, dark crows. Their heads followed us as we rode by the rotted picket fence.

Teta let loose with a fine string of Spanish curses. Most of what I knew of the language had to do with swear words and he'd hit them all. He sneered at the crows and hurled insults their way.

"You shouldn't do that," Selma admonished him. I suddenly realized she knew full well what he was saying.

He whipped out his Colt and fired a shot in the air.

The mule gave a strangled whimper and my horse flinched. The crows didn't even move a feather.

"Bad omen," I said, just to rile him up. It was easy to do, now that we were leaving. I'm not so sure I would have been so cocky if we were headed in the other direction.

Selma didn't see my humor, either.

Teta gave one last, *"Sucios, hijos de putas!"*

The land before us was flat and unbroken for miles. We waded through a narrow creek where the water had been reduced to a thin trickle. There was more dust than water in the creek bed.

I estimated how long it would take to get to Laramie, turn in the horses and leftover supplies, talk Selma's father down from laying into her for leaving, get a room at the hotel and grab a nice steak. Teta and I would drink ourselves into oblivion and find a train back East tomorrow. Somewhere in there, I'd take a nice, hot bath and wash Hecla off me. If I was really lucky, Selma would be there to wash my back, among other things.

Teta had pulled ahead to take the lead while I daydreamed.

When his horse reared up on its hind legs, whinnying like the devil was about to take a bite out of him, my dream of a soft bed and warm whiskey shattered into a million pieces.

CHAPTER TWENTY-SEVEN

Teta's horse tried like hell to unseat him but he held on for all he was worth. I was getting in close enough to grab his horse's bridle and help settle him down when my own horse went wild. As my line of sight went from east to north in a hurry, I heard Selma's horse cry out.

In fact, all of the horses were clawing at the air and behaving as if they'd lost their minds. I squeezed my thighs as hard as I could and tightened my grip on the reins. It would take a lot more than a little dance to knock me or Teta off. That didn't mean that the effort to hold on didn't send fire through my legs and arms.

To her credit, Selma was the first to regain control of her horse. I'm sure they'd been paired up for a good long time and were in tune with each other's inclinations. It took a little longer for Teta and me to settle our horses down, but we did.

My hat had flown off and the wind had carried it a good twenty feet behind us. I looked down at the disturbed dirt, the surface a mess of wild hoofprints. I got Teta's attention and pointed.

"What do you make of that?"

There was a solid line of prints that stopped at the exact same spot. "Was there a snake we didn't see?" he said.

"Snakes leave tracks. There's nothing on the other side of our prints."

"Something spooked them," Selma said. She had dismounted and was rubbing her hand up and down her horse's muzzle. "I've never seen Maria act like that before."

"Let's move down a ways and try again. Maybe something's under the ground that we can't sense," I said. The words even sounded preposterous to me. Horses reacted to things they could see and hear, not intuitions.

We skirted the area and went down a couple of hundred feet, putting good distance between us and the spot the horses refused to cross. I told Teta and Selma to move back while I moved ahead.

Again, my horse went plum crazy. I struggled to regain control and when I was done, I felt ready to turn in. The mind was willing but the flesh, well, it was a tad weaker than it'd been in years past.

"We keep this up and I'm going to end up flat on my back," I said. A Wyoming wind cooled the sweat on my face.

"This is *loco*." Teta jumped off his horse and walked over to the spot where my horse had stopped. "If we can't ride them, we'll just have to drag them."

He turned, took a step, and tumbled backwards.

Selma knelt by his side. "Are you all right?" She held his arm and helped him into a sitting position. His eyes were glassy and I could see he was having a hard time bringing things into focus.

"What happened?" he said, his words slurring a bit.

"I haven't a clue."

"It was like I was pushed, but at the same time something pinched my head and threw ice water on my brain. I know that doesn't make any sense, but that's how it felt. I need a drink."

Selma grabbed a canteen but he gently pushed it away. I tossed him a bottle of whiskey.

He fumbled and nearly dropped it.

"You *are* hurt," I said, concerned by the slight tremor in his hands.

"I'll be fine. Just need a moment." He took a long pull from the bottle and wiped his mouth with his dirty sleeve.

"Nat, what's going on?" Selma said. She stared at the way ahead, her eyes searching for anything that could explain what had happened to Teta and the horses.

"I'll find out," I growled, fed up with Hecla and its mysteries that plagued us even when we were fixing to leave. "Teta, you good enough to move on?"

He took another pull and tossed the half-empty bottle to me. "Right as rain, jefe."

"Selma, I want you and the other horses to keep at least five feet behind us. We'll move farther up the line and try again."

I went back to scoop my hat off the ground and we retraced our steps, passing by the spot where we'd first been brought to a halt. This time, we rode for about a quarter of a mile before stopping. I looked up at the sky and figured this little detour meant we wouldn't get into Laramie until sundown. I'd have to skip that bath.

I whistled to call everyone to a stop. Dismounting, I scanned the ground, looking for a decent-sized rock. I found one and hefted it in my hand.

Cocking my arm back, I lofted the rock. It sailed unimpeded and bounced on the ground with a loud clack.

"That's encouraging," I said. "Now let's see what happens to *me*."

"Nat, be careful," Selma said. One look at her round, tanned face gave me the needed boost to take that first step. Men were always boys just trying to impress girls. I let out a big breath.

Come on, Nat, it's just walking. You've been doing it since you were a baby.

The tip of my boot moved into the seemingly empty air.

A whirlwind of stars and pain came rushing to greet me. I cried out something unintelligible. Staggering on one foot, I did manage to stay upright.

Teta was right. It did feel like something had crawled inside my head and flushed it clean, while at the same time doing its damnedest to break my skull from the outside. Dizzy, I walked uneasily until I could rest against my horse. I grabbed the saddle horn to hold myself up. I didn't even feel Selma and Teta on either side of me.

"That put a spoke in my wheel," I said. Teta wafted the open bottle of whiskey under my nose and I took a drink.

"We keep at this and we're going to run out of whiskey," he said. There was no humor in his tone.

"And sunlight," I said, craning up to check its position in the sky. My father had taught me how to tell the time that way. Watches were a rare commodity in the Blackburn house. "I think we need to go back through Hecla and see if we can at least go west. Selma, what's the closest town in that direction."

She bit her lip and thought a moment. "The next rail stop would be in Centennial. If we got there, we could take the train back to Laramie."

"I don't suppose we'd make it there by tonight." My scalp was peppered with pins and needles, but the fuzziness in my head was clearing. My leg felt like it had been dipped in a bonfire and pulled out before the flames could catch. I had a strong suspicion that no matter which way we went, we weren't getting out of Hecla today.

How was it possible? What was behind it and why? Like the way the original miners had staked their claim on the Deep Rock Hills, Hecla had staked its claim on us. What worried me most was what it had in store for us.

One thing I couldn't deny was that the way east was blocked. Me, Teta and the horses had learned that sure enough.

Selma replied, "I'm not sure. I don't care if we have to ride all night. I want to get out of here."

She looked close to a flat-out panic.

We rode back to Hecla and tied the mule and extra horses up by the house we'd just vacated. We packed only the supplies we absolutely needed in case we did break through the invisible barrier. I promised Selma we'd come back with an army to retrieve the horses. She looked like she didn't believe a word, but she needed to hear it to ease her conscience, leaving them behind like that.

I shouted, "Hyah!" and we tore ass out of Hecla. We rode as clear as we could of the hills, keeping our noses due west.

When the mined-out hills were at our backs we slowed down. I had no desire to run into another one of those unseen walls with a full head of steam.

Any glimmer of hope I had was dimmed for good when all three horses pulled up short and kicked at the air.

"Well shit!" I spit into the dirt. My spit was able to cross the barrier, just not the rest of me.

"I hate to say it, but I think we're trapped," Teta said.

I pulled out my pistol and fired three shots dead ahead. My bullets tore into the distance, freer than us.

"What did you do that for?" Selma asked. I had no answer.

Instead, I turned south and put my spurs to my horse. Teta and Selma hurried to catch up to me.

There was no luck that direction, either. Hecla wasn't about to let us go.

CHAPTER TWENTY-EIGHT

The ride back to Hecla was slow and silent and tense. Teta saying we were trapped kept playing over and over in my mind. Whatever lived in Hecla, and I was now convinced this was far from a dead, empty mining town, had something in store for us. I'm sure it wasn't going to be pretty. It wanted to make us disappear like it had done with every other poor soul that had had the misfortune of crossing into its territory. No wonder the Indians wouldn't set foot here.

Indians. I almost had to laugh at my worrying when we first got here that Indians may have been behind everything.

They were the smart ones. Leave it to the white man to stumble into this nightmare.

We ended up back at the house. The horses and mule looked at us lethargically. Without saying a word, we unlashed our supplies and took the saddles off our horses. Teta led them to the trough.

Selma gathered everything she needed to cook as if she were in a daze. I tried to say something a couple of times but the words twisted my tongue and wouldn't come out. What the hell was there to say? There wasn't anything to do except wait. It wasn't something I was accustomed to doing.

We ate a little, had a smoke and moved everything inside the house just as night fell. I wasn't sure what kind of protection four rickety walls would give us, but none of us felt safe outside.

Teta went back to reading Teddy's book. "I'm not sleeping until I get through it all," he said.

In fact, none of us slept. Selma and I passed the time watching Teta page through the book by lamplight, counting the minutes until dawn.

★　★　★

Even though nothing happened for the rest of the night, my nerves were on edge. The future didn't bode well for us. The question now was, did we wait to die or go down fighting? If Selma weren't with us, the answer would be simple. With her to consider, things weren't quite so cut and dry.

My back was killing me when I decided the sun was up enough to go outside and look around. The strain of riding my horse when she went wild and of whatever the hell the invisible barrier did to me had taken their toll on my body.

I tipped my head back and looked up. Not a cloud in sight. The sun blazed an orange streak, dividing the night sky. Selma came out and stood beside me.

"Do you hear that?" she said.

I listened for a moment, then said, "Hear what?"

"Silence. When was the last time you faced a dawn without the sounds of birds chattering away? Do you think they're smart enough to keep away, or is the town chasing them out?"

"If it's the latter, I'd as soon disguise myself to look like a bird so Hecla can spit me out."

We shared a tired, awkward laugh. I looked inside the house and saw Teta dozing, his back propped up against the wall, the book on his lap. "Well, at least one of us is getting some shut-eye."

"Are you hungry?"

"Not at the moment." My stomach was tied in a hangman's knot. I couldn't have put food into it if I tried.

"Me neither. It's like I have to make something so I don't feel so useless, but I don't want to waste the food."

"Better to wait and see if our stomachs start rumbling later."

A strong breeze blew her hair into wavering black tentacles that covered her face. She pushed it back and stared at the Deep Rock Hills. "I feel like they're watching us. And I'm scared, thinking Franklin's part of it. Does that sound crazy?"

I put an arm over her shoulders. "If you said that before I came to Hecla, I'd have said yes. Right now, anything is fair game. If those hills are watching us, I'd like to find their eyes and poke one out. That'd help make things right."

With not much else to do, we walked around collecting wood,

then fed what was left of the carrots to the horses.

It was then I heard an odd sort of rumbling. It wasn't like the small earthquake we'd experienced before. It was farther off in the distance, a mechanical type of racket that had no place out here in the ass end of nowhere. Selma heard it too and looked at me with wide eyes.

"Can't be," I said. "Are you sure?"

"I'm not sure about anything anymore."

I ran over to the house and turned the corner. It had to be my mind playing tricks on me.

But it was real.

And it was headed straight for us.

CHAPTER TWENTY-NINE

"Teta, get up and get out here!" I shouted.

I don't think Selma realized she had my arm in a tight grip as we watched the dust cloud tear across the plain at a speed that was hard to comprehend. Teta ran out of the house with a shotgun in his hands.

"What is it?" he asked.

"Check that out," I replied, pointing.

Coming at us from the west was an open, black automobile. I could see two men seated behind the wheel. The car moved faster than anything I'd ever seen before. Being in New York for a few years, I'd taken a gander of my share of horseless carriages. I'd also seen quite a few cut down horses in the street, causing a bloody, horrible mess. I'd once had to put a horse down whose front legs had been wrapped up within the tire and front body of a car. It was hard to tell where the car began and the horse ended. The mare made a sound in its agony that I'll never forget.

"What the hell is a car doing out here?" Teta said. "Out for a Sunday stroll?"

The men must have seen us because the horn blared, an ugly, long caterwaul that made me want to put a slug in the engine. The driver raised his arm and waved. We didn't wave back.

"Do you think the barrier is down?"

"More like it just let another couple of fools into its trap," I said.

With a high-pitched squeal of metal on metal, the car pulled to a stop some twenty feet from us. A dirty, brown cloud of dust rolled over the car, hiding it from view for a few seconds. When it cleared, I could see the car better. It had an exposed engine with four heavy, round cylinders on each side. I imagined that the dry terrain would play hell with it. Long running boards ran along each side and there was a slightly raised rumble seat in the back. The tires were bigger than I'd seen on regular cars and narrow. It resembled the skeleton of a much larger car.

The driver leapt out and approached us, halting when he spied Teta's shotgun.

"Did we just ride into a Wild West show?" the driver said. He removed a pair of thick goggles and stuffed them in his jacket pocket. He was tall and lean with slicked-back hair that had more grease in it than the gears of a locomotive. A thick handlebar mustache framed razor-thin lips. Something about him screamed big money. Maybe it was the car, or the clipped accent, I wasn't sure.

"You're not that lucky," I said.

He clapped his gloved hands. "Cowboys and a cowgirl! This is unexpected."

Teta asked, "How did you get here?"

The man looked at Teta as if he'd asked the most nonsensical question ever dreamt up. "With the help of my Buffum Roadster. You did see me drive up, didn't you? It's right behind me, see?"

I saw Teta's grip tighten on the shotgun. If he thought he was being made fun of, he could get mean in a hurry. I wasn't in the mood to talk him down.

"I mean, how did you get through?"

The man cocked an eyebrow so high it almost reached his hairline. "Through? I just— drove. It's what one does when one is at the wheel of the finest car money can buy, eight cylinders of pure, unadulterated power. Why, if I had an actual road to drive on, I could go up to eighty miles an hour. It's a beautiful piece of machinery. I would have gotten here sooner if I didn't have to travel over God's untamed country. I'll have to take it in to have the shocks redone."

Selma looked at me as if to say, *Is this man out of his mind?*

"You said you would have gotten here sooner," I said. "Does that mean you were intentionally coming out to Hecla?"

He looked around, unfazed by the fact that his destination was a town in ruins. "Is that what this place is called? Hecla. Odd name. The answer is, yes, this is where my companion and I have been headed ever since we heard the Trumpets of Armageddon."

Trumpets of Armageddon?

Selma said, "When did you hear these trumpets?"

He smiled and regarded her with a patriarchal air. "Why, it was just the other day. Were you here at the time?"

"Yes. May I ask where you were when you heard them?" I said.

I suddenly remembered that terrible howling that erupted when the ground shook.

Funny how I could forget it. My mind had other puzzles to decode.

"My companion and I were up near Medicine Bow. We had a...business engagement when we heard it clear as day."

"But Medicine Bow has to be more than ninety miles away!" Selma said.

"One hundred nine, if I can trust my odometer," he said. He slapped his forehead with the palm of his hand and cried, "Where are my manners? Please, allow me to introduce myself. I'm Reverend Matthias Manning. My strong but silent companion is Angus Ibbs." He motioned for his friend to join us.

The car tilted to one side and groaned as Angus shifted himself out of the passenger seat. Angus was as broad as a barn, squat and thick, with a bald head burned by the sun and thick sideburns that sat like lost islands in a sea of flesh. His eyes were set deep under his brow and he approached us with a slow, even gait. The man was a beast. I expected he could lift a cow over his head just to pass the time.

He carried a wooden chest under one arm. It looked like something a pirate would use to store gold and stolen booty.

"Angus, I'd like you to meet—"

I put my hand to the brim of my hat and said, "I'm Nat Blackburn, and this is Selma Smartwood and Teta Delacruz."

Angus cocked his cannonball head. "Your name is *Tit*?"

"Language," the reverend scolded.

Teta said nothing. He was still deciding what to make of our visitors and I'm sure curious as to how they were able to get here so easily.

"I know the horn, or whatever you called it, was loud, but I'm having a hard time believing you heard it all the way in Medicine

Bow," I said. "And even if you did, Reverend, what makes you think it came from here?"

"Please, call me Matthias. Titles can be so restricting. To your point, I, in fact, didn't hear the *trumpet*. The hearing and the locating of its origin all fall under Angus's purview. He's, shall we say, gifted in peculiar ways."

"What were you hoping to find?" Selma asked.

Angus stood mute, a statue of flesh. I guess one of his talents *wasn't* conversing.

"The Horsemen of the Apocalypse? A dragon called from Satan's realm? An as-yet-undiscovered anomaly? Who's to say? It's the mystery that compelled us to come. 'And the heavens departed as a scroll when it is rolled together, and every mountain and island were taken from their place'."

I was beginning to wonder if they were just another creation born of the twisted heart of Hecla. It was getting to the point where I couldn't trust my own eyes and ears anymore. Maybe if I shot one in the leg just to see if they bled.

"You picked a bad time to visit," Teta said. "This place doesn't play nice with people."

Matthias looked around. "Oh, I can see that. Or rather, I can feel it."

I said, "Understanding that, you drove a long way to get here. And even though we just met, I need to ask a favor of you."

"I live to serve." He made a slight bow and a greased lock of hair flipped over his face.

"My friends and I have come across some difficulties getting past the town limits. Seeing that you didn't have any problems with your motor car, I was wondering if you could get them to Laramie."

Selma tugged at my arm. "We're not leaving without you."

"There isn't room for all of us. Someone has to stay behind."

"What kind of difficulty did you encounter?" Matthias asked.

"A painful kind," Teta answered.

Matthias sucked on his teeth and considered my request. He eyed the car, then us.

"It shouldn't take long. I'm sure whatever mysteries are here can wait," he said. "I'll leave Angus with you, Mr. Blackburn."

"Nat."

"Nat. I should be back in time for supper."

"I'd be much obliged."

I avoided Teta's and Selma's gazes. There was no room for arguing. If this half-mad preacher could get them out of Hecla without me, they were just going to have to lump it. Things were escalating here, and I didn't want the blood of their fate on my hands.

"Well, no better time than the present. I'll get her started."

Matthias strode over to his car while Angus plopped his pirate's chest down and sat upon it.

"Let Selma go," Teta said. "I'll stay with you."

I shook my head. "I'm not leaving Selma alone with him. He says he's a reverend and can quote Scripture, but that doesn't tell me squat about the man. Be sure to let him know when to slow down. I don't want you in a car wreck if the barrier is still up."

Teta's face paled. "Okay, but as soon as I get to Laramie and drop Selma off at her ranch, I'm coming back."

I smiled. "I expect nothing less."

Matthias gave his horn two quick honks. His goggles were back in place and he'd fastened a leather cap on his head.

"You better go," I said to Selma. She looked at me with pleading eyes, daring me to crack. I stayed firm.

"I'm going to be sick with worry," she said.

I put my hands on her shoulders and gave them a gentle squeeze. "I can take care of myself, even in a place like this. Besides, I have Angus now. He's better than a scarecrow."

A lone tear brimmed in her eye. She tried to laugh but lowered her head to wipe her tear away.

"Promise you'll stop by the ranch when you get back to Laramie?"

"I will. Now go on, before Matthias changes his mind."

Selma sat in the front passenger seat while Teta took the rumble seat. Knowing him, there'd be a gun quietly trained on Matthias's back. I waved at them as they sped off eastward.

Damn, that car was fast.

I turned to the mountain of a man and said, "Well, that just leaves us." Angus lowered his heavy eyelids in reply.

There was a soft, muffled moan and I could have sworn the chest moved slightly under Angus's considerable weight. I looked down at it, then at him.

"You mind telling me what's in the chest?"

The sound of a woman sobbing was definitely coming from the chest. I pulled my pistol and pointed it at Angus.

"I need you to get off that chest and take three steps back." Angus looked at me with arctic, dead eyes.

CHAPTER THIRTY

"Get off the chest, now!"

It seemed too small to contain a person, but that was definitely a woman I'd heard crying inside it. Maybe she was very small or, worse, busted up in a way she could be crammed into the chest. I was doubly glad I'd sent Teta with Selma.

"You do understand the implications of getting shot, don't you?" I asked.

Angus stared at me but didn't move. I couldn't tell if he could hear or understand me. But he *had* responded when we'd introduced ourselves. He wasn't a deaf-mute and he did speak the language.

"I've had a rough few days and my temper is wearing thin. If you don't do what I say, I'm not going to weep for you when you're gone."

Angus's shoulders heaved with a big sigh and he slowly got up. He took one short step to the side.

"A little more, big fella."

I could tell by the way his knees locked that he wasn't moving another inch. I'd just have to move the chest away from him. Keeping my pistol pointed at the center of his burly chest, I walked over to the box and tried to move it aside with my boot.

It didn't budge. The damn thing must have weighed well over a hundred pounds. But he'd carried it like he'd had a small sack of flour under his arm.

It had a thick padlock on the front. Bending down, never taking my eyes off Angus, I tugged on the lock. It was as immovable as the chest.

"You have a key?"

Angus continued with his silent treatment.

Suddenly, something thumped within the chest and it lifted off the ground, slamming back down hard. I jumped back. I had to swallow several times to dislodge my heart from my throat.

"All right, that's enough. Give me the key or I'll shoot the damn lock off!"

Still Angus didn't move. It was like talking to the wind. Well, I'd wasted enough time. I moved the barrel of my pistol from his chest to the lock.

"No!"

Angus's hand shot out with superhuman speed. He got my gun hand in a grip that felt like I'd been caught in a bear trap. He crushed my fingers into the steel of the gun and it took everything I had not to cry out in agony.

He released his grip and my Colt dropped from my mashed hand.

Angus spoke in a low, pleading voice. "You can't open the box. I don't want to hurt you."

I massaged my hand, trying to chase the pain away. "Well, it's a little late for that. Don't think I can't shoot with my left. Maybe I need to take you out first, before the lock. I'm not going to sit by and listen to a woman trying to get out of that chest."

"It's not...a woman," he said.

"And I'm not Momma Blackburn's pride and joy. Who's in the chest?"

I surprised him by retrieving my pistol and drawing on him again with my left hand. I wasn't as good a shot from the left side, but accuracy wasn't a problem when your target was the size of a bull and four feet from you.

"You can shoot me," he said with a disconcerting air of resignation. "Just don't open the box."

It was a bizarre reply. I was stunned into inaction. I couldn't recall any man willfully asking me, or anyone, to shoot him. I was growing more certain that Angus and Matthias had sprung from the twisted depths of Hecla and not from Medicine Bow.

A series of loud beeps from the returning car had us both turning our heads.

I wasn't happy to see Teta and Selma in the car. For once, I didn't want to be proven right.

The headlights on the car were busted. All of the glass had shattered and the metal casings were squashed flat.

"Barrier still up?" I asked.

Teta replied, "Sí," and jumped out of the car. He saw that my gun was drawn and pulled his own. "Trouble while we were away? That's record time for you."

I returned my attention to the chest. It was quiet now.

"Looks like our friends have a little surprise," I said, motioning with my gun to the chest. "I was just trying to convince Angus to open it up so we can see what, or who, is inside."

Matthias jogged away from the car and put himself between me and the box. "I strongly advise you, Mr. Blackburn, to desist with your line of inquiry. Nothing, and I mean *nothing* good can come of it."

To my surprise, Selma had gone and picked up my rifle. She had it pointed at Matthias. "What are you so afraid of, Reverend Manning?" she said.

"That we'll see the woman they've crammed inside and be forced to discuss a matter of justice," I said.

Selma said, "A woman? How?"

"I don't know, but I heard her clear as day. At one point, she struggled enough to make it move."

Teta spit at Angus's feet. "You like to hurt women? Open it up, *now*. I never ask twice."

"Gentlemen, and lady, if you'll all just put down your weapons, we can discuss this like civilized adults. You can plainly see that my companion and I possess no weapons of our own. I do believe that your cowboy culture calls for a certain set of rules when it comes to a fair fight. A cowboy code, if you like."

"The only cowboys I know who thought fighting had to be fair never lived long enough to learn the error of their ways," I said.

But he had a point. With great reluctance, I lowered my gun, but kept it in my hand.

Teta and Selma did the same.

Matthias broke out in an enormous grin. "There, don't you all feel better now? Tension is bad for the body and the soul."

"Tell us what's in the chest or get ready to be very tense, very fast," Teta said. With all of the shadows and sounds that had been dogging us, I knew he was itching to deal with something he could see, hear and feel. Like me, he was ready to take all his frustrations out on this odd pair if they didn't make things straight in an expeditious manner.

Matthias seemed indifferent to Teta's threat. Instead of revealing the chest's contents, he asked, "Do you believe in spirits?"

None of us answered.

"Let me be clear," he continued. "By spirits, I don't mean the type you imbibe. I refer to the continuation of the soul. Phantoms. Ghosts. Surely you have some opinion on the matter."

"What does that have to do with the chest?"

I noticed that Angus had angled a little closer to it. I'd seen how fast he could be. Was he fixing to make a dash with it, knowing we could easily gun him down from behind? Then again, he had said I could shoot him.

Matthias planted a foot on the chest and we all heard a soft groan. Except, this time, it sounded like a man.

Our guns were back up and pointed at Matthias and Angus. Teta had both pistols out and the hammers on each clicked back. Selma's face was pinched tight with grim determination. I was pretty sure she'd never shot a man before, but you'd never know it from the way she held herself. If they made so much as one suspicious twitch, they were going to be cut down to little, unidentifiable pieces.

"I think you better speed things up," I said. "Delays could be hazardous to your health." Matthias actually smiled and removed his foot. "I take it this is what you heard earlier while I was out getting my car into a bit of a sticky widget. She won't be much for night driving until I get those headlamps fixed."

"Not quite," I said through gritted teeth. I was beginning to think it would be easier to just shoot them both and get on with waiting for Hecla to play with us like a cat with a canary. Unless, of course, they were a part of Hecla, in which case, I really had no compunction about introducing them to a few bullets. "What I heard before was a bit more feminine."

Matthias nodded and said, "Yes, you did say you believed it to be a woman in distress earlier. What you heard was a facsimile of a woman, as well as of a man, for what's locked in that chest is no longer either. As it is written in the gospel of Luke, 'Behold my hands and feet, that it is I; handle me and see; for a spirit hath no flesh and bones'. My friends, what is contained in this chest no longer hath flesh, nor bone, but that's not to say they *didn't* before crossing into the realm of the afterworld. The reason we refuse to open the chest is because we cannot unleash the vile spirits that we worked very hard to entrap.

"Angus and I have made it our life's work to remove restless, and sometimes destructive, spirits so the living can carry on with their lives without interference from the dead. We were in Medicine Bow because we had been called upon by a Mr. Jedidiah Thompson who believed his factory to be haunted by the spirits of several workers who had burned to death in a fire several years past. These former workers spent a great deal of time and energy sabotaging the machinery of his factory, causing production delays, costly accidents and even the death of one of his workers.

"The spirits in that chest were contained within it at great physical, spiritual and emotional expense. These were not pleasant people when they were alive. They are downright malevolent in death. For your sake, and ours, it's best we keep them imprisoned where they can do no harm."

A week ago, I would have shot him midway through his little story. Now, here I was, listening and assigning a percentage, albeit small, to the possibility that he was telling the truth. Selma's percentages must have been lower than my own because she said, "Do you really expect us to believe you?"

Angus looked down at the chest. He said, "Do you really think a man and a woman could fit inside it?"

It seemed we had come to a bit of an impasse.

The next move, the next word, would set the course for better or for worse. I didn't mind being the one to do it.

CHAPTER THIRTY-ONE

"He's right about that," I said. Teta looked at me as if he thought I'd lost my mind. "Look at it. You could just about fit a grown raccoon in there, not much else. That still doesn't explain what we're hearing."

Matthias sighed, exasperated. "I just told you what's in the chest."

I raised the gun so it was level with his face. "You told me a humdinger of a cock-and-bull story, is what you did. You wouldn't mind if we tied you and Angus up for a spell until we figure things out, would you?"

Angus clenched and unclenched his fists. This was not going to be easy. "Selma, get the rope from my saddle."

She reluctantly put down the rifle and ran to get the rope. When she came back, I handed my knife to her and asked her to cut it into sections so I could bind their wrists.

"If you'll turn around with your hands at your back, I'd be very appreciative."

A look of warning passed from Matthias to Angus and the hulk turned. His wrists were about the width of my calves. "Cut one extra long piece," I said to Selma.

Teta and Selma kept their guns trained on our newfound friends while I tied them up and led them back to the house. Matthias's face cringed when he crossed the threshold.

"Is something dead in here? I don't mind going along with you, but I have my limits. I don't want to be locked in a charnel house."

"*Was* dead," I said, poking him in the back with my pistol to move him inside. "We cleaned it out last night."

Angus toed a bit of skull. "Not clean enough."

"It'll do for now," I said. "Besides, it's the only place in the whole damn town that won't come crashing down on your heads."

Matthias turned to face me before I shut the door. "Please promise me one thing."

I wasn't in the mood for making any promises, but I also wanted him and Angus tucked away so I could think. "If it's within reason."

"Whatever you do, don't open that chest. The contents and this place will make for a very unfortunate combination."

I let a moment pass, and saw the desperate honesty in his eyes. Whatever was in there, he believed it was bad.

"Fine. We'll bring you some water in a bit. Just sit tight and relax. If either of you try to go out the door or window, we'll put you down. Understand?"

Matthias nodded. "We're not men of violence. You'll get no problems from us."

I kicked the door closed before he could say anything else. The man made my head hurt.

Selma handed me a cup of water and I removed my hat, tilting it over my head. It was cool and should have felt good, but it only increased the sharp pain in my temples.

Teta was sprawled out on his back with his head against his saddle. "Now there are five blind mice."

I tapped the bottom of his boots and said, "Help me move that chest over here."

It had no handles so we had to dig our fingers underneath it to get a passable grip. I was wrong earlier. It weighed more than a hundred pounds. We crab-walked it near the fire pit, both of us grunting from the effort.

"Angus carried this like it was nothing," I said, huffing.

"With one arm," Teta added. "If I have to shoot him, I'm making sure it's from a distance."

Through all of our jostling, whatever was within the chest remained silent. I was tempted to blow the lock off, but I had made a promise. A dark part of me was also concerned about what Matthias had said. It appeared I was out of my depth as well as my mind.

"What do you think is really in there?" Selma said. She was on a knee, running her hands over the top of the chest. "You don't think it could be spirits?"

"Who ever heard of such a thing?" I said. "Matthias seems more like a con man than a right reverend."

"In my country, there are men who can capture souls and lock them away," Teta said. "For a price. It's the ultimate curse, to be denied proper rest even in death."

I cocked an eyebrow. "You ever see it for yourself?"

"No, but my mother did. One of her cousins married a terrible man. He abused her day and night. She wore her shame in shadows, rarely coming out during the day. One day, she'd had enough. She went to family and friends to beg for money so she could visit the witch doctor. To do something like this is very expensive, you see. My mother said her cousin's husband died in his sleep a week later, and that the witch doctor lured his soul into a bottle that he sealed and threw into the ocean."

It would have made a hell of a late night campfire story. Even during the day, my arms prickled a bit with goose bumps.

"So you believe Matthias?"

Teta shrugged. "I don't know. If my mother was here, she would. And I never doubted my madre."

Selma nudged the chest with her boot. When nothing happened, she gave it a little kick. Still nothing. She hit it hard with the heel of her boot but the moaning was done for the moment.

"Maybe we heard wrong," she said, her eyes glazed, staring at the mysterious chest.

"All of us?" I said. "Highly doubtful."

Teta waved his sombrero at a cloud of gnats. "I'll look in the window, see what they're up to."

I rested my hands on my hips and went from looking at the chest, to the house, to the hills. *There's got to be an answer somewhere in all of this. Think, Nat, think. Better come up with something soon because we're running out of tobacco and whiskey. And with two more mouths to feed and no game in sight, food isn't far behind. How long can we last on water alone? With the way our luck's running, that well will dry up by morning.*

Selma picked up some rocks and cradled them in her palm. She proceeded to throw them with surprising speed and accuracy at the wreck of a cabin across the street. The rocks popped and caromed off the rotted wood.

"What are we going to do with them?" she asked. Most women would be a ball of nerves and tears by now. Her courage made her even prettier. Was it wrong to feel that way about her when we were in such a state? I didn't know and cared even less.

"I don't know."

"I don't think it's a coincidence that they showed up today."

I plucked a rock from her hand and fired it at the mercantile down the street. It pinged off the metal sign above the door. "I don't think anything is a coincidence here. My question is what is it all leading up to?"

She glanced down at my gun and said, "You hoping it's something you can settle with that?"

"It's never failed me before."

Teta came back to report that Matthias and Angus were sitting on the floor, staring at the walls. "I listened for a little and they weren't even talking."

"Do we keep them in there and sleep out here tonight?" I looked up at the unrelenting blue sky. There wasn't a cloud for miles. "Doubt we need to worry about rain in the night."

"Or we could switch places. It's not like they can go far," Selma said. She had a point, and I'm sure she felt safer with four walls between us and whatever existed on the winds of Hecla.

"I don't like the idea of leaving the whole place to their disposal. I'd feel better if they were locked up tight," I said. Selma was crestfallen but she recovered quickly.

She said, "Does that mean I get to stand watch for a while?"

Teta was quick to put a damper on that idea. "Not alone. You can stand watch with me, if you want. Even with a gun, I think it's best you leave that to Nat and me."

She opened her mouth, I'm sure to put up a spirited counterargument, when she simply froze. Her eyes rolled up and up until she was practically staring straight into the sun.

There was no danger of her blinding herself.

Because the sun was disappearing, and not behind the clouds.

CHAPTER THIRTY-TWO

It couldn't have been more than an hour or so past noon, but night was falling on Hecla, fast. It looked as if a can of tar had spilled across the pale-blue sky. Deep, black rivers of night etched across the horizon, swirling over the surface of the sun, swallowing it whole.

We plunged into a darkness as thick and impenetrable as the grave. There were no stars to offer flickering light, no moon, nothing but the most terrifying pitch I'd ever laid my eyes upon. I felt Selma grab hold of me but couldn't see her at all.

"Nat, what's happening?" she whispered.

"It's not an eclipse," I said, my voice hushed as well. We didn't know what lurked in the sudden darkness and it was wise to keep as still and silent as possible.

"Jefe, you still have the matches?" Teta asked.

I fumbled in my pocket for the little matchsticks.

Matthias called out, "Would it be a bother if one of you told us what was going on out there?"

"Shut up!" Teta growled.

My fingers wrapped around a match and I struck it against the bottom of my boot. The tiny orb of orange light it gave off was just enough to make out Selma's horrified face. Teta was a fuzzy outline.

"You remember if there's any tinder nearby? I'll light a fire if I can."

"There might be some," Selma said.

I heard her scrape around in the dirt, feeling her way around the fire pit, looking for kindling. I crouched and tried to offer what little light I had.

"If you give me another match, I'll find my way into the house and get one of the lamps," Teta said.

"And give Matthias and his grizzly a prime opportunity to brain you? We'll make a fire out here."

The tiny flame fizzled out as it reached my thumb and finger. My hands were so calloused I couldn't feel it. We fell back into total darkness. This time, I was quicker getting another one lit.

"I think this should be enough," Selma said.

I got on my knees and saw the small pile of twigs and dried saw grass she'd arranged.

Before I could touch the flame to it, a loud, tortured howl pierced the false night. I dropped the match and it blew out.

Two metallic clicks sounded ahead of me. Teta had his guns drawn.

My chest felt as if someone was sitting on it. We didn't move, but I know we all wanted to run.

Reaching out, I found Selma's hand and pulled her close.

Another cry, a mix of a growl and a man screaming at the top of his lungs, came from the opposite direction of the first.

Selma was breathing hard. Her nails dug into the flesh of my hand. "Sounds like that thing in the mine," I said.

"Exactly like it," Teta replied.

"What thing in the mine?" Selma said. Her voice trembled.

"Just a little something we heard and saw before your brother-in-law stumbled out of the shaft."

When the third scream came, it sounded closer – and angrier.

We had to take our chances and get in the house. I liked our odds against two men rather than what I thought was making those noises.

I lit another match, sick to my soul that it might illuminate one of those beasts standing right in front of us. Thankfully, whatever was out there was still in the distance.

"Follow me."

Selma grabbed hold of Teta's shirt, her other hand still in mine, and we formed a little train leading to the front door of the house. Before I opened it, I said, "Matthias, Angus, we're coming in and we're both armed and anxious. I need you to back away from the door and move over by the window."

"We can't see the window," Matthias said.

"You're not a dumb man. You remember where it is. Just keep scooting in that direction until you can't move anymore."

We heard them knocking about. Angus must have walked into the far wall because the whole house vibrated.

Something crashed down the street. It sounded a lot like one of the smaller cabins being kicked to splinters.

We had to get inside. I turned the knob and reached for my pistol. Matthias and Angus were vague shapes, but I could see they had done what I'd asked. I pulled Selma and Teta inside and slammed the door shut.

Before the match died out, I grabbed a hurricane lamp and lit it. Matthias and Angus eyed us curiously.

"Teta, look for something to wedge under the door. We need to keep it jammed."

Teta took the lamp from my hands, scanned the scattered bits of wood he had brought over earlier and found a good-sized shard of timber. He buried it between the gap at the bottom of the door and the sill. Once that was secure, he found a couple more pieces and did the same all along the length of the door.

There was another loud growl and Selma gasped. Whatever it was, it wasn't far from the house. In fact, it sounded like it was just outside the door.

The horses, which had been unnaturally calm through everything, suddenly went wild. They cried out and there was no mistaking the fear in their tone. They were tied up and helpless, which made them only slightly worse off than us.

"Maria!" Selma exclaimed.

"There's nothing we can do for them now," I said.

We all jumped when something heavy hit the side of the house. "What the hell?" Teta shouted, his guns trained on the door.

There was a sharp pop on the roof, followed by an unsteady tapping as if a rock was rolling down it, then slipping off.

Heavy footsteps prowled around the house. We listened to stout grunts and labored breathing. I felt as if every muscle in my body had turned to stone.

Whatever was out there was patrolling the house, throwing rocks every now and then to rattle our nerves. It was working.

"Mr. Blackburn, it might be a good idea to untie us," Matthias said. I had almost forgotten he was inside with us.

My mouth wasn't working and my brain couldn't perform the necessary calculations for taking the risk of setting them free. I must have looked like a dim mute, standing there with my eyes popping out of my head and my mouth open wide enough to catch flies.

Matthias's eyes flashed with anger. "Cut these fucking ropes off us now! I refuse to face whatever abomination we've stumbled into tied up like a prize hog!"

I'd never heard a man of the cloth cuss like that before. That was assuming he was what he claimed to be.

Selma dug her fingers into my arm.

I whipped out my knife and sawed Matthias free. It took a little longer to get Angus cut out because I'd used extra rope to tie him up. When he rose, his body blocked the entire window. He rubbed his wrists, unaffected by what was going on outside the frail house.

He was the biggest son of a bitch I'd ever come across.

The next inhuman holler ripped right through the gaps in the front wall.

Looking at Angus and hearing that scream made something click together in my mind. Whatever fear that had taken hold of me was burned off by a burst of anger. Striding into Angus, I took him by surprise and pushed my gun past his teeth, hitting the roof of his mouth. He grunted and stumbled back a step.

"Call them off, big boy, or your reverend friend can spend the rest of the night cleaning you off the floor and walls."

CHAPTER THIRTY-THREE

I had Angus's full attention. When Matthias went to grab my arm, Teta snatched him by the back of his collar and yanked him back about two feet.

"What on earth do you think you're doing?" Matthias wailed.

"The question is, what have the two of *you* been doing?"

I pushed my Colt as far as it could go until the big man gagged on it. I can't say it didn't give me a small sense of satisfaction. I kept my eyes on his hands, wary of what he could do with those ham hocks. I wasn't about to let him take me by surprise.

The howling and the whooping and the hollering continued outside. The stone throwing had stopped, replaced by their hammering on the walls with their fists. Dust trickled down on our heads from the force of their blows.

"You can tell your friends the jig is up," I said. If I could breathe fire, I would have burned Angus to a crisp. I was tired of being jerked around like a toy on a string. "What do you have, some brothers with growth disorders like yours dressing up like wild men to frighten us off? I don't think you and Matthias showed up by coincidence. I think you were here to check up on us, and when you realized your little games hadn't chased us off, you told your gang to step things up."

Angus's lips worked around the barrel of the gun. Nothing but a few grunts came out of his mouth.

"This is preposterous," Matthias said. "How do you explain your inability to cross that barrier and the changing of the day into night? Think, Mr. Blackburn. I may be a reverend, but I don't have the powers of Jesus to do such things."

I lashed out and kicked Angus on the top of his kneecap as hard as I could. He staggered a bit but didn't fall. My foot throbbed. It was like giving the boot to a cannon.

"Maybe you drugged us," I said to Matthias. "Maybe you've been prowling around all this time and put something in the well. I've spent my time with the Apache and know the effects of some of their herbs."

The entire house shook. A chorus of shrieks rang out. I fought to concentrate on Angus.

If he got a swipe at me, I was done for.

Matthias said, "You've lost your mind. There's something very real trying to break into this house and you're wasting time accusing us of...of...sheer lunacy! Wake up. We're not your enemy. In fact, if you let us, we might be able to help."

Selma had come up behind me. I could feel her hot breath against the back of my neck. "Nat, let him go. We may need him if whatever is outside gets in."

I looked at Teta. He had a good grip on Matthias and I knew he'd go along with whatever I decided.

The front door shuddered. They were making their way in.

I pulled the gun out of the big man's mouth and pistol-whipped him across the cheek.

To my surprise, he fell to his knees, grasping his head.

Selma screamed and pointed at the window.

An impossibly tall, hairy creature with red eyes that burned like the sun crouched outside the window, staring at us with what I could only describe as hunger. It bared its teeth like a rabid dog.

I fired three shots into its face. The glass shattered and the beast dropped away from view. I turned to Matthias and said, "You're right, what's out there is real. For your sake, I hope they're not people you care much about."

"I told you—"

I pushed him away and went for the door. "Selma, light the other two lamps."

By shooting whoever was outside the window, I had riled up the gang. The fact that they were still shouting like creatures and not men didn't stop my resolve to put an end to this, no matter what was outside the door. I'd played my hand and it was time to take it to the bank.

The pounding at the door had stopped but I could hear plenty of movement outside. "Put the lamps down there," I said, motioning to the edge of the door with my pistol, "and hand me my rifle."

Selma did what I asked. I traded her my pistol for the rifle. I wanted to inflict maximum damage when I started shooting. Teta was on the same page and warned Matthias, "If either of you move, I'll turn around and shoot you in the eyes."

I kicked the wedges out from beneath the door. "You ready?" Teta nodded.

"Selma, step back to the corner and shoot anyone that comes near you." I hoped she understood that Teta and I were excluded.

"Do it," I said. My jaw clenched tighter than a virgin's pussy.

Teta threw the door open and the light of the lamps provided just what I needed.

Targets.

CHAPTER THIRTY-FOUR

There must have been a half dozen of them gathered outside the door. They were tall, broad, covered in matted hair and downright repulsive smelling. Man or beast, it no longer mattered. I'd had enough.

Teta and I didn't wait a beat. We pulled back on our triggers, hitting everything in sight. The noise was deafening. It should have echoed off into the distance, but it was like the darkness had come with thick walls and a close ceiling. I was past trying to make sense of things.

"Hurts, don't it?" I shouted as I took one of the beasts right in the gut. It jumped and folded in on itself, falling to the dust and dirt. Teta shouted something in Spanish, unloading his pistols into everything that moved.

The creatures, or men, took off in the direction of the hills. We shot as many as we could in the back. Fuck honor. Dying was dying and it made no difference whether you took it head on or looking away.

I threw one of the lamps and flames erupted in a long line as it shattered. It gave us a longer field of light so we could take care of business.

Teta took aim at a retreating beast. It was the tallest of the bunch, maybe a good eight feet tall. He squeezed the trigger and the top of its head exploded. It ran a few more steps before falling facedown.

The rest had dashed off into the dark. We could hear them but we could no longer see them. A half-dozen wooly bodies lay about the street. I saw the chest rise on one of them and shot it in the heart.

I should have been breathing heavily and my nerves should have been singing with adrenaline. Instead, I was filled with a warm sense of calm. It felt damn good to take matters into my own hands for once, no matter how brutal or messy.

"Mierda, jefe," Teta said, covering his nose and mouth with his dirty bandana. "It hurts to breathe. How can you stand it?"

The bodies were smoking.

A part of me knew I was standing in the center of one of the most malodorous shitpiles a man would ever come across. Instead of gagging, I savored it. The closeness of the air made sure the stink draped over us like a blanket dipped in skunk entrails, horse shit and spoiled meat.

I was so busy admiring our handiwork that I had forgotten about Selma.

Relief swept over me when I darted back inside and saw her standing tall, covering Matthias and Angus with my pistol. The gun quivered a bit in her hand, so I took hold of the barrel and holstered it.

"Did you get all of them?" she asked.

"Most. The rest will think twice before coming back."

Teta came back inside and slammed the door. He brought our two remaining lamps in with him. "We're going to have to move upwind. This place is going to get bad real quick."

Matthias stroked the ends of his dark mustache. I didn't like the cocky look on his face. "What's on your mind, *Reverend*?"

"I'm not quite sure you understand what you've started."

"I didn't start anything. For the first time since I got here, I sure as hell ended it."

Matthias poked his head out of the shattered window. I kind of hoped one of those creatures would come by and take his head as a souvenir.

I added, "You should be thankful we did what we did. At least now I'm convinced that you and Angus aren't behind everything. What we shot out there isn't human." I still wasn't convinced he and Angus were a pair of traveling oddballs with a chest of trapped spirits, searching for the source of the Trumpets of Armageddon. Putting it all together like that made me think I was ready for the nuthouse.

Matthias turned to me but had nothing to say. He looked uncertain – about what, I wasn't sure.

Selma broke our little stare-down. "Nat, what are those things?"

"I haven't a clue."

There was no need to tell her they bore a striking resemblance to the wild-man stories I'd been told by plenty of Indians from different tribes. All that mattered was that a good number of them were dead and the rest were gone.

What concerned me was how Hecla could control the sun and what we'd do when we ran out of lamp oil.

Teta said, "Maybe they're some kind of diseased bear. Could be a whole clan has some kind of sickness."

"A sickness that makes them walk on two legs?" Matthias interjected.

"Maybe they have a deformity. Nat, you remember that guy we met in Montauk who had his upper legs fused together?"

I recalled the poor soul. He had been leaning against a boathouse, begging for spare change. He wore shorts, both because of the heat and so passersby could see his deformity and take pity on him. Teta and I gave him a dollar as well as a fresh bottle of rum. He was happy for the dollar, but he was over the moon about the rum. We had both survived battle and disease in Cuba and were grateful to be able to give the guy a little something. We were quite the charitable pair for a while after landing in Long Island. Becoming cops wiped that all away.

"Could be just like it," I said.

"Do you two always run for the safety of the physical and mundane when you're faced with questions larger than your tired paradigms?" Matthias said.

What the hell was a paradigm?

"Big talk coming from a guy who professes to have a spirit in a box," I snapped back.

"If you're going to stand here arguing, I'm going to shoot you both," Selma barked.

Judging by the set of her jaw and the squint in her eye, she just might.

She continued, "What we all should be doing is figuring a way to get out of here. There's nothing natural about this place and we all know that the longer we stay, the better the chances that we never leave. So, for the moment, you need to end your suspicion of one another and think. And, Nat, you should apologize to Angus for hitting him."

I looked at the big man and gave a short nod. He nodded back. There was no lingering anger in his eyes.

Teta raised an eyebrow and gave an approving nod. The air seemed to go out of all of us. Selma was right. We were trapped in Hecla like insects on flypaper. The one thing we all had in common is that we were all of the same species, whereas Hecla was in a world all its own.

We cast our heads down like scolded children.

"That's more like it," Selma said. "The four of you all have very different takes on what's going on here. Somewhere in the middle is the key to figuring everything out. If we're going to get anywhere, we have to be honest with one another. Nat, Teta, that means you have to tell me exactly what happened in the mine. And then I'll tell Matthias and Angus about Franklin."

"Don't forget the dog," Teta said.

"Right, and the dog." She looked directly at Matthias. "I'm not entirely sure why you came here, but your lives are in just as much jeopardy as ours. You say you capture spirits. I believe Hecla is full of spirits. Maybe some are the miners or other people that have come through. And maybe it's the land itself. My mother came from a town that believed very much in the sanctity of the land and that it had a soul, just like you and me. Something's gone terribly wrong with Hecla's soul. The five of us need to make it right if we ever want to go home."

If I'd had eyes for the pretty half-Mexican before, I wanted to pull her into my arms and lock lips until the real Trumpets of Armageddon sounded and we could let the whole world crumble away around us.

Matthias cleared his throat and said, "Your candor and call for honesty has opened my eyes, as well as my heart. Gentlemen, she is absolutely right. Angus and I answered our calling many years ago, choosing to live in the gray areas between rationality and the preternatural. Please, fill us in on all you saw so we can help find our way out of this conundrum."

I had to grit my teeth and draw a big breath not to say

something wise to Matthias. When he wasn't quoting Scripture like some snake-handling false preacher, he was using words no normal person could understand to show his superiority.

Selma must have sensed my budding anger. She gave me a look with her big brown eyes that said, *Stand down.* So I did.

She said, "Teta, why don't you start?"

He dug his fingers under his sombrero to scratch his head and looked at me. "Should I tell them about the first time we went in the mine with the tommyknockers?"

"Might as well spill it all," I said. And we did. Selma grew a little more uneasy with each bizarre story. Matthias seemed very interested in the boy and girl with the black eyes.

"Eyes are the window to the soul. Their windows are shuttered up," he said.

"What the hell do you mean by that?" Teta asked.

"What you saw, the black-eyed kids, are children taken before their time by something sinister, trapped between heaven and hell."

"Did they ask for something strange?" Angus said.

"Not exactly," I said. "They wanted something to drink and eat. But when I offered it to them, they didn't take it."

"Trapped in a loop," Angus said, turning to Matthias who played with his mustache. "Selma, you must have had some interaction with the miners and their families, considering you're from the nearest major town," Matthias said.

"I did. A lot would come over once a month for supplies."

"Were there many children?"

"I saw some. I don't know how many were in Hecla itself."

"People out here like to breed, so I'll assume there were a good number. I think we know who those children were. The question is, how do we help them?" As I opened my mouth to speak, the entire house began to vibrate. Selma covered her ears, expecting the horn to sound again.

Angus threw his arms out, trying to steady himself. For the first time, he looked frightened.

He said, "Earthquake?"

Suddenly, a pair of massive arms crashed through the wall.

I fell back on my ass. The hands were dark and bloody, with fingers bigger than the length of my entire hand. Thick splinters pelted us like hail and I had to raise my arm to protect my eyes from being impaled.

Next thing I knew, Selma was screaming for her life.

CHAPTER THIRTY-FIVE

I looked up just in time to see the horror of those hands, attached to thick arms covered in long, dark-brown hair, as they grabbed Selma around her waist. Her eyes rolled up and she screeched loud enough to wake the dead. The ground was still shaking and we couldn't get our footing. The walls of the house moaned and swayed.

Fumbling for my pistol, I tried to find an exposed spot to shoot without hitting Selma.

She was thrashing in the thing's arms, hammering it with her fists.

Before I could get off a shot at the upper part of the arms, they pulled her back with a tremendous shattering of wood and the crack of what I hoped wasn't bone. In an instant, she was gone. An enormous hole had been blown through the wall. I ran into the dark, following the sound of her screams.

"Help me, Naaaaaaaaat!"

Her cries were so raw with fear, my heart felt like it was going to explode. My lungs burned as I forced my legs to move faster than they had since I was a young buck on my first cattle drive, chasing after steers for fun.

I couldn't see where I was going and tripped on something hard yet yielding. I landed face-first into what felt like a pile of wet rags.

I looked up and couldn't believe my eyes.

The night was receding, following the direction of Selma and the creature that had ripped her from the house. Daylight returned. There was a clear line between night and day, and I watched that line speed into the distance, straight to the Deep Rock Hills.

Selma's cries were swallowed up by distance and the wind. Whatever had her was moving so fast there was nothing known to man that could keep up with them. Not even Matthias's fancy car.

Teta, Matthias and Angus skidded to a halt behind me.

My blood was soaring through my veins and drumming a deafening beat in my ears. I had to get up and follow Selma.

When I balanced myself with my hands, they slid out from under me and I collapsed again.

Now, back in the light of day, I could see exactly what I had stumbled upon and fallen into.

It was Teta's horse, or what remained of it. Something had opened up a four-foot gash in its side and I was up to my elbows in its entrails. Black and red organs swam around my hands and I tasted its blood as it dripped down my throat.

A pair of hands helped me to my feet. I looked around.

All of the horses had been gutted. The mule had been torn in half, one part tangled amidst the branches of a nearby tree, the other emptied its insides into the trough. Its blood splattered the red-soaked earth in a steady, nauseating beat.

"Sons of bitches," Teta swore under his breath.

I'd seen and done a lot in my time, and I wasn't prone to squeamishness. Vomit hit the back of my teeth before I could even open my mouth, and then it was pouring in a hot torrent into the exposed cavity of the horse. I was so repulsed by the sight and smell that I threw up even more, heaving until my ribs ached.

I collapsed on the ground, rolling away from the defiled carcass. The sun was so bright I had to drape my arm over my eyes. I'd never felt so weak before, so completely helpless. Covering my eyes spared me from having to see Teta's reaction.

Where the hell did they take Selma? And why? How could we get her back from something that could control the goddamn sky?

It was Angus who offered me a cup of fresh water. The cup looked like a child's toy in his hairy-knuckled paw. I sat up so I could rinse my mouth out. I think I muttered a thank-you.

"They took her to the mines," Teta said. "I watched the hills absorb the dark like it was going down a funnel."

Struggling to my feet, I pointed at him and grumbled, "If you make the sign of the cross I'll tie your arms to your sides. God has nothing to do with this place and I don't think he much cares about anyone fool enough to end up here."

Teta's hand was midway to his forehead when he stopped. He

was a hard man and not one to take threats lightly, but we knew each other at this point better than our own mothers, had they been alive.

"We're going to have to find her ourselves, without divine guidance," I said, looking for my hat. It was perched on one of the stiff, upright legs of our spare horses. I dusted it off and thought better of putting it back on my head, which was covered in blood and guts.

"There's always divine guidance, Mr. Blackburn," Matthias said.

I walked to the water pump and ducked my head under the spigot. The water was cold as ice and chased away any fuzziness in my skull. It turned a dark pink as it sluiced over my head and hands.

When I was cleaned up as best I could, I turned to Matthias and said, "You keep telling yourself that. Maybe the hands of providence will raise you up and out of here, seeing as we can't escape any other way. Or maybe you have room in that chest of yours for whatever hell breathes in Hecla. You think you can stick it all in your spirit box?"

When Matthias rested his hand on my shoulder, I was too overcome with disbelief to twist it until his wrist broke. "I understand your anger, Mr. Blackburn, Nat. I know you're uncertain as to our intentions and how we came about this place. But where you see only evil and suspicion, I see the work of the Lord. There isn't anyone else in this whole country who could help you, and yet here we are. Brought here through the miraculous gifts bestowed upon Angus in your time of need. This is what *we* do. Don't turn away from us, and most of all, God."

I felt my face flush red and my hands began to twitch. They wanted to smash Matthias in his pious mouth. Teta whistled and narrowed his gaze at me. I rested my hand on the butt of my pistol and stepped away from Matthias's touch.

"You're going to help us," I said in as measured a tone as I could muster. "But if you talk to me about God or quote Scripture one more time, I won't be responsible for my actions. Are we clear?"

Matthias's swallowed hard, but he gave a half smile and said, "Crystal."

"You think your car can fit all of us?"

"I don't see that being a problem."

"Good. You fill up the canteens while we get the lamps and ammo."

"What about food?"

"If we have time for a sit-down meal, we're not doing things right."

"Angus, get the tools." The giant lumbered over to the car. "We'll need about an hour before we can leave."

"We don't have an hour!"

"Whatever has Selma will wait for as long as it takes for us to arrive. It doesn't want her per se. She's only a means to an end. You asked me if I thought we could fit the evil of Hecla in our spirit box and the answer is no. We need an hour to construct a bigger one using the scraps of the town. There's a special kind of power in that."

I didn't have the foggiest what he was talking about. All I heard was one hour. I was about to tell him to get in the car now when something made a thunderous crash behind us.

My head whipped around so fast my neck crackled with pain.

The house we'd been staying in, weakened now that one wall had been demolished, had finally fallen in on itself. A slow-moving cloud of dust carried itself to the soft but always present winds.

Angus came up beside us with a box full of various rust-flecked tools. Matthias said, "It appears we have fresh lumber for our purposes."

I looked around. "Where's Teta?"

The three of us turned 360 degrees on our heels. He was nowhere in sight. "I think he may have gone in to retrieve your lamps," Matthias said softly. "Teta!"

I ran to the ruin of the house, knowing that if he'd been inside he was never coming out alive.

$\star$ $\star$ $\star$

It was hard to make out anything through the dust and dirt that had been stirred up. My eyes stung from grit as I shouted for Teta, pulling on planks of wood, peering into the darkness below. Nails and shards of wood dug into my skin. My flesh was riddled with bloody pinpricks. Inch-long splinters stuck halfway into my hands and forearms.

"Teta, can you hear me? Make a noise so I can find you!"

Wood clattered behind me. It was Matthias and Angus, joining in the search. Angus hefted bundles of wood that would have taken three men to lift, casting them aside like they were toothpicks.

First Selma, now Teta. Hecla was picking us off one by one.

I stopped breathing when I saw his boot wedged between a heavy beam and a heap of fractured wood. Dropping to my knees, and ignoring the pain of a sliver that wedged itself deep below my kneecap, I tore at the wood, desperate to reach his boot. The bottom was facing up, which meant he was buried deep. It was the worst case scenario and my stomach lurched again, but I kept it in check.

"Angus, I need your help!"

His wiry sideburns were peppered with dust and bits of wood. He staggered on the uneven debris. I pointed at Teta's boot. "We have to dig down."

Angus nodded and thrust his hands into the remains of the house. Wood snapped and cracked as he pulled up an incredible amount of wreckage. With a great grunt, he threw it to the side. In one swoop, he'd managed to expose most of the area around Teta's boot.

It was empty.

I reached down and pried it out from under the beam.

Matthias had come up behind me and was staring at the boot. "Where's the rest of him?"

I got down on my belly and burrowed into the hole that Angus had made like a foxhound going in for its prey. Enough light filtered in through the gaps in the wood so I could see. And what I saw was nothing.

I was about to ask Angus to dig some more when I heard a groan. We all froze. "Did you hear that?" Matthias said.

I shushed him.

"Uunnngh."

"Over there!" I said, scrabbling to the edge of the pile. The south face of the house had fallen pretty much intact. The sound was coming from underneath it.

I jumped off the wood pile and barked, "Angus, Matthias, get on either side of this! We have to lift it up. Teta, can you hear me?"

The groaning had stopped. Bad sign.

It turned out, I didn't need Matthias. Angus squatted, gripped the end of the wall and rose to his knees. I knelt down and saw the top of Teta's head.

"Can you hold it like that?"

"Yes," Angus said.

"Matthias, help me drag him out."

We each grabbed a shoulder and tugged. For once, our luck held out and his bottom half wasn't snagged on anything. As soon as we got him free, Angus dropped the side of the house with a tremendous boom. A blast of dust swept over us.

Teta wasn't moving. I had my knees on either side of his head and pulled his eyelids back. All I could see was the whites of his eyes. I tapped his cheeks, trying to wake him up, if he was, in fact, still alive.

"You know how to check a pulse?" I asked Matthias.

He pulled up Teta's sleeve and placed his fingers on his wrist. I studied Teta's chest, looking for any sign of movement.

"Come on, partner. You're not allowed to check out on me yet. We've still got work to do."

Matthias solemnly looked at me. He still had Teta's wrist in his hand. He shook his head slowly.

"No!"

I slapped Teta hard across the face. His head moved to the side from the force, but his eyes didn't so much as flutter. His chest was still as stone.

"Dammit, Teta, get up!"

My hands and feet were going numb as I shifted over him and shook his entire body. He couldn't die. Not like this. The man had stared down the barrel of too many guns to count, had gotten in more scraps than he could barely get himself out of. Every man had to die, but the way you lived your life should determine *how* you died.

Matthias whispered, "Nat, he's gone."

CHAPTER THIRTY-SIX

I jumped to my feet. My hand was on my Colt before I even knew what I was doing. "Shut your mouth."

To his credit, Matthias didn't back down. He rose to meet me eye to eye and said, "It's okay to be angry. I could see the two of you were very close."

"I said to shut your mouth."

"He's in the hands of our Lord now."

I twirled my pistol so the barrel was in my palm. I pulled it back to pistol-whip him across the side of his head when my wrist was locked into a vise. I turned to see Angus had caught my arm in midarc.

He squeezed and no matter how much I tried to push the pain away, I could no longer hold on to my gun. That was twice now that he'd been able to disarm me like a weak child. He kicked my gun aside, then shoved me towards Matthias. The reverend caught me and kept me on my feet.

Angus eyed Teta's cooling body with confusion. He cocked his head, giving particular attention to his chest.

"Get away from him," I said, rushing the big man. He swatted me with the back of his hand and this time I did go down.

"He's hurt inside," he said, kneeling down.

He made a fist and I shouted for him to stop. Angus raised it above his head and brought it down into the center of Teta's chest like a blacksmith hammering an anvil.

"What the hell are you doing?"

Angus turned to me and pulled his lips taut against his teeth. "Starting the insides again."

He lifted his hand. I knew one more blow would shatter Teta's corpse. I'd be damned if I let him defile his body.

Then Teta coughed.

His body shook with spasms and he brought his hand to his mouth, then his chest. He winced, groaning with pain.

His voice was raw and parched. "What kicked me?"

Matthias clapped his hands and raised his face to the sky. "Praise Jesus! Miracles happen in your name every day."

More like, *Praise Angus.* I didn't know how he did it, but I was grateful that he did.

I helped Teta into a sitting position. He rubbed his head with one hand and chest with the other. He looked to me with glazed eyes and asked, "Why do I hurt all over?"

I pointed with my chin toward the remains of the house. "First, because that fell on you, and, second, because Angus punched you in the chest to get you breathing again."

"Breathing again?"

The next words were hard to say. "You were dead."

"That's not possible. You must have thought I was dead. I'd think the same thing if I saw you crushed under a house."

I shook my head. "No, we checked you out. You weren't breathing. Your heart wasn't beating. Angus brought you back."

His job done, Angus gathered wood for his bigger spirit chest. Matthias helped by gathering nails.

"You all right to get up?" I asked.

He took a moment to consider it, then said, "With a little help."

I draped his arm over my shoulder and lifted him to his feet. "Just lean into me until you feel steadier."

We walked slowly to where we'd pulled him out. "Well look at that, I'm not the only miracle around here."

The two lanterns were still very much intact. The shattered window frame boxed them in, but they hadn't gotten so much as a scratch.

Teta said, "I felt the house starting to go and tried to get out the window with the lanterns. I guess it's better it came down on me because I don't think Angus would be able to put them back together."

I laughed despite myself and our dire situation. The odds were sorely against us to start with. With Teta hurt, they got much, much worse.

Angus moved fast. He was already hammering away, with Matthias feeding him nails and holding slats of wood in place.

Teta reached behind himself and cursed when he got hold of his sombrero and pulled it over his head. It had been smashed flat and was torn in several places. He punched his fist to pop it out and tried his best to get it back in shape. "It's still lucky," he said, securing it to his head.

As we moved along to where the front of the house had been, we stopped and stared in quiet horror. Teta tensed and stepped out of my grasp. "This isn't good," he said, almost reverently.

"It most certainly is not."

I dug my knuckles into my eyes in a useless attempt to get them to see something that just wasn't there.

The creatures that we had shot were gone. In their place was a series of smoldering piles of ash. I counted seven in all.

"At least they're not disgusting like the dead dog," Teta said. "So much for getting a chance to look at one up close."

"Maybe that's for the best, huh, jefe?"

I turned around and called out for Matthias. He jogged over, his vest flapping open and closed, pulling up short just before he stepped into one of the wild-man ash mounds.

"Notice anything missing?" I said.

I thought the shock would crack his cocksure veneer, but I was wrong. He extracted a pencil from his pocket and dipped an end into the cinders. He sniffed it but didn't recoil. His sniffer must have up and left him a long time ago. Reaching into another pocket, he pulled out a glass vial and proceeded to gather as much of the stuff as he could into it. When it was three-quarters full, he topped it with a small cork.

"Very, very interesting," he said. "Definitely worth further study at a later time."

"At least you're optimistic that there will be a later," I said.

He almost seemed happy about it. What kind of man were we dealing with?

Matthias carefully tucked the vial in his shirt pocket. "I can talk more about that subject when we're in the car. If you'll excuse me, I have to help Angus. We should be on the road shortly."

The road. Selma.

I scanned the hills and felt a knife twist in my guts, thinking she was in there, somewhere, held prisoner by something only a madman like Matthias could understand. I was suddenly very anxious to get moving. I thought of hopping in the car and taking off by myself, but something held me back.

"That man is loco," Teta said. He was still rubbing his chest but he looked firmer on his feet.

"Before long, we all will be."

We watched Matthias and Angus work on the chest and I knew with certainty that none of us were long for this world. With that came a sense of clarity and an end to any trepidation I may have felt. If Matthias was right and whatever had taken Selma was using her as bait so it could have us, I was happy to oblige.

If we were the main course, I'd make sure we didn't go down easy.

CHAPTER THIRTY-SEVEN

Angus tied the new chest, which was big enough to fit a couple of good-sized men, to the back of the rumble seat. Teta and I climbed in back so we could keep an eye on the preacher and the creature, as Teta had nicknamed them while we watched them working on the chest.

Matthias got behind the wheel and turned to us. "She won't go as fast as she normally can, because of all the weight, not to mention the terrible terrain, but we'll get to the hills faster than your horses would have. We placed the smaller spirit box in the rubble of one of the homes for safekeeping."

I sighed and leaned forward. "Just go."

Matthias pursed his lips, his head bobbing up and down. "Right. You might want to hold on."

He started the car and hit the gas. The car lurched forward and Teta and I almost flipped over the rumble seat.

We headed down the deserted main street and hooked a left past the mercantile, through an alley that spilled out onto the flat plain leading to the Deep Rock Hills. I couldn't help thinking how the gray, jagged rocks in the distance resembled giant tombstones.

"I guess it doesn't matter where you're buried."

"What?" Teta said.

"Nothing."

The car bounced along at a pretty good clip. The engine made a hell of a racket. A couple of times we hit depressions and I thought the wheels would come off. Teta and I had to grip the sides of the rumble seat to keep our asses from falling out.

Give me a horse, even one with a bum leg and a nasty disposition, any day. Our faces were pelted with small stones and our eyes filled with dirt. We held on tight to our hats. I had no idea what we'd do when we made it to the mines, but I had to get there quick. The thought of Selma trapped and afraid made my blood boil.

Matthias tried talking to us but his voice was drowned out by the steady thrumming of the wind. At one point, the sun glared so hard off Angus's bald head it blinded me. I was tempted to square my Stetson on his head but thought better of it.

We'd been driving for a good while when Teta tapped me on the arm and leaned close to my ear.

"Maybe I'm still dazed, but does it look to you like we're no closer to the hills?"

The vision of those damned hills jounced as the car rocked along. It was hard to tell. "Maybe we're taking it from another angle," I said. "You know how sometimes a point in the distance looks like it's out of range until you're right on it."

Teta eyed the hills warily. "I don't know, jefe. I'd swear on my mother's grave that they look even farther away than when we started."

I was about to say that was impossible, then recalled all we'd seen and experienced.

I gave it a few more minutes, locking my eyes on a point at the top of the highest crag in the hills.

Either my eyes were going on me, or Teta was right. The hills were receding. I leaned up and tapped Matthias on the shoulder.

"Slow down a second," I shouted.

The brakes screeched and he took us to a stop. His goggles were flecked with grit. "The hills are running away from us," I said.

Relief swept over his face. "I thought it was just me. I was trying so hard to keep the car in one piece and headed on a straight line that I thought my perspective was off." He stood up in the car and looked behind us. "I can't even see the town, so we have put some distance between us and it."

I said, "We got to the hills and back on horseback days ago at a decent trot and would have been a lot closer than we are now."

Matthias settled back into his seat and the car jerked with a groan. "I say we try for a little bit longer and see where it gets us."

"Look," Teta said, pointing to our left.

A three-foot, black-and-yellow bull snake wound its way past the rear tire. Remarkably, it was the first snake we'd seen since we'd gotten to Hecla. It was nice not worrying about them crawling on you while you slept, but unsettling in their absence just the same.

Teta threw his knife and pinned the snake to the ground just behind its head. Its tail lashed back and forth, the body twitching with pain. Teta jumped off the rumble seat, put his boot on the snake's back and extracted the knife, wiping the blood off on the side of his pants.

"What did you go and do that for?" I asked.

"To see if my head was completely clear. I don't want to be in those mines if I can't protect myself."

"If they're full of snakes, you've proven yourself. Get in so Matthias can drive."

The engine roared back to life and we resumed our dusty trek. It felt like Matthias was pushing the car as fast as it would go. I looked past his shoulder at the speedometer. We were definitely double-timing it.

But no matter how fast we went, the hills never got any closer. After a good ten minutes, Matthias stopped again. I checked the crag and it was most assuredly farther away.

"I don't believe it," Matthias said, throwing his goggles on the ground. "They took Selma.

We're going exactly where they want us to go. So why make it impossible to get there?"

It was Teta who figured it out. "They're playing for time. Probably setting a damn good trap. Maybe one we can't get out of."

I got out of the car and heaved a great wad of spit. If everything here was somehow connected to whatever was in the mines and in the town, I wanted to show it as much disrespect as I could muster. It was a puny thing to do, but the place had me feeling puny – and old.

"At least we have something to eat," Angus said, leaning out of the car.

The snake Teta had killed was exactly where we had left it. Matthias's mouth dropped open.

"Don't look a gift bull snake in the mouth," I said. "You three set here. I'm going to go for a little walk, see if that changes things. I'll circle back in an hour."

Any objection died on Teta's lips the moment our eyes met. Instead, he tossed me the rifle and I headed on foot to the hills.

⋆ ⋆ ⋆

The sun baked any horse blood I'd neglected to wash off the back of my neck. When I went to scratch it, red flakes buried themselves under my fingernails. My clothes smelled something fierce and when a breeze hit me head on, my eyes watered.

I kept a steady pace that was just shy of jogging, determined to gain some ground on the hills. I hadn't realized I was talking out loud, and when I did, I kept the conversation going.

"Are you afraid of me? One man with a gun and a rifle? Come on, you chickenshits. Maybe if I was a defenseless woman you'd let me in."

The sun was heading west and I no longer trusted its movement in the sky to tell me the time of day. For all I knew, it would bounce off the hills and roll across the plain, taking the light with it.

"I'll tell you one thing. I'm not afraid of you. You've pissed off the wrong man."

When I thought of Selma, and the fear in her eyes when she was dragged out of the house, I wanted to shout my fool head off.

Instead, I whispered, as if my voice could be carried by the wind and secreted to her so only she could hear me say, "I'm coming for you, Selma. Your husband and your father may have abandoned you, but that won't happen with me. You stay strong. I'll be there soon."

But it became abundantly clear that I wouldn't. Despite having walked so long and hard that my feet ached, I hadn't gotten one step closer to the hills. I stopped and stared at them, trying to picture in my mind where Selma could be. Was she even alive? I couldn't bring myself to think otherwise.

I turned and headed back for the car.

Angus was tending to a fire. He had stabbed chopped portions of the snake onto the ends of three sturdy sticks. The skin had flaked off and the meat dripped juices into the flames.

When Angus saw me, he pulled one from the fire and offered it to me. I waved it off.

My stomach wasn't right for food. "No luck?" Teta said.

I shook my head. "Then we wait."

Matthias sat in the rumble seat with an umbrella over his head to keep the sun off him. He was reading a small, leather-bound Bible and looked the part of a church lady at the park. He didn't even glance my way.

I took off my shirt and asked Teta for the whiskey. Even though we'd packed for war, I knew he had a bottle on him.

"You think it's a good idea to get tight now?" he asked.

"It's for my shirt. I want to get some of the stink off." I poured a little whiskey on the bloodstains and hooked the collar on the edge of the car's window so it could air out. I also kicked off my boots to give my feet a chance to breathe.

"What I wouldn't give for a nice, cold creek," I said.

Angus smiled. Bits of snake meat dangled between his teeth. That smile was more sinister than any war face I'd ever seen a man make in the heat of battle. Hecla had its wild men. We had Angus. Things could be worse.

Night came fast, or maybe it was just my imagination. I no longer cared. Matthias finally closed up his umbrella and stuffed his Bible in the front seat. Teta and I watched the flames, listening to the wood pop.

"Read anything good?" I asked when Matthias sat between us. Angus lay on his back, cradling his head in his hands. He'd nodded off not long after eating the entire snake.

"I gave Revelations a thorough rereading and I've come to the conclusion that what Angus heard was not the Trumpets of Armageddon."

"No shit," Teta said, snapping a stick and throwing it in the fire.

I wondered how long Matthias had been a reverend, if he needed to reacquaint himself with one of the more popular books of the Bible. More proof he waved that title around for show.

"It was a call," he continued, "but it's not one heralding the end of mankind. I'd bet that Angus was the only person outside of Hecla who heard it, on account of his special abilities. The question now is, why?"

"That's all we've been asking ourselves since we got here," I said. "Maybe you should ask the spirits in your little box, they being closer to the unknown, so to speak."

Matthias didn't take the bait.

Teta said, "That reminds me, jefe. I found something in that book Teddy gave you, but I forgot all about it. It's not much."

"Spit it. Any little bit helps," I said.

He gingerly removed his sombrero and laid it on the ground, brushing dust off with the back of his hand. "I found out that Hecla is actually named after a volcano in Iceland. Except there, it's Hekla with a *k* instead of a *c*. Most of the book is a Norse story about a king who laid down a lot of laws and regulations. Pretty boring stuff."

"Where the hell is Iceland?"

"In the Atlantic ocean, way off the coast of Canada. Hekla, the volcano, was very active, especially a thousand years ago. When it would erupt, it would spill fire and smoke and great walls of steam would fill the sky when the flames and lava came in contact with the snow and ice. Nothing could be seen for miles, but everyone could hear the volcano burst like thunder from the gods. It was terrifying."

"Please don't tell me there are volcanoes here too," I said.

"Lucky for us, no. Here's the thing. It was believed that Hekla, the place where the world seemed to split open and rain death and destruction, was actually one of the two gates of hell on earth. People heard more than explosions in the mist and heat. They heard the cries of the damned and the shouting of demons."

The wind began to pick up and whistled as it raced across the valley. Matthias leaned into Teta, hanging on his every word. Even Angus had stirred. The firelight made hideous shadows on his wide face.

"So why on earth would they name the town after that?" I asked, not really sure I wanted to know the answer.

Matthias answered before Teta could take a breath. "Because maybe they knew that this *was* the second gate to hell."

CHAPTER THIRTY-EIGHT

I didn't need a gate to know that we had been living in hell on earth for the past several days. I wasn't much for fire and brimstone, or salvation, for that matter. Swallowing the story about Hekla, and Hecla, was a little more than I could take. I said to Teta, "You sure that's all there was in there?"

"From what I could tell."

"That Teddy can be one odd duck."

"Who is this Teddy person you keep talking about?" Matthias asked.

"None of your business," we said at the same time.

Matthias raised his hands in surrender. "What do you propose we do now?"

I looked at the sky and the now-full moon that shone brightly. It shouldn't have been a full moon at all, not at this time of the month. Again, I didn't know what to trust. When the heavens could be manipulated, all bets were off.

My tobacco pouch was pretty low. There was just enough for three cigarettes, four if I made them small. "You fellas smoke?"

They shook their heads. "Tobacco is a poison and I try to keep my body free of anything that can befoul it. It *is* a temple, after all," Matthias said.

"No skin off my ass," I said, rolling one for Teta, then myself. I bent close to the fire to light it and took a deep drag, holding the smoke for as long as my lungs would allow. For all I knew, this would be my last cigarette and I wanted to savor it.

"I think that whatever has been controlling things will come to us when it's good and ready. Until that time, we might as well get some rest." I lay back and tilted my hat over my eyes.

"How can you sleep?" Matthias asked.

"Easy. Just do what I do."

I felt him staring at me, but I was all talked out. All I wanted was a little sleep and hoped that my mind could work a way out of our situation. The moment I closed my eyes, I saw Selma and the way she'd smiled when we first saw her at the ranch. It was easy to obsess with worry, but she needed me strong if I was going to have a chance at saving her. So I only thought good things, and soon drifted off.

★   ★   ★

I woke up clinging to the remains of a dream about working a cattle drive. My ears pounded from the thunder of all those heads of cattle rushing in a dangerous mass. I felt the horse beneath me, smelled the shit and dust, tasted copper in my mouth from where I'd bitten my lip as I worked the herd. Years of working the Chisholm Trail never left a man, and it wasn't unusual to find myself back there where life was hard but I'd never felt freer.

When I opened my eyes, Teta did the same. He fastened his sombrero on his head and got to a knee.

The fire was just orange embers.

The ground carried the subtle vibrations of an oncoming herd.

"Guess I wasn't dreaming," I said, rising to my feet. I gave Angus and Matthias a nudge with my boot. It was still dark out. A hint of something foul drifted in the air.

I offered my hand to help Matthias up. "Looks like it's time."

"What's that sound?"

"Something's coming, but I don't think it's cattle."

"We better get in the car."

For once, Matthias had a good idea. The steady rumble grew louder, which meant whatever was on its way was getting closer. Teta asked, "Do we run? Try to find higher ground?"

"No sense. This plain is flat as my Aunt Abigail. Might as well face it head on. Matthias, you should have a gun."

"I don't believe in firearms."

The sounds of metal scraping on metal made the hairs on the back of my neck stand up. Angus slid a pair of long machetes and a curved, silver cavalry sword out from under the front seat. He handed one to Matthias. The spirit-box boys were full of surprises.

"You use that to battle spirits?"

Matthias gave a quick laugh, but there was real panic in his eyes. "Spirits are easy. It's people we can't always trust."

You couldn't have enough weapons. I motioned with my fingers to hand over the sword.

Angus gave it to me, handle first. I could see it had some wear and tear. The herd, for lack of a better description, was coming from the west. "Matthias, turn the car around so we're facing it."

"Are you sure that's wise?"

"Just turn it," Angus snapped, startling all of us. His meaty hand flexed as he adjusted his grip on the machete. Matthias kept talking about his special abilities. I hoped being a master with a killing blade was one of them.

Matthias started the car and made a tight turn. Teta and I stood in the rumble seat. He had the Winchester at the ready. I pointed the shotgun into the darkness. My shoulders tensed and I forced myself to relax them. If I was going to be shooting, I couldn't do it all locked up.

Angus stood on the running board with the machete at his side. He held on to the window frame to keep his balance. Matthias gripped the wheel, the machete across his lap. We waited. The ground vibrated. I could feel it in my bones. The smell was getting worse. It was the stench of death. It reminded me of our time in Santiago, sitting aboard ship, surrounded by men dying with malaria, left to rot in their own waste. "Come on, you little putas," Teta hissed.

Matthias revved the engine. I wished we had a cattle catcher mounted to the front. Hell, I wished we were on a train. The added weight and height would have us in a good position.

Angus shouted, "Here they come!" It was what I feared most.

"Matthias, I need you to drive straight into them."

"Have you gone mad? We may as well sign our own death warrants!"

"That's what they told us at Kettle Hill, yet here we stand. Sometimes the move that seems the least logical is the one that gets you to the other side." I clapped him on the shoulder. "Now do it."

He hunched closer to the wheel and put his goggles on.

About a hundred yards ahead of us, an army of those wild men stampeded. Their scarlet eyes bounced in the dark as they loped toward us. They ranged between seven and ten feet tall. Locked together like that, they looked like a wild herd of upright buffalo.

Of all the ways I'd dreamt I'd die, this had never been a consideration.

CHAPTER THIRTY-NINE

The wild men came at us, snarling and hollering for all the world to hear. My blood ran cold as their menacing cries hammered my skull. They had long, powerful arms that looked as if they could break a man in two as easily as swatting a fly. The moon glinted off their jagged teeth and my flesh crawled thinking about them tearing into me.

"Matthias, now!"

The car jumped forward and Teta and I nearly lost our balance.

The surge of wild men seemed to stall the moment they saw us riding *to* them.

When they were only ten yards away, Teta fired the first shot. It took off the top of one of their heads. The beast twirled from the bullet's impact. Its body became a cyclonic, black mist that scattered into the wind.

"Holy crap, they explode!" Teta screamed, then took down the one next to it.

I pulled the shotgun's trigger and caught two closely packed wild men right in their stomachs. They turned to smoke the moment they left their feet.

We hit the first line of wild men. Their bodies battered the car with resounding thuds before careening off into twisting mist.

"Hallelujah!" Matthias whooped.

Angus held his machete out so it was at chest height of the wild men. The momentum of the car and the strength of his arm allowed him to cut a dozen down in just a few seconds. Teta and I continued to pump round after round into the horde. The creatures parted like the Dead Sea as we cut through the masses.

One of them managed to drive a fist into the front windshield. A web of cracks fanned out across the glass.

"They're coming up behind us!" Teta said.

Sure enough, the ones we had passed, that we had failed to kill, were on our tail, running faster than any horse.

One of them leapt for me. Its sharp-nailed fingers got hold of my leg and tore a long rip down the front of my jeans. I swear it smiled at me just before I put a bullet between its red eyes. My leg felt like it was on fire. I looked down to see a jagged trail of blood between the open flaps of my jeans.

Angus grunted and I turned to see one of the creatures clamp its teeth on his forearm.

Teta spun and blasted it in the face, missing Angus's arm by a curly hair.

They may rupture into harmless vapor when they were mortally struck, but they could still inflict pain. Somehow, Angus managed to hold on to the machete and was back to slashing them into nothing at an alarming rate. Even Matthias cut a few down while keeping steady at the wheel.

No matter how many Teta and I shot at the rear, an endless number of beasts took their place. We were going to run out of bullets fast.

As I suspected, we were making progress toward the hills. Whatever magic that had kept us at bay was now happy to suck us in – if we could get past the bloodthirsty wild men.

"Matthias, give me your machete!" I barked.

He handed it back to me without a moment's hesitation. I gave it to Teta.

"Save ammo," I said, having to shout to be heard above the din of the speeding car and the howling mass of wild men.

We hacked away at them like butchers in a contest to see who could chop off the most steaks. The only blood was our own as they clawed at us. Four had managed to get a handle on the rear end of the car. I took the one on the extreme left, Teta the one on the extreme right. The other two used their powerful arms to propel themselves into the rumble seat with us. We collapsed in a pile, slamming into the front seats.

Matthias lost control and the car started to spin.

I was nose to nose with what looked to be a caveman. I'd seen depictions in museums back in New York, and its face was more human than I cared to consider. I clung to the fur that sprouted from its neck to keep its jaws from closing on my face. Thick, horrendous-smelling drool spattered onto my lips. We rocked from side to side as the car went out of control. Matthias screamed something. My machete was useless at this close range and my hands were too busy to reach for my pistol.

The beast grunted and its eyes went wide with shock. And then it was gone. I looked up to see Angus bury his machete in the back of the wild man that was clawing at Teta.

The car came to a sudden, awful stop and we were all thrown from it like from an untamed bronco. I rolled to a breathless stop. Angus slammed into me. Teta skidded on his back.

My head and side where Angus had collided with me barked with agony. But there was something else far more alarming.

The night was suddenly very still. All I could hear was the sound of our ragged breathing. When my eyes came back into focus, I saw that Matthias was still in the car. His head was bleeding. He was slumped on the front dashboard.

"My fucking sombrero," Teta moaned, holding the mangled thing in his hand. It was ripped in two.

"You're not going to need it where we're going," Angus said.

I looked around and if I'd been a cat I would have watched all nine lives scatter into the night.

We were surrounded.

The moonglow threw light over row upon row of the hell-bent, hairy beasts that had formed a tight circle around us. Hundreds of pairs of gleaming, crimson eyes bore into us with something this side of hate.

Even if we'd each had a Gatling gun, I didn't like our odds.

We rose slowly to our feet. I felt that if we made a wrong move, the madness and killing would burst forth. The big question was, what constituted a *right* move?

The car groaned, then spluttered.

"Gentlemen, it appears my Buffum is experiencing some major difficulties," Matthias said, trying to crank it back to life. His head wobbled a bit and one eye was clouded with blood.

Taking slow, tentative steps, Teta, Angus and I made our way to the car. Our machetes were scattered along the ground. I questioned whether I should even pick one up, lest that be the thing that set the wild men on us, but figured I'd rather die with a weapon in my hand than a regret in my mind.

Matthias tried to get the car started a few more times, but each time the engine coughed and went silent. To my surprise, I saw that we were on the outskirts of the tree line that surrounded the hills.

If we could somehow make it into the trees, there was a chance we could lose them. It was a chance slimmer than a bank note, but it was better than staying where we were.

"Angus," I whispered from the corner of my mouth, "you're a big man, but can you run?"

His bald head gave a solemn nod.

"You see those trees? I say we head for them as fast as we can. You lead and Teta and I will take everything out around us, with Matthias keeping our backs clear."

Teta stuffed the remains of his sombrero in his waistband and said, "You've gone off the deep end, jefe. Lucky for you, I have too."

The beasts regarded us like a four-course meal, but they didn't make a move. Their combined smell was stronger than ten tons of dynamite. "Matthias, toss us the guns."

We caught them and checked the chambers. Both needed reloading.

"When I count to three, I need you to run out of the car, grab this machete and stick to us. With Angus blocking, we're going to make for the woods. It's not a far shot from here to the mine. If anything, we can get to higher ground and try to defend ourselves."

"That's suicide," he said.

"It ain't if something else kills you," I reminded him. "God will forgive you."

He considered it, looking round at the angry, half-human faces that stood waiting like a living bear trap.

"Okay," he said.

I held up a finger. "One."

Angus turned to face the trees. Teta and I closed in on his hulking frame. "Two."

I thumbed the hammer back on the Winchester. I'd have to use the barrel to bash the creatures after I ran out of ammo.

"Th—"

The wild men behind the car swarmed like bees on a hive.

Matthias heard them before turning to face their savagery and screamed, "I'm stuck!" He pulled at his leg but he couldn't get out of the car.

The other wild men began their advance, taking up their chilling howls and screeches. Before I could get off a single shot, they descended on the car and Matthias. There were so many it transformed into a hairy, rocking mound.

Angus shouted for Matthias. But he was gone.

CHAPTER FORTY

As much as I hated to admit it, there was no saving the so-called reverend. I pushed myself into the big man's back and shouted, "It's too late! Go!"

Angus roared with pain and red-hot anger that equaled the cry of any of the wild men. He moved forward like a locomotive on full steam. Teta and I had to push hard to keep up. Angus squared his shoulders and decimated everything he came in contact with. We scooped up the fallen blades.

As we shot and smashed our way to the tree line, the wild men took their pounds of flesh. Swinging my rifle into the head of one, my elbow was caught by a row of teeth that tore a ragged line through my flesh, bouncing off the bone. The butt of the rifle connected with its temple and the spray of my blood mingled with the blast of smoke that the beast became.

To his credit, Angus never slowed down, nor did he stop bellowing like a wounded animal. At one point my face rubbed against his back and came away wet with his blood.

The air burned with the smells of gunpowder, burned hair, blood and vile smoke. The wild men converged on us and tried to slow us down, but Angus was not to be denied.

I slipped my Colt out of my holster and blasted a couple of the wild men in the face – tanned faces that looked much too human. I'd worked alongside big, hairy men who looked more like animals than these creatures.

"Jesus, that hurt!" Teta pulled his hand from the bloody maw of one of the beasts. I put a bullet down its throat and it burst into a black mist.

We ran and shot and hacked with the machetes and cavalry sword. The wild men screeched so loud my ears were ringing.

"Trees!" Teta cried.

Sure enough, they were just a handful of yards away. We had broken through the final row of the wild-man ranks and now it was just us and the rows of evergreens. Hundreds of the creatures were at our backs.

I was mad as hell and wanted nothing more than a ring of cannons to blast every last one of them away. If Selma weren't somewhere in the mines, I might have stopped to face them, taking out as many as I could until my strength was no more and they overtook me. Dried leaves and brown pine needles crunched as we made our way into the trees, winding around trunks, trying not to get tripped up. The moon couldn't penetrate the thick canopy and it was hard to see more than two feet in front of our faces.

We ran until our lungs burned. It was an uphill climb and we sounded like a trio of asthmatics.

I was the first to stumble. I don't know if my boot caught on something or if my legs just gave out. I skidded onto my hands and knees. My stomach heaved as I gulped the cool night air. Teta and Angus stopped next to me. Each went down on one knee.

"You all right?" Teta asked.

"Yeah, I'll be fine. Just need to catch my breath."

Pausing our flight gave us a moment to listen. There were no sounds of pursuit. Because of the drought, every step in the small forest was a symphony of noise. Now there was nothing. Not even the sound of crickets.

Teta said, "I think we lost them. Thank God. I'm so beat up inside every time I breathe in my ribs feel like they're going to snap."

I looked down into the dark alleys between the trees, imagining all those wild men crouched behind them, waiting. Any minute, I'd see a thousand burning red eyes, hovering like demonic fireflies.

"They let us lose them," Angus said.

He was a man of few words, but when he spoke there was an undeniable truth behind them.

"You're right, they did. How could the three of us outrun creatures that were capable of keeping up with a speeding car? We've been herded here. And I don't think it's by accident that we've been separated from the car," I said.

"Or my spirit chest," Angus added. He scooped up some leaves and used them to sop up the blood that covered most of his face, neck and arms. His shirt was torn in so many places it was a miracle it even stayed on. He had taken a beating, running through those wild men.

They wanted us to be here, alive, but not unhurt.

My own scratches felt like someone had poured salt in the wounds. Amazing how something made of smoke could inflict so much damage.

I struggled to get up and put a hand on Angus's shoulder. "I'm sorry about Matthias." He closed his eyes and went silent.

From our vantage point, we couldn't see the hills yet, but I knew we were close. There was only one way to go, and that was up. I patted my shirt pocket to see how many bullets I had left for the Winchester.

"You got any shells for the shotgun?" I asked Teta.

"Enough. When they run out, it'll make a good club."

"Next time we decide to go down shit creek, remind me to bring a paddle…and a boat," I said.

My thighs twitched and burned when I attempted to take a few uphill strides. My blood pulsed through every part of my body, increasing the pain in the deep gouges the wild men had painted on me. My knees shook, and I had to lower myself before I collapsed.

"Maybe we should rest a bit," I said, squinting my eyes to shut out the agony that had taken hold of me.

I was so close to Selma I wanted to press on, but my body was betraying me. I called out to her in my mind, praying she would know I was near and would guide me to her.

"Selma," I whispered.

When I looked over, Teta and Angus were asleep, and for a moment, I wondered if they'd died. I watched them, straining against the dark, and saw the slow rise and fall of their chests. They were in a deep, unnatural sleep.

My skull felt like it was filled with cotton and my eyelids kept dropping of their own accord. No matter how hard I tried to fight it, sleep was going to drag me under. My last thought was that there was poison in the wild men's sharp nails and teeth and we were going to rot up here.

At least there were no buzzards to peck away at our eyes and flesh.

★   ★   ★

"Nat."

I struggled to get out of a dream that was already fading into nothing. "Nat. Wake up."

My eyes snapped open. A grizzled face leered down at me, its white beard undulating in the wind. I rolled away, scrambling to get to my feet.

My heel clipped Angus's side and I fell over him. Angus sat up on his elbows, groggy and confused and unhappy that someone had dropped onto him.

I raised my hands. "It's only me, Angus."

I looked over to where I'd been sleeping. There was nothing. Teta was still asleep down where my feet had been. "Franklin?"

There was no sign of the man. He had been standing over me, calling my name. He couldn't have run away without making a sound. "Franklin!"

Teta bolted awake and drew his pistol. "What happened?"

"I…I think I saw Selma's brother-in-law," I said, unsure of my own senses.

"Do you know where he went?"

I looked all around. "No. One second he was calling my name, the next he was gone."

"That sounds like Franklin."

I was reluctant to say what I felt, but I knew Teta wouldn't laugh it off. "He's not alive."

"What do you mean, he's not alive?"

"I get the feeling we've *never* seen him alive. When I looked at his face just now, it was different."

"I don't understand." Teta reholstered his gun and rubbed his eyes.

"I saw his face, plain as day. But I could also see *through* his face, right to the stars above him."

"Like a ghost?"

I swallowed hard. Everything I'd come across since entering Hecla was counter to the core of my beliefs. It's not easy for a man half a century old to admit he's been wrong about everything.

"Yeah."

"What did he want?"

"For me to get up."

"That's all?"

"He didn't exactly stay around long enough to share some jerky and conversate."

"Spirit guide," Angus said. "Hard to know if they're good or bad. You usually don't find out until it's too late."

"Spirit guide? Like what the Indians talk about?" I said. Angus slowly shook his head. "Not really."

It didn't look like he planned to expand on things, so I dusted myself off and did a quick internal inspection of my body. I was still sore as hell, but the rest had done me some good. The blood had dried my shirt to my cuts and when I stretched, the fabric pulled free with tiny ripping sounds. If I wasn't wide awake when I saw Franklin, I was now.

"So what are we to make of Franklin being a spirit guide?" I asked. Angus shrugged his shoulders and walked off to relieve himself.

"He's the expert?" Teta said, his jaw working out some tension.

"He has special gifts, remember. Matthias is the expert, I think."

If I was right, we were getting closer to the evil source of Hecla's power and were at an immense handicap. That must have been why the wild men focused on Matthias and gave us a halfhearted chase through the trees.

When Angus came back, I suggested we make our way up the face of the cliffs and find one of the mine access points. "Teta and I will take the lead, Angus." I didn't want him in front. If he slipped, he would take us down like a boulder in a landslide.

It was still dark but I had no idea what time of day it actually was. There wasn't a bird in the sky, critter on the floor or insect on the wind. It was like being locked in a room with a lone window facing the moon. At least the breeze never let up. It was comforting to know at least something worked right out here.

Our boots made quite the racket as we emerged from the tree line and crunched the hard gravel around the hills' base. I saw what looked like a darkened opening up and to our left.

A winding road had been cut into the rock that circled the hills, leading to each of the shaft openings. We'd seen it when we'd done our earlier recon during the day.

"I'll bet we're expected to take the road," I said to Teta.

"All the more reason not to use it. If we're lucky, no one, or no *thing*, thinks we'll climb straight up. Less surprises for us, you think?"

"What I think and a dime is worth ten cents. But I do agree with you. It doesn't seem so steep and it looks like there are a lot of hand-and footholds. I'm pretty sure we can make it up and still hold on to the guns."

"I sure wish we still had one of those lamps. It's going to be hard to shoot what we can't see."

"We'll burn that bridge when we get to it. Since you're the younger, after you."

"You're too kind, jefe."

With the shotgun in his left hand, Teta used his right to find a depression in the rock and hauled himself up, wedging the tips of his boots where he could. When he was about five feet over my head, I tried to follow his path. It wasn't so bad. Everything was dry and sturdy. A few small rocks were dislodged as we made our way up, but nothing to worry about. I looked down and saw Angus right on my heels. He'd looped the blades through his belt and they clanged and scraped off the rocks. He took to climbing the hills like a duck to water. The man's size was very misleading.

I kept waiting for something to happen. Images of heavy iron pots filled with flaming oil tipping over us filled my brain. I shook it away. We weren't knights and this was no castle. What I had to worry about was what could potentially be waiting for us when we made it to the mine entrance. If it was filled with more of those wild men, we were done. There was no sense trying too hard to strategize because we were up against something that didn't make any sense.

And there was Selma. I had to get to her, no matter what the cost. If we were all going to die up here in these hills, we were going to die together.

"You know what this reminds me of?" Teta said, taking a cautious step with his right foot.

"I can't even imagine."

"Remember when we busted those guys who were smuggling guns for the Eastman Gang?"

The Eastman Gang was the terror of the Lower East Side back in New York. If there was a dirty racket, they had their noses in it. Those thugs were everything from thieves, to pimps, to killers for hire. We'd gotten a tip that a boatload of guns was coming into the harbor, all destined for the sweaty hands of the Eastman Gang. Big Monk Eastman was still the ringleader at the time, and he needed some heavy firepower to make a go at an all-out turf war with the Five Points Gang. The NYPD had a guy undercover who'd brought the shipment to our attention. Teta and I volunteered to be part of the squad that was to intercept both the boat and the gang members that were sent to get the guns.

We had men stationed everywhere along the docks. It was very hot that night, especially for mid-May. Teta and I were situated under the pilings, waiting for a signal from another cop on the neighboring dock to make our move. The smell of fish and oil was so heavy it would take four washings to get it out of my clothes.

The boat pulled in and we listened to footsteps above as men hustled back and forth.

When the signal came, Teta and I climbed up the pilings. We were to be the first line of defense should the men try to beat a hasty retreat off the bridge.

"We climbed up onto the dock like a couple of kids on a tree," Teta said, pulling himself up another foot. "I remember thinking, *What the hell are we getting ourselves into?* I mean, we knew everyone on that dock would have a gun, but we didn't know how many there would be or how they would react when they saw our pretty faces. We had no cover. It was just us and them and a shitload of guns."

I chuckled thinking about it. "Not our brightest idea. There were easier things to do to help stop the boredom."

"But that's just it. Guys like you and me, we need moments like this. You're only a few years older from when I met you in Cuba, but all I hear you talk about is what an old man you are. You never said it once that night at the dock. And your bones may be feeling things more now than they did when you were riding cattle, but you still have the fire, you know. And here we are again, climbing up to who knows what, and it's just me, you and some guns."

"You forgot Angus." The big man grunted.

"Yeah, we've got Angus."

"Hold on a sec. Let me see if I can climb up next to you."

I jammed my fingers into a fissure and pulled myself to the right, finding a good spot to support my feet. I managed to get myself in line with Teta. It was only another five feet until we got to the ridge.

"Now we'll hit the top together," I said, a little out of breath but ready.

He smiled and said, "If it comes to it, I'll shoot to the left, you shoot to the right and we'll meet in the middle."

"If our bullets hold out."

"They always do."

We scrabbled up the rest of the way, managing to keep our fingers on the triggers of the shotgun and rifle without setting them off. As soon as we hit the ridge, we got into a firing position on our knees. Angus hauled himself between us, brandishing a machete in each hand.

I looked around and sighed. "Ah shit."

CHAPTER FORTY-ONE

We didn't manage to get to *one* of the mine entrances. In fact, there were six.

This side of the hill was honeycombed with open shafts. Four were on the bottom ridgeline, each spaced twenty to thirty feet apart. A tall conifer sprouted between them, giving partial cover to the other two up top. This made my earlier assessment of the number of shafts very shy of reality.

"Why would they cut six shafts so close to one another?" I mused, walking the perimeter to make sure I hadn't missed any.

Teta pointed to the widest entrance. "I'll bet that was the one they first dug for the copper. They must have found multiple veins of gold inside and just tunneled into where they thought it led."

"Gold fever makes for dumb miners?"

"I don't know. I never read much about mines."

"I would think that by carving out so many tunnels so close together, it would make for a very unstable series of shafts. I'll bet there're a lot of bodies down there that never made it to the boneyard."

Angus leaned against the support beams of one of the smaller shafts. He tilted his head toward the interior of the shaft, listening.

"Hear anything?" I asked.

"Crying."

It's funny how one simple word could raise the hairs on my arms and neck.

"Does it sound like a woman crying?" If it was Selma, I was about to make a mad dash into the dark and hope I didn't fall down some pit.

"No. Men. Many men. All dead."

Teta came up beside him and took two steps into the shaft. He put his finger to his lips and stood quietly.

"I don't hear anything," he said in a hush.

"You can't," Angus said. "The dead don't talk to you. I'll go to them now."

Teta held his arm. It looked like a child trying to wrap his fingers around a bull's neck. "You can't go in there. We have to decide which shaft to take and go in together."

Angus stared at him, unmoving. Teta stared back, but I could see him starting to waver. He knew there was no way he could hold Angus back, short of shooting him. I decided to break their silent struggle.

I said, "What do you plan to do?"

He looked at me with eyes tinged with a sadness I'd only seen on folks who had lost someone close. "End their suffering. Send them home."

"Will you be long?"

"No."

"Do you want us to come along?"

"It's not necessary."

I may not have heard the crying, but looking at Angus, I didn't doubt that *he* did. He needed to exercise whatever ability it was that Matthias swore he'd been given. "We'll wait right out here, then. You call out if you need us."

His back heaved and he disappeared into the darkness. We heard the crunch of his heavy footsteps as he walked deeper into the tunnel. I had a sense that we'd seen him for the last time and desperately wanted to be proven wrong. If he didn't come back out, that would make it a perfect score for Hecla and the mines eliminating everyone who had been drawn to it thanks to mine and Teta's little expedition. Things like that could weigh a man's conscience down.

"This is crazy," Teta said. "We came here to find Selma, not wait for him to talk to dead people only he can hear."

"Crazy just about fits here," I said. "We've been trying to fight everything. We might as well take a different approach and go with the hand we've been dealt."

The wind started to kick up again. Teta's greasy hair flopped to one side of his face. "It would be nice to have a good shave and a haircut before we die," I said.

Teta huffed and absently fingered the remains of his lucky sombrero in his waistband. "I wouldn't mind a rare steak, good whiskey and an even better woman after that shave."

I had the same fantasy, only the woman in my dream was Selma. Angus's footsteps suddenly stopped.

"I hope he's not so far back that we can't even hear him. Be a fine mess if he needed us and we had to run too far in the dark to get to him," I said. We stood on either side of the tunnel's mouth, listening hard.

"When we get out of here, I'm throwing the biggest fiesta Wyoming's ever seen," Teta said softly.

"I hope gringos are invited."

"I've been around you so long I've become half-gringo myself."

The shaft was silent. The air coming from the tunnel was cold as well water. We waited a couple of minutes. It was as if Angus had been swallowed whole by the mine. He was no Jonah, and this wasn't Sunday school.

I cupped my hands around my mouth and shouted, "Angus! You all right in there?" My voice echoed down the tunnel.

The big man didn't reply. "That's not good," Teta said.

"Thanks, professor."

I called his name again and was met by my own voice responding back to me. Something moved in the trees below us and I tensed. If it was one of those wild men, or a bunch, we might be able to hold them off if they took the same route we had. It didn't happen again, though. It was a small relief.

When I sucked in some air to call for Angus again, I was stopped by the sound of murmuring. It was coming from inside the tunnel. It was a deep baritone, so I knew it had to be Angus. What I couldn't make out was what he was saying.

"At least we know he's alive," Teta said.

I shushed him. I wanted to hear what Angus was up to.

His muttering got louder, but no matter how hard I tried, I couldn't catch a single word. "Is he speaking Spanish?"

"Not any Spanish I know."

"Could it be French? He looks a little French."

There was a musical quality to the way he spoke, with hard

consonants and soft syllables riding up and down in a kind of wave. If I listened long enough, it might lull me to sleep.

"What's he doing?"

"Singing to ghosts, far as I can tell," I said. And then he went silent again.

"Nat, we're wasting time."

"What do you propose we do?"

"For starters, we have to decide whether we leave him there with his ghosts or get him out."

"We're not leaving him."

"Then it's settled. We get him out."

"You have a team of horses somewhere that can pull him out?"

"I'm sure he'll listen to reason." Teta clicked the hammer back on his pistol. I knew he wasn't going to shoot Angus. He just needed to make a point.

I scratched the bristly stubble on my chin and thought about mentioning option three, which was to do what I said we would before and wait for him to come out. But dammit, Teta was right. We needed to get a move on.

"Let's go then."

We'd taken no more than four steps when the tunnel rang with Angus's fevered shouting. The words, which were nonsense to begin with, blended into one another as the echo melded into fresh vocalizations. His voice was as fierce as he was big and if I didn't know it was coming from him, my bowels would have turned to water.

"LADALLL MISTRUCT! FELDAL UTAME BISCOOD! ENDAMANTE! ENDAMANTE MADOOL!"

We froze, stupefied by Angus's chant.

"ENDAMANTE MADOOL! ISHTOK UTAME SANSIDAR! ENDAMANTE!"

He was shouting at the top of his lungs. I was concerned that the vibrations of his voice could bring the whole works down on us. I grabbed Teta's sleeve and pulled him back, out of the tunnel.

"He sounds like he's lost his mind," Teta said. The whites of his eyes practically glowed in the dark. Angus continued with a litany of foreign words, yelling like an angry god amid the heavens.

"ISHTOK UTAM SANSIDAR!"

"That's definitely not French," Teta said. "That's not anything I've ever heard in my life."

"If the wild men didn't know where we are before, they do now."

Angus stopped for a blessed moment, then he roared. It went on louder and longer than any man should have been capable of doing, and I wondered if what we heard was, in fact, Angus at all. What we'd heard could be the language of the thing in the hills.

Fast, thunderous footsteps flowed from the mine. I hoped to hell it was Angus.

"Get back," I cautioned Teta. If it wasn't our giant friend, it was best to give it some room. We had our pistols aimed at the black tunnel. Again there was noise down by the trees. There hadn't been a single critter in sight, so it had to be something bad. Sometimes that was just the way luck ran.

I breathed a sigh of relief when Angus's bald head emerged from the gloom. He skidded to a stop when he saw our guns.

"We didn't know it was you," I said, pointing my gun to the ground.

"What the hell were you doing in there? It sounded like you were speaking in tongues," Teta said, slipping his pistol back in his holster.

"I was trying to set them all free."

"Did it work?" I asked.

He bit his lip, looked down at the ground and bit his lip. "No. There are too many and the hold on them is too great."

"How many is too many?"

"Hundreds."

"That's a lot of miners," Teta said.

Angus shook his head. "Not all miners. Women and children too. Everyone in Hecla." I peered into the shaft as though by staring long enough I'd be able to see the heart of things in these cursed hills outside a damned town. "You mean to tell me that everyone in the town is in there, dead?"

"They're all dead, yes. Their bodies aren't all there, but their spirits are trapped."

"Too bad we had to leave your spirit chest behind," Teta said.

"I'd guess even a whole town of spirits could fit in there since there's not much to them."

"Don't mock," Angus growled.

I asked, "So, are they all in that one shaft?"

"No. Within the center of the hills."

Damn. "What about Selma? Did you get any sense where someone *living* would be?"

He thought it over and my heart paused. The one thing I didn't want to hear was that he'd found her amongst the dead and disembodied.

"No. She's not in that shaft. I went to its end. It doesn't go far."

"At least we can rule out one," Teta said. He picked up a jagged rock and carved a big *T* into one of the support pillars. "They all look just about the same. Now we'll know not to go back in there."

"We're going to need some light and holding tiny matches isn't going to do it," I said. "Angus, give me a hand with that tree over there so we can make some torches."

CHAPTER FORTY-TWO

I pointed out a thick, low-hanging branch on a young pine tree. It would have taken an axe or saw for Teta and me to break it off, but for Angus it was only a matter of getting a good grip and pulling until it ripped free from the trunk. It made a hell of a racket and we stayed still for a bit to ensure we hadn't gotten any undue attention.

He broke the branch in half over his knee. Teta and I each took a section and went about carving off the bark with the machetes. We hacked the ends open so we could stuff the bark into the splits. When we were done, I gave the machete to Angus. He chopped a section of the tree away until he came to its stores of sap. We collected the sap with leaves and added them to the shards of bark.

I held a makeshift torch in front of me. "It's not pretty, but it'll do. We may have to load it up with more bark and sap within an hour or so."

"'And God said, Let there be light'," Angus said, barely above a whisper. I'm sure it's what Matthias would have said.

Teta struck a match and the end of his torch went up with a quick *whump!* I lit the second torch with the first.

"Guess we'll take the next one over," I said. "I'll go first, and Angus can take the other torch at the rear. If we have to turn about and skedaddle, we'll have a light leading the way."

"Good. That leaves my hands free for protection," Teta said.

The rifle was in his left and the pistol in his right. He was deadly from either side.

We stepped into the crudely constructed mineshaft. I could tell from the start it had been tunneled out in a hurry. There weren't as many supporting structures and the sides of the cave were ragged and raw. The ground was clear of tracks because they'd never gotten around to laying them.

"Must be another small one," I said. My voice sounded like a trumpet's blast in the cold silence of the tunnel.

"We can only hope," Teta said.

The torchlight flickered and popped and we had to make sure it didn't set the timber on fire. If there were any pockets of gas, we were in for a short trek into the hills. It was a concern I had to force to the back of my mind. There was no sense worrying about something you couldn't avoid.

Sure enough, the tunnel died a little over a hundred feet in. We turned and headed back outside, now with Angus in the lead.

"Must have been a bad vein," Teta said.

"Must have."

I felt an itch at the back of my skull. This wasn't what it seemed, but I had no way of knowing the truth. Why would miners take the time to blast their way in, then stop after such a short while? It was a lot of work for nothing and didn't make a lick of sense.

All the while, I couldn't shake the image of us being surrounded by the dead, begging to get out, but unable to set themselves free. I felt hundreds of sets of eyes on my back, imagining myself passing through their untethered bodies. It was chilly in the tunnel. Was that natural, or was I feeling the icy grip of death?

When we made it back to the false-night air, Teta got the rock from his pocket and etched another *T* on the outer beam.

We moved on to the next. It was the tiniest of the ones on this side of the hills and we had to crouch to get inside.

"What was this one made for, Chinamen?" Teta groused.

"You're the shortest one here. Quit your complaining."

It was narrow, to say the least. We were hemmed in by solid rock. Here, more than in the other tunnels, I could sense the spirits brushing past us as we inched our way down. The floor dipped into a sharp decline and I worried about us slipping into God knows where.

My arm scraped against the wall and my hand jerked up. I nearly set my hat on fire with the torch. My face was singed from the heat.

I motioned for everyone to stop so I could listen. If Selma was there, we might be lucky and hear her cough or move or, worse, cry. I could only hear the steady flapping of the flames, like a new flag atop a pole on a windy day.

The silence made my ears ring. Moving forward, I dug my heels into the loose-dirt floor to keep my balance as we descended.

"Angus?"

"Yes."

"What language were you speaking back in that first tunnel?"

With all of the unknowns before us, I wanted to scratch at least one thing off the list. If knowledge was power, I had all the strength of a baby calf.

"Deadspeak," he replied. A cold creek ran down my spine.

"You learn that in some special school?" Teta asked, all sarcasm in the face of fear.

"No. I was born with it. So was my mother. She called it deadspeak. Now I do."

I said, "And you use that to—"

"Talk to spirits."

Suddenly, I no longer wanted to know about his deadspeak. Hunched over, feeling claustrophobic and stepping into the bowels of haunted hills were not the ideal conditions for talking about the dead. It was bad enough I imagined them pressing against my face, their sightless eye sockets gazing into my soul.

The rock walls bled cold water. It ran down the declining tunnel floor. My torchlight played crazy games with the surface of the water. I didn't realize we had come to the end of the floor until I stepped up to my knees into an ice-cold pool.

"Dammit, that's freezing! Turn around, guys, this one is clear."

The hike up was even harder and we had to grip jutting rocks along the walls to haul ourselves along. When we got to level ground I tried shaking the water from my boots.

We could just about see the opening of the tunnel when the hills shook. Dislodged rocks and dirt rained on our heads. A terrific concussion rocked us off our feet and we collapsed in a pile.

"I don't want to die in here!" Teta shouted.

He scrambled to his feet and swayed from side to side, holding his hand out to us. "Hurry!"

Terror seemed to double his strength. He yanked me into a standing position with little help from me. Even Angus was able to get himself upright thanks to Teta.

We ran for the exit, ignoring the larger rocks that pelted us and the groaning of the failing wooden beams.

And then things took a mighty sour turn.

CHAPTER FORTY-THREE

The wild men had returned.

Their deranged caterwauling filled the air as we stumbled out of the shaft. We couldn't see them yet, but sure as shit they were making their way right to us. The woods were alive with the frantic sounds of their approach.

The rumbling had stopped and puffs of dust billowed out of all of the mine entrances. "I think the hills wanted us out so we could be served up to those things," I said.

Teta scrambled to the lip of the ridge and looked down. "I don't see them yet but the smaller trees are swaying pretty hard. There must be a thousand of them."

"Think we got too close for comfort?" I asked Angus.

"I wish I could tell you. If you want to take the path for the other side of the hills, I'll stay here and fight them off as long as I can."

Angus's words staggered me. We barely knew him, and in most of that time, we'd treated him with suspicion and doubt. Now here he was, willing to lay down his life for us. I'd been around countless brave men, but never one so willing to give up everything in the face of such mind-shattering madness for basic strangers.

"I can't let you do that," I said.

Teta was mesmerized by the wailing, rocking forest. "Too bad we didn't have more warning. I would have set the whole forest on fire and burned those sons of bitches."

"Teta, you're handier than a pocket on a shirt! Angus, use your machete to get some more bark and sap out of that tree."

We ran to the pine tree we'd used before and doused my torch with as much sap as we could collect. I burned my hand like an overdone steak when I wedged extra bark into the splits at the end of the torch. Pretty soon, the whole thing was blazing.

"Can you pull down some of those other branches?"

Angus broke off a pair of four-foot branches with ease. He rubbed them against the open wound in the tree, getting them slick with sap.

"How good's your arm?" I asked him.

"Very."

"I'll light the first branch and you toss it into the middle of that stand of trees. This place is so dry, it'll go up fast."

I touched the torch to the branch and stepped back when the fire rose above my head. Angus heaved the branch midway into a cluster of trees below us. They erupted into flames. The shrieks and cries of the wild men went up an octave. I don't think they were expecting that.

Teta held out his hand. "Me next."

I gave him the branch and set it alight.

"You should aim for the ground. With all that leaf litter, it'll create a wall they can't get through, while the rest burns them from above."

"Oh, I'll burn their asses up *muy bien.*"

He held the branch to his side. The flames crept dangerously close to his hand. He watched the trees wrapped in a halo of fire.

"What are you waiting for?" I shouted.

"I want to see their eyes, make sure they're good and close so they can be formally introduced to the flames."

I wasn't convinced it was the best thing to do and I was tempted to throw my torch and get things going. The army of wild men sounded none too happy. Their high-pitched shrieks were enough to raise the hairs on my neck.

Little dots of red came into view, weaving within the pitch black in the gaps between the trees. I tried counting, but they were moving around so much I lost track around fifty. I figured if I multiplied that by ten or more, I'd have a pretty good handle on the number of creatures coming our way.

"How can there be so damn many?" I said.

The first faces bled from the darkness. The orange light from the trees gave us a clear view as the first line of wild men broke from the tree line. To my dying day, it was a sight I'll never forget. They were tall, broad, hairy and angry as all get-out. They spotted us and, as one, bared their rotten teeth, baying like manic wolves.

I jerked when Teta howled back. "Here's something to cry about!"

The branch whirled end over end. At the top of its arc, it looked like the wind was going to extinguish the flame. My arm flexed as I prepared to follow with my torch if Teta's became a dud. But fate wasn't the mean old cuss I'd made him out to be, and the whole branch reignited a second before it hit the dry forest bed.

The forest floor blazed instantly. The first dozen wild men caught fire as the flame grabbed their long, matted fur. They screamed with an agony and intensity that should have severed their vocal cords. As they pinwheeled and ran in agonized circles, they set the others around them on fire as well. The line of flame continued to snake along their ranks.

Night turned to day as wild men and trees met in an epic conflagration. The heat was so intense I felt my face begin to burn.

"Holy cow."

"There's nothing holy about that," Teta said, spitting over the ridge and into the fiery melee.

It looked as if all the world were on fire. The air hummed with the shrieking of the dying and damned.

"I wonder why they're not turning to smoke," I said.

"They *are* smoke now," Angus replied, his gaze locked on the scene below.

Black, writhing clouds boiled into the sky and overpowered our noses. It smelled like rotten eggs and sizzling meat. My stomach roiled.

I said, "We should make our way to the other side of the hills while we have a chance."

"I think we did a pretty good job on this side," Teta said. The reflection of the devouring flames flickered in his wide eyes.

We were so busy staring into the flames and the flailing wild men that we never noticed what had crept up behind us.

CHAPTER FORTY-FOUR

When I turned to look for the best way to hit the road, I had to take a startled step back.

I was close to the ledge and Angus had to snatch my arm to keep me from falling.

The boy and girl with the black eyes stood silently a couple of feet from us. Their faces were so pale and drawn it was as if they'd lived in a world without sun or a decent meal all their lives. Their large, round eyes were as black as the heart of an evil man's soul.

They didn't move, didn't blink. The back of the boy's hand touched the back of the girl's. My gut told me they weren't here to ask for food and water this time.

"You kids shouldn't be here," I said. The words sounded as asinine coming out of my mouth as they must have to them. These weren't ordinary kids. They were Hecla's children.

Angus broke into an odd smile. He squatted down so he was eye level with them. He said, *"Madal intres avok."*

Their coal-black eyes swiveled in his direction and their bodies followed stiffly.

Angus closed his own eyes and tilted his head back as if he were listening to an old song played around a campfire.

The children smiled, and he opened his eyes again. *"Thesvud, thesvud."*

Teta and I held our breath. I wasn't sure what to make of the odd exchange between the giant and the eerie kids. Smoke burned my eyes. I stared at them through a film of tears. Angus mumbled something and the kids tilted their heads to the right in perfect unison. It was like watching a couple of windup toys. The big man nodded. I knew they were communicating with him somehow, even though their mouths never moved and they didn't make even the slightest sound.

All thoughts of making a hasty retreat left our minds. Despite their unnatural eyes and disconcerting mannerisms, by all appearances they were still children, no matter who, or what, had birthed them.

Teta, ever the realist, was the one able to break their spell. "Guys, we have to move our asses. Bring the kids if you have to, but let's go now!"

The moment he spoke, I could once again feel the heat of the flames at my back and hear the desperate cries of the wild men. Angus said something that was drowned out by the bedlam below us.

The boy raised his small arm and pointed to the blistering trees. "They're coming."

"We'll help you," the girl said.

I looked back and saw the boy was right. Hell was tramping toward us.

★   ★   ★

The out-of-control blaze only delayed the inevitable. The wall of flame wasn't enough to stop them. Granted, it did give them a moment of pause, but in the end, they took to the fire like a pig to slop.

Hundreds of them were fully engulfed in flames.

Their initial shock had worn off and they were no longer running around in mass pain and confusion. Now, they were an army of seven-foot, fiery behemoths, and they were climbing up the hillside.

Their eyes seared through the veil of fire that covered them from head to toe. They wore the flames as easily as I wore my shirt. When I was a kid my mother once showed me a painting of Hades in some old book she had. She'd said, "Nat, you have to mind your parents, and obey the laws that God has put before us. Otherwise, you'll end up in a very bad place, just like this, for eternity. Do you understand how long eternity is?"

"Forever," I'd answered, not comprehending how long the word implied.

"Good." She'd stroked my hair and squeezed my earlobes. "Hell is a place you never want to visit, much less live. I won't raise my boy to become one of the devil's playthings."

That picture and my mother's words had scared me good back then. It wasn't until she died the next year that their power began to fade, until I hadn't even thought of it at all for another forty years.

Mom, I'm glad you're not here to see this.

A picture in a book was one thing. Seeing a landscape choked with flames and smoke with inhuman creatures draped in fire climbing to take your life was a whole different animal. Their lips were twisted into demonic grins. I could feel their mad desire to tear us into pieces. They had fanned out into a wide arc around the base of the hill. It looked like they had formed a ring around the entire Deep Rock Hills.

Teta clapped his hand on the back of my collar and pulled. "We can't fight them off, jefe. We have to run."

Angus turned toward the mine and said, "We won't have to fight them alone."

The boy and girl opened their jaws until their mouths were wide open. I expected them to scream. No sounds escaped from their lips. A ferocious gust of wind blasted us and I clutched my hat before it blew off. The passing wind slipped into the various mine entrances, whistling a haunted melody.

From out of the mines poured dozens of tiny, pale forms. Their shuffling feet made no noise, raised no dust. They streamed out of the mines and gathered before us.

At least a hundred black-eyed children surrounded us. The smallest looked to be no older than two, while the oldest, a tall girl with long, blonde hair that glittered like sunlight off a fast-moving stream, was twelve, thirteen tops.

Teta stopped trying to drag me away. His mouth hung open, similar to the boy and girl that had called their friends from the depths of the mine.

"I am going to kick Teddy's ass when I see him," he said.

"Save some for me."

The black-eyed children gathered into tight rows and became still. It was as if they were waiting for an order – like we had back in Cuba, watching the Colonel ride before our ranks, waiting for the right moment to set us loose. All I wanted to do was yell at them to turn back and get away. I could hear the wild men getting closer. When we ran out of bullets, we'd have to turn tail and hope we could put a safe distance between us. Getting in close with the machetes or sword was out of the question. It was a safe bet that we wouldn't do so well if we were on fire.

Angus went back to his deadspeak and the children stared at him with unblinking attention.

He turned to us. "Be prepared. This is going to feel...strange."

"What's going to feel strange?" I asked.

Before he could answer, as one, the children swarmed to the edge of the cliff. We held out our hands in a futile attempt to ward them off.

They're committing mass suicide! Why are they diving headlong over the ledge into the clutches of the wild men?

My body was thrown into an ice-cold river as the first row of children ran *through* us. My organs froze as body after body became one with mine, passing out the other side. A sharp, stabbing pain pierced my brain and I felt myself losing consciousness.

I fought my body's desire to shut down. My knees threatened to go, but I refused to let them. Ghostly child after ghostly child violated the deepest parts of me, leaping from the ledge like lemmings. Teta was down on one knee, but Angus stood strong, beaming like a proud parent. The passage of the children seemed to have no effect on him at all.

I instinctively gulped for air like a drowning man when the last row of kids made their way over the ledge. Shivering uncontrollably, I wrapped my arms around myself and tried to lock my jaw shut to keep my teeth from chattering.

Angus peered over the ledge and pointed. "Look."

Teta and I stumbled to the precipice. I worried that I would pitch forward, I felt so weak, so trampled upon.

What we saw was a war never before waged on God's green earth, and I prayed it never would be again.

CHAPTER FORTY-FIVE

The children blazed with a brilliant light as sharp as the full moon on a clear night. They plowed into the burning wild men, passing through their bodies like they had done with us. Only with the wild men, the results were far different.

As soon as a child came in contact with a wild man, the flames extinguished themselves.

As the child emerged from the beast's back, the wild man exploded into dust and smoke.

The wild men cawed and screeched and hollered, but the children darted from one to the other without making a sound. The smoke of the vanquished wild men soon rivaled that pouring from the burning trees and ground.

Seeing as Angus was the only one who seemed to know what was going on, I said, "What should we do?"

"There's nothing we can do with the wild men. The children will take care of them for us."

Blurs of white light zigzagged through the throngs of wild men. It was a one-sided slaughter, and done without firing a single bullet or uttering a solitary word or command. "Who are they?" I said.

"The children taken from their families, from their futures." I was terrified by their silent ferocity.

Teta shook with chills. "Did they live in Hecla?" Angus nodded. "So, they're dead?"

He nodded again, smiling as he watched them lay waste to the wild men.

I said, "I don't think they're doing this just so we can watch them like fat field generals. We better search more tunnels and find Selma, fast. Angus, did you get anything from them that would lead you to believe that we can cross out the rest of the entrances here?"

He wiped beads of sweat that had collected on his smooth head. "She's not on this side of the hills."

"If we follow this path, it'll take us to the western side of the hills, where we first came," Teta said. "All of the openings here are half the size of what we saw there. If I was going to take Selma, that's where I'd go."

"Yeah, but we're not on the trail of a crazy Dominican gun hand." I raised my hand before he could object. "But you do make a good point and that *is* where we saw the first wild man, and Franklin *and* his diseased dog. Let's go."

It was harder than I thought, tearing ourselves away from the fight. The wild men's ranks were dwindling, and the ghost children moved like fluttering birds. The scene burned itself into my brain, and I was sure it would be my final memory before I breathed my last. We jogged down the cut in the hillside, searching for more shaft openings. It was difficult in the dark, made harder by the oily smoke that choked the moon and stars. If the fire continued to spread, there would be no difference in visibility between the interior of the mines and out here. I wasn't sure how long our torches would hold out, or if we had the time to make more.

Time.

I felt it slipping through my hands. How long would the hills hold Selma before they got tired of our bumbling around? Or would they be infuriated by the way the spirit children helped us and take their anger out on her? Up until now, we had been lured to the hills with zero assistance. I couldn't help but worry that the black-eyed children had saved us, only to doom Selma.

"Do you hear that?" Teta asked, keeping pace beside me.

All I could hear was my blood pounding in my ears and my breath laboring through old, tired lungs.

"It sounds like something growling," he added.

"Well, whatever it is, I don't have time for it. Shoot anything you see."

We kept running, the billowing smoke whispering at our backs. I wanted to make the west side with the main tunnel before the soot made it impossible to find.

My chest was burning and there was a sharp stitch in my side, but

I pushed the pain as far from my mind as I could. There was a very good chance that if I stopped now I wasn't getting up again. Every muscle in my legs twitched with exertion.

Just keep running, Nat.

"It doesn't sound like an animal," Teta said.

"It's just the fire. Sometimes when the flames get this big, they suck out all the air and it sounds like it has a life of its own."

Angus bumped shoulders with me as he sprinted past. Something either had him spooked, which was doubtful, or had drawn his interest.

Teta and I tried to keep up with him but he faded into the darkness fast. I shouted, "Angus, hold up! We don't want to get separated!"

And then I heard it too. It was a deep rumble that I felt in the center of my chest. *Please, not another earthquake.* Or maybe it was Matthias's Trumpets of Armageddon getting ready to blow. It sure felt like the end of times to me.

Whatever it was, it was coming straight for us. Angus would be our buffer if he didn't slow down. He was an asset I didn't want to lose.

I put my right hand on the butt of my pistol, pressing it against my side to deaden the pain that bloomed like a poisonous flower inside me.

Harsh light splashed against the side of the hill, momentarily blinding me. I put my hand up over my eyes to block it out.

When my eyes recovered, I saw what was hurtling at us.

I screamed for Angus, grabbed Teta's arm and dragged him off the path with little tenderness and no grace. It was either that or die.

★   ★   ★

To my relief, Angus made the same snap decision and leapt onto the trunk of a tree that lined the edge of the path. He clung like an oversized squirrel and retained life and limb with inches to spare.

Teta and I spilled over the edge, plunging ass over elbow through brush and sharp thicket. We came to rest in a slight depression, coming just short of braining ourselves against a fallen tree. The wind had been knocked out of me and it was an effort to roll onto my hands and knees so I could gasp for air. My stomach felt like it had been tied so tight it was going to burst.

"What the hell was that?" Teta said, struggling to get his footing.

When my diaphragm finally settled down, I replied, "That... was Matthias's car."

"Was Matthias driving? You grabbed me before I could see anything."

"I don't know. It was going so fast I couldn't tell if someone else was behind the wheel trying to kill us, or if they just couldn't see us."

"It can't be Matthias. We watched those wild men jump all over him. Even Wild Bill with an endless supply of rounds couldn't take on that many."

"Help me up and let's get back on the path."

I looked up and could see the depression in the brush where we had rolled. We had a twenty-foot climb ahead of us, but there were plenty of roots and bushes to hold on to, to make the climb easy. Thankfully, the rifle and shotgun were right in front of us. We were lucky they hadn't gone off during our fall. A pair of meaty hands reached out for ours when we were close to the top. We were pulled to our feet like a couple of rag dolls. "Thank you kindly, Angus," I said, picking thorns out of my side and chest.

Our torches lay on the ground, still burning but not as brightly. We'd need more bark and sap, and I hoped the wood could hold out a little longer.

Angus had a broad grin on his face and his attention was drawn to a spot off to our right.

Matthias's fancy race car was idling in the dark. A figure stood in the front seat and turned to us.

"Praise the Lord, he has seen fit for you all to survive!"

I bent to pick up a torch and walked cautiously to the car. The voice sounded like Matthias, but Hecla and the hills had taught me not to trust my senses.

My surprise was laced with wariness when my torchlight revealed his filth-covered face. His hair was a right mess and it looked like he'd been rolled in mud.

"Is that really you?"

He pounded his chest. "In the flesh! You didn't think those wild men could keep me down, did you?"

Teta had pulled up beside me. "Yes, we did. How did you get away?"

Matthias bounced back into the driver's seat. "A perfect question for our drive. Nat, you sit next to me. We have much to discuss. And please hold your torches outside the car. I don't want you to burn the upholstery."

I looked at Teta and he back at me. Neither of us knew what to make of our Lazarus. Angus didn't think twice, settling his girth into the rumble seat. The car tilted in his direction and the frame creaked.

Leaning close to Teta, I whispered, "If he does or says anything strange, don't hesitate to put a bullet in him."

"Everything he does and says is strange."

He had a point. "If it's anything stranger than his usual, you know what to do."

We got into the car and Matthias turned the car around, narrowly avoiding slipping over the edge of the path and down the side of the cliff. At least we were back in the direction we wanted to go, and our legs were spared for a spell.

If it was truly Matthias sitting next to me, I was thankful he was alive. He may have been a kook, but he was a dauntless one at that. If he wasn't, we'd have to take decisive action and hope Angus understood. If not, we were in for a hell of a fight. He wasn't going to turn to smoke if we hit him, and his bite was a lot worse than his bark.

"Where are you taking us?" I asked.

"On my way up, I came across a considerable shaft entrance. It looked big enough to drive the car through, if I was so inclined. I thought we'd try there."

We were on the same page, but I had more questions.

"If it looked like the most logical place for Selma to be, why were you driving here?"

"To look for you and Angus and Teta. I saw the flashpoint of the fire and hoped one or all of you were still around to have started it. I have to remember to say a few extra Our Fathers for his deliverance. Oh, but you should see the fire from below. Absolutely cataclysmic. Every scrap of vegetation is bursting into flame. It won't be long before every tree surrounding the hills is on fire. We're not getting down from here anytime soon."

The car shuddered as he cut the wheel hard to the right, keeping to a sharp bend in the path. I pulled my arm close in case we scraped along the hillside. I was hurt enough as it was.

"Which brings me to my main concern," I said. "How are you still alive?"

Matthias stepped on the brakes and the car came to an abrupt stop. My forearm caromed off the windshield. He fumbled with the inside pocket of his dusty vest.

His palm opened and in it was something round and made of metal. I couldn't make out any specific design in the dark.

"I survived because of this. And now I know at least part of what we're up against."

CHAPTER FORTY-SIX

Matthias leaned into me, so close that I could smell the staleness of his breath. His eyes sparkled with a mild sort of mania. "Have you ever heard of the Djinn?"

"I've had lots of gin in my time."

"I'm not talking about alcohol, Mr. Blackburn. The Djinn I'm referring to are spelled *d-j-i-n-n*."

I didn't have to turn around to know that Teta's hand was close to his gun. The air was unnaturally hot and we were shrouded by a haze of gray smoke. I didn't want to talk. I wanted Matthias to drive. But it didn't look like he had any intention of doing it until he'd said his piece.

"I can't say that I have, Matthias."

The metal disc was pinched between his thumb and index finger. He held it up to my face. "This is what put it all together for me. I was given this amulet as a gift from an Islamic Imam in California. We had worked together to rid a house of a very nasty spirit that had evaded every trick I had in my book. I've kept it on my person ever since."

"So what does it have to do with these Djinn?" I was growing irritable and had to suppress the urge to choke him. This confirmed for me that he was, indeed, Matthias.

"This is the fascinating part. The Djinn were a race of beings created by God after he made the angels, but before humans. They were made from fire and have coexisted with us for millennia. And, like us, the Djinn can be good, evil or indifferent. There are different levels of Djinn, each with their own powers and abilities. There are Sheytans, Afrits and the most powerful and dangerous of all, Marids.

"You see, if a Djinn makes up his mind to bedevil you, there are very few ways to drive him away. The evil Djinn are a nefarious lot.

Tricksters of the highest order. One of their greatest talents is that of a shapeshifter. For limited periods of time, they can take on the countenance of any living creature or even inanimate objects. Or, in our case, mystical man-beasts. I should have realized it when they turned to smoke and ash when we mortally wounded them. Beings of fire, when wounded, will return to some form of their core being. But you see, we weren't killing them at all, because they can't be killed. We simply broke their hold on the shape they had attuned their energy to become."

I must have gone mad because he had my full attention, and part of me was buying his story.

"So every one of those things that we shot, sliced and set on fire is still alive?"

"I'm afraid so."

"This is bullshit," Teta snapped.

"Let's hear him out," I said, locking my eyes on Matthias. If the Djinn were shapeshifters, could one of them be wearing Matthias's face right now? Angus coughed, rocking the car. The smoke was getting thicker.

Matthias continued, though with a little less enthusiasm. He cast a nervous glance back at Teta. "When the wild men overtook me, I offered my soul up to the Lord and gave thanks for getting you closer to Selma. I shut my eyes as I waited for them to rip into my flesh. When nothing happened, I opened my eyes and was pleasantly surprised to see them backing away from the car. That's when I put two and two together. I raised the amulet before me and it was like bearing fire to a wild animal. They cringed, they cried, they fled. I drove among them, attempting to keep them out of the trees, to afford you ample time to find where Selma had been taken. Then I saw the fire, and made a mad rush to find who had survived."

My lungs started to hitch and my eyes burned. "I think we need to continue this while you drive."

He looked back at the advancing dark cloud. "I think you're right." It didn't take much to get ahead of the smoke.

I said, "So, we're dealing with a bunch of Djinn? There isn't a chance you have more of those whatchamacallits is there?"

"Amulets. And no, this is the only one. Like I said earlier, the

Djinn are only part of the problem. I think we have a mix of Djinn and Sheytans, but I've never heard of so many working in tandem like this. It's as if they're being controlled by another higher power. There are two theories about the Djinn in relation to why the bad ones prey on humanity. It's said that the creator vowed he would bestow grace on the greater of his two earthly creations, man and the Djinn. Naturally, the Djinn want to claim that honor and have worked very hard at imposing their will on men. They feed on fear and blood, easy enough things to acquire when they make their presence known to an unsuspecting human."

"Well, they've gotten some of my blood already," Teta said. "Any fear I may have given them is long gone. I'm one pissed-off Dominican right now."

Matthias raised a fist. "Good! We all need to drive fear from our minds. It will keep us strong and protect us."

"But what about this other, higher power you mentioned? What do you think that could be?"

Matthias's lips pulled back into a tight line and his face paled in the light of the torch. "There's only one I can think of. Satan."

When I turned, Teta was making the sign of the cross.

"Matthias, the devil is something folks made up to scare people into doing right."

"Do you believe in God?"

"I have a strong suspicion he's real, yes."

"And you believe the supernatural origin of the things you've seen and experienced since you've come to Hecla?"

"Unless I'm having one hell of a hallucination, yes. And that's because I have the scars to prove it."

"Don't discount the existence of the devil. You can't have good without the counterbalance of evil."

His head swiveled forward and he stomped on the brakes. The car fishtailed and skidded to a stop. The large mineshaft that Teta and I had first explored loomed to our right.

"The devil is real, Mr. Blackburn, Nat, and he's here, in Hecla. The Djinn are acting on his behalf. They are, in fact, his slaves. We should pity them as much as the souls of the men, women and children that have fallen prey to the evil in this place. The question is, why is the devil here and what can we do to send him back to hell?"

The tall order of finding and saving Selma got higher than the peaks of the Rockies. What I didn't dare say aloud was that I chose not to believe in the devil because doing so was terrifying. As a kid studying the Bible with my mother, I tended to gloss over the fire-and-brimstone parts. I slept better that way. As an adult, I'd done my share of bad things, usually to bad people. It was easier to draw on a man if you didn't have to worry about burning in hell for eternity.

Now, if Matthias was right, I'd rode right into hell on a rented horse and damned some good people in the process.

And if the Bible was right, my soul was already good and tainted. I was, in fact, home. A man should be comfortable in his home.

We got out of the car and gathered at the opening of the mine. It stared back with the same black, fathomless mystery as the spirit children. A cold draft drifted up from its depths, chilling our exposed skin.

"You're not buying all of this, are you?" Teta asked.

I breathed deep, feeling the weariness in my bones. It would be so easy to just lie down and go to sleep. And if that sleep were permanent, all the better.

"I don't know. You're the one who couldn't make the sign of the cross fast enough."

"Catholic missionaries lived in my village. The only person that scared us more than the devil was our mothers. There are people in places I've left behind who would swear *I* was the devil. Kind of ironic, isn't it? But I never heard of Djinn or shapeshifters."

"I haven't either, but it's all we have at the moment. Maybe if we go with the worst-case scenario, the rest will seem easy."

"We can only ask the Lord for such a gift," Matthias said. "But I think he has other plans for us."

There were no pine trees, or any trees for that matter, around this opening. They had been cleared long ago to make way for men and their machines. It was the original one we had entered days earlier. I remembered when the tunnel went to hell and hoped we weren't met with a wall of fallen rock deep inside. The flames from our torches were growing weaker by the moment.

"I'll take the lead. We better move fast before we lose the torches altogether," I said. "I'll fix them," Angus said. He took both torches and ground out the flames under his boot.

Teta yelled, "Have you lost it? We need those!"

Angus paid him no mind. Instead, he went to the car and pulled a couple of shirts out from under the front passenger seat. There was a small kind of toolbox in the rumble seat and from that he got a long, thin hose. He wrapped the shirts around the ends of the torches, then inserted the hose into the car's gas cap. Sucking on its end, his chest heaved and he coughed, spitting out a mouthful of gasoline. He doused the torches with the gasoline and extracted the hose.

"Here, light them when we're inside the tunnel."

The odor coming from his mouth was strong enough to catch fire. I'd make sure to light them away from his trailing breath.

"Teta and I have been in here before. You really have to watch your step as much as your head. There are tracks everywhere, and in some places, the steel and ties are buckled. It's also wet and cold."

Teta snickered. "Funny, I never thought of being cold in hell."

Angus crouched by the entrance and waved us on. "This isn't the heart, but there is something here. I'll get the chest."

He unlashed the chest from the back of the car and had to hold it in front of himself with two hands. I wasn't sure if Teta, Matthias and I, combined, could have carried it.

"It gets narrow inside," I said. "I'm not sure you or the chest is going to fit."

"I'll take it as far as I can," he replied with a flat expression.

This time, I gave a torch to Teta so he could take the rear. Knowing that the wild men, or Djinn appearing as wild men, were still out there, gathering strength to re-form, I felt safer knowing Teta and his guns were covering our escape. I gave the other to Matthias. "Stay close to me. I'd rather have my hands free, if you get my drift."

"Guns to fight the devil. It's a novel concept," he said. So was introducing my elbow to his mouth.

*   *   *

We crept into the shaft. The temperature dropped considerably. It was a welcome reprieve from the heat that the forest fire had birthed in the past half hour. There was a good chance that we would be parboiled if we stayed outside much longer. My shirt, damp with sweat and blood, was cold against my skin.

Our footsteps sounded like thunder in the silence. The steady drip of water echoed back to us. My toes froze just recalling the last time we'd been here.

Matthias reached out to touch one of the wooden support beams. The tinder crumbled like dried leaves in his hand.

"The wood shouldn't do that," I said. "This mine hasn't been around long enough for that kind of rot to set in."

"There's a rot far more pernicious here," Matthias said. His breath turned to vapor the moment it left his mouth.

I suddenly felt a lot less safe, traipsing through the tunnel, knowing the heavy timber was more decorative than functional. I didn't know a man who wasn't terrified of the thought of being buried alive.

Angus grunted as the chest clipped the walls of the tunnel.

I said to Matthias, "How do you keep a spirit that isn't physical locked up in a box like that? Can't they just pass through the wood and be on their way?"

"The chest is almost symbolic. Angus binds them within it."

"Binds them? You mean he locks them inside?"

"Precisely."

"How does he do that?"

Matthias smiled. "I'm glad to see you're asking the right questions. Maybe there's hope for all of us." His torch scraped against one of the support beams along the ceiling and orange embers flittered down onto my hat. We stopped to make sure the rest of the beam didn't ignite. When we resumed, he continued. "Angus was born with an ability to communicate with the spirits around us."

"You mean his deadspeak?"

"You've spoken to him about it?"

"Heard him speak it, back on the east side of the hills. He used it to talk to those children spirits. I couldn't understand a word of it."

"No one can, at least no one who lives and breathes, with the exception of Angus, of course. I once asked him to teach it to me and he simply couldn't recall it. The words come to him when they need to, and leave no impression on his mind in their wake. I believe that the divine truly works through him, which is why I left my ministry to travel with him these many years."

We came to the fork in the tunnel and I hissed a string of cusses that made Matthias shrink.

Teta said, "Weren't there two tunnels when we came here?"

"Yes."

Only now there were three.

CHAPTER FORTY-SEVEN

It was obvious where the third tunnel had sprouted. It branched off at our extreme right, a good distance from the two that we had explored days ago.

"Shafts don't just make themselves," Teta said.

"I guess in Hecla they do," I replied. "Maybe that's what happened when we first came here. It wasn't a cave-in. The Djinn, the devil or whatever else is in here made a nice little corral for us to follow."

"That's *muy* polite of them. I don't like to have to think about where to go when I'm being led to the slaughter."

Matthias turned to him and propped a hand on his shoulder. "If it will make you feel better, think of it as we're already dead. At worst, we'll be brought back to the pain and suffering of life on earth. At best, we'll join our Heavenly Father, where we rightly belong, and enjoy a richness of the soul that could never be matched by the vainglorious wealth of the physical world."

Teta's eyes bored a hole through Matthias's hand, but the reverend didn't take notice. He replied, "That doesn't help at all."

Matthias gave his shoulder a final squeeze. "Have faith and it will."

It was easy to believe that I had been hit in the head back when we first rode into Hecla and had fallen into a deep dementia. The Deep Rock Hills were the bowels of a dank asylum, and I had three inmates to keep me company.

Just keep your mind on Selma. Stay angry. I am not afraid of the mines.

"Faith or not, let's go," I said. I pulled the hammer back on the rifle and kept my finger on the trigger guard. I could pull it in less time than it would take to blink.

The unrelenting stream of ice water didn't meander into the new tunnel, which was also absent of tracks or timber support. It was as if a giant, rock-eating mole had carved its way through, chomping stone in a desperate bid to find the center of the earth. We hadn't gone far before our balance wobbled. The tunnel, though high enough to stand upright, took a sharp decline.

I had to reach a hand out and dig my fingers into the sharp corners and niches in the uneven wall to steady myself. I thought of Angus and his chest and how he'd roll over us if his feet went out from under him. Hopefully his own massive gravity kept him sure-footed.

When I looked back, I saw that he had to step sideways down the tunnel so the chest could go through.

We had to walk slowly. The tunnel reverberated with the sound of our footsteps, heavy breathing and the fluttering of the torch flames. I shivered. It was starting to feel like winter in the mountains.

$$\star \quad \star \quad \star$$

Something else was with us.

The sound came as quickly as it went. I whispered, "Whoa, stay still a moment." Angus stumbled and the chest dinged me in the back.

Teta asked, "What did you—"

"Shhh!"

There it was again – so soft you could easily miss it or mistake it for the passing of air through the shaft that shouldn't be here.

There was a staggered breath, then a quiet, muffled cry. Someone was sobbing.

We listened some more. It was definitely a woman crying, but in a way that sounded as if she was trying to hold it back in case someone heard her, someone who would give her an even better reason to weep.

It had to be Selma. I wanted to shout for her, but if she was being cautious, there had to be a good reason.

The tunnel was dark as a root cellar and seemed to go on forever. There was no telling how far she was from us.

If her sobbing was being used as a way to draw us in, so be it. Almost more than seeing Selma again, I wanted to face the bastard that had turned Hecla into a chasm of no return. I nudged Matthias to resume walking.

"Would you like me to absolve you of your sins before we go much farther?" he asked. I didn't answer.

Instead, I squeezed by him, my back raking across the jagged wall, opening up a new set of welts. I wanted to be the first. I had to be the first. Even with his torch behind me, it gave off enough light to see by.

Selma's quiet weeping came and went as we descended. She sounded hurt, scared, lost and, worst of all, alone. With every step, I hoped she would hear us coming.

"This has to end somewhere," Teta grumbled from the back. He was anxious. We all were. Selma's crying suddenly cut off in midsob. If I didn't know better, I would swear someone had clamped their hand over her mouth and whisked her away.

"Come on, you son of a bitch," I rasped, grinding my back teeth so hard pain radiated from my jaw to the top of my skull.

The tunnel curved ahead, and in the bend I saw flickering light.

I wanted to run, but I slowed instead. We were close. I had to be smart about this. "Teta, switch places with Matthias."

There was a lot of huffing and grunting as Teta wormed his way past Angus and the oversized chest. We inched our way to the bend. When we got there, I poked my head around, had a quick look and pulled back.

"There's an opening on the left. Looks like it leads to either another tunnel or a chamber. That's where the light's coming from."

Matthias said, "Here, take the amulet. It will protect you if there are any Djinn waiting for you."

I waved his offer off. "You keep it. If those wild men-Djinn decide to clog the tunnel, you can drive them back with it and get us out of here."

To Teta, I said, "I'm going to scoot past the opening. You pull up on this side and we'll go in together, barrels first."

"*Comprendo*, jefe."

I patted him on the chest, took a deep breath and ran around the bend. I glanced into the opening and saw that it was, indeed, a chamber, and a large one at that. I slammed my back against the wall and watched Teta do the same on the opposite side of the opening.

My head was spinning. Wavering tongues of light danced along the rock face. I imagined fireflies swarming around me like they would during hot nights on a cattle drive. My legs were rubber and my teeth chattered so hard my jaw hurt.

In the instant I had been able to see inside the chamber, my world, which had been turned upside down, was thrown spinning.

It can't be!

I tried to settle down, but my body betrayed me. My mind wasn't far behind. Death no longer had meaning.

★   ★   ★

"Are you all right?" Teta whispered.

I wasn't. At all. My nerves tingled and my skin felt like it was on fire. It was hard to draw a breath. An invisible hand had reached inside my chest and was slowly crushing my heart, making black spots float around the edges of my vision. I couldn't seem to keep my head up and the thought of moving was as unwelcome as having a tooth pulled.

"Nat," he said, his voice rising.

I ground the inside of my lip to give my system a jolt. The taste of copper flooded my mouth.

I didn't want to look inside that chamber again. And yet more than anything in the world, I did.

For the first time in my life, I was paralyzed with indecision. I wasn't doing anyone, including myself, any good leaning against the wall, wondering if I was going to pass out or not. I collected myself as best I could and looked at Teta, nodding.

Before I could second-guess myself, I pivoted around the entrance and entered the chamber.

It was roughly the shape of an oval, with a ceiling that must have been at least ten feet high. A half-dozen torches burned along its curved walls, their handles jammed into fissures in the rock. Two tunnels branched off at the end of the chamber, dark voids to deeper recesses under the hills.

But it wasn't the chamber that shook me.

A lone, pale stalagmite rose from the center of the chamber floor. A woman was lashed to the stalagmite with long leather straps. Her head rested on her shoulders and her eyes were closed. Someone, or something, had knocked her out cold.

It wasn't Selma.

Her curly, blonde hair obscured half of her face, but I'd seen enough to know exactly who it was, and it was impossible.

My Lucille, as young and beautiful as she'd been the day she died almost thirty years before, lay at my feet, her dress in tatters, exposing her pale, tender flesh. Red welts and bruises blossomed across her arms, back and neck.

You can't be here, Lucille. I watched you die. After I buried you, I spent five years doing my damnedest to get killed so I could be with you again.

I put you in the ground myself. I buried everything I ever wanted to be or hoped to have with you that day. I still see your face every night before I fall asleep, clear as if we'd just said good night.

Why are you here?

I didn't notice Teta come in behind me. He ran to the back of the stalagmite and had his knife in his hand. He was going to cut the straps that bound Lucille's wrists.

I shouted, "Wait!"

Teta paused, the sharp blade resting against the leather. "Matthias, come here now!"

Angus and Matthias entered the chamber. Angus placed the chest on the ground. I held out my hand.

"Give me the amulet."

He pressed it into my palm. Teta stared at me, questioning, but trusting enough to back away from Lucille. There was no way he could know who the woman was, but he must have seen the choked panic in my eyes.

"You said this thing repels the Djinn?" I asked, turning to Matthias.

"Most certainly."

All eyes were on Lucille. Her skin was almost translucent. If I hadn't seen her breathe, I would have sworn she was dead.

But she is dead!

My boots scraped across the floor as I got closer. I pushed her hair back behind her ear. There was her face. The delicate jawline I'd traced my fingers along, the line of sun freckles that marched over the bridge of her nose and eyelashes so long they could almost touch her eyebrows.

It couldn't be Lucille. I knew that. The dead don't rise from the grave.

My hand shook as I brought the amulet closer, waiting for her eyes to flutter open, waiting for her to turn to smoke like the other Djinn. Their image of her was so heartbreakingly perfect it would be like watching her die again.

I held the amulet to her cheek. Her flesh was warm and supple. Alive. Nothing happened.

I turned to Matthias. "If she was a Djinn, she would have reacted, right?"

He came over and looked Lucille over. He took the amulet from me and laid it on her forehead. Her brow twitched, but that was all.

"This woman is no Djinn, Nat."

"Teta, cut her free."

I pulled her into my arms, burying my face in her hair. She smelled like sun and crisp spring air and the homemade soap she always used, made from wild flowers and honey. I could feel the bones beneath her flesh, savor the rise and fall of her chest against mine.

I kissed her lips, tasted her breath.

"Nat, what's going on? Do you know her?" Teta said. He'd rolled the straps around his hands and was crouched down next to me.

"It's...it's Lucille," I said, my voice trembling. He shuffled back.

"You said she died when you were a kid."

"She did."

I wanted to cry. I wanted to shout. I wanted to scream at a God that could take her from me, only to deliver her when I was in the bowels of hell on earth.

"How long ago did she die?" I heard Matthias say. My eyes were closed, lost in the tangle of her hair, in the rush of having her in my arms.

"Twenty-five years, maybe more," Teta replied.

Something heavy scraped across the floor. When I looked up, Angus stood over us, the chest open and by my outstretched feet.

"Please," he said, "let me talk to her."

He flinched at the sound of my pistol's hammer being drawn back. "You stay away from her!" I snarled.

I didn't want Angus or his damn spirit chest to come anywhere near Lucille. And despite the situation we were all in, I was ready to make things much worse.

CHAPTER FORTY-EIGHT

"Nat, don't be crazy," Teta urged. He motioned for Angus to step back. "That can't be Lucille. You know it can't."

"Don't you fucking tell me it can't!" I shouted, pulling her closer to me. Any harder and I'd crush her. "You saw it with your own eyes! The amulet didn't do a thing to her. I don't know how this is happening, but she's real. For Christ's sake, look at her. She's breathing."

As I smoothed her silky hair with my rough hand, I detected a large knot on the back of her head. Someone had hit her pretty hard.

"But you said you saw her die."

"I did. Or, maybe I was wrong. Maybe I buried the wrong woman. I don't know." And I didn't care. All that mattered was that Lucille was alive.

Matthias eased closer. "I can only imagine the emotions that are running through you right now, Mr. Blackburn. In light of everything you've experienced, I think it would be prudent if Angus took a moment to examine her."

"He a doctor?"

"No, he's not."

"Then fuck off."

"Does any of this seem natural to you? If the devil is truly here, he's using her to play with your mind."

I didn't allow his words to sink in. "Jefe, what about Selma?"

A dull pressure built behind my eyes. Selma.

Finding Lucille, I had completely forgotten about Selma, the reason we were here in the first place. Gazing at Lucille's fair skin and golden hair, I was finding it hard to recall what Selma even looked like. Searing pain knifed through my skull. Every thought felt fuzzy around the edges.

Teta said something to Matthias but I couldn't make out the words. I kept my eyes on Angus.

The ground began to vibrate and the walls sang a hideous chorus of stone being compressed to the breaking point.

"Shit, shit, shit!" Teta yelled.

The hills above us grumbled and shook. A cascade of loose rocks and dirt rained from the ceiling. Something roared in the tunnel where we had come from. We jumped when a boulder the height and width of the chamber entrance rolled into sight, wedging itself into our only means of escape.

Angus picked up his chest, looking to Matthias for a course of action.

Holding Lucille to my chest, I shouted above the din of the quake, "We have to make for those tunnels!"

I had to shift Lucille so she was over my shoulder. I grabbed one of the torches from the wall and ran for the tunnel on the left. "Come on!"

No sooner had I stepped inside than the entire façade came crumbling down. I turned to sprint, my instinct to take my chances and try for the other tunnel where everyone else had gone. But I was too late. The way out was blocked by a mound of heavy rocks.

I'd been separated from the others. But I still had Lucille.

★ ★ ★

When everything settled down and the Hecla mine was satisfied that it had sequestered our little rescue party, I hammered the butt of the rifle on the wall.

"Can you guys hear me?"

If they said something, I couldn't hear it, but I did hear three sharp raps against the wall. At least I knew they'd made it. Hefting Lucille into a better position across my shoulder, I started walking. My choices were limited at this point. I was truly at sea, mentally, physically and emotionally. The only thing to do was see where the tide took me.

After every few feet, I tapped on the wall to show them I was advancing down the tunnel. I was met with responding knocks as they kept pace. The farther I walked, the lower the ceiling became. It would be hard if I had to crouch with Lucille on my shoulder, one hand on my rifle and the other on the torch.

I kept walking and listening to the steady rhythm of Lucille's breathing. Words were too inadequate to describe how I felt, holding her once again. No matter how high my joy, there was a sinister low lurking around the corner.

The tunnels must have diverged, because the taps began to grow weaker as the wall between us grew thicker. Pretty soon, I didn't hear any at all. I had to bend my knees to keep from hitting my head. Lucille's dead weight was almost too much for me to handle. I had to set her down and see if I could wake her up.

I laid her across my lap, cradling her head in the crook of my arm. The lump on her head hadn't gotten any bigger, which was a good sign.

"Lucille," I whispered. My shaky fingers touched her cheek, her chin, her nose. "Baby, wake up. Can you hear me? It's Nat. Please open your eyes. I know it might be hard to recognize me. A lot of hard years have come and gone since I last held you like this. Me, I look like an old horse put out to pasture. But you're just as beautiful as the day we met. Lucille."

I leaned over her face and softly blew the hair from her forehead. I moved down to her neck, just the way I used to wake her up in the morning. She'd said it tickled, and she'd rather wake up to a tickle than a holler or a raggedy cock crowing.

"Come on, Lucille. Come back to me."

Something shifted in the darkness up ahead. It could have been rocks still falling after the quake.

It could have been anything.

I kept blowing on her neck and rubbing her wrists, anything to get her blood flowing. There was a narrow crack in the wall opposite us. I wedged the torch handle into it. The flame was still burning strong, which was a good thing. Aside from giving the only light, it meant there was ample air in here, at least for now.

Lucille's lips were dry and chapped. I pressed my lips against them. They were cold, but not with the chill of death.

As I pulled away, her eyes flashed open. The hazel of her eyes burned with an intensity I'd only seen when she was angry or frightened.

"Where am I?" she said, looking about, trying to make sense of her surroundings.

"You're with me, Lucille. Just stay calm."

My heart trip-hammered at seeing those eyes and hearing her voice. When she tried to lift her head I said, "Take it slow. You took a pretty good shot to the head."

She settled back into my lap and seemed to see me for the first time. "I know you," she said.

"I don't look the same."

Her hand brushed my stubbled cheek. "Nat," she said.

"Yes, it's me."

"I've missed you."

"Not any more than I've missed you."

"What is this place?"

"We're in a mining tunnel, I think. When you feel up to it, we'll start moving again, try to find our way out."

"How did I get here? I can't remember anything."

"I don't know, honey. Maybe you'll recall when your head clears up."

It was as if there weren't a thirty-year gap since the last time we'd seen one another. I didn't want to say anything that would be too big of a shock to her system.

She rolled to her side and pushed herself into a sitting position. She winced and her fingers flew to her head.

"Does it hurt?"

"Some."

"I wish I had some water or something to give you, but I've kinda been playing things by ear ever since I got here."

Her eyes went to the rifle. "There's trouble."

"Of a kind, yes. It's nothing I can't handle, now that I have you back."

"Back?"

"Never mind. God, you're as beautiful as ever."

"I must look a mess." She gave a disappointed glance at her clothes.

I tucked my hand under her chin and lifted so I could look into her eyes. "I've never seen anyone more beautiful."

She smiled and I felt the blue birds fluttering in my stomach. She could always do that to me with such ease, make me feel like a kid gawking at the first pretty woman who caught my fancy.

Something shuffled in the distance. I picked up the rifle, aiming it over her shoulder. "Teta, is that you?"

My voice raced down the tunnel with a low, deep echo. All was quiet again.

"Who's Teta?"

"A good friend. We'll find him, or he'll find us. You think you can walk?"

Even though the tunnel was getting smaller, she was slight enough to be able to walk without bending over. I took her hand in mine and tried to help her to her feet. A snap of electricity threw out blue sparks at her touch and she snatched her hand back.

"Well, that shows we still got it."

Her eyes were wide as saucers. She seemed to shrink into herself and her lips curled back

"I'm so sorry," she said.

"There's nothing to apologize for. It only hurt for a second."

"Not that. For everything. For now."

"I don't know what you mean."

"He – forced me to do it."

That got my dander up. "He? Who is *he* and what did he force you to do?" I felt the slow boil of red-hot rage start to simmer. She must have been talking about the man who'd beaten her up before I found her.

"I loved you, Nat. I never wanted to hurt you." Her hand trembled as she reached out to touch me. She pulled it back when I stepped closer.

I couldn't bring myself to say she never hurt me, because her death damaged me in more ways than I could count. But it hadn't been intentional. I'd never stopped loving her. I never blamed her for dying.

Tears rolled down her cheeks. "It hurts so much to see you. He wanted me to hurt. He wants everyone to hurt."

"Lucille, I don't know what you're talking about. You have to help me out here."

She shook all over. Her head dropped and she looked away from me. "You have to find Selma. I won't help him anymore."

"How do you know about Selma? You have to tell me who you're so afraid of. I won't let anything happen to you again."

Now she looked up, and her eyes swam with tears. "I love you, Nat. He brought me back to hurt you, to hurt us."

"Lucille, I've never loved anyone but you."

The rustling in the distance started up again. I squinted to see if I could make out anything, but it was darker than night past the flickering circle of light.

"Save Selma, Nat. Only you can. You went where no other man has gone and found me. Keep going. Find her."

"Lucille, you're starting to scare me. Just let me hold you and we can talk this through. I'm worried that bump on your head has you all confused."

There was a sharp crack, as if part of the tunnel wall had broken free.

"Who's there? Teta? Matthias? Angus? Say something before I start shooting."

Lucille's lips quivered, and this time she did touch me. Her hand wrapped around mine. "You were always there to protect me."

Something enormous and black and vile smelling catapulted from the darkness. Lucille gasped, but her face showed a grim acceptance that made my heart sink. What looked like a hand, one big enough to curl around her from her waist to her neck, pulled her into its grasp.

"Lucille!"

I aimed at the hand, but any shot I took would hit her as well.

She looked at me one last time. Her mouth moved but no sound came out. I couldn't make out what she was trying to say.

And then the hand pulled her into the darkness faster than any bullet could follow.

She disappeared in utter silence. One second she was there, the next she was gone. I shouted until my throat was raw; until flecks of coppery blood coated my tongue. I fired a shot into the dark. The report was deafening.

It was a blessing I didn't have to hear my own cries.

CHAPTER FORTY-NINE

I plunged into the tunnel, going as fast as I could without falling or cracking my skull. I had to keep wiping my eyes with the back of my hand to clear the tears that blurred my vision. I called out for Lucille. I tensed, waiting for the black hand to reach out for me next. The tunnel narrowed, and I had to get on my hands and knees to proceed. The uneven rock floor stabbed my knees and palms. I barely registered the pain, didn't even realize how bad it was until I went to lift the torch a little higher and it slipped from my hand because of all the blood. "Lucille!"

She'd kept talking about *he* and how *he* made her do it and *he* brought her back. Could a Djinn be a he? I knew she wasn't one of them. Or was it the higher being that also controlled the Djinn? There was nothing higher about giving Lucille back to me, only to take her away. With my fury came a cold, black numbness that surrounded me. I had killed men in my time, but never did I desire to see someone die at my feet like I did now. I had always killed out of self-preservation or for a cause greater than myself.

Now, I just wanted revenge.

Save Selma.

How did she know about Selma? If she was aware that Selma was held captive, did she also know how I had felt about her? Could she sense the betrayal that twisted my heart?

★   ★   ★

When I was thirteen, I was with my father riding cattle up to Kansas City. We'd taken a late afternoon break so my father could get some supper together. It was one of the rare times he told me I didn't have to help him, so I was free to do what I wanted. Not that there was much to do on an open trail, surrounded by farting cattle and tired, dirty cowboys.

We'd had a couple of dogs that followed along with us, two mixed breeds that actually helped keep the herd in line. It was like they'd been cowboys themselves, now trapped in mangy dogs' bodies. I was playing with one of the dogs. We didn't give them names. We wrestled over a stick, the dog baring its teeth and snarling while I tried to pull the stick from its mouth. Its tail wagged as it whipped its neck from side to side, trying to break my grip.

I realized I'd need two hands if I was going to win the tug-of-war. The moment I put my other hand on the stick, the dog's tail stopped wagging. I guess it didn't like the thought of losing. Its jaw released the stick and it snapped at me. One of its canines caught the soft spot between my thumb and index finger and tore a ragged hole through it. I yanked my hand back, and my blood splashed into my eyes, stinging me.

My next recollection was my father pulling me off the dog. When I looked down, it was dead. I had beaten it to death with the same stick we'd been having fun with just a minute earlier.

As my father cleaned the wound, he said, "Son, you're not going to be long for this world if you don't learn to control your temper. Dogs bite. You can't get mad at nature for doing what it was made to do. And you can't go around killing everything that hurts you."

★   ★   ★

I kept on. When my back scraped against the top of the tunnel, I bit down on the pain. I put it out of my mind that I could be wedged down here, trapped, and die a slow, maddening death.

My father died when he was forty-one. He was a kind man who never hurt a soul. I'd outlived him by ten years and had more notches in my belt than I cared to consider.

"You were wrong, Pa," I huffed, pulling myself forward with my arms, having to toss the torch ahead of me. "Sometimes nature has to be put down."

My rifle raked across the ground and I grunted with every thrust forward. My lungs were on fire. It was an effort to draw a full breath.

Save Selma.

Had I been too late, too slow to save Selma?

He would have to answer for that.

The tunnel walls had boxed me in. I could barely move forward, and there was no chance of turning around. Trapped like one of Angus's angry spirits.

My fingers jittered as I groped to find something to latch on to, to keep moving, even if it was just an inch.

The flames from the torch dwindled. It was either burning out or there simply wasn't enough air to keep it lit. I watched it dim from orange, to blue, to the soft glow of dying embers. It was darker than dark, a total nothingness that made me feel as if I'd left my body. If it weren't for the crushing grip of the tunnel, I would have felt weightless.

I was so damn tired. I couldn't breathe. Darkness curled at the edges of my mind.

Keep moving, damn you!

Save Selma!

I'd always done whatever Lucille had asked.

My fingertips scoured the edge of – what? It was probably a raised part of the rock surface. I gripped it as hard as I could and pulled. My body inched ahead, slowly, painfully.

I wasn't afraid to die.

I just didn't want to disappoint Lucille. And I didn't want to fail Selma. My chin ripped open against a serrated stone.

I kept pulling.

I let go of the rock and reached ahead. There was nothing. The tunnel floor simply fell away. A cold breeze made my hand tingle.

The end of the line. I laid my head down, conscious of every labored breath, wondering how many more I still had in me.

"I'm sorry, Selma," I rasped.

I'm sorry, Lucille. Sorry that I can't do what you asked. Sorry that you've been damned to a place like this just because you made one wrong, fatal decision.

If this was hell, it tore me up inside to think that this is where she ended up, just like the preacher had warned me when we made plans for her burial. Well, at least I wouldn't have to travel far to be with her again.

It was time to let go, and I was fine with it.

I tried to cough but my ribs were too constricted. White spots swirled before my eyes.

I laid my head down and waited for the inevitable.

The tunnel began to vibrate.

The floor abruptly gave way. I instinctively clutched my rifle. And then I was falling.

Spinning end over end into nothing.

CHAPTER FIFTY

I landed on my back on something that gave way with a tremendous crack. A sandstorm of dust clogged my nose and mouth, choking me.

I mustn't have fallen far or else I wouldn't have been alive to cough out half my lungs. I was just grateful that I could still draw a breath, and a good one at that, even if it was laced with something that smelled old and musty and plain terrible.

Live to fight another day.

My ribs were sore, both from the fall and racking coughs. I spit the chalky crap from my mouth. If I dragged my tongue over my teeth, I could feel a cake-like residue left on them.

There was no light, and no way for me to tell where I was. When I tried to move, whatever I was laying on shifted and pitched me forward at an angle. I didn't want to fall again, so I lay still, gathering myself and waiting for the dust to settle.

Matches! Carefully, I felt around my pockets. My empty tobacco pouch was still there, but the matches I kept next to it were gone. They must have dropped out when I fell.

Blood rushed to my head and I realized I was hanging upside down. I slowly raised myself and got into a position where the rush of my pulse wasn't deafening. My ears were still ringing from firing my rifle in such tight quarters.

"This place just gets better and better."

My voice rebounded all around me. Wherever I had fallen, it must have been big. Something scuffled. It was impossible to know from which direction.

"Jefe? Nat?"

A pinprick of light appeared to my left. It looked low and far away. "Teta?" I said. My throat burned.

"Where are you?" he answered.

"I'll be damned if I know. Just try and follow my voice." I saw him holding a blazing torch high above his head. "I'm up here," I croaked.

Matthias and Angus were right behind him. They also had torches. Matthias called out, "Don't move! Hold steady until we can figure this out."

Not moving sounded like a fine plan to me. Every bone in my body hummed with agony.

"I'll come up to you," Teta said. He handed the rifle to Matthias and clenched the torch between his teeth.

I joked, "It's a good thing your sombrero isn't here to see this. You'd burn it up with that torch."

"It's still here and it's still lucky," he said, scrabbling up to me.

"Lucky?"

"We're still alive, aren't we?"

After being with Lucille, I wasn't sure anymore. Maybe we had all died back there in the shaft, or maybe the wild men had overtaken us. Maybe this was a hell we'd never imagined. When Teta climbed next to me, everything began to slide. He grabbed hold of my shirt collar as we slipped a few feet. When it stopped, he took the torch from his teeth and held it out.

"Are you hurt?" he asked.

"Yes, but not so much as I can't move. I'll be all right as soon as I get off this pile of rocks and get my boots on the ground."

He shook his head, moving the torch around. I followed its path and immediately wished he'd kept things dark.

We were sitting atop a heap of bones that had to be at least forty feet high. From what I could see, it was a grisly collection of both animal and human bones. My hand rested on a human skull with a crushed eye socket. I jerked it back.

"We're going to have to slide down," he said. "I'll hold you so we go down together."

"I'll jump clear off just to get away from here."

Thinking that the dust I'd inhaled was actually ground bone powder made my stomach roll. My skin itched and it felt like tiny fingers were dancing up my spine. I wanted off. Now. I maneuvered myself so my feet pointed toward the ground. Teta and I clasped hands.

We only needed to shift our body weight to start the plunge.

Sharp bits of ribs and femurs nicked us as we slid. The descent was mercifully quick and my feet hit hard. We both stumbled but managed to stay upright, thanks to Angus's assistance. He placed a hand on our chests and bore the brunt of our fall.

"Thank you, Angus, again," I said, clapping him on the shoulder. "I'm sorry about what happened back there."

He nodded and went back to his chest.

"Where's Lucille?" Teta asked, dusting bone off his shirt and pants.

"She wasn't mine to keep. Something took her from me. But I think she knew that was going to happen. She kept saying *he* made her do it. She also said to save Selma." I turned to Matthias. "Are we dead?"

"No. But whatever is in control here wants us to wish we were dead. It wants us so frightened we'd rather pass away than face another moment. Of that, I can assure you."

"I just can't figure where Lucille fits into all of this," I said.

Matthias said, "If I may be so bold, I believe she was presented to you to break your spirit, to confuse you, to distract you from your one true purpose. Whatever is here needs you unbalanced and afraid."

I massaged the back of my neck. "Then I'll do my best to prove it wrong."

I heard a sharp click, then the whining of hinges. Angus had opened his chest. "That can't be a good sign," I said.

"There are no good signs down here," Teta said. "Where there are bones, there are spirits."

Angus stared at the mountain of bones, transfixed.

"If they're angry spirits, they're no more pissed off than me," I snarled. I wiped the blood from my palms onto my jeans. "What's he waiting for?" I asked Matthias.

"Sometimes, he has to let the spirits come to him. He can sense them. But I daresay they're not angry spirits."

"No? Then what are they?"

"Tortured. I can feel it myself. Angus is going to take them from here, and release them to a better place."

"Are there any other tunnels?" I asked Teta.

"No, just the one we came through that led to here. There might be something on the other side of those bones, but it's buried."

"So what's the sense of jamming that box full of spirits when we have nowhere to bring them?"

"Faith, Mr. Blackburn. Faith."

He was wrong about me. I did have faith.

I knew for sure we were never going to see the light of day again.

CHAPTER FIFTY-ONE

Angus's voice boomed with his creepy deadspeak, his echoes gaining intensity. Some of the bones on top of the mound began to shift. If he kept it up, he was going to bring the whole thing down on us.

"Ubataya singnot futool!"

He repeated the phrase over and over, until the air became electrified. Every hair on my body pricked. I felt like we were being watched. It was a far-from-pleasant sensation.

"Ubataya singnot futool!"

"Maybe he's calling more of those black-eyed kids to save us," Teta whispered. "For their sakes, I hope they're not down in this pit."

"Stop!"

It was the voice of an old man, grizzled by years, made weak and thin. From the bottom edge of the bone mound, something white, almost glowing, appeared. As it came closer, it grew, took shape, until it was a man.

Franklin.

He stopped before Angus, looked at me and smiled. It was enough to chill me to the core.

"You'll bring them all," he rasped. Then, to me he said, "I never wanted to be here. But where my brothers went, so did I. They said I was acting like an old, scared man. And now here I am. Punishment for not succumbing to the lure. They scared me then. They scare me now."

Matthias stood with openmouthed fascination. I reached out to Franklin. My hand passed through his chest, to an unseen, frigid core.

"But you're dead," I said. "What's left to be scared of when you die?"

His eyes grew sad and the smile faded. "So much more."

"Why do you keep appearing to us?"

"We need your help."

"I don't think we're in any position to help anyone. In fact, if it wasn't for those spirit kids, we'd probably be dead. If they can't help you, you're shit out of luck."

He considered me for a moment with an expression that was impossible to read. Matthias pulled a small leather Bible from his back pocket. "Is there anything I can read to you that can give you rest, perhaps comfort – help?" Franklin looked at him but didn't answer.

Matthias opened it to a random page and began to read from the Gospel of John. Franklin considered him with tenderness. The words flowed from Matthias as if he'd memorized every word.

Franklin put up a hand to stop him. "Thank you."

He looked at Angus's spirit chest. "The weight will be considerable. I can call them for you."

Angus was stoic. One hand rested atop the open chest.

"The others, they will follow, but there's nothing I can do about that." Franklin turned to the bones.

It was as if tiny fires spontaneously flickered to life within the hundreds of dark gaps. Small points of white light began to glow. The lights poured out of the bones, converging into the center of the mound until they formed a continuous streak of light that touched down to the floor. Human shapes made entirely of that light stepped from the flowing spring. We couldn't make out faces, but by their builds we could see some were men; others, women; and so many were children. Angus stepped back as they filed past Franklin, melting into the chest. Franklin reached out to touch them as they passed, his fingers drifting through them.

Dozens, then a hundred, and still more stepped into the chest.

I saw a man in uniform, then another. Teddy's troops. They didn't look my way as they followed the somber parade into the chest.

When the last spirit – a willowy woman by the looks of it – made its way, Angus knelt and carefully closed the lid. He muttered some deadspeak, too low for us to hear.

"He's sealing the box," Matthias said.

Then Matthias prayed over the chest, resting his Bible on the lid, his hands clasped together.

It was an amazing thing to see and, for once, I didn't have a hard time believing my eyes and ears. Maybe some of that faith was starting to rub off on me.

I said, "Franklin, why didn't you go in the chest?"

"I have more work. I can't see Momma until I'm done. Where's the dog?" he asked.

There was no soft way to put it. "We had to put him down. He turned. He was bad."

"Yes. Yes he was."

He began to walk back to the mound.

"You may want to protect yourselves," he said with his back to us.

"From what?" Teta asked.

"The glue has been undone. Even Jericho fell."

We looked at one another. Teta looked over his shoulder. "Shit, the bones," Teta said.

They had started to tremble. Skulls bounced crazily onto the floor, exploding into clouds of dust.

"Back to the tunnel!" I said.

Angus tucked the chest under his arm and was the first to run out of the cavern. We weren't far behind.

There was a tremendous explosion, and a whirlwind of bone dust blew over us. We tucked our faces into our shirts, shutting our eyes against the onslaught. It took several agonizing minutes to pass. I was grateful that it hadn't blown out our torches.

"If that bone mound collapsed, maybe there's a way out now," I said.

"I think we have to go deeper before we can rise," Matthias said.

"Nobody likes a pessimist."

Teta ducked in and out of the entrance. Then he craned his head back inside, his body following.

"Nat, you have to come in here." I ran into the cavern.

The entire bone mound was gone. It was as if it had never been there. The floor was gritty with white and yellow dust.

Teta pointed, and my eyes followed.

A small shape lay amongst the ruins. I ran to it, heedless of what might happen.

Worrying about what would befall us next was no longer a concern.

I skidded along the bone dust, stopping inches before the figure on the ground. "Selma."

CHAPTER FIFTY-TWO

Her head turned to me the moment she heard my voice. Unlike Lucille, she was conscious, and as I helped her up, she seemed, impossibly, unhurt. We looked at each other for what seemed like hours, then her eyes melted into tears and she fell into my chest. I held her, rubbing her back, trying to calm her sobs.

"Oh, Nat, I thought I'd never see you again."

It was disconcerting, hearing that for the second time that day, from another woman. I'd be damned, if I wasn't already, if I let something snatch her from me again. Whatever had tried to scramble my heart and brains with Lucille would have a hard time getting to Selma. She was alive, and here, and possibly my last shot at a future. Hecla's plan had backfired. Lucille was gone, and not to a better place. I couldn't be her savior now, just as I couldn't the day she decided to take her life. It was her telling me to keep searching for Selma that had lifted a weight from my soul, a dark shroud that many times had sabotaged my chances for a normal life.

I did like you asked, Lucille. I found her. Now comes the hard part. Saving her.

"Did the wild men hurt you?"

She shook her head against my chest.

"Do you remember what they did, where they took you?"

I couldn't imagine her surviving under the weight of all those bones. Again, wondering if we were all dead troubled my mind. Matthias couldn't know everything.

"I...I don't even know where we are now."

"Somewhere in the lower intestines of the Deep Rock Hills," Teta said, keeping his eyes peeled for anything to come out of the darkness.

"Whatever is in charge of Hecla and the mines used you to get us here," I said. "Now that it has us, I'm not sure what its next move will be."

"I'm just glad you're here," Selma said, wrapping me in a hug. She felt real. But so had Lucille. I wondered how I felt to her.

Teta shouted, "Hey, there's another tunnel back here!" Matthias and Angus came jogging up to us.

"You're all here," Selma said.

"A horde of wild men couldn't keep us away...literally," Matthias said with a grin.

Angus touched her face. "I'm happy to see you're okay."

"I guess there's only one way to go," I said. "Can you walk?"

"Yes, I'm fine. It feels like I've been sleeping. I remember being carried off by those creatures, and calling out for you, but that's it. The rest is blank."

"It's probably better that way." I whistled and Teta turned to me. "You want to take point this time?"

"Sí."

We followed him into the next shaft. This one was larger than the main access tunnel outside. We could easily walk four across, even with Angus. This was nothing that miners had ever dug out. It felt ancient. It reeked of centuries of decay and secrets. This had been here before the hills settled into position above us. It couldn't lead to anywhere good.

*   *   *

As we walked, Matthias explained his theory about the Djinn to Selma. He said knowledge was power and there was no reason to hide anything from her just because she was a woman. I wasn't in a mood to argue.

"So the Djinn are bad?" she asked.

"Not all, and I suspect the ones we've encountered are under a kind of spell. That doesn't mean they can't hurt us."

"If one of them tries to drink my blood, I'll make sure they choke on it," Teta said.

Our torches were growing dim. They had long outlasted their burning time, but like everything here, nothing about them was typical. I suspected they'd last just as long as they needed to in order to move us along.

The coolness of the tunnel had taken a turn, and the humidity began to rise. Our footsteps echoed down the vast passage. The more we walked, the hotter it became, which was a welcome relief for my joints. The cold had stiffened them up. Now I could walk a little easier. Tiny beads of sweat danced on Angus's shiny head as he lugged the full chest.

"Any theories on what we can expect?" I asked Matthias.

He sighed. "None, I'm afraid. Angus and I have seen a lot of strange places and done our fair share of odd deeds, but nothing like this."

"I keep wondering why they don't just come out and kill us," Teta said. "Or at least give it a real try."

"It's because we're not afraid," I replied, startled by my own words.

Matthias snapped his fingers. "I think you might be right."

"Of course I am. Whoever *he* is, he may have us where he wants us physically, but he can't get us there emotionally. He's not going for the grand finale until he pushes us exactly to the point he wants us."

It was like someone was talking through me, using my mouth and lungs and throat to put voice to the bare truth behind our predicament. I knew it was me. I just wasn't sure what part had taken control.

And to my surprise, I kept going. "You told me that the Djinn feed on fear. Maybe that's what kept drawing them to us, until they pushed us too far and the fear turned into something else. They thought they were dealing with regular people. I've been told more times than I can count that I'm not regular people, and it's usually not meant in a good way. Teta and I, we've survived off a controlled recklessness and learned how to use anger as a tool. In the lines of work that we've done, it's the only way to even hope of seeing another day. The Djinn, or whatever is controlling them, were doing a good job keeping us off-balance, what with the wild men, ghosts and that strange dog. When they took Selma, they overplayed their hand. Teta and I don't get scared, we get angry. And from what I can tell, you two actually *want* to be in the mix of things like this. I don't think they factored four folks like us coming together into their odds."

"Exactly why I can't understand why they don't kill us now," Teta said. "It would be easy. Just drop the roof on us. Problem solved."

Selma looped her arm through mine. "Maybe they can't."

Matthias said, "I get the feeling this has all been a game, and the prize is whatever amount of terror that can be induced in us. It's not so much that we die, more so that we die consumed with fear. So if we follow Mr. Blackburn's line of thinking, which I think we should, there is going to have to be an escalation of scale."

"Meaning?" I asked.

"I would think that if everything else has only succeeded in stoking your anger, the *he* in Hecla is preparing to up his ante."

The words hung in the air like a death sentence. Teta and I had been through a lot, but every man had his breaking point. I had no idea what Matthias and Angus's would be, and I worried about Selma.

I said, "I think it's best if we all just shut up and keep walking."

So we did. It felt like we were starting to ascend, if only slightly. The gradient of the tunnel was too minute to tell for sure. Rivulets of water wound down the cracks and crags in the walls, but didn't touch the floor. The walls swallowed up the water before it could collect at our feet.

It was getting hotter. My clothes stuck to my skin, the salt of my sweat stinging the wounds that covered me from head to toe.

I knew that lava was formed underground. Even though there were no volcanoes around, could there be a river of lava nearby? There was no way of knowing how deep underground we were. I was tempted to ask Teta. Maybe he'd read it in a book somewhere. But I was the one that told everyone to keep quiet, and I wasn't going to be the one to break the silence.

I looked over at Selma and offered a weak smile. Her hair was plastered to the side of her face, but she still looked beautiful. She smiled back and clutched my arm, as if to tell me she was all right and knew I would lead us all out of here.

Then I thought of Lucille, and a dull ache settled into my chest. It seemed an odd thing to fixate on, considering our situation.

That's exactly what Hecla, *he*, wanted. Why else bring Lucille back, only to snatch her away? Play with a man's emotions enough, you rob him of his ability to function.

I reached down and laced my fingers through Selma's. Her palm was damp and warm. "When we get you back to your ranch, I think me, you and your pa have to have a talk,"

I said softly.

"About what?"

"Certain long-term things."

It took her by surprise, and a welcome one at that. "I know I'm no spring chicken, but I can provide."

"I know you can."

The emotional turmoil that had been boiling inside me began to subside. For the first time since stepping off the train in Laramie, I felt sure of something.

Hecla and the Djinn could suck on that for a while.

Teta had moved ahead of us but not so far that we couldn't see his back, except when there were bends in the tunnel. I could hear each boot step clear as day, and I was immediately aware that he had stopped walking. We rounded the bend and he motioned for us to stop. The tunnel ended five feet from where he stood. Another tunnel sprouted to our right.

"We have company," Teta whispered.

★　　★　　★

I let go of Selma's hand to look into the next tunnel.

Seven men were gathered in a circle. But they weren't ordinary men.

These men glowed, like ghosts, but they appeared as solid as me or Teta. Their heads were bowed and they were muttering some kind of chant, but it didn't sound like English to me. One of them lifted his shaggy head, and I stepped back, out of sight.

"Franklin's in there."

"He keeps popping up like a bad penny," Teta said. "Except I don't think he's the bad one."

Selma tried to nudge past me. "I want to see."

I held her back. "Just hold on. We have to think before we do anything."

She slipped out of my hand and turned the corner. Her mouth dropped open. She covered it with her hands.

"Hank."

There was no sense hiding now. Teta, Angus, Matthias and I filled the entrance to the tunnel.

We faced what could only be Selma's husband, Hank, and his brothers. Judging by their appearance, they hadn't fared so well when they came searching for gold. Something else had found them first. To say they were a ragged bunch was putting things mildly. They broke their little circle and fanned out the length of the tunnel, forming a barrier between us and the next leg of our journey.

"What do you think, Matthias, Djinn?" I said out of the side of my mouth.

"Possible. Show them the amulet."

I took it from my pocket and flashed it at them, like I used to do with my badge back in New York. They responded the way most criminals did, with utter indifference.

They were all relatively young, with the exception of Franklin. They stared at us with empty, emotionless eyes.

"Hello, Selma," the one in the center said. He was tall and stocky with longish hair and a heavy beard. He didn't look happy to see her.

Selma's hands fluttered by her mouth but she couldn't say anything.

"You just couldn't keep away," he said. "I told you I'd find riches here. Oh, but it wasn't gold. It was so much more. Are you here to take it? Do you think you can?"

"Hank, what happened to you? What *are* you?"

Hank smiled, and there was only menace in it. "I'm exactly what I want to be. We all are. And we're not going to share with you. Do you hear me?" he shouted, his voice exploding in the tunnel and repeating itself.

"Nobody wants what you have," I said flatly.

"Angtha fithool!" Angus bellowed.

Hank and his brothers flinched, taking a step back. "They're dead," Matthias said. "Not Djinn."

Selma stiffened.

To Hank and his kin, Matthias said, "We can offer you peace and eternal rest." The brothers glared at us.

Angus opened the chest. Teta said, "Hey, isn't that going to let the spirits out?"

"They choose to be there," Angus replied in his rich baritone. "These spirits won't. This will be the last time I can open it."

Hank and his deceased brothers took a defensive stance. I wasn't sure how to fight a ghost. I was hoping Angus would have that covered.

Selma's voice shook when she said, "Hank, you have to help us. Please, as your wife, I'm begging you. Tell us how to get out of here."

Hank laughed. "I don't have a wife. You're just a half-breed whore who couldn't say no." The muscles in my shoulders tensed. I clenched my fists.

"There's no getting out of here," he said. "I'll make sure of that."

Selma looked like she wanted to rush him, and not for a warm embrace. I held her back with a tug on her elbow.

Teta spoke up. "Oh, we're getting out of here."

He walked to the line of incandescent brothers with a steady stride, as if he planned to pass right through them. The brother to the right of Hank, a squat man with arms like logs, punched Teta in the chest when he got too close. Teta stumbled back, clutching his chest.

That's when things went deeper into the shitter.

CHAPTER FIFTY-THREE

When Teta regained his footing, he lashed out with the butt of his gun, swiping it across the man's face. His cheek caved in and his nose flattened to one side. There was no blood. Teta pistol-whipped him again, this time caving in his eye socket and putting a considerable dent in the side of the man's head.

"I'd expect more from Selma," the brother said.

Teta hammered at his face, landing blow after blow. It was like his head was made of soft clay and Teta was resculpting it into something too grotesque to look at.

Hank and his brothers laughed when Teta stopped, winded. All but Franklin. The man's face was a deformed ball resting atop a thick neck.

Hank lashed out and smacked Teta to the ground.

That's when I leapt into them. They converged on me like it was a game of pile-on. I punched and jabbed and kneed my way out of the pile. At one point, I saw Teta join the fray and we both fought like there was no tomorrow, which seemed a distinct possibility.

I growled like an animal, taking all of my frustrations out on the solid ghosts. Faces, heads, arms and legs twisted into bizarre shapes. Their punches were very real, and my ribs and face ached. Unlike them, Teta and I were bleeding.

"Enough!" Matthias shouted.

We scrabbled, six on two, neither side willing to give in. I spotted Franklin off to the side, looking too old and frail to fight, even though he'd been the youngest. It had turned into a regular saloon brawl, except Teta and I had no chance of winning. How could you hurt someone who was already dead?

When Angus spoke, the men paused.

"Angtha fithool!"

It gave Teta and me a chance to stumble out of the pile. Selma grabbed our collars and pulled us to her. Matthias had his Bible in hand and was reading from it. Angus kept on with his deadspeak. Hank and his brothers looked like they wanted to attack him but were powerless to make a move.

They also didn't move toward the chest. From the way Angus was shouting and gesturing, I got the feeling he was ordering them to get in, but they wouldn't budge.

"These men are possessed," Matthias hissed.

"They're not men, they're goddamn spirits," I said, though the pain radiating throughout my body said otherwise.

"They died possessed, and their souls have been claimed. I have to cleanse them if we have any hope of getting past."

"Hank." His name fell from Selma's lips, heavy with sadness. He had been her husband.

At one time, she had loved him.

"Hank's gone," I said, draping an arm over her. "Believe me, nothing you see down here is real."

We all flinched when the crack of gunfire broke whatever stalemate we had achieved. Smoke spiraled from Teta's pistol. His bullet went through Hank and ricocheted off the wall behind him, pinging from wall to wall and down the tunnel.

"Well, Matthias, unpossess them!" Teta shouted.

Hank looked down at where the bullet would have shattered his rib cage and grinned.

Teta fired off two more shots, this time at Hank's brothers.

"Teta, stop wasting bullets," I snapped. "You can't kill them with that."

Matthias flipped through his Bible. "Oh my," he croaked.

"'Oh my' what?" I said.

"I always kept the rites of exorcism tucked into the pages of Ezekiel. They're missing.

They could have fallen out anywhere."

I grabbed his arm and turned him towards me. Hank and his brothers watched us, I'm sure having a good time seeing that we'd lost the one thing we could use against them. "You can quote chapter and verse from the Bible. You mean to tell me this is the one thing you haven't committed to memory?"

"I've only had to use the rites twice before. I don't spend much time reading it when I don't need it. There's not much comfort to be drawn from reading the passages, Nat."

"I hope you're nice and comfortable down here, because this is where we're going to rot."

He gazed at me with a look I'd seen many times before. He was sure I was about to hit him and didn't know whether to defend himself or run. That was good. I wanted him to be afraid. I'd seen fear make a man suddenly remember things he couldn't recall for the life of him moments before.

His eyes moved to the top of his head like he was inspecting his brain for the information.

Come on, Matthias. Think!

I kept an eye on Hank and his brothers, waiting for them to make a move toward us. If they did, I hoped Angus's deadspeak could get them back in line. "We're running out of time, Reverend."

"You don't understand. The rites of exorcism are very specific. One wrong or misplaced word can undo everything. Even if I tried, I could do more harm than good."

I let him go.

"So you're telling me there's nothing we can do."

"I'm afraid not. Angus could hold them in place for a spell, but they'd only come right back once he stopped."

"Nat." Selma melted into my side.

I took a deep breath, squared my shoulders and adjusted the brim of my hat. I pointed at Hank. "I've lived a long time, longer than even I expected. A lot longer than you. I've seen my share of dumbshits, and I've put a few of them where you are right now. Did I regret it? Can't say that I did. The world needs only so many dumbshits, and I figure I was put here to keep things in balance. You and your greedy, dumbshit family are just another to add to the heap. But the best part is, you already did it to yourselves. So why don't you come on over here and do your best. But know this. The minute you kill me, I'm coming right back, right here, and we're going to be even. You're not going to like what I do to you in a fair fight. No, sir, you're not going to like it at all. Dumbshits like you, dead or alive, you're worth about a drop of sweat to men like me."

I had them riled up. They seethed with hatred. I'd bet they'd turn down a chance at heaven just to have a go at me. So be it. We'd come pretty far and the Promised Land wasn't even a given for Moses. And he was someone God liked.

"Let's go, boys. Teta and I will have us a real hog-killin' time making you work hard for the first time in your sorry lives."

Angus balled his hands into fists and narrowed his eyes. He would certainly help to even things up. I meant what I said to them. Once I couldn't fight anymore and took my last breath, I would return to make their eternity a misery. Nothing ever seemed to escape Hecla's grip. At this point, I was happy to stay.

Both sides took a step to one another. I turned to Matthias and whispered, "If you can, take Selma and start looking for a way out. We'll keep them very occupied."

The reverend looked like he was about to soil his drawers, but he nodded and moved closer to Selma.

She'd heard what I said and looked about to protest, but I had something else to tend to. We took another step and were driven to our knees. The tunnel was filled with the overwhelming roar of a massive horn. It was the same sound we'd heard aboveground. Down here, the chest-rattling note was more than any of us could take, dead or alive. We rolled on the floor, our hands clasped over our ears. My head felt like it was going to explode from the inside out. The walls and floor of the tunnel shook. Even Hank was squirming on the ground, his face a mask of distress.

It was a nice sight to see.

My vision was going dark. The horn continued to blare, one long, deep, steady blast that sounded like the world was being split in two.

I fought to stay conscious. I couldn't let my mind run from the pain. That horn was blowing for a reason, and I wanted to make damn sure I was awake to find out what it was.

CHAPTER FIFTY-FOUR

When I was a kid, my mother used to call me *the defiant one*. She and my father often talked about what I'd done that day or what they hoped my future might entail, considering my stubborn streak. My father agreed that I could be an ornery little cuss, but he said it was the one trait that would serve me well in a world that was dead set against good men trying to scratch out a living.

Rolling on the tunnel floor, I heard my mother say, *"Do you know what your defiant one did today?"*

I answered in place of my father. "Yes, Ma, I do."

Phoooooooooommmmmmmmmm!

The horn kept on blaring.

I turned onto my stomach, tucking my knees under me and forcing my head from the dirt and filth. My balance was all off, but I got myself to one knee, then shuffled a bit before getting both boots on solid ground. Standing, the vibration of the horn rattled down my spine like an order to lie down and die.

That wasn't going to happen.

Every muscle burned as I struggled to stand, fought to keep my wits.

Defy the pressure of that horn.

Matthias thought it was the call to Armageddon. I was beginning to think he was right.

My heart quivered in my chest, punching the breath from my lungs. Still, I wouldn't go down. The next time I was on that floor, I'd be too dead to realize it.

I reached for my pistol, my hand quivering like a drunk in the dry, head-splitting morning. The tunnel stretched into infinite darkness. A gust of wind, kicked up by the bleating of the horn, hammered my face. It was down there. *He* was down there, hiding like a coward. My elbow felt like it would pop as I got the pistol from my holster, holding it up so it pointed straight into the black.

My heart jumped and I choked, desperate to find my next breath. The pistol almost slipped from my fingers. I eased the grip into my palm and raised it as far as I could, which was about hip high. My finger felt like it was crippled with arthritis. The trigger was an immovable object, no matter how hard I pulled.

Something tugged at my ankle. I rolled my eyes to look down. If I moved my neck even an inch, I knew the rest of me would collapse.

It was Teta. His face was twisted with pain, but he had dragged himself to my side. He had his pistol out, his arm straight along the tunnel floor. He struggled with the trigger too. His hand twitched, but he didn't have the strength to pull it back.

I wanted to say something to him, some last words before our souls were swallowed up by the mines. There was no way to be heard over the constant thrumming of the horn. Our guns would have to be our final say.

Concentrating with what little strength I had left, I directed all of my energy into my trigger finger. The hammer moved back as the trigger gave way. It went off with a sharp crack at the exact same moment as Teta's pistol.

Our bullets sailed into the unknown. And just like that, the horn stopped.

The pain and the humming in our ears went away just as fast. It was as if it had never happened.

"Did we hit it?" Teta asked.

I turned and helped Selma to her feet. "I'll be damned if I know."

A man's voice came from the darkness. "That's a curious choice of words, Nat Blackburn." Everyone had recovered, the living and the dead. We all faced the unfathomable tunnel, waiting for the owner of the voice to emerge.

How did he know my name?

He continued, his voice thick with a Southern drawl that would have been just as out of place aboveground in Wyoming's towns as it was in the shafts beneath the mines. "You're about as close to damned as one can be, but I have to give you credit. No one has lasted this long, or gone this far before. You should be proud of yourselves. But we all know how pride goeth before the fall."

The torches that had been burning to their quick flared up and we were bathed in harsh, golden light.

We could see the man walking toward us. He was tall, dressed in a black vest and jacket, with a shine on his ebony boots that reflected the firelight. His hair was long and dark, like an Indian woman's, swept off his high forehead and trailing down his back. A dark, wiry beard dangled off his chin, but the rest of his face was clean-shaven. The closer he came, the more I could see the sharp contours of his face and the almost catlike tilt of his eyes.

This was the *he* Lucille had spoken about.

The big question was who he was exactly, and what he planned to do with us.

"That's far enough," I said, aiming my pistol at his chest.

He stopped, raised his hands to show he wasn't heeled and laughed. "I have to say, I've enjoyed every second of you."

"If you've been responsible for everything down here, I can't say the same about you," I replied. I positioned myself so most of my body blocked Selma. There was no telling what our host could do and I wanted to keep her from his direct line of sight. Matthias and Angus were alongside me. We ignored Hank and his brothers, who regarded the stranger with doglike obedience.

Matthias whispered to Angus, "Can you get the name of this demon?" Angus remained silent.

The man tucked his fingers into the lapels of his vest and raised his chin. He said, "Probe all you want, Angus. You won't find what you're looking for."

Angus grunted and slammed his eyes shut. Sweat poured off his head in buckets. His body shook. His breath exploded from his mouth and he panted. "I can't," he said.

"That's right, you can't," the man said. "But if you truly want to know, all you need to do is ask."

For the first time since I'd met him, Matthias looked unsure and afraid. "All right, who are you?" I asked.

His lips curled into a perverse smile. "I have more names than you can count."

"I'm not a banker, so one will suffice."

He laughed, loudly and wickedly. "You really can't know how much you've entertained me. You may call me Belial."

Matthias gasped, pulling his Bible to his chest.

"I see it rings a bell with one of you. How about Abaddon? No? Somebody didn't go to church like a good boy."

Matthias leaned in to me and said, "Nat, that…man, is the—"

"Devil!" the man shouted. "In the flesh. This is quite the honor...for you, I mean."

Teta spit on the ground. "I don't think so. I think you're trying to make us afraid of you. Everything we've seen so far has been an illusion, and you're just another part of it."

The devil, or whoever he was, stared at Teta with steely eyes. Hard. Uncompromising. "I merely assumed a form that I thought would be more suitable for you. A mortal mind can bear witness to just so much, and then it breaks as easily as a freshly laid egg. You've trespassed into my home, created havoc with my sycophants. I would expect a little more gratitude. I can be so much worse, if that's what you wish."

No one moved. No one spoke.

"I thought as much. Breaking you has been the most fun I've had in ages. So much more rewarding than, say, the children."

He must have been talking about the kids with the black eyes. I didn't want to think that they had once been happy, innocent, living children. But they had, and he'd taken that away from them.

"Taking the little ones is easy, almost too easy. They're so simple to shatter. But their souls! That's another matter. Soft on the outside, the children are harder than steel on the inside. It doesn't stop me from trying. And, of course, there's the added pleasure of ruining the adults they leave behind. First the children, then the poor weeping mommies, then the vengeful daddies who no longer believe in a just God. Suffering is a sweet delight."

"You're one twisted bastard," I snarled.

"I *invented* twisted bastards," he replied. His eyes flashed red and my heart paused, wondering if he was going to morph into the vision of the devil I'd grown up seeing in my mother's Bible.

I took a step forward, but Matthias touched my arm. "Not that way." He opened his Bible and started chanting the same verse, over and over in a low and steady rhythm.

"How you are fallen from heaven, O Lucifer, son of the morning! How you are cut down to the ground, you who weakened the nations!"

The devil's upper lip curled and he went stiff. "Shut up," he said.

Matthias spoke louder, faster, the words running into one another.

"I said shut up!"

Matthias was lifted into the air. The Bible fell to the ground. His body was thrown into the wall. He cried out and tumbled to his knees.

"Do you believe who I am now?"

I sensed we all did. A dark power radiated from him. I felt sick being near him, tainted, like I'd been thrown into a deep pool of shit and rotting carcasses.

No one spoke. Being the devil, I was sure he could see right through us. "What do you want with us?" I said.

"What have I ever wanted?"

"And if we say no?"

Again he laughed, a terrifying rumble that filled the tunnel. "You have no choice. When you come to the doorway to hell, you don't get to run back home. Consider this your home. Or at least it will be, once we take care of one last formality."

The devil directed his gaze at Hank, breaking him from his stupor. He and his brothers bowed their heads as one.

"Selma, your husband will make sure we see each other very soon." At the mention of her name, Selma gave a muffled start.

The devil smiled, then blinked out of existence. The mad howling began.

CHAPTER FIFTY-FIVE

Hank and his brothers leapt into action, picking up right where they'd left off. They swarmed over Teta and me. There was no stopping them. They were a pack of mad dogs answering the dinner bell. I saw one of them grab Matthias by the throat and drive a knee into his chest. He was pinned, helpless.

Only Franklin stayed out of the fray – again. I caught a glimpse of his face and I could tell it was a real struggle for him not to join in. I didn't know whether it was out of fear of disappointing his master, or if he simply didn't have it in him, no matter how damned his soul. All that mattered was that he was one less indestructible brother we had to deal with. Angus swung his oak-tree arms from side to side, sweeping two of the brothers clear of Selma and the spirit chest. He was too massive, even for them, but he was human, and he couldn't keep the pace up forever.

I struggled with two brothers, one wrapped around my legs and the other landing glancing blows on my face. I threw a punch into one of their chests that would have stopped another man's heart. It only slowed him for a moment. He retaliated, launching a haymaker at the side of my head that I blocked with my forearm.

I had to get my legs free. No matter how hard I kicked, the wild-haired brother wouldn't let go.

And then they were both lifted from me. I watched their bodies sail to the other side of the tunnel, landing on top of four others. Angus did the same with the brothers pummeling Teta. For a moment, we were all free.

Something thumped against the chest.

Whump! Whump!

"Great," I said, taking hungry gulps of air. "Now your spirits want to join the party." Angus leaned over the box, chattering in his creepy deadspeak.

"Matthias, you got anything in that Bible that will throw the boys off-kilter like it did to the devil?"

Every part of that sentence sounded wrong – strange, alien. A great part of my mind was still miles behind what we were facing, back where the devil was a story to scare people into following the rules and abandoned mines were just that, empty and abandoned holes in the ground.

He looked at me with haunted eyes. "What's the use? We'd only delay the inevitable." I slapped him across the face. "Because we're still alive for a reason."

Hank was the first one to his feet. He wiped his jaw with the back of his hand, growling like a madman. He ran for Selma. He was too fast. I had no way of getting between them. She brought her hands up and clapped her fists over his ears. Hank barreled into her midsection, driving them both to the ground. I ran to pull him off her, shouting incoherently.

With a quick swipe, he knocked me off my feet.

"No!" Selma shouted as he dragged her by her hair. With his other hand, he grabbed her by the throat and lifted her to her feet. She threw an elbow into his stomach but it was useless. You couldn't harm a man whose body was worm food, probably rotting in one of the tunnels under the Deep Rock Hills.

Hank scampered backwards with Selma positioned in front of him like a shield.

"You don't mind if I have a little reunion with my wife, do you?" he said. His face shined with sickening glee.

"I might," I said.

Teta picked up the cavalry sword and sliced it through the air. I reached over so he knew to drop it. There were no weapons made by man that could stop them. Selma, on the other hand, could get hurt if he started swinging it around.

"So it would bother you if I wanted to have conjugal relations with my woman?" Hank sneered. "It has been awhile."

"I believe you'd need a real, working cock in order to do that."

I watched his hand tense as he applied more pressure to Selma's throat. "Hank, if you ever loved me, let me go," she croaked. "You don't want to do this. I know you."

"You *knew* me," he said. Hank looked at his brothers, motioning with his head in our direction. "Keep them busy. I want to break my little Selma in."

Out of the corner of my eye, I spotted Angus reaching down to grab the chest's lid. "Angus, don't!" I shouted.

It was too late. The spirits were loose and filling the tunnel.

★   ★   ★

Hundreds of wispy, alabaster shapes swarmed on top of Hank, his brothers and Selma.

She screamed so loud I thought her lungs would burst. "What the hell did you do?" I screamed at Angus.

He stared back with wet eyes. He was crying. "They chose this. I can't put them back."

Franklin materialized between us. "He did what he had to do. Come on, let's make sure this wasn't for nothing."

The echoing cries and hungry keening made it almost impossible to hear. Hank and his kin were being tossed about the tunnel as a whirlwind of white tore at them, taking small pieces with every turn. Teta ran into the tempest, hooking an arm around Selma's waist. Even though she'd been in the center of the storm, she hadn't been touched by the spirits Angus had unleashed.

Franklin ran ahead of us, his old legs rejuvenated. "Follow me."

He headed down the long tunnel. Back where the devil had come from.

There had to be another way. If we backtracked, there might be a passage we hadn't seen before.

"There isn't," Franklin said. Now even my thoughts weren't my own.

We had to act fast. There was no telling how long those spirits could keep Hank and his brothers occupied, though it looked like they were doing a thorough job of obliterating them.

"Nat, we should go with him," Selma said.

"And do what, shake hands with the devil?"

"Better," Franklin said. "You're going to close the gates of hell."

CHAPTER FIFTY-SIX

We skirted around the melee of spirits. I thought I heard Hank shout my name and hoped one of the spirits used that as an opportunity to tear out his tongue. Teta pushed Angus and Matthias ahead of him so he could guard our rear. Matthias had regained some of his color, though Angus didn't look so good.

And then it hit me.

How could I see them so clearly when our torches were back where the fighting was taking place?

I turned and saw it was Franklin. A soft but bright white light poured out of him. He moved fast, and I had to remind myself that even though he looked like an old man, his ghost, or whatever he was, wasn't bound by the frailties of age. I went to grab his shoulder but my hand passed right through him. He spun around to face me, so he must have been able to feel my attempt.

"Franklin, I don't know if we can even trust you. You're going to have to explain some things before we take another step closer to the gates of hell," I said, wincing at the words that kept tumbling out of my mouth.

"I will, but first we have to put some distance between us and my brothers."

We trailed after him, our only beacon in the dank shaft that got hotter with each step. This tunnel had a lot of twists and turns, but it stayed level. Had we already gone down so far we were flush with hell itself? The thought made me queasy. Everything made me queasy at this juncture.

I thought of Teddy and that book of his and how Teta said Hecla was similar to Hekla, the volcanic gate of hell. There were no coincidences. Did Teddy know he was sending us on a one-way trip, or did the early settlers know exactly what they were standing on? I would have given anything to be in Teddy's cozy study right about now, asking him just that.

After jogging for what I felt must have been a quarter of a mile, Franklin stopped. We were out of breath. He *had* no breath.

"Can we talk now?" I asked. Sweat danced down my spine and stung my eyes. Selma's hair was matted to her scalp.

"Yes." He looked at Angus. "Don't be upset. You did the only thing you could. You can still free them all. If you close the gates, you can free every enslaved spirit, Djinn and human alike."

The big man closed his eyes and nodded, but he looked doubtful.

Matthias said, "You spoke about closing the gates of hell. I'm just a reverend without a flock, but I'm almost positive that there's nothing a handful of mortals can do against the ultimate evil. Only the archangels or God himself have the power to seal Satan within his den of iniquity."

"It's true, you will need help," Franklin said.

"From you?" I asked.

"No, not me. There's not much else I can do beyond getting you to the gates. My soul is trapped, damned. I can't raise my hands against my master. Even now, I wonder why he's let me go against him without consequences."

"You're the carrot, the devil's the stick," I said.

Teta stepped up to Franklin, drenched, tired, bruised and bloodied. I suspected I looked the same. "You seem to be doing pretty well for someone, or some*thing*, that was a babbling old bastard when we first brought you to town."

"It's because I'm not supposed to leave here. When I do, my strength is sapped away. The hound was sent to stop me by scrambling my thoughts, weakening my will. It was a parasitic demon. Satan uses them as spies and siphons, absorbing energy and information like sponges. You've heard of vampires?"

We nodded.

"Parasitic demons are the inspiration for the myth. That particular one made it too difficult for me to maintain any semblance of coherence. I'm glad you put an end to it."

I could see the jagged wall through his face. It was unsettling.

I said, "This gateway to hell, how long has it been open? And what can we do to close it?"

"It's been here a very long time. There are gateways all over the earth. Most, thankfully, are sealed. This is the second time this particular gate has been opened. There were people that lived here thousands of years ago. They were the ancestors of the different Indian tribes that are all over this part of the country. One day, the earth shook and the opening cracked wide. Satan feasted on them like a hungry wolf in a henhouse. But they fought back using the ways taught to them by their fathers, handed down by their grandfathers and so on.

"They knew all about Djinn. In fact, they had found a way to live in peace with the Djinn for many generations. Banding together, they battled Satan and his demons, pushing them back, down and down into the lone portal that stretched from hell to the surface. They won, but it came at a price. Everyone who came in contact with the demonic army was infected. Djinn and human went mad, became evil. The men were put down like rabid animals. The Djinn were sealed into the stone of the hills by their elders, what we would call medicine men. And the land was left barren, for a long, long time.

"When the rush for copper and other minerals swept through Wyoming, the Deep Rock Hills were once again split open. The main copper mine went too far, shattering the ancient seal. The devil used gold as a lure to attract more people, planted ideas in their minds to bore as many holes into the hills as they could. What the miners didn't know is that they were unleashing the tainted Djinn, as well as Satan's demons, and, ultimately, *our* doom."

Selma reached out and tried to touch his lined face. "Franklin. You were always so gentle, so sweet. I'm so sorry."

"I went with my brothers because I wanted to. What man doesn't dream of being rich? I'm not as good as you remember me. That's why I'm here."

Matthias paced back and forth while Franklin talked. His hands were wrapped around his Bible so hard his knuckles were white. "You said we needed help to close the gates. What kind of help are you inferring?"

Franklin stared at Selma. "When I first knew you were here, I left the mine to see you, and to warn you. But Satan robbed me of that, just like he stole my life from me, watching me grow old and suffer and die when we came across him in the mine. I was pulled back here before I could gather enough strength to tell you to leave. But when I sensed their arrival—" he pointed at Angus and Matthias, "—I knew there was hope. You all just needed to live long enough to make it happen."

"Make what happen?" Matthias asked.

"His gift." He walked until his face was inches from Angus's chest. "He can talk to the spirits, but he can also talk to the Djinn. They'll follow him as they did with the Indian elders. He'll show them there is a way to break from their captivity. He can turn them against Satan. If he can unite the living, the dead and the Djinn, we can close the gates."

Matthias's eyes went wild. "A horrible destiny, for sure, but proof there is always a purpose behind a calling."

Franklin had neglected to mention the most important thing, at least to me. I wasn't sharing Matthias's enthusiasm. I said, "If we close the gate, how do we get out of here?"

"I don't know," Franklin said.

Matthias put his hand on my shoulder. "If we're meant to escape, we will."

I bored holes into him until he got the hint that I didn't want him touching me or telling me I had to have faith.

"The final tunnel is just down there. It will be protected by a variety of demons," Franklin said.

Demons. Of course. The ability to shock me had long worn off. "So what do we do now?" Selma asked.

"Angus needs to call on the spirits and the Djinn to bring them here. And Matthias should prepare you."

Matthias went through the thin pages of his Bible. Franklin began to step away. "Where do you think you're going?" I said.

"He's going to quote God's words. I can't be around when he does it. It hurts too much for someone like me who's been denied heaven. I won't go far."

By his moving away, we lost a good deal of light, but that didn't stop Matthias from finding his prayer. He said, "Please, everyone gather in a circle around me. Angus, while I pray, call them."

Teta reached into Matthias's pocket and pulled out the amulet. He tossed it down the tunnel. It clinked off the cave wall. When I looked at him, he said, "If we need the Djinn's help, we can't have that around."

"Good thinking," Matthias said, beaming. Guess he thought he had a new convert.

I pulled Selma close to my side and we huddled around Matthias. Angus bowed his head and started with his incomprehensible deadspeak.

"Nosfaung entdulas, edmane, thikool."

The Bible's spine lay in Matthias's hand. "This is from Psalms. I'm going to bless each one of us, as well as our weapons, to assure victory." He made the sign of the cross over our guns, blades and the few spare bullets we had left. Then he started to read, "'The Lord hear thee in the time of trouble, the name of the God of Jacob defend thee'."

I watched Franklin standing apart from us and it appeared that the light emanating from him dimmed. His face was twisted in a grimace. Matthias went on, with Angus a steady drone under his prayer. I hoped the prayer would work, even if I hadn't paid it much mind.

"'They are brought down and fallen, but we are risen and stand upright'. Amen." We all responded with a somber "Amen".

"This is how we're going to do it," I said. "We're going to form a cross, keeping Selma in the center. Teta, Angus and I will be the forward facing parts of the cross, with Matthias keeping track of the rear." I gave Selma the shotgun and the last shells. "When you run out of ammo, swing it like a club at everything you see. Don't grab it by the barrel or you'll fry your hands."

"Thank you, Nat."

"Scared?"

"Strangely, no. I'm just glad I'm with you."

"You just keep thinking about getting back to Laramie and you'll be fine." I smiled and rubbed my thumb across her cheek. Talking to her father would be a piece of cake after this.

"Teta, you all set?"

"Oh, I'm ready, jefe." He'd given the rifle to Matthias. He had a pistol in one hand and the sword in the other. Angus gripped the machete, still muttering.

I nodded at Franklin. "Lead the way, spirit man."

We walked another fifty feet, keeping our formation. Franklin paused at a sharp turn, then motioned for us to continue. There was a dull, pulsing orange glow against the far wall of the tunnel. When we rounded the corner, I had to swallow hard to keep my heart from leaping out of my throat.

It was bad. Real bad.

CHAPTER FIFTY-SEVEN

Until this point, we'd been moles running through tiny burrows. What stretched out before us was so dizzying, it made me feel like an ant gazing up at the base of the Rocky Mountains.

The tunnel was enormous. The ceiling was so high, it couldn't be seen. Its width could have accommodated a dozen trains riding side by side. It was long, but we could see a wall of angry flame at the other end. The flames illuminated the tunnel with blinding light. I squeezed my eyes shut, reopening them slowly to give them time to adjust.

The walls were covered in a thick layer of ice, but the air was hot and arid. Fire and ice.

Death and damnation.

Large, dark shapes moved back and forth, across the curtain of fire. Even from a distance, they looked big. Impossibly big.

"I take it that's the gate up ahead," I said. Even Franklin stared at it with terror. "Yes."

More shapes walked through the flames and were gathering. The welcoming committee was getting itself in place.

"I'll take an army of entrenched Spaniards any day over this," Teta said.

"Yeah, but the food's been better since we came to Hecla," I said, nodding at Selma. "I'd even eat a hundred cans of that terrible beef and come down with malaria over this."

I noticed Angus had stopped chanting. Matthias let out a startled yelp. I turned around to see what had scared him. Selma and Teta turned with me.

"Looks like the posse has arrived," I said.

Behind us, hundreds of luminous spirits filled the tunnel's entrance. Some were on the ground, but more floated above us, swaying about and circling around our heads. Men and women, hardened miners and Teddy's tattered troops swept about. Everyone who had ever been lured to Hecla only to find a fate even worse than death came to join our ranks. Behind them came a procession of the black-eyed kids. They walked in eerie silence, proceeding to our right and left until they formed two solid rows ahead of us.

"I don't want those kids on the front line," I said, "Dead or not. It's not right."

"Their innocence is our best shield," Matthias said. "They may be stuck here, but the devil was denied full possession of their souls."

I still didn't like it.

More figures joined the ranks outside the flaming gates. My stomach tightened when I saw they were scampering up the walls like bear-sized lizards.

A black explosion of foul-smelling smoke erupted between us and the spirit children. In an instant, a wall of wild men materialized. Wild men were perched on each other's shoulders, reaching up well over thirty feet.

The Djinn had arrived. I wondered if Djinn always looked like wild men, or, like the devil had said of himself, it was just a form they took so as not to rattle our feeble human senses. Were the wild men of legend all Djinn, or had the Djinn just copied them?

It was a question that would have to wait for another day. "Is there anyone else coming to the party?" I said.

Angus shook his head. "Every available soul is here. They want their freedom. They believe in us. We can't let them down."

"Nothing like a little pressure," Teta said, spitting against the wall. I knew Teta. He wanted the fight to start. Win or lose, he wanted to take action.

Selma pulled on my shirt. "Nat, there's something I want to tell you before we go down there."

I looked into her big brown eyes, leaned down and pressed my lips against hers. They were soft and sweet and trembling. "Save it for later. We'll have plenty of time to talk then."

Turning to Angus, I said, "You might as well tell them to make the charge."

He smiled. "They answer to you now. You're the fighter."

I'd never commanded an army of the dead and Djinn. I looked

around at the strangest regiment ever assembled. From what I could tell up ahead, we were about to clash with hell's most nightmarish creations. Even now, I wasn't afraid. I wanted to show the devil what an old cowboy was capable of when you pushed him too far.

I used what I thought was the universal language to plunge ahead. "Heyaaahhhh!"

The tunnel rumbled as we ran, bellowing loud enough to split the world in two.

★   ★   ★

The adult spirits swept over us like a wave, jumping ahead of the children. It made sense. They had been their parents at one time, and were going to protect them even beyond death.

The Djinn disassembled as we plunged ahead, running and snarling. Some moved so fast, they were able to sprint along the tunnel walls. Others moved to the rear, either to protect the back of the small band of the living or as a last line of defense should we fail.

The demons ahead of us roared as one mad, angry beast. The shock waves of their howls pushed back at us like a hurricane wind. It didn't so much as give the spirits and Djinn pause. For those of us still in possession of our flesh and bones, it was hard to keep our balance. Selma screamed. I reached behind and pulled her closer.

A colossal report rattled the tunnel as the first wave of spirits slammed into the swarming mob of black, demonic bodies. My ears popped and rang with head-splitting intensity. The opposing forces met midway to the gates and transformed into a swirling mass of light and dark. We ran as hard as we could, but we were still too far to make out any detail.

"Shoot anything that moves!" I shouted, barely able to hear my own voice.

We got closer, and the first line of black-eyed kids darted with lightning speed into the fray. Demons wailed and the ground shook.

It wasn't until the wild men broke their formation ahead of us that we could see what we were up against.

Nothing in Sunday school could have prepared us for this.

The demons grappling with the spirits were enormous, at least twice the size of Angus. They resembled fat-bodied spiders, except they had eight long, multiple-jointed human arms in place of legs. Their mouths were crammed with deadly incisors, dripping with some kind of fluid that smoked when it touched the rock, frying the ice along the walls.

A pair of Djinn jumped onto one of the demon spiders' back, plunging their arms into its sides. The spider's mouth stretched wide in a scream of pain. The Djinn extracted their arms, yowling as whatever acid that lived inside the spider chewed away at them. The spider and the Djinn collapsed, the spider melting into a pulpy puddle and the Djinn bursting into smoke before the acid finished eating their arms up to their shoulders.

A spider leapt over a row of black-eyed kids, headed straight for us. Selma pumped a round into it, catching it square in its single, green-glowing eye. It flipped in midair, crashing to the floor and knocking over another demon.

"Holy shit!" Teta shouted. His pistol went off and another spider dropped from the wall. Above us was a tempest of madness. A host of spirits had gathered up as many of the spiders as they could hold and circled around them like a tornado. I don't know what went on in the eye of the storm, but it didn't sound like things were going well for the spiders.

Parts of their bodies shot out from the cyclone, splattering against the frozen tunnel walls.

We pressed on.

The demon spiders were reluctant to touch the black-eyed kids, stepping back every time the kids stepped forward. As the spiders paused, the Djinn shrieked and scampered on top of them, ripping arms, pulling out incisors and tearing into their pregnant bodies with abandon.

A machete sang to my left and I saw Angus cleave a spider's head in two. He put his foot on its eyes for leverage as he pulled the machete free. The eye gave way with a loud plop.

Matthias prayed above the din, shooting at any spider that got past us. Turns out, he was a good shot.

If hell was worse than this, I wasn't sure I wanted to get closer to the gates.

Thanks to the spirit children, we were able to keep a steady pace forward, never stopping, never going back.

A spider galloped toward us, leaping over the kids. I fired one shot in its open maw, and another into its eye. It skidded to a stop by my feet. We kept formation as we skirted around the body, careful to avoid stepping into the gelatinous goo that pooled from its fangs.

"Nat, look out!" Selma screamed.

She pointed over my left shoulder. A spider, chewing on the remains of one of the Djinn, flexed its arms like it was about to pounce. Teta shot out two of the joints in its front arms and it rolled down the side of the wall. He hacked at it with the sword for good measure when it hit the ground.

The spirit tornado broke apart, and with that, a rain shower of spider bits sprinkled to the ground. I put out an arm to stop everyone. I didn't want us to get caught in that poisonous mess.

As the spirits settled to the ground, I could see what lay ahead.

The flames guarding the gate flared a hundred feet high, higher. We'd made good progress, but there was still a ways to go. The demon spiders had been reduced to scattered piles of coagulating blackness.

But hell wasn't done with us. Not by a long shot.

CHAPTER FIFTY-EIGHT

"Teta, Selma, Matthias, how are you on ammo?"

"I have two shells left," Selma said, her voice quaking. "Four bullets, one sword," Teta replied.

"Three," Matthias took a break from his praying to answer. Angus tapped his machete against my leg.

We were going to need a lot more than what we had to get past the next part.

Before us stood a dozen gray, knobby creatures. Each stood well over twenty-five feet high. Their heads were flat-topped, with eyes on each side. An opening under their heads held long, lashing tongues. Their bodies were a cross between a man and something from the sea and open range. Their chests were ten feet wide, and from them flowed a series of tentacles and antelope legs with cloven hooves. It was as if the devil had taken a little bit from every living creature and molded them into one hideous, enormous creation.

A tongue whipped out, wrapping itself around one of the black-eyed kids. It scooped the silent spirit child into its mouth and went for another.

"No!" I shouted, creasing its fast-moving tongue with a bullet. The tongue snapped back, and the kids moved from its feeding zone.

For a moment, there was a complete break in the fighting. The appearance of these monstrosities even made the dead and the Djinn stand still, taking them in with dreadful awe. In the stillness, I thought I heard a man laughing.

I shouted, "It's too late to turn back! Show them you're not afraid! Let's make hell fear *us!*"

That stirred up the spirits, who took to the air once again, flowing over the beasts. The demons rolled out their tongues, catching two, three, four spirits at a stroke before stuffing them into their mouths. I didn't want to think what happened to the spirits once they were inside the demons.

The Djinn went for the demons' legs, clawing and biting and chewing anything they could get their hands on. One of the massive demons was brought down, crashing next to us and almost flattening Teta. He and Angus leaped onto its monstrous head and went to work with their blades.

"Guys, get back!"

By breaking formation, Selma was exposed. It seemed a lost cause to try to protect her through all of this, but I wasn't going down without giving it everything I had.

The rifle cracked as Matthias whirled around to blast a tongue that was a few feet from connecting with my head. It retracted, and two Djinn jumped onto the tongue, tearing it to shreds as it tried to pull back to the safety of its mouth. A blur of spirits carried the Djinn to safety before they were consumed.

Angus and Teta rejoined our sides, but we couldn't move. The monsters were too big and the spirits and Djinn were in a hell of a fight. The black-eyed kids could do nothing against them, so I ordered them to the rear, hoping the Djinn back there could watch over them better than us.

These demons were too big for us to handle. At best, we could defend ourselves when they attacked. It was hard to find a weak spot when your opponents were the size of city buildings.

"I don't know about this," Teta said.

"And what's behind *them*?" Matthias said.

"Just keep pressing. Until we get to the gates, we fight like Kilkenny cats," I said.

We stood our ground, watching the battle explode. The spirits and Djinn were doing a good job pestering the giant demons, but only the one had been taken down. A tongue lashed out at us and Selma filled it full of buckshot. The tongue made a sharp left over our heads and pulled back.

Another was right behind it. I fired but missed. It went straight for Selma. She jammed the hot barrel into its soft flesh and I heard it sizzle. It smelled like flaming shit. The shotgun fused itself to the monster's tongue and it reeled it back, gun and all.

"Nice work," I said, keeping an eye out for more hungry tongues.

"The rest is up to you," Selma said, hooking her fingers through my belt.

A second creature was brought down by the weight of the spirits that had collected on its head. Immediately, the wild-men Djinn went for its eyes, kicking them in and tearing through the sockets like wolfhounds.

This time, one of its beastly brethren reached to help it back to its feet. Teta emptied his pistol in its face. Nothing slowed it down. The creature whipped a tentacle leg at him, wrapping its tip around his arm, and pulled.

Teta's scream ripped through the war cries. We watched in revulsion as his arm tore free from his shoulder. A geyser of blood painted the ground red. Teta staggered, his remaining hand clutching the stump, trying to stop the flow of blood. He fell to his knees. His eyes rolled up into his head and he dropped onto his back. "Teta!"

Selma and I ran to him, ignoring the creature hovering over our heads. "He's going to bleed to death," Selma said. Teta's body spasmed with shock.

The amputation ended right at his shoulder, so there was no way to tie it off. We had to stop the bleeding.

"I'll be right back," I said, handing Selma my pistol. I ran to the demon spider bodies, catching sight of Angus as he chopped off the end of a tongue while Matthias shot the beast in the eye. A fountain of iridescent green flowed from the socket.

I put on my leather gloves and kicked through the broken bits of the spiders. I found a fang, its end still dripping and steaming.

I ran back to Teta and Selma. "Hold him down. This is going to hurt worse than having his arm yanked off."

Selma straddled his chest. Teta, for the moment, was out, but I knew the pain would bring him right back.

I touched the tip of the fang to the gaping wound in his shoulder. His flesh and muscles and tendons hissed. It smelled sickeningly like barbecue. Teta woke up screaming and bucking, but Selma kept him down.

Sure enough, the acid did the trick, stopping the flow of blood and sealing everything up. At best, I probably saved him enough time so we could say goodbye properly. He passed out again.

"We have to hide him," I said.

We picked him up and placed him within the jumble of legs of the fallen monster. "I'll come back for you." I bit back the bile that splashed against the back of my teeth. I took the remains of his lucky sombrero and put it on his chest, draping his arm over it. "Stay lucky for just a little longer."

Selma handed my pistol back to me and we regrouped with Angus and Matthias. "We're never going to get past them," I said. The spirits and Djinn fought wildly, but even they couldn't escape becoming food for the beasts.

"It doesn't look like it, no," Matthias said. He took aim at a beast and the hammer clicked. It was empty.

"Did you say the Djinn were shapeshifters?" I asked.

"Yes, that is one of their powers."

I pulled Angus's shirt to get his attention. "You need to talk to the Djinn for me. We need some from the rear to come up and get us past these things. They need to be big, and fast. You see where I'm going with this?"

Angus nodded, and deadspeak flowed from his lips.

"Selma, I want you to stay back here. If things don't work out, stay close to the black-eyed kids. They can keep you safe and may even help you find a way out of here."

"I'm not going anywhere without you!"

"Listen, what I need to do next requires my total attention. I can't give that if I'm worrying about you. Be wary of the Djinn. They may turn on you if we get taken out. Now go!"

She ran reluctantly to the waiting flock of spirit children. Her eyes shimmered with tears. I had to put it out of my mind for now. She was safer with them.

Angus tapped my shoulder and pointed. Three Djinn appeared next to us.

Yep, he had understood exactly what I meant.

CHAPTER FIFTY-NINE

These Djinn were not the wild men of Indian lore. Now they were exactly what we needed.

Horses.

But not ordinary horses. The Djinn were double the size of Clydesdales, with heads like battering rams. They pawed the floor with hooves the size of anvils.

Matthias looked at them nervously. "What are we supposed to do with them?"

I ran and jumped onto one of their backs. The flesh was cold, the texture nothing like horsehair.

"We're riding them past these big old bastards and shutting the gates down."

"That's insane!"

"Since we got down here, it's the sanest thing I've seen. Mount up. We may need you." Angus was already on his Djinn horse. He had to move next to Matthias to help him up. "Let's go!"

I gave the Djinn a kick and it took off, accelerating like no living horse. My hat flew from my head and we galloped headlong into the brouhaha. A tongue punched the ground ahead of us and the Djinn swerved around it, taking us to the side of the tunnel and riding along it, past another monster as it swiped at our heads. I looked down to see Angus and Matthias weaving between the uncountable legs of the creatures.

Gripping on to the Djinn's black mane with everything I had, I fought to keep myself from slipping off its back. If I did, I was going to tumble off the side of the wall. It was a hell of a long fall. I didn't want to get this far, only to die from a tumble off a Djinn horse.

I yelped when we made it past the line of monsters and saw the fiery opening ahead. The Djinn kept its breakneck pace and guided us back to the ground. Angus and Matthias pulled up beside us.

A lone man stood before the gate, his arms crossed over his chest. The Djinn horses pulled up and stopped.

We dismounted. The devil stood not more than ten paces away. He was not happy.

But neither was I.

"Still having fun?" I asked.

The devil sneered and hissed.

"Vile serpent," Matthias whispered.

"How dare you," the devil said.

"You're the one who wanted to play," I said. "We just changed the rules a little."

The devil burst into flame with a loud *whoosh*. As the flames died, the exterior of the man he'd worn melted away. In its place was, I assume, his true form. He was deformed beyond imagination, his limbs twisted and gnarled. Sickly yellow eyes burned from a face lined with scars and pockmarks. His flesh was the color of a corpse burned by the sun. His teeth, rows and rows of them, gleamed white.

He was death made flesh.

"I can close the gate," Angus said softly.

I didn't see how. The fissure itself was forty, fifty feet high and encased in flame. "Keep Satan occupied."

For a moment, I almost laughed at the absurdity of it. My hand moved to my hip, inches from my holster. I looked the devil in his jaundiced eyes and said, "You and me have something to settle."

"If you're talking about your death and eternal damnation, I agree."

I shook my head. "Back up in the real world, I was an officer of the law. I can't say I enjoyed it so much, but I did like the part about righting wrongs. The city has strange, inefficient ways of handling justice, though. I like it better out here, without lawyers and judges. What's right is right, and what's wrong, well, usually ends up hanging at the end of a rope or standing on the wrong side of a gun."

The devil chuckled.

"I'm going to shit your soul, over and over, until this world is nothing but dust."

"Are you sweet-talking me?"

That wiped the smile from his hideous face. Matthias took his Bible from his vest pocket and took one step from me. "I don't think mocking Satan is such a good idea," he said.

"You have a better idea?"

Angus had crept off to the side, using the Djinn horse to conceal his movements. The devil paid him no mind. He only had eyes for me. Angus managed to get past where the devil stood and was making his way to the opening.

"You'll suffer more than Christ when I'm through with you," the devil said.

"We do have the same father. Look, I might as well come clean and let you know that I'm about as afraid of you as I am of a field of flowers. I heard you've been beat here before. Looks to me that you're ripe for a repeat."

The devil roared. It sounded like the cries of hundreds of tortured men. Fire erupted from his eyes, a deadly line of flame directed at me.

"Look out!" Matthias shouted.

He jumped in front of me, holding the Bible outward. The flame slammed into the Bible, sending him crashing into my chest. We tumbled across the ground. My ribs felt like they'd been broken.

Matthias lay sprawled next to me. The Bible had been reduced to ash. I couldn't tell if he was breathing. Smoke wafted off his body.

The devil laughed, licking his lips over his rows of teeth.

"Pretty easy to hurt a man who only has a book to defend himself." I saw the fire build in his eyes.

Getting to my feet, I grunted when I straightened, my ribs poking into my lungs. I wanted to cough, but I knew if I did I might pass out.

I stared back at him, hoping he could see the anger that burned in my own eyes. We stood, motionless, staring at one another. I could feel his hatred.

Flames sputtered from his eyes, coiling over his head.

He geared up to take his final shot at me. No more playing around. We'd taken things too far and he was no longer amused or entertained by me.

My body relaxed as I exhaled.

I drew my pistol and fired twice.

The devil staggered back, his hands clutching his face. When he pulled them away, it was my time to smile.

Two direct hits. Thick gobs of yellow pus dripped from his shattered eye sockets and down his black and grey cheeks.

The sound of hammering echoed in the tunnel. I looked up. Angus was held above the gateway by the Djinn. It had once again taken the form of a wild man. Angus hammered his bare fist against the arch, and bits of rock tumbled down.

Holy shit. He was going to bring it all down by himself.

★ ★ ★

Angus punched and jabbed at the stone with all of his might. The entrance groaned as more rocks were dislodged, falling into the flames.

A large crack zigzagged across the entire arch. Angus saw it, and the Djinn moved him closer so he could concentrate his fury on the weakened spot.

I looked into the chamber of my pistol. One shot left.

"Angus!" I shouted.

I raised the gun, aiming at the widest part of the fissure. He nodded, and moved back.

I pulled the trigger and watched the rock explode. There was a tremendous *crack* and it all began to crumble like loose shale. Angus continued working on it, knocking boulders loose. His hands were a bloody mess, but he never let up.

"You fucker!" the devil said. His eyes were back, but it was too late. The gates were closing. The boulders doused the flames.

"Guess you'll have to find someone else to shit out for eternity."

Angus and the Djinn hung from the arch. Together, they dislodged the weakened rock face. The ground rumbled as the cave-in thundered in a shower of stone and smoke.

"No!" I shouted.

Angus swung one last time. Everything gave way and he lost his grip.

The big man tumbled through the air, his body bouncing off the great falling rocks until he disappeared amidst the crumbling rubble.

Smoke and dust filled the tunnel like a wild fire. I dove over Matthias.

The bones in Satan's body cracked like fireworks. He twisted round himself like a snake around a tree branch. He pointed a long, sharp finger at me. I winced, expecting flames to shoot from his finger, but nothing happened.

A great wind came from nowhere and everywhere, all at once. It pushed at my back as it was drawn into the rapidly closing gates of hell. I had to lay as flat as I could over Matthias to keep from getting picked up by the wind like a toy kite.

In the maelstrom, the devil rose, struggling to stay erect. He took an uneven step toward me.

I had nothing left to defend myself. If I so much as tried to push myself up, I was going to be carried by the hurricane straight into the bowels of hell.

I heard more of the tunnel collapse around the fissure. Black smoke choked the air. The devil sneered against the backdrop of unholy carnage.

And then he spread his distorted arms wide, letting the wind carry his wicked body home.

In the darkness, I heard great beasts roaring and flailing, felt the tunnel quake like it was going to explode.

It hurt to breathe, and when I did draw in air, it was tainted with dust. I couldn't stop coughing. The pain was excruciating. My mind, mercifully, went black.

CHAPTER SIXTY

"Nat?"

Something touched my face. I tried to swat it away. "Nat?"

The pain was back in my chest. I wanted to curse whoever had resurrected that particular agony.

"Please, Nat, wake up." Selma.

I opened my eyes. Her face hovered over me. Her tears dripped onto my forehead. "Oh thank God," she cried, cradling my head in her lap.

"Is it—"

"Yes."

It hurt to move, but I forced myself to look over to the opening. The smoke had settled and hovered a few inches above the ground. A great pile of rocks and boulders covered the entrance.

"Angus?" I said.

"I haven't seen him."

He hadn't made it. I think he knew that all along. Never once did he hesitate. I was sorry I'd never get the chance to know him better.

Someone groaned and I saw Matthias move onto his back, coughing. "He saved my life," I said.

Selma smiled. "You saved everyone."

The tunnel glowed with the presence of the spirits and black-eyed children. They surrounded us, sealing us in a cocoon of warmth. Now that hell's fires had been extinguished, the tunnel had grown mighty cold.

"They're going to show us the way out," Selma said.

"How do you know that?"

"They told me."

"And the Djinn?"

"They left. I don't know where. One minute they were there,

the next they disappeared in a cloud of smoke."

She helped me up and, together, we were able to get Matthias standing. His eyes rolled in his head and he couldn't talk yet, which was a good thing.

The spirits guided us through the tunnel. The demon bodies were gone. It was as if they'd never been there. I saw Teta lying unconscious. I tried to lift him, but the pain in my ribs was too much.

The spirit children gathered round him and picked him up. It didn't look like he was breathing at all. The stump where his arm used to be was a charred mess.

"Lead the way," I said to them.

Together, we walked for what felt like miles until we emerged into the bright sun.

Birds flew in crazy circles above the mine entrance. They whistled and chirped and sang.

It felt like the perfect time for the clouds to burst and the rain to finally come down and wash away all of the evil that had gripped the land for so long.

The sun blazed in a cloudless sky.

Who the hell was I to tell the weather what to do?

The wildfire from the night before had burned itself out. The trees were black and twisted and smoking. The air was bitter, but, damn, it was fresher than anything down in the tunnels.

I peered into the dark mineshaft.

Goodbye, Lucille. I hope somehow your soul broke free like the others. I'll pray for you every day.

An orange-breasted robin landed by our feet, cocked its head and twittered.

"I never thought I'd appreciate that music so much," I said before collapsing on the hot, dry ground. Teta was laid next to me and the children and adult spirits slowly disappeared. I hoped it was to a place of rest, somewhere they could have a hell of a family reunion.

I wished Angus was with us to watch them dissipate into the sun's rays. After all I'd seen, I figured he was somewhere close, enjoying the moment.

CHAPTER SIXTY-ONE

We pulled outside the gates of Sagamore Hill. Winter was still a week away, but it had already snowed the night before.

Matthias was at the wheel of his new automobile, a Buffum Model E touring car. Unlike the one he'd driven to Hecla, this one had a roof, but it was still pretty open to the elements. We draped blankets over ourselves during the drive.

I got out of the car, my boots crunching in the snow.

Selma leaned into me and said, "Do you want me to go inside with you? I can't lie and say it wouldn't be a thrill to meet the president."

"Not this time, darling. I promise, another time."

I turned to face the snow-covered estate. I could see the soft glow of a fire in one of the windows and a track of Teddy's prints marching to and from the house. The man had to walk, no matter the weather, day or night. He just couldn't sit still.

I pulled up the collar of my coat and kicked the side of the car. "Be careful, Nat!" Matthias said.

"I didn't hurt your precious car. I wonder what Jesus would say about your lust for something as material as a car."

"He'd say if it made me happy and didn't hurt anyone in the process, it made him happy." I shook my head.

"You coming or what?"

Teta woke up with a snort. The arm of his jacket was pinned to his side. I helped him from the car. He was still weak, but he would get better. The infection in his arm had kept him in a hospital for two months. Selma and I brought him back to the ranch in September and helped build him back up to strength. Her father played cards with him and Matthias every night. For the first time in my life, it felt like I had a family, even if our kids, for now, were a one-armed Dominican and an itinerant reverend who looked for ghosts.

"I wouldn't miss this for anything."

I kissed Selma and told Matthias to keep the car running. We wouldn't be long.

Teta and I walked up the path to the estate. Our breath steamed from our noses and mouths.

I knocked on the door. It was answered by an older woman, one of the housekeepers.

"We're here to see the president," I said. "And you are?"

"Teta Delacruz and Nat Blackburn," Teta said.

Upon hearing our voices, Teddy turned the corner and walked into the vestibule. "They're fine, Anna, thank you. Come in. You look like a couple of ice blocks. Anna, take their coats."

"It's not necessary," I said. "We just wanted to give something back to you."

We had already debriefed a man that Teddy sent to Wyoming back in the summer. I didn't know if he believed us, but I didn't care either. We didn't lie when we told him there was no gold, and to stay away from Hecla at all costs.

Teta handed the book, *Konungs Skuggsjá: King's Mirror,* to him.

"You came all the way out here to return a book? Please, come inside, have a drink, warm up. We have a lot to talk about."

I didn't move. "You're right, Teddy, we didn't just come to give you the book."

We both reared back and punched him square in the face. Teddy toppled over. His pince-nez broke in two and flew off his face. Anna screamed for security. Teddy sat on his ass with his face in his hands.

"That's the first step toward being even," I said.

He looked at me, blood dribbling from his nose, and nodded.

We walked back to the car and I pulled Selma onto my lap, covering us both with a wool blanket.

"That was fast," she said.

"Wasn't much to say."

The sun came out from behind the clouds and made the drive to the city bearable. I couldn't wait to get back on the train headed for Laramie.

AFTERWORD

I want to thank you for reading this here yarn about a cowboy living in a changing world, a place where roping and wrangling have given way to driving and what most folks might call a more civilized way of life. I try not to listen to most folks.

Like any good tale, there's a bit of truth within every fabrication. I thought I'd end this story as the campfire dies down with a list of the truths. Some of them are far more fascinating than anything I can dream up and worth picking up a history book or trolling through the Internet to learn more.

Okay, here are the people, places and things that are verifiable fact: Teddy Roosevelt did exist, was one of the leaders of the Rough Riders in the Spanish-American War and did become president. Yes, that was an obvious one, but it gave me a chance to say this country needs another T.R. to make mincemeat out of the human train wrecks we call our modern congressional and executive parties.

Hecla is an actual abandoned mining town in Wyoming. Copper was mined there in the 1800s. I don't suggest you head out there now searching for gold.

For you cattle-trail enthusiasts, there was a Chisholm Trail, made famous in about every other John Wayne movie.

Of course, the unfortunate Apache Wars lasted decades.

The legendary Nock-ay-det-klinne did stir up a good deal of trouble with his ghost dance and was indeed serious about raising fallen Apaches from the dead.

Depending on whom you ask, the Djinn exist, though on some sort of interdimensional plane that sometimes intersects with our own. No one knows what they really look like, but whenever you hear about genies in a bottle, you're hearing about the mystery of the Djinn.

Wild men – or Bigfoot, or Sasquatch, or one of any dozens of names – may or may not live in the deep forests of just about every country in the world. Almost every civilization has tales of large, hairy, manlike beasts living on the outskirts of society.

Native Americans have believed this to be true for longer than we've been on this continent. If it's good enough for them, it's good enough for me.

Last but not least, again, depending on whom you ask, the devil is very real, and very active nowadays. If that frightens you, remember, you can't have evil without good, so give God a shout-out from time to time.

Now, if you'll pardon me, it's time I treated myself to some whiskey and a hand-rolled cigarette.

FLAME TREE PRESS
FICTION WITHOUT FRONTIERS
Award-Winning Authors & Original Voices

Flame Tree Press is the trade fiction imprint of Flame Tree Publishing, focusing on excellent writing in horror and the supernatural, crime and mystery, science fiction and fantasy. Our aim is to explore beyond the boundaries of the everyday, with tales from both award-winning authors and original voices.

•

•

Join our mailing list for free short stories, new release details, news about our authors and special promotions:

flametreepress.com